To Scott,
Thanks for coming out &
enjoy your first case!

This Thing
of Darkness

Barbara [signature]

An Inspector Green Mystery

BARBARA FRADKIN

RendezVous
Crime

Cover design: Emma Dolan

Le Conseil des Arts
du Canada
depuis 1957

The Canada Council
for the Arts
since 1957

Canadä

We acknowledge the support of the Canada Council for the Arts for our publishing program. We acknowledge the financial support of the Government of Canada through the Book Publishing Industry Development Program for our publishing activities.

RendezVous Crime
an imprint of Napoleon & Company
Toronto, Ontario, Canada   www.napoleonandcompany.com

Printed in Canada

13 12 11 10 09   5 4 3 2 1

Library and Archives Canada Cataloguing in Publication

Fradkin, Barbara Fraser, date-
          This thing of darkness / Barbara Fradkin.

(An Inspector Green mystery)
ISBN 978-1-894917-85-8

          I. Title. II. Series: Fradkin, Barbara Fraser, date- . Inspector Green mystery.

PS8561.R233T45 2009   C813'.6   C2009-904767-5

To my mother, Katharine Mary Currie,
for letting my spirit roam free

One

"Pumpkins!" Tony shrieked, his dark eyes dancing as he struggled to get out of his bike trailer. "Daddy, look at all the pumpkins! Can we buy three?"

Ottawa Police Inspector Michael Green leaned on his handlebars, red-faced and gasping for breath. Sweat poured into his eyes and soaked through his Bagelshop T-shirt. The mere thought of lugging three huge pumpkins all the way back home in the bike trailer alongside his four-year-old son exhausted him. The Sunday morning bike excursion to the Byward Market had been his wife's idea. He'd been angling for the car, but Sharon had ladled on the guilt. The environment, fitness, family togetherness. "How many more gorgeous sunny days will we have before the snow falls?" she'd said. "Besides, we'd never find a parking place."

Looking out over the crowded streets, he privately admitted she was right. September was the peak time for local fruits and vegetables, and people fought their way along the street stalls looking for the best bargains in brightly-coloured sweet peppers, fragrant apples and cauliflower so huge, it would take all winter to eat one. Street buskers cashed in on the crowds, playing everything from classical flute to African drums, and the musical chaos rose up over the roar of engines and the chatter of farmers hawking their goods.

Green had grown up in the heart of old Bytown, and twice a year he liked to bring his son down to the inner city to experience the authentic old farmers' market. Once in the spring, when the maple syrup and flower vendors first brought the market back to life, then again at harvest time. In these brief visits, he saw it once more as a source of life and colour, and not as a dishevelled, dissolute playground of drunks, hookers and predators. It took a conscious effort to set aside the twenty-five soul-battering years in the trenches and to reclaim the innocence he'd felt as a youth, but his own son's joy was the only reminder he needed.

"Gelatos first, honey," Sharon said with a laugh. A mango gelato from Piccolo Grande had been the bribe she'd offered Green to tip the scales. They navigated their bikes cautiously down the busy street that bordered the market, past the hideous barricades of the new American embassy and down a street of limestone heritage buildings, formerly nuns' cloisters but now converted into trendy shops. Inside the gelato shop, it took ten minutes to debate the choices, but they finally emerged with mango, chocolate and strawberry.

As they sat on the bench to eat their cones, Green found his cop's gaze roving, picking out the darker parallel world beneath the bustle and cheer of the marketplace. The bearded pan-handler on the corner, the tiny, almost prepubescent sex trade worker advertising her wares at the traffic light, two skinheads in leather and chains swaggering down the street with a muzzled pit bull tightly held in hand. Perhaps the two were innocent, but more likely they were looking for sport. A solitary black, or a woman in a hijab. I have my eye on you punks, he thought, as his son chattered excitedly beside him.

Green claimed it was a curse, but in truth, the menace of the streets set his pulse racing. Here, amid the diesel fumes and crumbling streets, the eclipsed dreams and discarded hopes, he'd first felt his calling. He thought ahead to his week of meetings within the corporate walls of the Elgin Street mothership. Meetings with the RCMP, with his NCOs, with his boss, Superintendent Barbara Devine, who was shoring up her bid for the vacant Deputy Chief's job. Would he even survive?

"Daddy, listen!" Tony cried, jumping off the bench. "A police car! Maybe it's an accident."

Green grabbed his hand to restrain him. There was no sign of cruisers, but in the distance, he picked up the sound of sirens. One vehicle, then a second and a third. His own curiosity stirred.

"Is it an accident, Daddy? Or a fire?"

"Could be lots of things, buddy." A collision, a fight, a brazen robbery at the height of weekend shopping? Green scanned the area, but business was continuing as usual. The sounds appeared to be concentrated farther east and south, perhaps on Rideau Street.

"But we have to go see," Tony insisted, his forgotten gelato dripping down his hand.

Sharon drew her son to her and rescued the gelato. "Other police officers are taking care of it, honey." She cast Green a wary look. Her dark curls had been whipped by the wind, and a smudge of strawberry gelato clung to her delicate chin. "Daddy is busy helping us today."

He reassured her with a sheepish grin. How well she knew him. He swooped his sticky son into his arms and turned to the bicycles. "Yes, we're on the hunt for a pumpkin!"

"Three pumpkins!"

"Peppers and cauliflower too," Sharon said, laughing. "Do you think we can fit everything in the trailer?"

Green contemplated the long ride back along the Ottawa River bike path. The view was inspirational, the terrain gentle, and the breeze a mere whisper. It should be manageable, if only he weren't in such abysmal shape. He uttered a small prayer of resolve to hit the running track more often. Let the guys laugh.

As they walked their bikes along the crowded sidewalk stalls, Sharon gradually buried a gleeful Tony with brightly-coloured apples, peppers and squash. Between his knees, one long-faced, doleful pumpkin. The trailer grew heavier and heavier.

Another siren went by.

There was still no sign of the source of trouble, nor of public concern. No one was whispering or running to look. Green forced his thoughts back on track. Half an hour later, every cranny of the trailer and Sharon's backpack was stuffed, and even she laughed ruefully about whether they were going to survive the ride home. She was barely five-foot two, and although she kept herself trim and fit, her fortieth birthday loomed.

Two more sirens sounded up ahead, and now even Sharon noticed his distraction. They were stopping at a red light, waiting to cross over Confederation Bridge and down beside the locks to the river path. Green twisted around, trying to see down Rideau Street behind him. In the distance he could distinguish a forest of flashing red.

"Not every emergency in the city is your responsibility," she said.

"I know. Occupational hazard. But it looks major. That's at least six responders."

Tony was also craning his neck to see. "It must be a humongous fire, right, Daddy?"

Sharon snorted. "I've known a police car, ambulance and two fire trucks to respond to a cat in a tree."

Green gave her an apologetic smile as he turned back to the light. Not in this neighbourhood, he thought. On his hip, his cellphone rang. He glanced at the ID. Ignoring Sharon's warning scowl, he snatched it up. On a Sunday morning, a call from Staff Sergeant Brian Sullivan could only mean one thing.

4

*   *   *

Screech had slept poorly, curled up in his usual spot behind the Rideau Street grocery store. He'd woken far earlier than he'd wanted, still awash in the vodka he'd bought the night before but freezing cold. His hand had groped around for his sleeping bag, but closed on empty air. He cursed. Some worthless bum had stolen it right off his back! He unfolded himself and struggled stiffly upright, supporting himself against the rough bricks of the store wall. The sun was climbing overhead, and it cut harsh lines through the buildings on Rideau Street. He squinted as he scanned the shadowy nooks and crannies where the traitor might have settled. Nothing.

He limped to the sidewalk and headed up the block, dragging his left foot, which refused to obey him any more. He'd given up caring. Lots of things didn't obey him any more, including his brain, which dropped things faster than he shoved them in, and his tongue which no longer formed the sounds he wanted. His fingers, frostbitten more times than he could remember, had trouble doing up zippers or opening bottles, so he never bothered to wrap himself properly in his sleeping bag. This wasn't the first sleeping bag he'd lost, but it was the warmest. With the autumn frosts coming, he was damned if he would give it up without a fight.

A little ways up, he spotted it in an alleyway, almost hidden in the window well of a building, like the bum had tried to get out of sight. Outrage propelled him forward, a string of insults already forming on his lips. The culprit was completely wrapped in the bag except for his stockinged feet. Not a single hole in those fancy socks, Screech thought, adding fuel to his outrage. He propped himself against the wall so he could aim a good kick. His foot connected with soft flesh, but there was no grunt. No recoil. Understanding penetrated Screech's brain. He'd felt that dead weight before. Either the guy was totally wasted, or he was dead.

Either way, it was not Screech's business, but there was no point in a good sleeping bag going to waste. But when he leaned down to grab a corner, the bag felt crusty and damp. He snatched his hand away in disgust and stared at the red stains on it. Then he noticed the red all over the ground in half-dried streaks and pools spreading from beneath the body.

Fuck! He reeled back and tripped on the curb, twisting his good ankle and landing hard on his rear. Crablike, he scuttled backwards into the middle of Rideau Street. Horns blared, tires squealed, and a car swerved by him so close he felt its heat. He scrambled back to the curb. Waved a hand to flag someone down. What was everybody's goddamn hurry?

Finally a car veered over to the curb, a door slammed and boots stomped around the car.

"What the fuck, Screech?" A familiar voice shouted.

Screech recognized a beat cop who brought him food and supplies when times were tough. Surprised at his relief, he tried to get his rattled brain in gear. "There's a sleeping bag," he said. "Bleeding. Dying." Then he gave up and used his trembling finger to point.

Two

Green locked up the bikes and piled Sharon, Tony and the vegetables into a cab. Although her eyes were glum, Sharon hadn't uttered a peep of reproach, but Tony had to be cajoled into the back seat, squirming and protesting that he wanted to see the fire trucks. He was slightly mollified by the promise of lunch with Zaydie later on, but Green could still see his face pressed against the rear window as the cab pulled away. Trying to push guilt out of his mind, he called for a cruiser to take him to the crime scene.

There was a well-established protocol for homicide investigations, and Green knew it would be some time before he'd learn many details about the victim and the crime scene itself. But from the distraught patrolman who was first on the scene, Brian Sullivan had learned enough to make the call to Green. "It's a homicide all right," he'd said, "and not your usual homicide around here. An old man beaten beyond recognition. I thought under the circumstances, in this neighbourhood..."

Sullivan hadn't needed to say more. While Green waited for the cruiser, he phoned his father. When he heard the familiar, singsong Yiddish voice, he felt a wash of relief.

"You okay, Dad?"

"I shouldn't be?"

"You been outside today?"

"I'm watching a black preacher cure a blind boy. Maybe when that's over."

"Okay." Green paused. No point in alarming his father, who lived with enough fears of his own making. Fears planted long ago, by jack boots and train whistles and the barking of guard dogs along the barb wire of the death camp. "I'm in town. How about we go to Nate's for some cheese blintzes?"

"Why?"

Green kept his tone light. "I need a reason?"

"No. Why are you in town? It's Sunday."

"Business, Dad."

"*Oy,* Mishka. Always business."

The cruiser pulled up, leaving Green no time to counter the rebuke. By now, Rideau Street was in gridlock, and even the cruiser's roof lights did little to speed them up. Curious pedestrians clogged the sidewalk as they tried to get a closer look. Cars jockeyed for space amid the rumbling trucks and buses that inched through the lights. Only the cyclists wove in and out, gleefully dodging potholes and cars on their way to the tree-lined bike paths along Ottawa's river system. The eclectic jumble of shops that brought Rideau Street to life— the tattoo parlours and African restaurants next to dance clubs, bakeries and body piercing salons—were all wide open, their displays spilling onto the sidewalk before them.

Some were new, catering to the tougher elements that had taken over the neighbourhood in recent decades, but others, like Nate's Deli, clung stubbornly to their immigrant, working class glory days. When Green was a little boy growing up in one of the dilapidated Victorian redbrick townhouses just to the north, his mother had sent him to the Rideau Bakery for *challah* and to Nate's for *varenikes* and white fish. Many of the tenements had been bulldozed to make room for the subsidized slums that masqueraded as urban renewal, but the shops were still there, familiar landmarks on the evolving street.

Also familiar, unfortunately, was the scene that greeted him just a block from King Edward Avenue. Three police cruisers were flashing blue and red in the sunlight, and parked next to them was a white Forensic Identification van. Assaults, muggings, burglaries, drug disputes and booze-fuelled brawls were all common on the volatile bar strips of the Byward Market.

This time, however, a black coroner's van had joined the line of official vehicles.

Green directed the cruiser to the curb behind the coroner's van and scanned the officials gathered in the corner behind the yellow police tape. In their zeal to prevent scene contamination, the first responders had secured not only the alleyway but half a city block, and two uniforms had been deployed to conduct traffic in a vain attempt to ease the snarl. Green could see Brian Sullivan standing just outside the secured area, conferring with an Ident officer. Behind them, Green could see more officials in white Tyvek suits bent over something in the alley. At the mouth of the alley, abandoned except for a numbered forensic marker, lay an old-fashioned wooden cane like the one Green's father used. In spite of himself, his gut tightened.

His father's gentle rebuke came back to him now as he stood at the edge of the crime scene. He'd been investigating major crimes for nearly twenty years and had stood at the edge of countless crime scenes, waiting for the coroner's report. The crime scene both repulsed and fascinated him, each one a new challenge, each one a clash with villainy. Now, as an inspector, he no longer attended crime scenes; Brian Sullivan and his major crimes detectives took the calls and worked the cases, while Green sat around committee tables, overseeing the broader picture, allocating resources and planning future initiatives. Even the catchwords irked him. Yet he also knew that after twenty soul-battering years on the front lines of rape and murder, he'd had no choice but to retreat.

Standing outside the Rideau Street crime scene, however, he felt not exhilarated but slightly sick. In his mind was the image of an elderly man walking down the street, perhaps on his way home to some modest seniors' residence in Sandy Hill, much like the one Sid Green lived in only a few blocks away. With his cane, he had probably walked slowly and stiffly, his head bent to watch his footing. He might even have been a little deaf, easy prey for the punk who'd crept up behind him. Not just knocked him down, which would have been appalling enough, but beat him to death. Green felt a tremor of rage at the affront.

Brian Sullivan turned and glanced around the street thoughtfully, no doubt trying to judge where the killer had come from. Had he been lying in wait in the alleyway and somehow lured the victim into an ambush? The killer had chosen a particularly disreputable corner populated by street people, drug dealers and low-end hookers working the fringe of the club district. A corner decrepit by day, dangerous by night. Both a beer and a liquor store were within a couple of blocks, and desperation sometimes drove alcoholics to extreme actions. But no sooner had the thought crossed Green's mind than he dismissed it. This was no simple mugging; from Sullivan's description, it had been a rage out of control.

Other than the all-night grocery store and a pawn shop, there was nothing in the immediate vicinity that would have attracted the killer to that corner. Possibly a drug or sex deal in the alleyway, which the old man had the misfortune to witness. But again, that hardly justified the violence of the beating. More likely, the killer had spotted the old man a few blocks earlier, trailed him and used the cover of the alley to strike.

Movement at the crime scene caught Green's eye, and he glanced back to see Sullivan striding towards him. The big Irish farm boy still moved with a footballer's grace, but twenty-five years of fast food, hasty snacks and beer had added a substantial gut to his mammoth frame. It strained the buttons of his white dress shirt beneath his open sports jacket. High blood pressure had mottled his freckled face, and for the first time Green saw glints of silver in his tufted, straw-coloured hair. Sullivan shook his head grimly as he ducked under the yellow tape.

"It's not my father," Green said.

"I didn't think so. This man looks much larger. I estimate five-ten, one hundred and seventy pounds. He has white hair, but he doesn't seem as..." Sullivan paused as if looking for a neutral word.

"Withered?" Green supplied. His father was in his late eighties, and years of chronic illness and depression had whittled his body to a wraith. "Any ID on him?"

Sullivan shook his head. "Pockets are empty, watch gone—you can still see the indents of the links on his wrist. The bastard even took the rings off his fingers."

"Wedding finger?" Not that it would mean anything. Green's father still wore his wedding band twenty years after his mother's death.

Sullivan nodded. "And on the pinky finger of his right hand. On the surface, it looks like a mugging turned ugly."

"How long has he been dead?"

Sullivan turned to nod towards the white-suited officials clustered over the body. Two Ident officers, two morgue assistants, and in the middle, looming larger than any of them, the flamboyant, white-maned figure of Dr. Alexander

MacPhail. Green could hear his booming Scottish brogue from a hundred feet away, admonishing Lyle Cunningham's junior Ident assistant not to vomit on the hands.

"Bag them, laddie! That's all I asked!"

Sullivan even managed a chuckle. "Lyle's breaking in a new lad, but I don't think he'll last a week. He's already puked in the corner twice."

"So they're a bit behind schedule."

Sullivan shrugged. "MacPhail's not giving us a thing yet, till he gets all his calculations in, but I did our usual simple test—"

"The toe test?"

Sullivan nodded. "He's stiffened up nicely. Rigor's pretty complete. With the cold last night, I'd guess he's been dead eight to twelve hours."

Green considered the implications. Eight hours made it four o'clock in the morning, an unlikely time to be out for a stroll. It made more sense that the old man had been assaulted a couple of hours earlier than that, when innocent passersby were safely tucked into bed and the streets were overrun with punks. The question was—why hadn't the old man been tucked into bed too?

"What does he look like? Homeless?"

Sullivan's brows shot up. "Oh, no! He was wearing a three-piece suit, a tie and a nice camelhair overcoat. All about twenty years out of date, according to MacPhail, but in perfect shape. Expensive, MacPhail says, and he should know. Probably didn't get stolen because it was covered in blood. His shoes are gone."

"Pricey Italian leather, I bet. A lowlife with taste?"

"Well, they could have been stolen after the fact, by some street bum in need."

"For that matter," Green said, "all the stuff could have been stolen after the fact by someone who stumbled upon the body."

"But then we don't have a motive for the attack, do we?"

Green shrugged. He wasn't sure Italian shoes, some rings and a dress watch were motive enough to obliterate a man's head. "Not till we find out who this guy was and what he was doing out that late." He broke off as he watched a tall, slender woman stroll languidly towards them, flicking her cellphone shut. She was nicely packaged in a navy jacket and beige pants — or as Sharon would have scolded him, taupe—and a simple gold scarf at her neck. She wore no make-up that Green could detect, but her skin was like flawless cream. She had long legs, a straight back, and everything about her flowed, including her blonde hair, which was loosely clipped in a long ponytail down her back.

Green shot Sullivan a look to see if he too was watching. Sullivan grinned. "Our new sergeant wanted to take the lead on this herself, so I figured why not? This will hit the media—are the elderly safe on their own streets?—and they'll lap her up."

"Not to mention our new police chief. The Force's 'diversity in hiring' program visible for all to see, and she's fluently bilingual to boot."

Sergeant Marie Claire Levesque frowned fleetingly at the sight of Green before pasting a determined smile on her face. Green had met her only once, at her transfer interview the month before, but he'd analyzed her file and sought the opinion of colleagues. Determined was the word most frequently mentioned. Along with smart.

"Good morning, Inspector," Levesque said with a hint of French lilt. She extended her hand. "Nice to see you again."

Ambitious too, the file had said. Nothing wrong with ambition, as long as it was tempered by competence. At five-

13

foot-ten, she matched him in height, yet with her high cheekbones and long, patrician nose, he almost felt as if she were looking down on him. Conscious of his sweaty T-shirt and bike-helmet hair, he drew himself up.

"Your first case is a sad one."

She nodded. "And messy. Forensics says there is a lot of physical evidence, and they were able to lift some tissue from under the nails. It seems the victim fought back. His cane has a crack in it, and what looks like blood on the tip."

"Any leads from Missing Persons?" Sullivan asked her, nodding towards the cellphone in her hand.

She shook her head. Her pony tail swished distractingly. "I just checked with them again. No one called in a missing senior."

Green wasn't surprised. How long would it take before his own father was reported missing? Sid Green lived alone and rarely went outside any more. The circle of cronies he used to meet for card games had dwindled through illness and death. Green tried to phone him every day, but some days there weren't enough hours in the day. If this old man had a wife or lived with someone, he would probably have been reported by Sunday morning, but if he lived alone, it might take days.

"Do we have anything to go on?" he asked. "A monogram on a handkerchief, an ATM slip in a pocket?"

Levesque nodded. "They may find more when they examine the clothes and the body, but we found one item in his coat pocket—a receipt from the Rideau Pharmacy from last April. I asked Detective Charbonneau to follow up with them. And..." She paused, then slipped her hand into her handbag and withdrew a plastic evidence bag. Inside, Green could make out an object on a gold chain.

"We found this beside the body. It looks like gold." She

held out the bag. "It's a Jewish star, right? What's it called?"

Sullivan cast Green a sharp look, but Green barely noticed as he took the bag and held it up to the sunlight. He twisted the piece this way and that. It was hammered gold, exquisitely delicate and old. Dread crawled down his spine.

"A *Magen David*," he said, then grimaced at the irony. "Literally, Shield of David. It's meant to protect."

*　　*　　*

Mort Fine, the owner of Fine Antiques, was just flipping the sign in his shop window to "Open" when Green pushed through the door. He scowled as if a customer were an inconvenience, but then his pig-like eyes lit up at the sight of Green.

"Mr. Yiddish Policeman!" he exclaimed, trundling his squat body along the narrow aisle of his shop. "More mysteries for me?"

"You remember me?" A few years earlier Green had enlisted his help in identifying some old keys found at a crime, and since then Fine had provided the occasional tip about the fencing activities of his more dubious competitors.

"How could I forget? I get so many customers here?"

Green glanced around the shop. The place was a fire trap. Curios, figurines, tarnished silver and old lamps were still jumbled without apparent order on the shelving that crammed the aisles. Antique chandeliers covered the ceiling like stalactites in a cave. It didn't look as if a dust mop had passed over anything since Green's last visit. He could feel his bronchial tubes closing up at the mould and dust.

"Business good?" he asked, trying to keep the irony out of his voice.

"*Oy...*" Fine scrunched up his rubbery face. "So what can

I do for you? We'd better talk fast before the crowds come through the door."

Green laughed. "You know anything about jewellery?"

Fine's eyes danced. "You want to buy your wife a special something? I could give you a very good price on a sapphire ring that just came in."

Green laid the evidence bag on the counter at the cash so that the small gold Star of David was visible. "What can you tell me about this piece?"

Fine picked the bag up with pudgy but surprisingly nimble fingers. He turned it over and over, frowning. "Besides that it's old, not much unless you let me take it out of the bag."

Green had him sign the evidence log, then followed as the man carried the bag into the workshop at the rear and turned on a powerful light. He slid the contents out onto a white enamel tray. The chain tumbled out along with the star Fine weighed first the whole pendant then the star alone. He held it up to his jeweller's loupe and peered at each square millimetre of it. In the small, stifling confines of the workshop, the silence was broken only by his asthmatic breathing and the occasional grunt.

Green sneaked a peek at his watch. Tony and Sharon were expecting him at Nate's Deli at one o'clock, and he had tried their patience enough for one day.

"You in some kind of hurry?" Fine demanded, without taking his eyes off the star.

"How long will you be?"

"Can you leave it with me? I can research in my spare time."

Green shook his head. "It can't be out of my custody."

"I don't work miracles. It's good quality. Twenty-two carat gold maybe, not the *dreck* they make nowadays. Hand shaped and hammered by a goldsmith, not off the assembly line in China."

"China makes *Magen Davids*?"

"China makes everything. *Mezzuzahs, yarmulkes...* You go to Israel today, half the Judaica in Old Jerusalem is from China. But this..." he smiled enigmatically, "this is from Russia."

"You can tell that? Something different about the gold?"

"Probably, but who knows?" His smile broadened, showing a row of unnaturally straight, white teeth. In his lumpy, pockmarked face, their perfection was jarring. He stepped back, removed his loupe and held it out to Green. "Have a look. There's a jeweller's monogram on the back. Cyrillic letters. ASM, I think. There's an inscription as well."

Dutifully Green peered through the magnifying glass, astonished that he could see every scratch and speck of dust on the gold. At first he could make out nothing beyond a few faint etchings, well worn by the passage of time. Then slowly a pattern emerged. He couldn't read Russian, couldn't recognize anything but a few loops, but he took Fine's word for it.

"Can you photograph this?" he asked. "Would that help you research it?"

Fine scowled, but Green could see the glint of intrigue in his eye. Objects told a tale, and the older and more widely-travelled they were the more fascinating the tale. Without another word, he had his state-of-the-art digital camera out and was fiddling with lenses.

Ten minutes later, Green left the shop deep in thought about the elderly victim. Having an old piece of jewellery from Russia meant very little, of course. The old man could have purchased it in an antique store here or in any one of the hundreds of Judaica shops in North America. He could even have purchased it online. Fine might be able to pinpoint who the goldsmith ASM was, and when and where he had lived, but that would tell the police nothing about where the victim was from. Green himself had bought a pair of antique silver

Shabbas candlesticks from Fine, who claimed they had come from the Ukraine. Green had never been near the Ukraine.

Reluctantly, he forced the mystery of the dead man from his mind. The routine homicide investigation was being capably managed by Sergeant Levesque and overseen by Staff Sergeant Sullivan, who had fifteen years in major crimes under his belt. The body had been removed to the morgue, and before heading off to the Britannia Yacht Club for his Sunday afternoon sail, Dr. MacPhail had scheduled the autopsy for Monday morning.

The Ident Unit was still at the scene, painstakingly collecting cigarette butts and trying to lift footprints from the tiny patch of dirt between the sidewalk and the building. The killer might have hidden there, pressed up against the wall in the shadows, waiting to ambush the old man. A team of uniformed officers under Levesque's direction was conducting a street canvass, searching for anyone who might know the old man or might have witnessed the assault. In the middle of a weekend market day, a near-futile task.

Against Levesque's obvious but unvoiced objection, Green had taken over the tracing of the Star of David, arguing that he had the connections and knew more about the significance and possible origins of the religious piece than either she or Sullivan, both lapsed Catholics. But the truth was, he couldn't resist the lure of the case. It wasn't simply the desire to be back in the trenches, following up leads and tracking down killers instead of sitting behind his desk. This victim felt special to him. The death of a courtly old Jewish gentleman out for his evening stroll hit a little too close to home for him. Who knew what this man had accomplished and endured over his life? To meet such a brutal and pointless end was an affront to all that Green believed just and fair.

His resolve hardened as he helped his father through the

glass doors of his seniors' residence and into the staff car parked illegally at the curb. Nate's Deli was a mere five blocks away, but at his father's creeping pace, too far for him to walk now. The deterioration had been slow, almost imperceptible, but every spring, Sid Green seemed never to bounce back to the form he'd had the autumn before. The snow, ice and bone-chilling cold of winter sapped his strength more each year.

Sid leaned on his cane and eyed the alien car with dismay. "Where's Sharon? And the baby?"

The baby was now nearly five years old and had just begun kindergarten, but in Sid's eyes, he would always be the new arrival.

"They're going to meet us at Nate's."

A smile spread across Sid's face, momentarily erasing the pinched frown and the perpetual melancholy in his rheumy brown eyes. "And Hannah?"

Green didn't know where his daughter was. She was not answering her cell, and in typical eighteen-year-old fashion, she had not come home Saturday night. She had called just after the eleven o'clock news to say she would be staying at a "friend's". Judging from the loud chatter and the booming bass music, it was "friends" in the very plural.

At least she had called. When she'd first arrived on their doorstep, fresh from a fight with her mother and spitting mad at the world, she had planned to stay only long enough to punish her mother, Green's ex-wife, and put a face to her father. Two years later, she was almost finished high school, had found a part-time job as a special needs companion and had learned to meet them halfway on rules. Most of the time.

Green too had made progress as a father in the past two years, but he knew the main reason Hannah had slowly been won over was Sid Green. She adored her grandfather almost as much as he adored her. In looks, she was the incarnation of his dead wife, for whom she'd been named —small and delicate, with an elfin innocence that hid a steely spirit. In Hannah's presence, Sid shed ten years and half a century of sorrow.

When Green had to tell his father she wasn't coming, he could see the old man deflate. Sid lowered himself into the passenger seat with a sigh and barely spoke as they drove to Nate's. Green knew the sight of Tony would reinvigorate his father, but he'd asked Sharon to come a little later, because he wanted a few minutes alone with his father before the energizer bunny burst in, full of bounce and chatter.

He waited until Sid was settled with his customary weak tea before broaching the subject on his mind. He was still summoning the words that would not alarm his father when the elderly man raised his hands expressively.

"*Nu,* Mishka. You look worried."

Green hesitated. Nodded. "Just wondering, Dad. There's a case..."

"*Voden,*" his father said softly. "The old man killed on Rideau Street."

Green suppressed his surprise. "You know?"

"I heard it on the morning news. You want to tell me not to walk alone on Rideau Street. Never mind I haven't done it for five years."

"I know. But just in case you should feel like it..." Green toyed with his spoon, avoiding his father's skeptical eyes. "But also I wanted to ask if you know a well-dressed Jewish gentleman maybe ten years younger than you, who lives alone around here, walks with a cane and wears a beige camelhair coat."

Sid looked thoughtful. "Well dressed. What—a tuxedo maybe?"

"A suit and tie. But expensive. Classy."

"So, rich."

"Well off, probably. His camelhair coat is a Harry Rosen."

"That you can buy off the rack at Neighbourhood Services."

Point taken, Green thought. MacPhail had thought the suit was twenty years out of date, so it was possible it had been given away to a charity shop and snapped up by an elderly man with tastes beyond his current means. But the Star of David had also been good quality gold, and the shoes had been nice enough to steal.

"I think he had—or used to have—some money, and whatever he'd done for a living, expensive clothes were important." Green was grasping at straws, but he hoped some small detail might twig Sid's memory. "It's possible he was also from Russia."

"Ach." Sid waved a dismissive hand. "Russian Jews are everywhere."

"He had an antique gold *Magen David* from Russia. Think, Dad. Well-off, well dressed, lived alone, might have had a Russian accent, used a cane." Sid was still looking blank. "Could he have lived in your building?"

"Not in my building, no. But you could ask at the *shul* up on Chapel St. If he lived downtown around the old neighbourhood, they might know. The *alter kakers* go there for services, to say *kaddish* for their wives and parents who've died." Sid said the word for old men with contempt. He had tossed his faith, and his trust in old men, on the funeral pyres of Auschwitz.

The suggestion of the Chapel Street synagogue was brilliant, and Green was just about to thank his father when the front door burst open, and a shriek filled the restaurant.

"Zaydie!" Tony came charging down the aisle, his dark curls bouncing and his chocolate brown eyes shining. Sharon scrambled to deflect him from waiters laden high with trays. A good ten seconds later, to Green's surprise, Hannah slunk through the door, her orange hair plastered up one side of her head and last night's mascara still smudged beneath her eyes.

Sid clapped his hands, all trace of irritation gone. His day was complete.

Three

Omar Adams rolled over to the wall and pulled his pillow over his head. He still couldn't block out the incessant natter of his three younger brothers, who were crouched on the floor in the little space between their beds, playing *Warcraft II* on their Play Station. In the background he could hear his mother and father arguing, his mother in Somali and his father in English. As usual, his mother shrieked like a demented crow, but the scary one was his father, who got quieter the angrier he was. The old man was deadly quiet this morning.

Morning? Omar lifted the pillow to check. No sunlight was poking through the small, narrow window in the corner of the room, and the smell of spices and onions filled the air. Fuck, had he missed half the day? His stomach lurched, and he had to swallow hard to keep the bile down. His head ached, and his mouth tasted of stale puke. When he shifted, pain shot through his arms. He couldn't remember why. He couldn't remember a fucking thing about last night, after that last bottle of vodka and the weed they'd passed around. Special weed, Nadif had said, scored from a new source. Some special!

He wondered how the other guys felt. Besides Nadif and Yusuf, his street buddies, he knew there were others, even though he couldn't remember who. Or how he'd got home, or what time. He remembered them all sitting around drinking in the gazebo in Macdonald Gardens, talking about Nadif's court case, about the brothers who were refusing to testify against him and the old man with the lousy eyesight who'd fingered Nadif. He remembered them all walking down Rideau Street, ogling the hookers. Yusuf said he did one once, for fifty bucks behind the construction fence for the new condo, but then Yusuf's big brother ran a slew of them himself, so he probably got a family discount.

The thought of drinking brought the bile up again, so Omar tried to make his mind go blank. Blank out the pounding in his chest and the pain in his hands. Blank out the flashes that danced behind his eyelids, the clenched fists, long, glistening ropes of blood, jagged bone, panicked eyes. And the long, thin glint of steel.

It was the last image that forced him out of bed, tripping over his brothers and staggering down the hall to fling himself over the toilet. For five minutes he heaved, resting his head on the bowl, tears and snot mingling with God knows what as he tried to purge last night from his system.

What the hell had they done?

Afterwards, he flopped back against the wall and cradled his head in his hands. That was when he noticed the crusted stains on his hoodie. He must have fallen into bed last night fully dressed. He pulled at the baggy shirt and peered at the stains. Blood. A shiver ran through him. Grabbing the edge of the sink, he hauled himself to his feet and propped himself against the bowl. A freaky sight met him in the mirror—his face, smeared with dirt and crusted with puke. Dark red was caked around his swollen nose. He touched it carefully, swore out loud as the pain shot through his brain.

The bathroom door opened silently, and his father loomed in the mirror beside him. Omar recoiled in shock and gripped the sink. His father fixed him with his pale blue eyes. Those cold, creepy eyes. The only sign of trouble was the vein pulsing under the skin of his neck. "Where were you last night?"

Omar tried a little shrug, but his shoulders screamed in pain. "Just out with the guys."

"Nadif." He said the name like it was a cockroach. "What did I tell you?"

"Not Nadif. Just Yusuf."

The flat eyes never blinked. In a contest with Omar, they never blinked. Omar knew he could see right through the lie. "You got in at three o'clock. That's unacceptable."

Omar wanted to ask what he was like when he got home, but he didn't dare. He just nodded, hung his head, and his father turned away.

"Clean yourself up before your mother and your brothers see you."

The bathroom door closed. Omar reached for a towel, wetted it and began to dab at his face. Slowly his ebony skin emerged from behind the puke and blood. It was scraped. Raw. What the hell? He tried to think, but his brains felt fried.

He could phone Nadif and try to find out what he knew. But Nadif was already up for attempted murder on that Rideau Centre knifing, and he was going to cover his own ass. No matter what happened, he'd lie or rat out someone else, rather than add to his sheet.

He could phone Yusuf, who at seventeen was still a young offender and under the cops' radar. Yusuf would tell it straight, and he'd be on Omar's side if it came to ratting anyone out.

Or he could just lie low. Nurse his hangover. Wait till the fog lifted and the crazy jumble of flashbacks faded away. Maybe then he'd remember what had happened. What was real and what was from a horror flick he'd seen in some freaked-out, wasted state.

Maybe nothing was real at all.

As Green expected, the old synagogue on Chapel Street was locked up tight on a Sunday afternoon, but he had a back-up plan. He had a personal connection with the rabbi who'd served the aging inner city congregation for twenty-five years before being forced to face old age himself. Rabbi Zachary Tolner had not slipped into retirement easily but spent most of his spare time, when he wasn't training for marathons, badgering the new rabbi and the board to ensure they didn't forget how things should be done.

When Green's mother had been dying of breast cancer more than twenty years earlier, Rabbi Tolner had tried to visit her in hospital. Sid had thrown him out in a rage.

"Where is your God!" he'd screamed, in one of the rare moments of animation Green had seen during his mother's long ordeal. "Where was He in Auschwitz? In Majdanek, where she was a girl—a fifteen-year-old girl who had to sell her soul for..." He'd never said for what, but it was more than Green had ever learned in the years before. Or since. The rabbi had tried to calm him and simply to be with him, but Sid had retreated back into that numbness which had probably served him well in Auschwitz.

At twenty-five, intoxicated with police work and with Hannah's featherbrained but perfectly-formed mother, Green had been no more receptive to Tolner's spiritual overtures than his father had been, but that had not dampened Tolner's belief that he had a personal line of influence in the police department. Green had a stack of letters Tolner had sent him over the years complaining about everything from drug dealers on the synagogue steps to bums sleeping under the tree by the back door.

Green knew where to find the man. Now it was time for a little payback.

Tolner had changed little in the ten years since Green had last seen him. He was bent over the postage stamp-sized garden outside his townhouse, wearing a warped Tilley hat pulled down snug over his bald head and a pair of powder blue jogging pants concealing his spindly legs. His arms stuck out from his T-shirt, sinewy and tanned almost nut brown from a lifetime worshipping the outdoors. As Green approached, he straightened and drew every inch of his five-foot-four-inch frame to attention. His face was a web of wrinkles, but in their midst, his pale blue eyes lit with interest.

"The mountain comes to Isaac!"

Green laughed and extended his hand. "How are you, Zak?"

Tolner peeled off one gardening glove and encased Green's hand in a powerful grip. "Bored! I hope you brought something interesting." Worry flickered his gaze. "How's your father?"

"Fine. Going to live to be a hundred, *kvetching* all the way. This is another old man. Maybe you've heard? Beaten to death just off Rideau Street?"

The ready grin fled. "A Jew?"

Green tilted his palm in uncertainty. "Possibly. We're trying to identify him. Early seventies, five-ten, a hundred and seventy pounds, thick white hair, used a burled maple cane. Harry Rosen suit, out of date?"

Tolner had been listening intently, his blue eyes flickering with each new description as though he were searching through some internal database. At the end of the list, he shook his head slowly. "You could try being more specific. You're describing everybody."

"His hair was long and frizzy. Picture Einstein."

This time a faint glimmer of recognition shone in Tolner's eyes, but still he shook his head. "Can't you show me a picture? Even of the corpse?"

"Too much facial damage."

Tolner winced. "*Oy.*"

"You have an idea, don't you?"

"No, I don't."

"Yes, you do. You blinked."

"Nothing that I'm going to tell you based on 'Einstein's hair'. What makes you think he was even Jewish?"

Green extracted the evidence bag containing the Star of David from his pocket. "He had this in his possession."

Tolner took the plastic bag and held it at arms' length. He squinted, and Green saw another flicker of recognition. "Ahh."

"What do you mean, ahh?"

"Just..." Tolner lifted his shoulders in a classic Yiddish shrug. "This I recognize."

"Does it fit with the Einstein hair?"

"Yes. Damn it, yes. And with the out-of-date Harry Rosen suit." Tolner handed back the evidence bag. "Sam Rosenthal. Been a member of the *shul* for years, although he doesn't come very often. Busy man, back in the days when I knew him. Travelled a lot to medical conferences, lectures and stuff."

"So he's a doctor?"

"Psychiatrist. Very well-respected years ago, when he was at the height of his career. Got a little wonky near the end, but then half those guys are wonky to start with, so it wasn't far to go."

Green had been jotting notes. "Wonky how?"

Tolner hesitated, and Green suspected he was weighing the wisdom of discretion against his love of gossip. He brushed at some specks of dirt on his T-shirt. "This is from congregants, you understand. When his wife was dying, he got Eastern religion and started meditating and searching for the deeper meaning of life. I gather he started to question all the drugs his psychiatric colleagues were prescribing. Claimed we had to respect nature's diversity and the patient's right to be different. Became the darling of the new age types, I think, but his colleagues were less amused."

"You said his wife is dead?"

"About ten years ago. Her death was a long ordeal— " He broke off, as if remembering Green's mother.

"We're going to need DNA for a positive ID. Does he have any other family?"

"A son somewhere in the States." Tolner nodded towards the west. "Sam used to live in one of those mansions on Range Road overlooking the Rideau River—it's an embassy now— but he sold it and gave half the proceeds to some group researching meditation, and he bought a falling apart Victorian dump in Sandy Hill near the university. He lives in a cramped one-bedroom on the bottom floor and rents the rest of it out to students for *bobkes*. I often see him out walking along Rideau Street."

"Was he still practising?"

Tolner shrugged. "He might have been, but I'd be surprised. He'd be up around seventy-five by now."

"Do you know the son's name?"

Tolner shook his head. "Like I said, he moved to the States to study right out of high school, and he never came back. That was maybe thirty years ago."

"Study what?"

"Oh, I don't know. Sam wasn't very active in the synagogue and his son was even less so. I met the son exactly once, at his mother's funeral. Didn't even stick around for the Shiva."

"Can you remember *any* details? A first name maybe?"

"David? John? Some common name."

Green sighed. There were probably hundreds of John Rosenthals listed in the United States. He had to hope that a search of Sam Rosenthal's apartment would yield a lead.

"One more question," he said. "Did Sam Rosenthal have any enemies or recent disputes with anyone? Assuming it is Sam, can you think of anyone who might have done this?"

Tolner had leaned down to yank a weed from the edge of the walkway. He straightened slowly, squinting into the slanting afternoon sun for a few long seconds. Finally he shrugged. "He spent years dealing with the mentally ill. Maybe one of them? He could be a little... arrogant, you know how doctors can get. Maybe some punk accosted him on the street, and he didn't give in quick enough. What a crying shame. It's always the good guys, isn't it? Like the coyote, nature's bad guys are too wily ever to be victims."

*   *   *

Green could have phoned the information in to the station. It was his day off and, as everyone kept reminding him, he was an inspector, whose job was to oversee and administer, not to scrabble around in the streets unearthing leads, but he was curious to see their new Sergeant Levesque in action to reassure himself that she hadn't booked off early or settled in to conduct the investigation with her feet up on her desk.

The Major Crimes squad room was deserted except for the familiar sight of Bob Gibbs bent over his computer. The young detective's head shot up in alarm at his superior officer's arrival, but he looked relieved when Green asked for the sergeant.

"She's out, sir. Checking s-security tape from the pawn shop on Rideau Street."

"Has Staff Sergeant Sullivan been in this afternoon?"

Gibbs shook his head, and Green suppressed his frustration as he pondered his next move. He felt restless and dissatisfied. So many dangling unknowns. He should go home to spend the rest of Sunday with his family. He could simply phone Sergeant Levesque to pass on the information on the victim's possible identity. Or he could check out just one more little piece of information to round out the story before he handed it off to her.

His little alcove office smelled stuffy as he squeezed inside and booted up his computer. Stacks of rumpled reports, files and official manuals overflowed the bookcase beside his desk and teetered on the guest chair just inside the door.

In the Canada 411 online directory, there were two listings for S Rosenthal in the Ottawa area, but neither were anywhere near Sandy Hill. Well, well, he thought. Dr. Samuel Rosenthal might have an unlisted phone number. Not so unusual for a psychiatrist, he supposed, since like cops, they would deal with the troubled and potentially unpredictable underbelly of society.

He tried a standard Google search—Samuel Rosenthal, psychiatrist—and received 442 hits. He added Ottawa to narrow the search down to 164 hits. A quick scan of these revealed that Dr. Rosenthal had been a prolific author of academic papers on depression, schizophrenia, the role of stress, and the efficacy of various unpronounceable drugs. He had given public lectures, sat on the boards of mental health and community agencies, and taught at the university medical school. Almost all the references were more than ten years old, but the most recent ones dealt with drug efficacy in the treatment of adjustment disorders in adolescence.

What the hell is an adolescent adjustment disorder, Green wondered in astonishment. Is it a label for kids like me, who'd run a little wild in rebellion against the obsessive overprotection of panicky parents? Out of curiosity, he clicked on the reference but couldn't access the article without subscribing to the journal. The brief abstract that preceded the article, however, was illuminating.

Adjustment disorders are by definition short-lived reactions to stress, characterized by mood and anxiety symptoms or acting-out behaviour. Despite the well-documented stress of adolescence, the diagnosis of adjustment disorder in this population is generally overlooked by mental health practitioners in favor of old standbys like anxiety disorder, mood disorder and even the major psychoses, thus squandering the opportunity to provide genuine help. In this rush to pathologize them, the adolescent's own analysis of his or her experience is viewed of no account.

And I thought police lingo was indecipherable, Green thought, but there was no denying the challenging tone. He scanned the bio that followed. Samuel Rosenthal had been born in Capetown, South Africa and had been educated at Capetown University and Maudsley Psychiatric Hospital in London before emigrating to Canada in 1964 to accept a post in Montreal. He had moved across the country, working his way up the academic ladder, before ending his career as professor and a chief psychiatrist at the Rideau Psychiatric Hospital, where Sharon worked.

Green wondered if Sharon had known him before his retirement, and if she knew anything about his reputation as a man and as a psychiatrist. He was tempted to call her, but her reaction to his mid-afternoon detour into work had not been encouraging. He could tell she was hiding her annoyance for

Tony's sake, but neither of them needed what remained of their weekend further invaded by his work. Besides, Rosenthal's work as a psychiatrist was probably utterly irrelevant to his death at the hands of street punks.

Green smiled wryly at the irony. Street punks—homeless, drug-addicted and alienated from the world—were the ultimate example of adolescent adjustment disorder.

As interesting as the information was, however, none of it yielded any clues as to Rosenthal's current address or telephone number. Green reached for his phone. It took him a few minutes to round up his back-door contact at Bell Canada and secure a listing for the doctor. Rabbi Tolner was right. Sam Rosenthal lived on Nelson Street, only a block from Rideau Street. And also, in a coincidence too close for comfort, only a block west of Sid Green's seniors' home.

*　　*　　*

I'm coming home, I'm coming home, he promised Sharon silently as he drove to the old doctor's home. He knew the building, a grand old Victorian mansion that would once have housed a member of Parliament or senior civil servant in burgeoning post-Confederation Ottawa. In its heyday, it would have seen its share of soirées and political intrigue, but it was now divided into six flats, each with its own doorbell and mailbox in the front hall. The apartments were probably occupied by a mix of university students, fixed-income seniors and new immigrants. From the medley of smells in the hallway, some East Indians and Latin Americans were among them.

The front yard betrayed the same descent from elegance to pragmatism. Most of it was paved over to house a jumble of bicycles, garbage and recycling bins, but under the bay window was a well-mulched rose garden still producing vibrant pink and red blooms at the end of the season. Someone must be weeding it, fertilizing it and encouraging it to grow in this toxic waste of asphalt and dust. Probably Dr. Rosenthal himself, accustomed to the stunning perennial gardens that surround the houses overlooking the Rideau River.

According to Tolner, Dr. Rosenthal occupied the ground floor flat, but there was no name on his buzzer or mailbox. Anonymous to the end, Green thought, and wondered whether it was professional paranoia that had lingered into retirement, or simply a sense that this place would never be home. Ringing the buzzer brought no response. His fingers itched to ring one of the neighbours. This was not his investigation, he castigated himself, and the follow-up really belonged to Sergeant Levesque.

He was rescued from his dilemma when one of the interior doors opened, and a young woman came out into the hall. Small, blonde and impossibly skinny, she was dressed in jeans and a frilly purple jacket, with the trademark book bag slung over one shoulder and a bike helmet under her arm. Her weary eyes widened with alarm at the sight of him. He hastened to introduce himself, which reassured her only marginally. She edged towards the door as he recorded her name—Lindsay Corsin—and asked her about the occupant on the ground floor.

"The landlord? He's quiet and nice, but he keeps to himself." Lindsay had a breathy, singsong voice that phrased everything as a question. "I've talked to him like maybe three times? Since I moved here. Why?"

"Can you describe him? Height, weight, hair colour?"

She shrugged. "I don't know. Medium, you know? About

the same as you, only way older."

Green suppressed a smile. In the past, his fine brown hair, freckled nose and medium build had made him look deceptively youthful, but recently strands of grey had appeared at his temples. It was reassuring to know that seventy-five still looked a long way off.

"What can you tell me about his clothes?"

"He's a funny dresser. Always has a suit, even a tie. He's old-fashioned that way."

Mentally Green was ticking off the points of confirmation. "Have you seen him today?"

"No, but I've been upstairs. I don't think he's in."

"Does he have visitors? Go out much?"

She wrinkled her brow as if puzzled by the question. Her gaze darted to his closed door, and she seemed to vacillate. "Sometimes he has visitors. I hear them talking, like? You can hear everything through these walls."

"Talking about what?"

"I couldn't hear. Just, like, conversation? But mostly he's alone." She shifted uneasily. Took the helmet in both hands and twirled it. "Umm, I gotta go. I'm late for my study group."

"I won't keep you much longer. One last question. Does he go out at night?"

She frowned as though trying to figure out why he was asking. "Sometimes, I guess. I think he has trouble sleeping, because he gets on my case when I have friends over. Keeps pounding the ceiling with his cane." Her face cleared with sudden understanding. "Oh, this is about last week, eh?"

"What happened last week?"

"Well, someone trashed his place. Broke a window in the back? Boy, was he mad. But you guys know all that. He wanted you to fingerprint his whole place."

Having now run roughshod over Levesque's first homicide investigation long enough, Green realized the sergeant needed to be brought into the picture. The obvious next move—checking out the apartment and the Break and Enter investigation—was hers to make. So he thanked Lindsay and handed her his card with the usual request to contact him if she remembered anything important. She snatched it and scurried out the door without a backward glance. She and her bicycle were already out of sight by the time he got back into his car.

He found Levesque crammed into the small utility closet that passed for the security and housekeeping office at the back of the Rideau Street pawn shop. She looked up with excitement, and if she was unnerved or annoyed by his appearance, she betrayed no sign. All business, she gestured towards the grainy monitor in front of her.

"Lucky for us, the shop has the tape on a two-day loop over the weekend so the shop owner can check for intrusions or missing merchandise when he arrives Monday morning. So we have coverage for the critical time period between ten p.m. Saturday and five a.m. Sunday."

Green peered at the monitor. The date and time, down to the second, were stamped in the bottom right corner of the image. The camera seemed to be mounted in the upper corner of the main door frame, and its wide-angled lens showed a blurry, fisheye view of the barred entranceway to the store along with the edge of the shop window and the sidewalk beyond. As it rolled, Green squinted, trying to make out details. "Any sign of the victim?"

She shook her head. "He must have been on the other side of the street at this point."

That makes sense, Green thought, since his home was on

the other side of the street. However, in his experience, elderly people with canes were careful to cross at a traffic light. "I wonder what made him cross in the middle of the block," he mused. "Any sign of trouble?"

"Just the usual Saturday night. Half a dozen drug deals, a girl having a shoving match with her boyfriend, I don't know how many drunks pissing in the gutter, sex trade workers strolling by..." Levesque tapped the screen as a figure limped by, trundling a pull cart behind him. "There's Screech, on his way to his sleeping quarters. Time is 1:33 a.m. He still has his sleeping bag."

"Have we talked to him? He may be able to ID some of these people."

"We took his statement, but his memory is unreliable."

An understatement, Green thought. Screech was a proud Cree from Labrador who'd once worked the mines in Northern Quebec until his lungs gave out, but ten years on the street had not improved his health. Nor his mind. But even so, sometimes Screech knew things about the street that no one else did. The trick was in persuading him to share them. Money usually improved his mood, a fact Green mentioned to Levesque.

She reached over and rifled a stack of papers at her side. "I've printed off stills, and once the pathologist gives us a better idea on time of death, I'll show them to him. I've also put a call out on the street. But we did find one promising lead." She leaned over and began to fast-forward the tape. Green watched the jerky flashes of people scurrying past the shop.

In the silence, he plunged ahead. "I have a probable ID, address, and next of kin on the victim."

Her finger jerked off the button, freezing the frame, and she swung around to gape at him. In terse, professional clips, he summarized his discoveries of the day. She had the discipline to listen without interruption, but her jaw grew tighter with each revelation. Beneath her dispassionate gaze, he knew she was fuming. Her blue eyes smoked.

"So I leave it in your very capable hands." He flourished a grin he hoped would take the sting out. "Public records should turn up the son easily, and the B & E follow-up may give you some very useful information about motive."

"I appreciate all of this, Inspector," she said, not bothering to fake sincerity. "We'll get a warrant for that address as soon as possible, and I'll have one of my detectives pull the B & E file. But I have a much more promising lead right here on the tape." She tapped the play button, and within a few seconds a group of young black males slouched by the camera, their hoodies bagging and their shoelaces trailing. They jostled one another as they fought for space on the narrow sidewalk.

"Street gangs," she said with a smug smile. "That's what this is all about. It isn't important who he was or what went on last week. It's only important that at that moment of that night, he crossed their path."

Four

Green's late night walk around the block with Modo was a ritual he'd grown to love. His huge dog padded peacefully at his side, stopping to browse the scents in the bushes along the way, unhurried and unconcerned. Their street of modest old homes tucked behind overgrown maples and shrubs was never busy, and by ten o'clock it was a morgue. Not a single person passed him in the crisp autumn night. It was a time he could lose himself in thought, sort through the events of the day and ready himself for the next.

Some nights when Hannah was home to babysit, Sharon would join him, and they would walk hand in hand. She'd talk about a difficult patient, or he'd talk about a heart-breaking case. It was a refuge in their busy lives, for which he was grateful.

He hadn't expected to like Modo. When he'd agreed under duress to take in the abandoned hundred-pound mutt—half Lab, half Rottweiler, as close as the vet could tell, but with the temperament of a dwarf rabbit—he'd sworn it was only for a month or two until a proper home could be found. Green had never had pets as a child. His home had been full of irrational fears and long, secretive silences that were oppressive to an only child. His mother had flinched at the mere sound of barking. Forever seared into her brain was the memory that dogs had terrifying magical powers to sniff out hiding places and hunt down fugitives. But Sharon had grown up with dogs in her happy suburban Mississauga home, and she'd taken to the traumatized animal instantly. Modo and Green had needed much longer to trust and value each other.

That evening, Sharon was still doing laundry in preparation for the busy week ahead when he set off for his walk. Random threads of the homicide investigation drifted through his mind as he walked. He considered the theory he was constructing about the victim, once a respected psychiatrist but torn from his moorings by the death of his wife. Like a man of faith, he had questioned the very nature of his professional beliefs. He'd sold his gracious home and bought instead a rundown turreted mansion, where he had to tolerate garbage bins in his front yard and student parties overhead. A solitary man who went out for his daily walk dressed in a suit from his professional days. A creature of habit like Green's own father, but proud, elegant, unafraid, and unlike Green's father refusing to be intimidated by the human dangers on the street. Refusing to be violated, even when the violators came to his own home. Ready to fight.

Tragically, ready to die.

For once, the walk did not put Green in a better frame of mind. It did not energize him for the week ahead but left him feeling outraged and ready to fight as well. When he came back inside, he found Sharon curled up on the living room sofa with her petite feet tucked under her, sipping a cup of tea. Finally at rest. He made himself a cup and sank down beside her, reluctant to drag her back into the ugly reality of murder. In the end, his expression must have given him away, because she snuggled against him.

"What is it, Mr. Bigshot Detective?"

"You know the man who died on Rideau Street? We still need a positive ID, but it looks like he was a psychiatrist named Samuel Rosenthal. He used to work at Rideau Psychiatric."

She pulled back, looking puzzled. Recognition widened her eyes. "Dr. Rosenthal! Of course. I didn't know him while he worked there, but everyone knew *of* him. My God, poor man."

"Was he controversial?"

"Well, I remember we often had to patch up patients whom he'd taken off their meds. He was into patient empowerment and natural remedies. St. John's wort for bipolar disorder, for example."

"Do you remember anything about what he was like?"

She took a slow, thoughtful sip of tea. "It was awhile ago. His patients were very loyal to him, so I think he meant well. And he was right, sometimes we are far too quick to pump patients full of drugs when psychotherapy or a healthy lifestyle change would be better. Drugs are faster and cheaper for the healthcare system."

She was slowly waking up. She uncurled herself and set down her tea as if to better marshall her arguments. Sharon had been on this high horse before, railing against a public healthcare system which funded doctors to dole out pills during fifteen-minute sessions but not other therapists who might actually talk to the patients to help them sort out their lives. It sounded as if Sam Rosenthal had shared her view.

"Still," he said, "he must have made some enemies that way."

She chuckled. "Looking for a colleague driven mad by him contradicting their advice?"

Or a patient. The thought came out of the blue and seemed far-fetched the moment he formed it. Rosenthal had barely practised in years. "Did he treat all kinds of problems?"

"I don't know. Most of the trouble came with his young

patients. Misdiagnosed bipolars or first-episode schizophrenics. Those were the real tragedies." He must have looked blank, for she twisted around to study him dubiously. "Do you really want to know all this?"

"I don't have much to go on with this guy. The working assumption is a random gang assault, but you know me. Never overlook the longshot."

She laughed. "Yes, the champion of zebras. Okay. Schizophrenia can be a devastating lifelong disease, but if there's any illness where proper drugs can make a huge difference, this is it. But to have the best outcome you should catch them early, before or during their first psychotic break. Typically that's in their teens or early twenties, where it can be hard to distinguish from other problems, especially if there is illicit drug use. Kids, even their parents, don't want to accept the diagnosis either, so they're willing to grasp at straws."

"Like a nice herbal remedy."

"You got it. Megavitamins or some fancy diet. My favourite is Bach's flowers, based on some guy's wacky ideas from the 1930s, as if we haven't learned a thing about the disease in the decades since then. I'm not saying Western medicine has all the answers in the treatment of mental illness and there's no place for alternative approaches, but the field is full of quackery and fake science, trading on people's fears and hopes. That was the biggest problem we saw with Rosenthal's patients. They'd been treated at the hospital for schizophrenia or bipolar and stabilized on the latest drugs. Then after discharge they'd trot off to Rosenthal complaining of side effects, and he'd take them off. A few months later, bingo, they're hearing voices again and they're back inside. With each psychotic break, their life spirals down. Jobs are lost, marriages destroyed, dreams and plans shattered."

Green had seen enough schizophrenics to know they often stopped taking their meds of their own accord anyway. They'd cross his path when they ended up on the streets acting crazy enough to scare people. He'd heard their reasons often enough. They felt so good after awhile on the meds, they decided maybe they'd been cured and they didn't need them any more. Or they hated the side effects, which gave them the shakes and made them feel they were living their life inside cobwebs. A doctor like Rosenthal, who told them they didn't need the meds after all, would have been greeted like the Messiah.

If they ever realized they'd been duped, however unintentionally, they would have felt betrayed.

Betrayed enough to seek revenge? he wondered, then shook his head at his own crazy thoughts. Blame it on the midnight hour. Levesque had her own, much more sensible line of investigation.

*   *   *

A shadow fell across his desk. "You've been a busy beaver."

Green looked up to see Brian Sullivan lounging in the doorway. To his relief, the head of Major Crimes had a crooked grin on his freckled face and a twinkle in his blue eyes. Green hadn't known what the fallout might be from his foray into the trenches yesterday, but now he guessed Sergeant Levesque was too smart and ambitious to complain about the meddling inspector to her NCO directly, particularly when it was common knowledge in the ranks that Green and Sullivan were not only former partners but close friends.

He returned the grin with a shrug. "What's a little help between friends? It was my day off, and I just used my connections to speed things along."

"She's smart and she's good, Green, even if she doesn't know about your legendary investigative skills. Before her time." He grinned. Nice payback, Green thought. "She looked into that B & E you mentioned, had read the whole file before roll call this morning. Doesn't look like there's much there. Might have been a random thing, or maybe they were looking for drugs or a prescription pad. They turned the place over, but Rosenthal didn't have either."

"He wasn't a big fan of prescription drugs," Green said.

"We're concentrating on the gang thing, trying to ID the four punks on the security camera."

Sullivan's six-foot-four footballer's frame filled most of the doorway, but nonetheless Green could get a glimpse of the bustling squad room behind him. Tilting his head, he signalled Sullivan to come in and shut the door. Sullivan obliged, sinking into the plastic guest chair and propping his huge feet on the corner of Green's desk. The grin had faded from his face, leaving a wary, questioning look.

"There probably is no connection between the break-in and the attack," Green said. "But I think Levesque should send someone around to reexamine the apartment and reinterview neighbours. The guy made enemies, or at least pissed people off with his manner, and in today's hopped-up, macho drug culture, that can be enough."

Sullivan's expression turned smug. "Already done. She's got Jones working on a search warrant for his place right now. We still need to confirm the ID, so she'll be looking for the usual— dentist's name, personal papers, date book, and next of kin."

"Any luck tracking down the son?"

"Not yet, but Levesque assigned it to Gibbsie. He's checking public records. So far there's no record of a birth, so it must have been out of province."

"Maybe even out of the country," Green said, remembering Rosenthal's roundabout academic journey from South Africa through the UK. "But if he's in a system anywhere, Gibbs will find him." Green wondered how the son would react. Losing a family member to murder was a horrifying shock, no matter how estranged the family was. "MacPhail doing the autopsy this morning?"

Sullivan nodded. "But it will be weeks before we get any DNA results back from the lab. There is a hell of a backlog, even when we mark top priority on it. I still think those surveillance tapes and forensics are our best bet. We're also talking to Lowell from the Guns and Gangs Unit and getting the names of all the known members operating in the neighbourhood, and all the wannabes—"

"That's just about everybody!" The Byward Market was one of the central clearing houses for the drug trade. Hardcore addicts and weekend partygoers alike headed down to its narrow, jumbled streets to make a score.

"These men are black—possibly Somali or Ethiopian from what we can tell from the piece of crap tape—so we'll concentrate on those groups first. We also think Rosenthal inflicted some damage. There's tissue under his fingernails, which he kept well manicured, by the way—the guy was a class act—and some blood and hair on the rubber tip of his cane. Our punks may have some visible war wounds, so we want to get a look at all possible suspects ASAP."

"Sounds good. Keep me posted, especially if you locate the son. Meanwhile I'll poke around into this guy's background using the connections I have. If I turn up anything, I'll pass it on."

Sullivan lifted his feet off the desk and took a deep breath as if gathering his forces for the day ahead. "Sure, Mike. Whatever makes you happy."

Green laughed and waved towards the door. "What can I say? Most times the hoofbeats are horses, but you got to keep an eye out for zebras. Now get out of here. I've got some pointless action proposal to prepare for Superintendent Devine. She's revving up her campaign for Deputy Chief into high gear, so I have to solve the spike in domestics by five o'clock today."

*   *   *

Omar twitched aside the curtain and peered down the street. The cop car was still there, parked in front of Nadif's house. Omar hadn't seen them go in, but they'd been in there an awful long time. Omar itched to phone Nadif to find out what was up, but he didn't dare. For one thing, his fucking father would probably hear the phone click and pick up in the middle. For another, Nadif wouldn't be able to tell him a thing with the cops standing two feet away.

He paced back into the bathroom to stare at himself in the mirror. He'd cleaned up the snot and blood the best he could and spent most of Sunday in bed, but he still looked like he'd hit a brick wall. There were scrapes on his arms, his nose was swollen, and one eye was half shut. He'd thought of washing his hoodie and jeans in the bathtub, but he was afraid his father would freak out at the mess. Instead he'd bundled them in a ball and shoved them in the back of his closet to deal with when he could sneak out to the garbage bin in the alley behind. His father had slapped him under house arrest for a month, and even now he was downstairs keeping an eagle eye out.

Omar wished he knew what story Yusuf and Nadif were telling the cops. Maybe they'd all settled on a story Saturday night, but he couldn't remember. Just like he couldn't remember what the hell they'd done after they left the park or how the hell he'd gotten blood all over himself. His stomach still felt like the bottom of a sewer, but at least his headache was gone and his brains were back in place. If the cops came, he'd have to wing his version, admit to all the stuff he could remember that was legal—probably even cop to the joints, no big deal—then say he went straight home. Tripped on the curb and fell down on the way. He'd stick to that, say it was all he could remember. Nadif always said if you're going to lie, best to stick as close to the truth as possible.

Maybe Nadif wouldn't squeal on him. Maybe the cops just wanted to talk to him about his court case, or check if he was following his bail conditions. Jeez, Omar you little dick, that's probably it. Nothing to do with you and the blood and the hole in your memory.

But then he saw Nadif's door open, and two cops came out. Plain clothes, not uniforms. Shit, what did that mean? He watched as they stood on the sidewalk looking up and down the street, before one of them pointed straight at Omar's house, and they started this way.

The asshole had ratted him out after all.

Omar dropped the curtain and pressed himself against his bedroom wall, hoping to be invisible. Maybe he could hide and pretend he wasn't there. But he had three stupid little brothers downstairs who'd be happy to show the cops the way, and a hardass father who always believed in paying the price for all the bad you'd done and then some. His father had seen the blood. Knew he'd come home at three a.m., drunk, wasted and puking his guts out. His father had barely said a word to him all weekend; the cold shoulder was his favourite father-son thing, and he'd forbidden Omar's mother to talk to him either. Not that she did much anyway.

But the old man would turn him in over a fucking marijuana joint, for chrissakes.

He was beginning to feel that slow burn that happened every time he thought about his father, and just then the doorbell rang. Squeals of excitement from his moron brothers, a yell for silence from his father, then nothing but voices in the hall, too quiet for him to hear. Footsteps scrambling on the stairs, the bedroom door bursting open, two brothers bouncing up and down, excited because the cops were here. They were asking for him. Dad was talking to them.

Omar clamped his hands over his brothers' mouths. "Just wait!" he whispered. "Don't make the cops' job easier. Let's see what Dad's going to do."

He signalled his brothers to stay put, and he sneaked out of the room onto the landing, then edged down the first few steps of the narrow staircase. He stopped just above the stair that creaked. The voices in the hall were clear. His father didn't yell, but his voice could crack stone it was so cold.

"Sorry, gentlemen," he was saying. "I wish I could help you. I've raised my boys to respect the police, although Lord knows that's hard around here sometimes. Lots of temptations and problem kids to lead a boy astray. But Omar's not here at the moment. I sent him on an errand to the store. Lentils. My wife's making lunch, and suddenly there are no lentils."

Omar heard the easy humour in his father's voice, like one guy talking to another about the whims of women. But the cop that answered had no humour in his voice. "When will he be back?"

"Well, my wife likes a particular kind of lentils, so he may have to go all the way to Vanier. On his bicycle. I told him not to come back without the lentils, so it may be an hour. What's this about?"

"Can you tell us where he was Saturday night?"

"Right here, in his room."

"He didn't go out any time between 10 p.m. and 5 a.m.?"

"He was here doing homework, and I saw to it personally. Twenty years old and still in adult high school because he thought he'd take the scenic route through his education. I want to make sure he crosses the finish line. That's the least a father should do."

"So he was here all night? You're sure of that?"

"Absolutely."

Omar heard that dangerous little edge creeping into his father's voice, but the cops wouldn't recognize it. There was silence in the hall. Omar realized his heart was almost breaking his ribs. What the hell was this about? Dad, who hammered them on the head about honour and honesty—Dad was lying? Bold-faced, calm, friendly. Lying, like it was natural as day.

"We would still like to question him about an incident his friends were involved in," the officer said. "Here's my card. Have him give us a call as soon as he gets back."

"Absolutely, officers. I'll pass it on. What incident is this?"

"Thank you for your time, Mr. Adams. Have him give us a call." The door squeaked open and closed again. Omar found he was holding his breath. Waiting for his father's next move.

It wasn't long in coming. Omar had barely made it back to his room when his father was on him, hauling him by the ear into the bathroom. "You little turd," he hissed. "You're going to scrub this room until every speck of dirt and whatever else you brought home Saturday night is gone. Then you're going to scrub it again. You're a disgrace, and if you bring trouble to your mother and brothers, I'll cut you off like you never existed. Don't think you'll ever see us or a single dime of support ever again. You were here all Saturday night studying for that math credit you've been working on. And if your worthless gangsta friends say different, they're lying. Got that? Lying. That's your story, or you'll wish you'd never been born."

I already wish that, Omar thought through the pain ricocheting through his head. I've wished that ever since I was old enough to wish.

Five

Sergeant Levesque was a good actress. She stood in the middle of Sam Rosenthal's living room, surrounded by stacks of files and textbooks, her hands on her hips and her head cocked. Her lips smiled, but her eyes smouldered, midnight blue and threatening. Like a distant thunderstorm, Green thought, chuckling at the image that had leaped to his mind.

"Inspector Green," she said. "Not much to report yet. We just got the search warrant, and we've been here only a half hour."

"I know," he replied blithely. "I'm just visiting on my lunch hour." He looked around at the work already done—drawers opened, filing cabinets emptied and cushions overturned—and felt a twinge of frustration. He remembered when he searched a victim's home, back in the days when he didn't sit on committees or jump to fulfill every whim from the brass above, but instead spent his shift on the road, running his own cases and calling his own shots.

Back then he would have spent half an hour just studying the apartment, getting a sense of the occupant, sketching and absorbing impressions before he disturbed a single thing. Sullivan used to call it "communing with the dead", and he wasn't far off. The victim told him a lot in those thirty minutes, from what pictures he chose to hang where and what books he had on display to what kitchen utensils were near at hand.

In most homicide cases, the victim's identity was key to his death. In this one, Sergeant Levesque thought it irrelevant. She might be right, but it disturbed Green's sense of due respect. He began his own walkabout, trying to picture the room as Rosenthal would have left it. Everything had an old, slightly-scuffed appearance, but the man had clearly once had money as well as taste. A dining room set of mahogany and velvet was shoehorned into the small nook allotted to it off the living room. An antique roll-top desk with leaded glass bookshelves and cubbyholes for stationery and supplies sat beside the bay window, and matching wing chairs bracketed the cavernous Victorian fireplace. A Persian rug in faded blue and red tones covered the scuffed oak floor.

The man had chosen a soft blue paint throughout the apartment to complement the many paintings that hung in every space. Green was no expert in art but recognized an eclectic mix of styles and subjects. Some were from Israel— a soft watercolour of the Jerusalem skyline, a vibrant acrylic of Jews dancing at the Western Wall. Some were rugged Canadian landscapes of pine trees and lakes. But the most striking were the portraits. Not happy or posed but raw and real. People lost in thought, lonely, isolated and in pain.

Rosenthal had spent his whole career dealing with human pain, yet he had not created an oasis in his own home. His home reflected his experience with life. Raw, lost, lonely. None of the artists were recognizable names, at least to Green, but he suspected Rosenthal had not bought the paintings for their investment value but for the feelings they evoked. Love of his spiritual homeland, awe of the Canadian wilderness, and above all, compassion for human pain.

In contrast to the living area, which was stuffed with treasures, the bedroom was stark, as if it were not a place he enjoyed. Tiny and utilitarian, it held only a single bed against one wall covered with a frayed blue duvet, an antique dresser with a sculpted mirror, and an entire wall of shabby bookshelves stuffed with books. Medical and scientific tomes shared space with philosophy, mysticism and provocative works like *The Mindful Brain, An Unquiet Mind* and *The Doctor and the Soul* by Victor Frankl. Green picked the latter up idly. He was familiar with the Viennese psychiatrist who had found a path to spiritual meaning amid the horrors of the Nazi death camps. Perhaps Rosenthal had a more profound grasp of human health and illness than his detractors understood, Green thought, replacing the book reluctantly before resuming his search.

Neatly arrayed on top of the dresser were a hairbrush, comb, shoe horn, some pill bottles and a small leather box, which the detectives had already opened. It contained cufflinks, tie clips, a gold watch with a broken face and a man's opal ring with an engraving inside the band. *"To my darling, June 16, 1980"*. A birthday or anniversary present from his wife?

Green peered at the labels on the pill bottles. Advil, multi-vitamins, Allegra, Tums and an herbal medicine that claimed to guarantee sleep. He jotted down the name. Not surprisingly considering his recent concern with over-medication, Rosenthal did not appear to be taking a single drug prescribed by a doctor, which was unusual among today's elderly. At last count, Green's father took eight pills a day.

Beside the bed was a night table on which sat a glass of water, a pair of reading glasses and a teetering stack of novels, one of which lay open face down, *By the Time You Read This,* by Giles Blunt. Green glanced at the back cover. A Canadian mystery set in a northern town and featuring an apparent suicide. So the man didn't shy away from the anguish of his profession even in his minutes before sleep. Also in the stack of novels were other Canadian literary titles, along with classics from Dickens and Dostoevsky. Just like his art, his reading tastes were eclectic and sophisticated, yet a touch sad.

The dresser drawers had already been opened to reveal a jumble of underwear and socks, all either black or white. Green was mildly surprised that the clothes were not folded, since he had formed a picture of a solitary, fastidious man with set routines and perhaps too much time on his hands. Lower drawers contained sweaters, cotton slacks and golf shirts, in blacks, blues and beiges. Not a man inclined to flamboyance, certainly. There were no jeans or T-shirts in the mix, suggesting a degree of formality in the appearance he presented. Fits with the three-piece suit, Green thought.

Green glanced in the closet, under the bed, and in the bathroom, but none held any surprises. Except one. He returned to the living room.

"There's no sign of a computer. I know he's over seventy, but he's educated and worldly. Seems unlikely."

Sergeant Levesque looked up from the stack of correspondence she was sorting. "A laptop was on the list of things he reported stolen."

Green felt a flash of annoyance. A laptop was an obvious target for thieves, but nonetheless one that might contain crucial information. He should have been informed. "What else was on the list?"

"Some jewellery—his late wife's diamond necklace and ring—a box of silverware and some papers from his filing cabinet. Typical stuff."

Green frowned at her dismissive assessment. To his mind, it was not typical at all. The paintings had not been taken, which suggested the thief was not an art connoisseur, but papers would be of little value to a thief. "What kind of papers?"

She shrugged. "He wasn't sure. When he came home, there were papers from the filing cabinet all over the floor. Most of that stuff he had not looked at since he retired. There were professional articles, patient files, workshop notes."

The filing cabinet had now been emptied into piles on the floor, and Sergeant Levesque's partner was sifting through them. Bafflement and frustration showed in his face. "He doesn't seem to have bothered sorting them out when he put them back after the break-in," the young constable said. "Just stuffed them all back in. I'm looking for personal papers like his will and insurance policies, but so far all I've found is this." He held up an empty file folder. "It's labelled 'will', but there's nothing in it."

Levesque let out a low whistle and brandished a paper she'd picked up. "Well, somebody might want to find the will. He owned this house completely—and in this neighbourhood that's probably worth over a million—and this investment statement says he's got almost three and a half million in an account. His son is going to have a nice surprise."

"How's the search for him coming?" Green asked.

Suspicion flashed across Levesque's face, and for an instant she even hesitated to answer. "Nothing yet. Gibbs is still trying to find out his name."

"Likely David or John. I'd concentrate on the States somewhere."

Levesque swung around on her junior partner, her ponytail snapping. She gestured to the papers strewn on the floor. "There should be a name somewhere in there."

"Find any kind of legal document, and that'll give you his

lawyer's name," Green said. "The lawyer will have his will on file and probably the son's coordinates as well."

The junior detective began pawing through papers, obviously eager to impress. "I found his income tax records for the last few years. They show lots of donations to charity —United Way, Canadian Mental Health Association, United Jewish Appeal and a bunch of charities in Israel. No lawyer's name, but I found a dental bill."

"Good. Call to see if he has recent X-rays." Levesque left the young man dialling his cell while she turned her attention back to the correspondence on the dead man's desk. Green resumed his stroll around the apartment, not gathering impressions this time, but searching for clues to the son's identity. Photos or letters. There was a large portrait of a woman he assumed to be the late wife hanging on the living room wall, and several photos of her in silver frames on the dining table and desk. She was always hamming it up, as if she hated formality and enjoyed teasing the photographer. To Green's surprise, however, there was not a single photo of a boy or younger man, nor of small children who might be grandchildren.

Green thought about his own father, an elderly widower , for whom Green, Sharon and the children were his whole world. Every spare surface in Sid Green's small senior's apartment was proudly covered with photos. In contrast, Sam Rosenthal's apartment felt extraordinarily lonely.

As he stood in the centre of the bedroom, he noticed piles of boxes stored at the back of the closet. Shoe boxes of old correspondence, cartons of old clothes, and at the very back, an old dusty banker's box tucked beneath a plastic bin of winter scarves.

He dragged the box into the room and peered inside at

the yellowed stack of old files, inwardly cheering at the sight of the word "Will" scrawled across the tab of one of them. Inside was a sheaf of legal-sized papers, with the words "The last will and testament of Samuel Yitzak Rosenthal" printed in old-fashioned script across the front page. He pulled out the papers and scanned for the date: November 16, 1999. Written not long after his wife's death, it was probably his most recent will.

Green flipped rapidly through the pages, noting that Rosenthal had named the lawyer who'd drafted the will as executor of the estate. The executor was instructed to sell his property, pay all the bills and distribute the remainder of the estate as follows.

Large sums had been bequeathed to charities. Three were predictable—$100,000 each to the Rideau Psychiatric Hospital, the Canadian Mental Health Association, and the United Way—all of which helped troubled people in need. But others, like the Humane Society and the Bytown Association of Rescued Canines, were unexpected. Green had seen no sign of pets in the apartment.

Besides the half million dollars to various charities, two million were to be used to endow the Evelyn Rosenthal Memorial Chair in cancer research at the University of Ottawa. Green wondered if the man had been grateful for the care his wife had received at the Ottawa Hospital or if he'd found it profoundly lacking.

The final page was most telling of all. Whatever crumbs were left over after the disposition of the specific bequests, had been left to the son, David Joseph Rosenthal. By Green's rough calculations based on the worth of the house and the investments, that was still close to two million. Hardly pocket change. However, a line had been drawn through his son's name and the word "no" had been scrawled over it. Green's excitement surged.

He took the will into the living room, where the junior detective had made little headway with the pile of papers on the floor. "Here's the will, the son's name, and the lawyer. A lot was left to charities, but the rest is slated for his son. But I think you'll find the last page interesting."

Sergeant Levesque plucked the will from Green's hands. "Where did you find it?"

"In the back of the closet." Green could see that she was bewildered and suspicious, but unwilling to challenge the serendipity of his find. He shrugged. "Old people have their quirks. My father hides his passport and bank records in a cavity under the floorboards as if he's still in the Warsaw ghetto."

Levesque scanned the will, arching her eyebrows briefly at the last page before setting the will aside. "I will follow this up, of course, and contact the lawyer for the son's address. But the will doesn't seem too relevant to our investigation at this time. We have a whole list of gang members to check out first."

"Beneficiaries are always relevant in a homicide investigation."

"He's been a beneficiary since 1999. I don't see why he'd suddenly decide to kill his father now."

Green frowned at her. "It looks as if his father may have had second thoughts. And the son needs to be investigated, whether Rosenthal wanted him disinherited or not." He studied the resentment and uncertainty on her face and tried to soften his tone. "The way the economy is now, the son may have fallen on hard times and recently incurred huge debts."

She flipped her ponytail in exasperation. "With due respect, sir, we don't know what that 'no' means. Maybe the father was angry, then later regretted it. It was all a long time ago."

"I'll give you more men, if that's an issue."

"It is not an issue. Priorities are the issue. For sure this son will get my attention, along with all the gang punks in the city." She caught herself and forced a tight smile. "But thank you for the offer, sir. I will let Staff Sergeant Sullivan know if I need it."

Green caught the borderline insubordination in the woman's retort and was tempted to call her on it, but stopped himself. She was like looking in a mirror, ten years ago, when he thought he knew everything. If she was as good as Sullivan believed, she would learn better soon enough.

*   *   *

Green forced himself to behave for the rest of the day, and by five o'clock he had a passable action plan drafted for Superintendent Devine to address the spike in domestic assaults. It would never be implemented, of course, but that wasn't the point. It was ammunition for debates on the police budget at City Council, not to mention feathers for Barbara Devine's Deputy Chief nest. Of course, the real way to prevent the spike would be to get rid of September, with all the stresses it placed on families after the casual, relaxed days of summer. He and Sharon had only two children, of very disparate ages, and yet they felt the stress of finding new schools, resuming full-time work hours, and juggling after-school activities.

To Green's astonishment, Tony was going to kindergarten, and Hannah, true to her word, was trying out full-time Grade Twelve in the regular neighbourhood high school. For the occasion, she was letting her hair grow out, transforming the orange-tipped spikes into softer waves. She'd cut back on the black eye-liner and heroin-addict make-up, allowing her freckles and innocent hazel eyes to shine through. For the first time, Green saw not only his mother but himself in her face.

Naturally, the transformation required a new wardrobe. Hannah was a social animal astute enough to recognize that black rags and metallic studs would not earn her acceptance with the earnest children of the organic-food, eco-conscious set in their neighbourhood. Tony too needed brand new clothes, since last winter's wardrobe was now several inches too short. The strain on their family budget and their time was enormous.

In fact it was Green's turn to pick up Tony from the sitter and take him to The Bay for a fashion outing that Sharon had dubbed a father-son bonding experience, no doubt with tongue firmly in cheek. Green's fashion sense did not extend beyond matching his cleanest pants to his favourite T-shirt, and Tony's two-minute attention span, together with his determination to do as he pleased, made any excursion a test of endurance and willpower.

Sometimes domestic assault was a simple matter of tipping the balance too far.

Nonetheless, Green had managed to outline a five-point action plan for Devine that involved changes to police response at several levels, from first responding through laying of charges, and he'd thrown in enough buzz words— community partnerships, alternative dispute resolution, strategic intervention—that Devine would be salivating. He was just locking up his desk when he heard the elevator open and saw Brian Sullivan stride out, the tell-tale hint of high blood pressure on his dusky face. Sullivan spotted him and veered over, his colour deepening further. Green wondered if Levesque had complained again. He decided on a pre-emptive strike.

"You're here late! The autopsy done?"

Sullivan flopped in the guest chair with a groan. "Just came from there."

"And?"

"The man was healthy for his age. Some arthritis in his left hip which might have slowed him down a bit, but otherwise strong and fit."

"Explains the cane. So what was the cause of death?"

"Blunt force trauma to the head. Repeated blunt force trauma, a dozen blows in total as near as MacPhail can tell. Fractured his skull, his jaw, some ribs and his collarbone."

"Same instrument or several?"

"That's hard to tell from the hamburger that was left. MacPhail's taken lots of photos, so he'll take a closer look."

Green winced at the image. "Any specs on the type of instrument?"

"Again, he has to examine his tissue samples, but there's nothing obvious to the naked eye. Something cylindrical and about five centimetres thick—about the size and shape of a baseball bat."

"Not something that's readily at hand on Rideau Street unless you brought it along." Green mulled it over. Drug dealers and other punks normally didn't carry baseball bats or obvious weapons that might draw attention to themselves. They preferred knives and guns. More deadly and easily slipped into the belt out of sight.

Sullivan's scowl was easing, and his dusky colour was fading, as if he'd forgotten to be annoyed. "It may make it easier to find witnesses. Somebody walking along with a baseball bat would stand out."

"I don't remember any of those kids on the tape carrying baseball bats."

"But we couldn't see them all clearly. Sergeant Levesque is going to break the tape into stills, see if we can see anything."

Green visualized the sequence of the assault. Rosenthal had tried to fend off his attacker with his cane before the killer got a good swing in. The earlier blows were likely less forceful, the latter ones would have produced the carnage.

"It would take a strong person to hit hard enough to break his skull like that," he said.

"Strong or enraged." Sullivan paused. "Some of the blows were post-mortem. The one that likely killed him was to the base of his neck, delivered when he was already lying down. Snapped his neck."

Green tasted bile. "Coward. Attacking an old man in the first place, then hitting him when he's down. This wasn't a simple mugging, Brian. This was an assassination."

Sullivan ran his broad hand through his bristly hair, frowning dubiously. "Well, it might have started as a mugging, but when Rosenthal resisted, the killer lost it. Maybe Rosenthal got a good hit in, and the attacker saw red."

Green was silent. He knew Sullivan was right. They'd both seen enough bloody destruction to appreciate the power of flash rage. But to keep hitting once the old man was already down, already dead, suggested a dangerously unstable man. Green finally broke into their grim thoughts. "What's his calculation on time of death?"

"More or less what we figured. Sometime between midnight and four a.m. Sunday morning."

"Anything else of note?"

"We got the dental records, and we've couriered everything over to the forensic odontologist. Probably have a confirmed ID by Wednesday. MacPhail says Rosenthal had an iron constitution and kept himself well. Even got regular pedicures. Heart, liver and arteries all in excellent shape, would have lived another ten years. Even had all his own teeth. 'A lifetime of clean living, the silly bugger' is what the old Scot announced when he was finished."

Both men laughed, grateful for the lighter mood. MacPhail would see that as a lifetime of wasted opportunities. But in Green's mind, it all fit with the image that was beginning to form, of a thoughtful, philosophical man who had few vices and took meticulous care of himself.

None of which explained what he was doing walking along Rideau Street during the most dangerous small hours of the night.

Six

"Stop the Carnage!" The Tuesday morning headline stopped Omar cold. He was just heading to the cash with the bottle of laundry detergent his mother had asked him to buy and the jumbo bag of chips that was his reward. She wouldn't know about the pack of DuMauriers he'd pick up too. Using his own money, so what business was it of hers? What other twenty-year-old man was grounded to the house for a month anyway?

It had been less than three days, but he was already going insane. He'd practically begged his mother to let him go to the store for her. She was as scared of his father as he was, so it had taken some persuading, but when the old man went off to work that morning, she'd slipped Omar some house money and sent him up to Rideau Street.

His mother didn't read English, and his father said the newspapers were all lies, so there weren't any in the house. Since part of his punishment was no TV, he hadn't heard any news either. That headline was the first he'd learned of the old man's death on Saturday night. That fucking black-hole Saturday night.

The *Ottawa Sun* screamed the headline in its usual half-page type, followed up with more hype. "Roaming gangs to blame in senior's death." Beside that, there was a photo of a building with a body sprawled against it. Details were fuzzy so it took Omar a moment to recognize Rideau Street, but then fear shot through him. He pretended to be cool as he bent to look at the more conservative *Ottawa Citizen* on the rack below. No headlines about gangs, but a recap of the progress the police were making into the brutal beating. "We are looking at video footage and at known gang members operating in the vicinity," some cop was quoted as saying.

Video footage. Fuck! Omar nearly bolted from the store. He snatched up the paper, and it took all his willpower to put his stuff down at the cash and wait for his change. He completely forgot about the cigarettes.

Back at the house, he shut himself in his room and read the story five times, his brain refusing to take it all in. This was bad. The guy had been beaten with a bat over a dozen times, even after he was dead. His body was pulverized, then robbed. An innocent old guy out for a walk, just minding his own business. Omar felt a dumb surge of anger. Well, that was the old man's first mistake. What the hell was he thinking, going out for a walk on Rideau Street in the middle of the fucking night?

Then he felt guilty for the anger. The old man's actions may not have been too smart, but no way he deserved to get beaten to death. This wasn't Somalia, where his father said your life was in your hands every second, where just to show your face in the wrong place to the wrong person could mean a machete or a strafe of bullets. Which was why his mother never complained about his father, no matter what he did, because he'd rescued her from that. Picked her from all the village girls in the camp, brought her back here when he transferred back to Canada. Omar had already been born by then, but not too many soldiers married the village women they'd fooled around with.

His father said it was a matter of honour after the things

the military had done in Somalia, and maybe that was true. His father still sent half his money over there for a village school. But Omar knew it wasn't that simple. His dad liked to be king of the heap, and he knew he had them all by the short and curlies.

He raised his head from the newspaper. How many times had he asked himself if they'd have been better off if the old man had left them in Somalia? He knew the answer, but it was a game he played whenever the bastard tightened the screws. Martial law, that's what this was. Once a soldier, always a soldier, and his father had been with the worst. The government hadn't disbanded the Airborne Regiment after Somalia because the guys had handed out lollipops. They knew all about beating. And killing.

Omar wrenched his thoughts back to Saturday night. He raked his memory. He remembered something metal, something shiny like a knife. But not a baseball bat. Who the hell had been carrying a baseball bat? A knife could be concealed, but a bat was pretty fucking long to hide under your shirt. Not to mention uncomfortable when you're sitting down. He tried to picture the four of them sprawled on the grass in Macdonald Gardens, smoking weed and talking about getting laid. He remembered jokes about the size of their hard-ons, about how far up a girl they could go. If anyone had had a baseball bat, it would have come out then.

Omar shook his head, feeling a bit better. It was possible one of them had picked up a baseball bat later during their walk, but not likely. Not too many baseball bats lying around in alleyways around here, especially when it wasn't even garbage day.

He heard his mother's soft bare feet on the stairs. Quickly he folded up the newspaper and stuffed it under his mattress.

He pulled his math textbook out of his bag and had just flipped it open when there was a light tap on his door. As always, his mother waited silently outside his door until he opened it. She was tall, and even after four kids—plus two who died in the refugee camp, but no one ever talked about them—she didn't have an ounce of fat on her.

Even inside the house, she kept herself wrapped head to toe in browns and blacks. His father sometimes bought her bright scarves and pretty clothes, but they sat in her closet. She looked at Omar now with her huge, sad eyes.

"You have laundry?" she asked in English.

He glanced around his room. His brothers had left their own clothes strewn around, but Omar's own corner was army shipshape. Just one more sign of his father's double standard. He handed her his bag of laundry, then remembered the clothes from Saturday night, still in a ball at the back of his closet. He said nothing.

She peered into the small bag and frowned. "Your jeans?"

Panic shot through him. "I'll check if they're dirty, I'll bring them down to you."

She went out and he closed the door. He ran to the closet and fished out the clothes. They were stiff with dried blood now and gave off a sickening smell. They were probably a write-off, except his father would ask him where they'd gone. He could make some excuse, but he'd never hear the end of it. The jeans had cost good money and were nearly new. He shook them out and peered at them in the light from the window. Against the dark blue fabric, it was hard to tell the stains were blood. They could have been...

He shook his head. His mother wasn't born yesterday, she knew blood when she saw it. She'd figure he was into something hot and heavy. But she wouldn't say a word to his father. She'd wash the stuff and never ask. It didn't pay to ask.

He began to empty the pockets to make sure there was no weed or folded bills that could get ruined in the wash. In the third pocket, his hand closed around something heavy and cold. He pulled it out. He stared at it a moment then yanked his hand away like the object was hot. It clattered to the floor.

Heart pounding, he picked it up again. Stretched the gold band, cradled the heavy disk. It was still ticking, the hands on the gold face keeping perfect time.

Which was no surprise, because below the dial, in sleek, classy letters, was the word *Rolex.*

*   *   *

He was on the phone before he'd even thought it through. "Nadif! What the fuck happened Saturday night!"

"Sh-h!" Nadif hissed and slammed the phone down without saying a word. Omar raced down the stairs, stopped for a moment to listen for his mother, who was busy with the laundry in the basement. He ran out the front door. Only when his bare feet hit the cold pavement did he realize he'd forgotten his shoes.

Ignoring the cold, he headed diagonally across the street and had almost reached Nadif's townhouse when he saw the curtains twitch in the upstairs room. A few seconds later Nadif came barrelling out his front door and ran at him, grabbing his arm and dragging him behind a van parked in the laneway beside the house.

"Fuck, man! You want to get us arrested? The cops are everywhere!"

"Sorry," Omar said. Sorry was always the first word out of his mouth when trouble started, but now he took a few seconds to process what Nadif had said. His mouth went dry. "You think my phone's tapped?"

"I don't know about yours, but you can sure as hell bet mine is. The cops were all over me about that old man's death on Saturday night."

Omar grabbed his arm. "What the fuck happened? What was in that weed! I don't remember a thing."

"Nothing happened. Got nothing to do with us."

"But I got blood all over me. All over my clothes!"

"You fell off the sidewalk. So wasted you didn't even see it coming. Fell flat on your face."

Omar was silent a moment, testing this theory against his memory. Didn't ring any bells. "But what about the knife?"

Nadif's face hardened. "What knife?"

Omar felt panic rising. "I remember a knife. I remember blood."

Nadif gripped him by both arms and dug his fingers in. "Listen to me. Nothing. Happened. Nothing. We were out partying, we came home, you tripped and fell, end of story."

To his shame, Omar felt hot tears gathering behind his eyes. "But I have a Rolex watch in my pocket. I don't know where it came from."

Nadif released him and stepped back from him almost like he was pushing him away. "I don't know nothing about a Rolex watch. I don't know where you got that. But my advice? Get rid of it. Now. Throw it down the sewer, chuck it in the river. Just get rid of it. And don't ever, ever talk about this again."

*   *   *

The phone was ringing on Green's desk when he reached his

office that Tuesday morning. Fearing it was Devine with another last minute demand before her job interview, he debated letting it go to voicemail, but after a long, stuffy meeting with the Provincial Crowns, any diversion was welcome.

A dulcet Southern drawl greeted him. "Inspector Green? Agent Jim Benoit of the FBI here."

The name rang no bells. "Yes, sir. How can I help you?"

"Your department put in a search request for a David Joseph Rosenthal yesterday?"

Green masked his surprise. There was a protocol for requesting assistance from south of the border. Had Levesque deliberately circumvented it? "Yes, he's next of kin in a death up here. Any luck?"

"Well, we found him for you. That is, we found his residence, and local police paid a visit to his wife. According to her, he's out of the country on business, and she doesn't know for how long. Do you want us to trace him?"

"She isn't able to contact him herself?"

"That's correct. According to her, that's normal. He's a busy man, apparently. Flies all over the world."

"But surely—" Green stopped himself. There was no point badgering the FBI with his skepticism. He asked for the woman's phone number, then thanked the FBI agent and asked him to carry on the search.

Afterwards he studied the information he had jotted down, an address in Baltimore that meant nothing to him. He dialled the number, listened for five rings, and braced for voicemail. He was thrown off-guard when the phone was snatched up.

"Yes!"

"This is Inspector Michael Green of the Ottawa Police. May I speak with Mrs. Rosenthal, please?"

"Who?"

Green repeated his introduction, as gentle and polite as she was abrupt.

"Oh. Is this in relation to his father?"

"Yes. We really need to get in touch with Mr. Rosenthal."

"It's Dr. Rosenthal, even if his father never admitted it. Two PhDs and half an MD weren't good enough for him. Why do you want David? Did the old man die or something?"

Green abandoned courtesy. "Yes. That's why I need to find him."

"Huh." The woman paused. "Well, I don't know where he is. New Dehli, Frankfurt, Tel Aviv? He doesn't keep me informed."

"Does he have a cellphone or Blackberry?"

"I don't have those numbers." Another pause, the sound of smoke dragging into lungs. "Look, you might as well know. He doesn't live with us any more."

"Where does he live?"

"Take your pick. He's got six houses. Well, maybe only four or five now. He's had to sell a couple off. But he may not be at any of them. He has his own plane, and he's always off wheeling and dealing."

"Who might know how to reach him, Mrs. Rosenthal? His secretary? Executive assistant?"

"I can give you the company number, that's all I have." She was silent a moment, presumably tracking down the number. When she came back, her voice sounded more excited. "I don't suppose there's money or...whatever involved?"

"That's not my area. But the sooner I can contact Dr. Rosenthal, the sooner you'll know."

That little nudge proved useful. She rhymed off the number, then added as an afterthought, "I never even met his father. David hadn't talked to him in years, but sometimes that's the worst kind of loss, isn't it? For what it's worth, at this time of year, David is usually up in Canada, duck hunting. The man loves to hunt."

After he'd hung up, Green sighed. Duck hunting up in Canada—that really narrows it down. Hoping for more details, he dialled the number the ex-wife had given him. He got the runaround through an automated phone response system before finally snagging a real person. She passed him on, like a hot potato, to Rosenthal's executive assistant, who was as treacly smooth as the ex-wife was blunt. But impressions could be deceiving. After oozing out the obligatory expressions of dismay, she began to stonewall.

"I will pass on this message as soon as possible, and I'm sure he'll contact you as soon as he's able."

Able, thought Green with disbelief. What, when it reaches the top of his "to do" list? "Give me his cellphone number."

"I don't believe he's in cellphone range. But I assure you, he will call you. Is there anything else I can help you with?" She'd reverted to her script, so he thanked her and hung up. He headed off to alert Levesque and Sullivan, hoping the secretary was right. He was anxious to get his own read on David Rosenthal, who was emerging as more peculiar by the moment.

*　　*　　*

By noon the rumour mill on the third floor was going full tilt, and snippets of gossip were seeping down to the Major Crimes Unit on the second. The first round of interviews for the Deputy Chief's job had been going on all morning, and the faces of candidates parading in and out of the Chief's private conference room were being minutely analyzed for signs of hope and defeat. Green heard that Barbara Devine had swept into the interview wearing her most conservative navy suit and practical pumps, with neutral polish on her nails and only the subtlest hint of red on her lips. He had to smile, thinking the Chief would have to have been blind not to notice the woman's penchant for scarlet and stilettos in the past three years.

She had emerged from the interview an hour later—the longest among the candidates so far—and had flashed a discreet victory sign at her secretary. Victory was far from assured, everyone knew, but the prospect of a new boss to fill her shoes left Green feeling ambivalent. A Chief of Detectives who actually knew something about major crimes would be nice, but on the other hand, Devine's ignorance, together with her blatant self-absorption, left him with a free rein to run his section as he chose. A new boss might be a pain in the ass.

Green was preparing for an afternoon meeting with his NCOs when his telephone buzzed. "A Mr. Fine on the line, sir. He said he left three messages." The major crimes clerk sounded dubious. Green wondered if Fine had asked for "Mr. Yiddish Policeman".

Green pounced on the phone. Fine's singsong voice came through. "So, you don't have private secretaries any more? A bigshot like you?"

"What can I say? Voicemail, automated menus... Thanks for calling. You got something for me?"

"Nothing that will do you much good, but yeah, I looked into your piece."

"And?"

"It comes from Russia, like I thought. I'd estimate turn of twentieth century. Czarist Russia."

"You can tell that from the gold?" Green asked, impressed.

He knew metallurgists could work wonders these days. Microscopic impurities and variations in colour and content could be traced to specific locations or processing methods.

Fine chuckled. "I can tell it's good quality gold, yes, and the workmanship suggests old-style hand-tooling. But no, I can tell that from the lettering on the back of the piece. It's an inscription, roughly translates as *To life and hope, my darling*. It uses some old Cyrillic letters and spelling which the Revolution tried to eliminate when they standardized things in 1918. Not everyone gave up the old ways, so it's not absolutely certain that it's Czarist, but I'm guessing there wasn't much call for these religious baubles after the proletariat took over. Jews, you know—always at the forefront of new ideas. Always hoping this one will be better."

Green didn't see how all this shed much light on Rosenthal's past. The Star of David had been made before the old man was even born. "So it's probably an heirloom passed down from immigrants who sneaked it out of the old country with them when they came."

"Yeah. Or not so romantic, he could have bought it in any antique Judaica shop. It makes a nice gift. The chain isn't old, by the way. Your standard gold chain you can pick up anywhere. It's a woman's Star of David. For one thing, the 'darling' is feminine, and for another, it's more delicate than most men would wear."

"It was worn by the victim."

"What can I say? Some men..."

"He had a wife. At least, did have."

"Then maybe it's hers."

Green turned the idea over in his mind. It made sense. Even the inscription *To life and hope, my darling* could have had special meaning to them as his wife struggled with cancer, and when she died—the love of his life in whose memory he had endowed an entire cancer research chair—he had taken to wearing it himself. Just as he continued to wear his wedding ring despite the passage of years.

"I wonder why the killer didn't steal it too," Green said. "He took the poor man's shoes, watch, and wedding ring."

"Maybe he didn't see it. These are normally worn inside the shirt."

"No, it was lying on the sidewalk beside his body."

"Ah, that explains it."

"What?"

"It was damaged. The chain was broken, and it takes more force than you think to break those things, like it was ripped from his neck. Plus the surface was bent and scratched. I found tiny particles of sand embedded in the gold."

Green tried to picture the chain on the ground. "Maybe it got stepped on in the struggle."

"Possibly, but the amount of scratching and the way the sand was embedded, it was almost like someone ground it in with their shoe. A pretty violent act, yanking it from the guy's neck and grinding it into the pavement."

*   *   *

That image stayed with Green afterwards, troubling him. The whole attack had been unusually vicious, beginning with the bat smashing the old man repeatedly when he was already down. Then the rings had been pried free, the Star of David ripped off and deliberately crushed into the ground.

Was there a message in this, or was he being paranoid?

He reached for the phone and dialled Sullivan's cell. The staff sergeant answered on the first ring.

"Where are you?" Green asked.

"Over in Vanier. About to go for lunch." Sullivan sounded wary.

"Meet me at the Rideau Street crime scene. Then we'll go to Nate's Deli."

"The crime scene's already been released, Green. There will be a hundred people walking over it."

"Doesn't matter. Humour me. There's a big, juicy smoked meat on rye in it for you."

Sullivan chuckled. "You springing for it, I'll have two."

Green printed off the stills Levesque had made from the pawn shop security tape, tucked them into a folder, and headed downstairs to sign out his staff car. He parked a block from the corner where Rosenthal had been beaten and walked slowly up Rideau Street, passing under the security camera of the pawn shop about sixty feet from the alleyway of the crime scene. He studied the photos and tried to recall the movements of the four young suspects. They had been drunk, jostling one another, oblivious to their surroundings. If the old man was standing sixty feet in front of them, they hadn't noticed him yet. That seemed unlikely. Most people walking down Rideau Street after midnight were instinctively on guard.

Sergeant Levesque had dissected every inch of the security tape for the night in question. Besides Screech and the young black males, dozens of other parties had passed by. Couples, singles, hookers waiting for the patrons from nearby bars. Levesque's team had been trying to track them all down, but in truth no one believed any of the others were guilty. Two were simple working girls, a couple were late-night revellers and still others looked like students from nearby University of Ottawa, stumbling home to their dorms. None had carried bats, none had looked poised for violence. None of them looked like skinheads or white supremacists who would target Jews for sport.

This morning, Screech had taken up his usual position cross-legged on the sidewalk about half a block from the liquor store. He had an empty Tim Hortons cup today, and kept his cart close at his side. The Ident Unit had confiscated his bloody sleeping bag but had given him a brand new one in its stead, so he was taking no chances. At his feet was a stack of stained pencil drawings, mostly poor imitations of Native animal art. Green doubted he sold many, but it allowed him some dignity.

Green had crossed paths with him in court a few times in his earlier days, but Screech had a vague look this morning, as if not enough brain cells were firing for him to recognize anyone. Green squatted in front of him and introduced himself, trying to ignore the stench. "Have the cops been around to ask you about what you witnessed the night the old man died?"

It proved too long a sentence, because Screech wrinkled up his nose and presented a gap-toothed smile. "Spare a loonie for a dying man?" he asked, his head bobbing as he extended his Tim Hortons cup.

Green extracted a ten dollar bill, held it out and tried again. "The night the old man was killed, did you see anything?"

"Eh?"

"Screech, come on. Did you see or hear the fight?"

Screech's smile fled, and he whipped his head back and forth, spittle flying. He eyed the bill, but made no move to take it.

"Where were you?"

"Behind the wall." He pointed to the brick building of the

grocery store up the block. "Didn't want no trouble."

"From who? Was somebody giving trouble?"

Screech clamped his cracked lips shut. Green took out the photos and laid them all out on the sidewalk in front of him. "Did you see any of these people?"

Screech flicked a glance at the line-up, then averted his eyes. "Didn't see nothing."

"Come on, now. We've helped you out a lot in the past. Got you this new sleeping bag, bought you food, we even buy your drawings sometimes. If you can help us out this one time..." He registered the fear in Screech's eyes. The street was a dangerous place for the homeless, particularly in the dead of night. Scores were settled in brutal ways. Green tucked the ten dollars into Screech's shirt pocket and softened his voice. "I won't tell anyone you told me. But you saw what they did to the poor old man. I just want whoever did it off the streets."

Screech cast a wary eye up the street then bent over to study the photos one by one. Green said nothing as nearby an idling transport truck spewed hot fumes into the air. Screech paused at the four black males. "I seen them."

"That night?"

"Yeah. Drunker than me. Hassling some hooker." He gave his gap-toothed grin.

"Is that hooker in the pictures?"

Screech shook his head. Too fast, Green thought. "What was her name?"

"Don't know her. Not a regular."

"Did any of these kids have a baseball bat?"

"Eh?"

"A baseball bat? Did you see one?"

"Didn't see nothing. Didn't want no trouble."

Green could almost picture Screech hiding, anxious to stay

out of the way of four drunk young men fuelled by testosterone. "I know you didn't, and you're doing great. Did you see anyone else in these photos?"

Reluctantly, the man returned to the photos. He moved along the line-up, then shook his head and shoved himself away. "Nope."

Green thanked him, packed up the photos, and headed up the street. The yellow crime scene tape had been removed, although a small tatter of it still hung from the pole of a nearby bus stop. The alleyway had been hosed clean of all traces of blood and brains. People walked over the spot without a care, sneakers shuffling, snakeskin boots clicking, stilettos tapping a pert rhythm. A bus pulled up and disgorged another crowd, which surged forward over the place of the old man's death.

Green walked over to the dusty patch of weeds where the body had been dragged. A short distance but still a very cold-blooded act when you'd just pulverised the man's brain. The body had been rolled on its side against the concrete wall, likely so that it would appear to the casual passerby like a drunk sleeping it off.

This killer was cool and collected, anticipating the angles.

Green studied the concrete wall of the building. It was spray-painted with gang tags, like dogs marking a hydrant. The Market was a free-for-all. No turf was safe.

"Recognize them?" came a deep voice from behind him.

Green turned to see Sullivan. The big man was looking rumpled and tired, flushed, as if his blood pressure was up again. "Some," Green said. "Not all. The city is getting new wannabe gangs every day."

"I don't think the tags have anything to do with the case," Sullivan said. "None of the paint is fresh."

"Still, are there any neo-Nazi tags among them?"

Sullivan frowned, his dusky colour deepening. "Neo-Nazi? Where did that come from?"

"Rosenthal was a Jew. That's a target for some people, especially after a dozen beers."

"Not obviously a Jew. No *yarmulke*."

"Maybe they spotted the Star of David. Or, with his expensive clothes and jewellery, he looked as if he had money. For some, that stereotype is enough."

Sullivan leaned against the wall, silhouetted against the midday press of Rideau Street. Belching transport trucks, growling buses, and lunch goers scurrying along the sidewalk. He studied Green thoughtfully. "I assume you have a reason for this line of inquiry?"

Green broke into a sheepish grin. "A couple of flimsy ones. The viciousness of the attack, the overkill, and the fact the killer stomped Rosenthal's Jewish star into the ground. Didn't steal it but destroyed it. It smacks of contempt."

Sullivan raised an eyebrow. He looked skeptical, but he was too good a detective not to consider the less obvious. "I'll ask the Hate Crimes guys if they have a lead on any Neo-Nazi groups hanging out around here."

Green nodded. "Ask if there's been any reports of vandalism or harassment. These guys don't usually start with a full-fledged attack."

They don't usually end with one either, he thought with a chill.

Seven

Brian Sullivan was on his cellphone when their smoked meat sandwiches arrived, thick, fragrant and spilling over with succulent pink meat. Green picked his up in both hands, sank his teeth in and closed his eyes in ecstasy.

Sullivan glared and covered his mouthpiece. "Nothing should interfere with a man's lunch."

Green stifled a chuckle with his mouth full. "What are you talking about? At least we're getting lunch. That's progress."

Sullivan was about to reply when the party came back on the other end of the line. He listened a moment, thanked the individual and snapped his phone shut. Without a word he picked up his sandwich and shovelled it into his mouth. Green watched him chew, shovel in another mouthful and slurp down half his coke.

"*Nu?*" Green said finally.

"Mmm?"

"What did Deepak say?"

"Not much. There have been no major anti-Semitic incidents in Lowertown recently. The usual spray-painted Swastikas, eggs thrown at the synagogue door, but nothing directed against people. There are some white power punks strutting around—you couldn't call them a gang—but they're mostly targeting blacks and Arabs."

"Is it a similar MO? Beating with a baseball bat?"

Sullivan shook his head. "Mostly threats with knife or gun, sometimes a minor beating meant to scare the guys off. Or pay them back. Mind you, the Somalis are doing some nasty shit of their own."

Green nodded, thinking of the high-profile case currently before the courts in which a young Somali had knifed a Lebanese youth allegedly for making a pass at his girlfriend. Too much testosterone and not enough purpose. However, he knew that most incidents of racism and anti-Semitism went unreported. Whether from fear of further retaliation or lack of confidence in the police response, most victims just shrugged and endured.

He persisted. "Did these white power punks have unusual tags, like the ones at the crime scene?"

"Deepak is emailing me their most common graffiti, and we'll take it from there." Sullivan belched, then fished a Rolaids from his pocket and popped it into his mouth with a rueful smile. "Can't do this like the old days."

They ate in silence, savouring the last of their sandwiches. After a few minutes, Deepak's email of recent graffiti popped up on Sullivan's cellphone. The two men scrolled through the tiny attachments. Art, or subtlety, was not the Neo-Nazis' strong point. Most of the tags were stylized swastikas or the skull-and-crossbones insignia of Hitler's ss. None of them looked like the graffiti on the wall at the crime scene. But Green couldn't dispel his sense of unease.

"I think Sergeant Levesque should get photos of that graffiti over to the Hate Crimes Unit anyway. See if we can connect it to any group here or elsewhere."

"Waste of time, but why not?" Sullivan shrugged as he drained his coke. With a grin, he wiped his lips and crumpled up his napkin. "This buys you a bit of wasted time. Thanks, Mike."

Green suppressed his annoyance. "Muslims can get into some pretty serious anti-Semitism too," he added. "Including the scary belief that all Jews are legitimate targets in the holy war to destroy Israel."

"That's what most anti-Semitic incidents are about these days. Muslim kids, not white power punks. Must be nice to be so popular."

Green managed a wry smile. "As they say, couldn't God choose someone else for a change? I'm not saying it was an anti-Semitic attack. Just that it's an angle we shouldn't overlook."

Sullivan gathered up his cellphone and his jacket. "I'll pass it on. She's good, Green. Let her do her job."

Green watched the big man thread his way through the crowded tables. He looked marginally more relaxed now, but Green knew he had a lot on his plate, with several dozen active cases to supervise and other units to liaise with. Unlike Green, who trusted no one to work a case as well as him, Sullivan was a natural leader who thrived on coordinated teamwork.However, Sergeant Levesque also had a lot on her plate. Green didn't doubt that she would follow up, but he chafed at the low priority she was likely to assign to the anti-Semitism angle. It would be a simple matter for Green to find out whether Jews were being targeted in the old inner-city neighbourhood, which had once been heavily Jewish but was now taken over by more recent immigrant groups.

Rabbi Tolner looked surprised to see him for the second time in two days. This time Green found him in the shed at the back of his building, oiling his bicycle. A colourful knitted *yarmulke* had slipped a little on his bald pate.

"I should be getting paid. Police consultant," he laughed, wiping his greasy hands on a rag hanging on the handlebar. "Any word on who killed Sam?"

Green shook his head and chose his words carefully.

Tolner had a love of gossip and far too much time on his hands. For someone as energetic and outgoing as him, it was a dangerous combination. Green erected the standard police stonewall.

"We're pursuing a number of leads. But so far we haven't been able to connect with his son."

Tolner's eyebrows arched. "He's a suspect?"

Green shook his head again, intrigued that should be Tolner's first thought. "He's next of kin."

He thought the man looked faintly disappointed. "Well, I haven't seen the son in years. Not since the wife's funeral."

"And how were things between father and son then?"

"Tense." Tolner hesitated. "I don't think it's easy growing up with a psychiatrist for a father. Especially one who specializes in young people. And Sam—may he rest in peace —Sam could be arrogant."

"Know-it-all?"

Tolner rolled his eyes. "And how. But David was no pushover either. Wore blinkers his whole life through so he would see only what he wanted to. Nearly killed the family dog once, I remember, kicked it down the stairs in a fit of temper. The fights in that house must have been stupendous. Poor Evie was the glue who kept that family together."

And when she was gone, it flew apart, Green thought. However, that was no reason for murder years later, and that line of speculation was better saved until Levesque's team had located the son. He switched gears, trying to sound as casual as possible.

"Do you know if there have been any threats or attacks around the neighbourhood against elderly people? Or Jews?"

Tolner's eyes narrowed shrewdly. "Attacks against Jews? You think it was a hate crime?"

"No, we don't," Green said, moving quickly to squelch Tolner's overactive imagination. "I'm casting a broad net, looking at all possibilities. You hear things. Anyone had a minor attack or threat?"

"What's an attack? 'Hitler should have finished the job, pig'? We get a few of those, mostly those of us who wear a *yarmulke* or other visible sign."

"Anything worse? Intimidation? Physical threats?"

Tolner bent over his bike and spun the wheel, watching its alignment. "Nothing much. Every time Israel does something not so nice to the Palestinians, we feel it on the streets. Mostly a glare here, a slur there." He raised his head thoughtfully to study Green. "Intimidation is a subtle thing, Mike. A group of youths come the other way down the street, black kids swaggering along, or Arabs talking loud and excitedly, and I feel afraid. They stare me down, and I want to take my *kippeh* off, cross the street and keep my eyes on the ground. I don't. I force myself to walk towards them, and in my head I pretend they're a group of chattering school girls. I smile at them, and I step out of their way. So far nothing has ever happened to me. Not even a muttered racial slur. But they own that little strip of street that we're on, and boy, you feel it."

"What if you didn't step aside? What if you tried to stare them down?"

"I'm not fool enough to test the idea. You're a cop, you know all about this top dog game. They don't want to beat you up, they just want you under their heel. All the rest—the Swastikas on the graves, the eggs on the synagogue door—is designed to further put you down. So they can build themselves up."

Green nodded. He was very familiar with the psyche of the bully and the street punk, who used the only tools at hand

—their size, numbers and body language— to capture some of the power that belonged to others. It was primitive, caveman psychology, but on a dark street corner, all of us were hardwired to respond. Fight or flight.

Green could almost hear Sharon shaking her head and muttering "you men". Since the caveman days, men had banded together, puffed up their team and strutted in front of the other side, testing their power and comparing their strength. Society was more complex now, and power was measured not just in brute strength but in money, possessions, jobs and trophy women, but that basic instinct still lay just below the surface. How did a man feel when his power faded? When he was alone, old and frail, no longer with the job and status he had enjoyed? How would he respond to a group of young men swaggering down the street as if they owned it all? Flight, like Tolner?

Not Rosenthal.

Eight

"Look, Daddy! I tied my new shoes all by myself!" Green bolted awake just in time to intercept his son, who was making a flying leap into the middle of his parents' bed. Grey daylight was barely peeking around the edges of the blinds, and Green shivered as he groped his way to peer out the window. Wednesday morning looked blustery and raw, an early hint of the winter to come. Charcoal storm clouds were billowing in from the west, scattering dry leaves along the street. Overhead a horde of Canada geese honked southward.

Sharon was still fast asleep, and with her stretch of evening shifts, he knew she needed all the sleep she could manage. In the background, he could hear the sound of the shower running. Miraculously, Hannah was up.

Tony talked in dramatic stage whispers as Green led him back into his own room and helped him select some of his brand new X-Games clothes for school. The choice proved so difficult that they had no time for breakfast, and Green ended up piling Tony into the car with only a bagel and juice box. His protest was loud enough to wake the neighbourhood until Green threw in a bribe of two Oreo cookies for snack. Sharon would not be impressed. It was Green's turn to do the school car pool, and by the time he had delivered all three chattering five-year-olds to the school yard, his head felt as if it had been jackhammered.

As abruptly as the chaos had begun, it was quiet again. Heading in to work, Green slipped in a Sarah Slean CD and balanced his bagel on the steering wheel as he savoured his coffee with his free hand. Thank God for solitude, he thought, letting the gentle lyrics wash over him.

He was anxious to get to the station before Brian Sullivan did his morning parade. Whenever there was a major new homicide investigation, Green liked to attend the briefings. However, by the time he'd delivered the children to school and fought his way past all the downtown construction, the preliminaries were over and Sergeant Levesque was just getting up to summarize the Rosenthal case to date. She used the most modern computer software and entered the updates on a smart board as they came along.

"The dentist has confirmed our ID of the victim. And we have identified two of the four men on the pawn shop video. One's a frequent flyer—our good buddy Nadif Hassan, currently out on bail in the Rideau Centre assault, and the second is a YO named Yusuf Abdi. Both of these men had preliminary interviews on Monday as part of our canvass of known gang members in the area. Nadif Hassan claimed he was home all Saturday night, and his mother corroborated that."

Eyes rolled. Mothers and their little darlings. Levesque smiled and flicked her ponytail to show she wasn't duped. "Since there are eight children in that household, I'm not sure she'd even notice. We will interview him again."

"This morning?" Sullivan asked.

She shook her head. "I want to get some leverage on him first, so I asked Detective Jones to get warrants for a wiretap and a search of his residence. We're looking for a bat or some other long, round weapon, bloodstained clothes, plus the items stolen from the victim—his shoes, watch, rings." She nodded towards the unit's warrant drafting wizard, who had just rushed into the room clutching some papers. "Any luck, Detective?"

Jones waved the papers, grinning. "I got Judge Olds. I knew he'd just bought a retirement condo for himself and his wife in that upscale new high-rise in the Byward Market."

Appreciative laughter rippled through the room. While Levesque lined up the logistics and personnel for the search, Green leaned in close to Sullivan. "Who's feeding the media, by the way?"

Levesque swung around from the smart board screen on which she'd been writing assignments. It was her first notice of him, and she didn't miss a beat. "I am, Inspector Green. I wanted to shake the gangs up, see who panics."

After yesterday's headlines, the mayor and city council are the most likely to panic, he thought, but he said nothing. From Levesque's point of view, it was the right thing to do, and it might even net them more resources for the fight against street gangs. She clicked, and a mug shot flashed up on the screen. The man had skin as smooth as polished ebony and large eyes fringed by long, almost delicate lashes, but those eyes were cold as they stared at the camera. Marie Claire Levesque tapped the screen.

"Nadif Hassan is our number one guy right now. He lives and operates in the area, and he does not hesitate to use violence. So I also want a canvass of the whole neighbourhood. Find someone he bragged to, find some place he tried to fence the proceeds."

Green could stand it no longer. "Hassan is a businessman. He commits crimes to settle a score or send a message. He doesn't beat an old man twelve times with a baseball bat, adding one for good luck at the back of the neck, just to make sure he's dead."

She was ready even for that. "He's also a hothead, and he's under a lot of pressure right now. The old man fought back, maybe challenged him to the very end. And Hassan knows any more felonies while he's on trial for the Rideau Centre knifing will make things much worse for him. He probably realized the old man could identify him, so what started as a mugging finished with this. Twelve hits with a baseball bat. And..." Levesque glanced at him with the merest hint of a smile, "there is also the anti-Zionist feelings. Hassan is a Muslim, Rosenthal was a Jew. A supporter of Israel. The destruction of the Star of David suggests that Hassan was angry at that."

Green nodded. She hadn't thrown out his wild speculation. Sullivan was right; she was good. Nadif Hassan was not going to know what happened to him once Marie Claire Levesque got him by the balls. Nonetheless, Green didn't expect the house search to bear much fruit. At twenty-three, Nadif was a wily veteran of numerous police raids, which began with schoolyard assaults at age ten, and he would have learned to keep his premises clean.

Green had barely worked his way through his morning's emails, however, when his phone rang.

Sullivan was chuckling. "Never underestimate the stupidity—or greed—of your average bad guy."

"Levesque found something on the warrant?"

"Not much. Our boy Nadif thought he'd covered his tracks. Not a trace of bloody clothes or sneakers, not even in the trash out back. No weapon longer than a six-inch paring knife."

That's because his father had confiscated all the knives after the stabbing incident, Green recalled. As if that would somehow keep his son in check. Green remembered the tall, slender, dignified man who rarely spoke above a soft murmur. He drove a taxi and was an elder in the Somali

Community Association, helping his fellow immigrants adjust to Canadian life. He had been ashamed of his own son's behaviour and made constant attempts to steer the boy back on the right path. The efforts had merely driven the young punk deeper underground. He became more adept at lying, crying racism and mistranslating official documents brought to his parents' attention.

"To judge from the sports equipment in the basement," Sullivan was saying, "the kid's never heard of baseball. Just basketball. His room was clean—too clean if you ask me—and he's got no visible scratches or bruises."

Green had been waiting impatiently for the "but". Finally he supplied it himself.

"There were fresh ashes in the fireplace," Sullivan replied.

Green perked up. In September, when the city had been enjoying glorious, sunny summer weather, people were putting on shorts and sandals, not lighting fireplaces. "Any trace evidence?"

"Nothing visible to the naked eye, but Ident has swept it clean and taken every last ash for analysis. We may get lucky."

"Fireplaces aren't great for burning clothes," Green observed. Or anything else, he thought, remembering his dismal efforts to start or sustain a decent fire in his own living room. Of course, what did he know from fires, Sharon would say, laughing from the sidelines. He refocused. "Not unless the guy got it burning full tilt. And that presumably would attract his parents' attention."

"Doesn't really matter," Sullivan said. "He doesn't have to know what we managed to find in the ashes."

"No, could be the thin edge we need."

"It could." Now Green could hear the merriment in Sullivan's voice. "But we've got something even better. Down in the basement, hidden in a box behind the furnace in among the spider webs, where he thought we wouldn't find them, was a nice shiny pair of black Gucci dress shoes. Now, if we can tie them to Rosenthal, I'd say the little prick is toast."

* * *

Levesque did not bring Nadif in for questioning right away. She knew there was not enough to tie him to the murder itself—no blood on his clothes, no murder weapon—and that even a semi-competent newbie legal aid lawyer could walk right through the holes in the police case. Instead she let him stew while she waited for the preliminary results from Ident.

The scales tipped in her favour late that afternoon. Sullivan was in the field checking out a call, and Green was just returning from a meeting with the RCMP. He spotted Levesque on the phone and could tell from the glow in her eyes that something had broken. After she hung up, she pumped the air with her fist. At the sight of him, she cut the celebration short.

He grinned. "News, Sergeant?"

She didn't hesitate. No suspicion of his motive, no jealous guarding of her turf. "The shoes, sir. The bastard tried to clean them up, but he couldn't get into the cracks and the stitching around the sole. Ident found traces of blood. It still has to be analyzed at the lab, but—"

"Our suspect doesn't have to know that. The fact we can ID it as blood should be enough to rattle him. What about the ash?"

Her face clouded. "No luck. Just paper of some sort, too burned to read any of the text." She thrust back her shoulders and flicked her blonde ponytail irritably. "But we have the shoes. That's leverage. I'm going to pick him up." She reached for the phone.

"It's not enough for a charge."

"No," she said, "but I can also threaten him with breach of his bail conditions. Maybe I can shake some other names out of him. Or a confession."

No way was Nadif going to confess to murder unless it was nailed down. The way he was fighting the Rideau Centre assault charge, despite the testimony of the victim and an eye witness, was proof of that. And with all the hype about the newly minted anti-gang laws, he'd know he was facing life inside. "This is premature. Have you made inquiries on the street? Anyone see him Saturday night? Any corroboration from the wiretap yet?"

She shook her head. "This is the first step. I want to keep at him, wear him down. Each time I'll have a little more evidence he has to explain, until he's so tangled up in lies he can't think straight." She punched in Dispatch's number and ordered a police cruiser to pick up Nadif Hassan.

"Staff Sergeant Sullivan is on a call," Green said. "But he'll need to be informed."

"I'll do that," she said. "But at this moment I have to set up the video room." She paused and looked at him darkly. "You're welcome to watch yourself. But it will be pretty late."

Green had been heading for a record—three consecutive evenings home for dinner with his children, if not his wife, who was still on the evening shift. But he couldn't resist the challenge Levesque had tossed at him. Confident and cocky, she thought she knew what she was doing, just as he had thumbed his nose at the stuffy caution of his own superiors in his early days. And indeed, hers was a time-honoured police tactic—wear the subject down with endless interviews and repetition until he was caught in a lie he couldn't escape. But Green preferred a more subtle approach: gather evidence and build a web of facts that traps the suspect inside before he sees the trap. Slam every door closed as he rushes towards it. He suspected Nadif still had plenty of escape hatches and might lead them a merry chase.

While elsewhere on the streets, there was evidence waiting to be found. And a prodigal son who, despite his assistant's assurances, had so far made no attempt to contact them about the murder of his father. That, even more than his apparent disinterest in his two million-dollar inheritance, cried out for follow-up.

*   *   *

Nadif Hassan slouched in the hard plastic interview chair and tried to look bored as Levesque ran through the introductions, the Charter caution, and other legalities for the record. He made no effort to demand his lawyer, acting instead as if the whole process were a waste of his time. His arms were folded across his chest and his legs stretched out in front, so long they hit the opposite wall in the tiny room. Not much of an actor, but Green had to admit he was a handsome young man, with clean, elongated lines, huge black eyes and flawless skin the colour of black coffee. He had a face that could have graced the cover of fashion magazines, right down to the sulky pout.

Really, Nadif, Green thought, your mug shot doesn't do you justice.

Marie Claire Levesque was sitting in the chair opposite with a laptop and a thick file open on the table before her and a paper bag on the floor at her feet. Behind her by the door stood Charbonneau, his notebook open. Charbonneau was a fixture in Major Crimes, but never had Green seen him so enthusiastic and alert as he'd been since Marie Claire came on the scene.

Charbonneau and his notebook, the laptop, the file and the paper bag were all part of the theatrical props, Green knew. After she'd finished the formalities, Levesque stared the suspect down for a few moments, but his eyes were fixed on the wall behind her. When she spoke, her voice was soft.

"Well, Mr. Hassan, you're in a lot of trouble here."

It was not a question, and Nadif was experienced enough to give no answer. Not even a flicker of an eye.

"Your trial for attempted murder has barely begun, and here you are committing another crime."

Still Nadif said nothing.

"Where were you last Saturday night, between ten p.m. and four a.m?"

"You know that. Home with my mother."

"Will your father confirm that?"

A heartbeat's hesitation. "He was out at work. Blue Line Taxi."

"An elderly gentleman named Samuel Rosenthal was beaten to death not six blocks from your house."

"Lot of people live six blocks from my house."

"So you were home with your mother. You're sure?"

"That's what I said."

Levesque opened her laptop and pressed a few buttons before swivelling it so Nadif could see the screen. She pressed "play".

Nadif only had to watch the screen for ten seconds before his coffee-coloured skin took on a grey tinge.

"This is from a pawn shop on Rideau Street," Levesque said conversationally. "You notice the date and time are stamped in the corner."

Nadif sneered. "Gee, I forgot. I went out with some friends for a couple of hours. That a crime?"

"For you, yes. It's a breach. Plus lying to the police, in your circumstances, might be too."

"Like I said, I forgot."

"Okay. So you admit you weren't home with your mama all Saturday night, but were out on Rideau Street at 2:17 a.m?"

"Maybe for a bit. But I didn't see nothing."

"No old man walking on the street? No old man lying in the alley by a building?" Nadif had been shaking his head. Levesque flicked her pen toward the camera in the corner. "Yes or no for the record."

The young man pouted into the camera and mimed, "No. Bitch."

Levesque closed the laptop as if she hadn't noticed and set it aside. Quietly she reached down into the paper bag and extracted a pair of black dress shoes in a clear plastic evidence bag. She placed them on the table without a word. Nadif's pout vanished.

"What are these?" she asked.

"I don't know, pigs' feet?" She waited. He looked away. "Shoes."

"Whose?"

"Never seen them before. Not my style." Nadif managed a smirking motion with his lips.

"They were found behind the furnace in your house."

"Don't know nothing about that. Never go down there."

"Hidden."

Nadif shrugged. "How do I know you pigs didn't plant them? Can't get me on the Rideau Centre beef, so you figured—"

"Your fingerprints are all over them, Nadif. Don't you watch *CSI*?"

The man grew sullen.

"Lying again. Remember what I said?"

"I forgot. I bought them for my dad. A present, you know? For all the trouble I caused him."

In the video room, Green laughed aloud. To her credit, Levesque didn't even blink. "Bought them."

"Yeah."

"Where?"

Nadif sat very still. Green could almost see him calculating, wondering how much she knew and what story he should tell. "From a guy."

"What guy?"

Nadif rolled his eyes as if the question was stupid. "I didn't ask his name. He got a nice pair of shoes at a good price. I don't got much money to spend on things, you know."

"Well..." Levesque picked up the shoes and turned them this way and that, as if examining them. "This nice pair of shoes just happens to have blood on them. Sam Rosenthal's blood. Someone tried very hard to clean them, but you know, you can never get blood out of all the little cracks. That's another thing you should know from *CSI*."

Nadif unfolded his arms and thrust his chair back as if trying to get away from the shoes. He looked angry. "Fuck."

"Fuck what?"

"The asshole screwed me!"

"What asshole?"

"The guy sold me the shoes. Told me they belonged to his father. No wonder the fucking price was so low!"

"Did you clean the blood off?"

"No, no! I never saw no blood!"

"We can test the cleaners, you know. Compare residue on the shoes to the cleaners in your house."

Green smiled. It was a stretch, especially if it was a common cleaner, but the witness wouldn't know that. *CSI* had made lots of things seem possible. She was good.

"So? Maybe he used the same cleaner as we have. You can't prove nothing!"

"His name, Nadif."

Nadif's eyes flashed. "I don't know his fucking name!"

Levesque stared him down for a good thirty seconds. "Okay, here's what we have for the courts, Nadif." She raised her hand to tick off points. "First, you breached your release conditions and lied about being out on Rideau Street Saturday night. Second, you lied about hiding the shoes. Third, you lied about not cleaning the blood off the shoes. Fourth, you say you bought them from a man but you don't know who he is." She waggled her fingers accusingly. "This is not looking good, Nadif. The shoes tie you to the dead man sure as a noose. You took them right off his feet—"

"No."

"After you beat him to death with a baseball bat."

"No!"

"Your prints, his blood, hidden behind the furnace? Come on."

"I told you, someone gave them to me."

"Gave them or sold them?"

"Sold them." Nadif swallowed convulsively. "Sold them!"

"Who? That's all we need to get you out of this mess."

The man hesitated, cunning flitting across his handsome features. Lightning fast, Levesque slapped the table in front of him. "One name."

"Omar!" He shot back. "Fucking Omar Adams. He told me he found them."

*   *   *

Green was on the living room sofa, fast asleep in front of the late night news, when Sharon arrived home from her shift. She snuggled in beside him, chuckling.

"I don't know why you bother," she said. "You miss all the good stuff."

"I catch the headlines," he said, fighting a yawn. He returned her kiss and felt a sleepy stirring in his groin. "Mmm. How tired are you?"

For an answer, she slipped her soft, delicate hand under his shirt. "Where's Hannah?" she whispered through a kiss.

"Asleep," he murmured, taking her hand and heading for the stairs. Upstairs, he surrendered himself to a delicious fifteen minutes in her arms.

Afterwards he felt wide awake and followed her down into the kitchen while she fixed her midnight snack. She wore that doe-eyed, sated smile he loved so much, and she flashed it at him as she opened the fridge. "That was a nice surprise."

"Feel free to surprise me whenever you like," he replied.

She twisted around to face him. "You know, I've been thinking—"

"Always unwise after a long day."

She hesitated then allowed the slow smile to return. Shaking her head, she bent to peer into the fridge.

Green cast about for a diversion. "How was your day?"

She fished out a block of cheese and two eggs. She shrugged as she cracked these into a bowl. "No catastrophes. I count that as a good day."

He debated, reluctant to bring work issues into this languid erotic moment between them. In the end, she herself broke the spell.

"Any more developments on the Rosenthal case?"

"We're looking at a group of black youth who live in the area, including the young man who did the Rideau Centre knifing."

"So you're not looking at any of his former patients after all?"

"Well, I'm looking at everything, including Rosenthal's son, who can't even be bothered to contact us to claim the body, let alone care about who might have killed his father."

She dropped butter into a pan and began to whisk the eggs. "Who knows what goes on in families?" She paused to test the eggs. Her movements were pensive. "We had an interesting admission at the hospital last night. Remember I was telling you about having to patch up Dr. Rosenthal's patients when he had them on some off-the-wall herbal remedy?"

He nodded. "Right. The difficulty of deciding when to drug and when to talk."

"Well, there's no contest in this case. The woman's a paranoid schizophrenic, been in and out of hospital for years. On her previous admissions she responded pretty well to meds, but she'd gone off them again, and she was completely off the rails. Her thoughts were so jumbled, I could barely do the admission. Screaming, ranting about plots, and soldiers of Lucifer..." She poured the eggs into the pan. The sweet scent of butter and egg rose with the steam. "I've rarely seen anyone so agitated. She wasn't making much sense, but I distinctly heard the name Dr. Rosenthal."

He stiffened, all senses alert. "What are you thinking? That she may have really seen something?"

"What?" Sharon swung around in surprise, her spatula in hand. "Oh, no. It was the way she said his name. *Dr. Rosenthal*. As if she knew him. I got to wondering if he'd been treating her, professionally, I mean."

"But I thought he hadn't practised in years."

"I know, and this could have been from years ago. But maybe he still was, in the odd special case. Maybe he was still preaching his new age illusions to some unsuspecting souls."

Nine

As he walked to the police cruiser, Omar Adams shoved his hands into the pouch of his hoodie to hide their shaking. Maybe it might even make him look cool, he thought, although he was sure the cops could hear his heart hammering against his ribs. It was too early in the morning to even think straight. His mouth was so dry, he could hardly talk, so it was a good thing he'd decided to say as little as possible. More than one side could play that game, he thought with a defiance he didn't feel. The cops bringing him in hadn't said a word. Two big guys beefed up by Kevlar vests, with caps pulled down to their eyes, had muscled their way in the door past his mother. She'd shrieked and cried and hit them with her fists until he came out of his hiding spot and told her to stop. No point her getting in trouble because of him. This wasn't Somalia.

If the old man had been there, it might have been different—he would have demanded to know what this was all about—but he'd gone off to his delivery job. The cops just said Omar was wanted for questioning. Period. Plus other cops had turned up with a search warrant for the house at exactly the same time, as if they'd arranged it. They hadn't taken no for an answer from his mother either, even when she said she didn't read English. Omar only got a quick look at the warrant before the first cops hustled him out the door, but what he read made him go cold all over. They wanted all the baseball bats and other long bats in the house, all his clothes, even his shoes for fuck's sake. A couple of rings.

And a fancy chainlink watch.

Fuck. What did they know? How had they found him? The video in the pawn shop? Fingerprints? Or Nadif.

On the ride into the station, staring through the cage at their black and red police caps, he tried to pull his galloping fears back under control. What could they have on him? He'd thrown the Rolex into the river as Nadif had suggested. Lucky his mother had washed his clothes and his father had made him scrub every inch of the bathroom with bleach. Omar had cursed him the whole time, but it had proved a good thing.

He didn't remember finding any rings anywhere in his pockets, and the only baseball bat they owned was in the basement, and he hadn't touched it in years. So there could be nothing there to nail him. The shoes...the brand new, high top, black Nikes that he'd worn that night. The shoes were a problem, because he hadn't checked if they had blood on them and he knew the forensics guys could match blood and footprints found at the crime scene. The shoes could be a problem.

But the biggest problem was the hole in his memory. How could he make up a convincing story that covered all the angles if he couldn't remember what he'd done? Over the past couple of days, hoping to jog his memory, he'd read every word he could get his hands on about the murder of the old man on Rideau Street. There wasn't much. The cops were playing this really close to the chest. Either that, or they didn't know fuck all, and they were just shooting around in the dark.

There was lots of stuff on Sam Rosenthal the guy himself. Former shrink, former professor at the university, nice guy who believed in old-fashioned talking to people instead of pumping them full of drugs. Omar could relate to that. Their doctor wanted to put his mother on Prozac to stop the nightmares that woke her screaming and made her run all over the house hiding knives, but his father said over his dead body. He sat up with her himself, trying to rub a giant eraser over her mind.

Maybe if there were more doctors like this Rosenthal, there'd be some help for her. Omar got to feeling sorry for the guy and thinking whoever did this should pay. He hoped to hell it wasn't him. How could he smash a guy's head in and not remember a fucking thing? It wasn't like he got in so many fights that they got to be no big deal. He usually tried to stay out of fights because they scared him, and one fight leads to another and pretty soon it's what everyone expects of you. But this time he remembered fists, a long flashing metal thing that seemed like a knife, and lots of blood. All over himself. His nose had bled, he was sure of that now, but he couldn't remember why.

That put him in serious trouble when he had to face down the cops. Which should be very soon, he realized as the police station came into view—an ugly, concrete shithouse as menacing as the cops in front of him.

In fact, they stuck him in an interview room, brought him a glass of water, and left him. He'd been hustled out of the house before he could grab his cellphone, and there was no clock in the stuffy little room where they put him—nothing but three plastic chairs and a table—so he had no idea how long he'd been waiting. He suspected the bastards did it on purpose. Let him sweat, let him imagine the worst. He shut his eyes, leaned back in his chair, and vowed to outwait them. This is one time that his father's silent treatment would come in handy.

*   *   *

"He's looking way too calm," Sullivan observed from inside the video control room, where he, Levesque and Green stood watching. Green was not so sure. The man was too still, as if it were a deliberate effort of will.

"Anything from the search yet?" Sullivan asked.

Levesque shook her head. "All his shoes and clothes are being sent right to Ident, so we won't know for a bit. Cunningham is cutting out some samples for the lab and said he'd do the luminol right away. However, all the clothes were washed."

"If there was blood on them, luminol would still show it."

"Ruin the DNA, though," she replied. "But one pair of black sneakers looked to have stains on them, so we may get lucky there."

"None of the other items were in the house?"

"They're still looking, but so far they've discovered nothing. Except a baseball bat, but it's so covered in cobwebs, I don't think it's the murder weapon."

"Did anyone ask him about his black eye?"

"No," Levesque replied as if in triumph, "but believe me, I will."

Green was still watching Omar, who had now opened his eyes and was surreptitiously studying the walls and ceiling until his one good eye stared straight out at them from the screen. Understanding dawned in it. It shuttered, partly in fear, partly in defiance.

"How long are you going to let him stew?" Green asked.

Levesque too was watching him. "At least until the search and the luminol results are in. Maybe longer."

Green nodded. There was still too much defiance in that gaze. Not enough apprehension. The police computer database had four hits on the man, but all as witness or bystander. The guns and gangs unit did not have him listed even as a gang affiliate. This was his first time inside a police station. It shouldn't take long for the defiant act to crumble.

Green was already late for a community outreach meeting, and he was about to head off to put in an appearance when there was a sharp knock at the door. Levesque opened it to admit Cunningham himself, holding an evidence bin containing some folded clothes and a pair of crisp new black basketball shoes.

"Some blood on the right shoe near the toe, and on the soles of both shoes," he announced deadpan, as though he were reciting stock prices. Cunningham showed excitement only in the slightest lift of his eyebrow.

In contrast, Levesque pumped the air. "Can you tell us anything about the blood? Sprayed? Dropped?"

"I don't want to second-guess my blood spatter guy—"

"Come on, Lyle," Sullivan exclaimed. "Live dangerously. We've got our suspect in there waiting to be blown away."

Cunningham pursed his lips and pointed at the shoe thoughtfully. "The blood on the toe looks like a smear, like the shoe was rubbed against something bloody. The blood on the soles is pretty thick—it penetrated the cracks in the tread. I'd say your man stepped in a pool of uncoagulated blood."

Green could see the disappointment on Levesque's face. Drops or sprayed flecks of blood would put Omar on the scene as the assault was ongoing, whereas smears could have been obtained afterwards by simple contact with the body before the blood dried. It still left Omar with a lot to explain, but it did not clinch his guilt.

"I've collected a dozen samples of the blood to send to the RCMP lab. They tell me they can have type by Friday, DNA by six weeks."

Green rolled his eyes. Funding and staffing shortages were

the bane of criminal investigations, delaying the discovery of crucial leads until witnesses had either forgotten or disappeared. The lab results would solidify the case for court, but meanwhile they'd proceed as if the blood was Rosenthal's.

"What about the clothes?" Levesque nodded to the folded clothes, already moving on from her disappointment. Sullivan was proving right about her skill.

"There had been blood on them, for sure. A heavier concentration on this shirt. Minute traces on the jeans, but nothing localized. If I had to guess—" Cunningham glared at Sullivan to express his distaste of guesswork, "I'd say the blood transferred to the jeans, maybe during storage."

All three detectives digested this, trying to visualize likely scenarios. Levesque spoke first. "What was the pattern on the shirt?"

Cunningham shook his head. "There we do have to wait for microscopic analysis. Bigger than sprays or smears, I think. It looks like the blood penetrated deep into the fibres."

Green brightened. They were still a long way from Omar wielding the murder weapon, but he knew that analysis of the blood patterns, even on washed fabrics, could establish how and when the blood had been transferred from victim to perpetrator with amazing precision. He looked at Omar, who had peeled off his hoodie. He sat staring at the wall and flicking the occasional wary glance at the camera. He was struggling to hang on to his defiance, but Green could see the glossy sheen on his chocolate skin and the trickle of sweat at his temples.

"How much did you jack the heat up?" he asked.

Levesque smiled. "Wouldn't dream of it, sir. But he looks ready, don't you think?"

She gave him an extra five minutes while she checked her notes, before she gathered up the evidence bins, her laptop and her clipboard and headed down the hall. Green could feel Sullivan's gaze upon him as the two of them settled in to watch.

"You've changed your mind," Sullivan said.

"About the Somalis? I agree, it's looking bad."

"I mean about Marie Claire. She's growing on you."

Green considered the observation in surprise. Levesque was not his kind of detective. She seemed too casual, too cocky, too quick to form conclusions and close off the less obvious lines of inquiry. But yes, he had to admire her instincts and her unerring nose for the route that yielded results. Perhaps she was on the right track. Maybe after all his years behind a desk, he was losing his touch, wandering into blind alleys and wasting valuable time and resources on dead ends.

In the interview room, she set the clipboard and laptop on the table and the bins on the floor underneath. She smiled companionably as she recited the interview details for the video record and cautioned him about his right to remain silent and consult counsel. Omar was sitting upright now. He shook his head at the offer of a lawyer, but his expression was wary.

Levesque leaned back in her chair and looked around the room. "Sorry about the delay, Omar. A number of things came to light in the searches that I needed to verify."

Omar shrugged. Green saw his uninjured eye blink several times in rapid succession.

"Last Saturday night. Tell me about your Saturday night."

The blinking increased. "Nothing to tell. I was home studying. I think my father already told you that."

"Where were you born?"

Omar grew very still. "Somalia." A pause. "So?"

"How long have you been in Canada?"

"Since I was four. I'm a Canadian citizen—same rights as everyone else. Besides, my father's a Canadian."

"Have you got a job?"

"I'm still in high school."

"High school." She let the silence run. "You're how old?"

Omar scowled. "Twenty. I had some trouble, but I'm finishing this year."

"What trouble?"

"I failed a few things."

"How many things?"

He shifted irritably. "You going to ask me about something or not?"

"Relax, Omar. I'm just trying to understand why you were studying Saturday night, when every twenty year-old man I know would be out partying. Is your father on your case?"

"Yeah, my dad's strict. He doesn't want me to screw up."

"What does he want you to do after high school? College?"

"Join the military. Army, like him. Get an education and do good stuff around the world."

"Is that what you want?"

"Pay's good, and they're looking for visible minorities. Dad says I could go far."

It sounded like a rote recitation, a mantra that his father had drilled into his head, but not his heart. Something about the young man didn't ring true. He tried to act like a punk and talk like a punk, and yet, sometimes in an unguarded moment, in his choice of words and grammar, a hint of intelligence shone through. Green wondered if Levesque saw it.

He watched her slow smile. "But that sure is different from your friends. Like Nadif."

Omar's eye popped wide. He stiffened, as if he feared some kind of trap. "Nadif and I are not... We just hang out, that's all."

"Is that what your other friends will tell me?"

"Well...yeah, we hang out."

"Since Nadif is on trial for attempted murder, I bet your father's not too pleased about that. Not too good for your chances with the military."

Omar didn't seem to know what to say, so he stayed quiet. Levesque reached below the table and brought out the bin with Rosenthal's shoes. Green scrutinized Omar's face as she placed them in front of him. No reaction immediately, then faint puzzlement. His brow drew down over his swollen eye. He went on the offensive.

"What's that?"

"You tell me."

"I don't know anything about them. Shoes, that's all."

"We have a witness who says you sold them to him."

Omar snorted. "I don't sell stuff. And where would I get shoes like that?"

"That's the question." Levesque waited, but Omar didn't bite. He looked too relaxed for Green's liking.

"Who told you I sold them?" he demanded finally.

"Nadif Hassan."

The young man's serenity vanished in a spasm of panic. "He's lying."

Levesque leaned forward to point to the seams of the sole. "This shoe has blood on it, which can be matched to Samuel Rosenthal, the man who was killed near Rideau Street early Sunday morning. Nadif Hassan had them hidden in his house, and he claims he bought them from you."

"Bullshit." Omar crossed his arms. "I wasn't even out that night."

Levesque didn't argue, merely opened her laptop and replayed the scenario with the pawn shop video just as she had with Nadif, with the same effect. Omar finally admitted to having sneaked out without his father's knowledge on

Saturday night to go for a short walk with his friends. However, he denied all knowledge of Rosenthal.

"How did you get those bruises on your face?" Levesque asked.

"I tripped and fell on my way home." Omar picked at his fingers. "I did—we did—have something to drink."

"How much?"

He looked relieved. "Some vodka, some beers... I lost count. Over the evening, you know?"

"Any drugs?"

The young man seemed to deliberate, a dead give-away. "A joint or two, yeah. One of the guys brought it. Not me."

"What time did you get home?"

"I didn't check. I was...pretty wasted."

"Midnight? One? Two? Three o'clock?"

Green watched Omar shaking his head, sheepish and relieved that she had moved on. He nodded at three o'clock.

"Please take off your shirt."

The young man looked confused. He plucked at his shirt as if trying to remember if he had anything to hide. He seemed to think a token objection was required, because he tugged his shirt down tight. "No way!"

"Have you got something to hide?"

"No, it's just...you can't make me do that. It's a violation, like."

Levesque regarded him gravely. Finally she nodded. "I understand. I'll leave the room, and you can show Constable Murphy here."

Before he had a chance to counter her offer, she scooped up her clipboard and left the room. Murphy, recovering from his own surprise, left the corner and loomed over the table. At nearly six-foot six, he cast quite a shadow. Omar flinched.

"Why did she ask me that?" he whined.

"Make it easy on yourself," Murphy said. "She could book you and strip-search you if she wanted."

"She's got nothing on me!" But he began to roll up his T-shirt, revealing first his torso and then his hairless, concave chest. Green winced at what a military doctor's verdict would be. Murphy prowled around to see all the angles. Omar stopped as the T-shirt reached his armpits.

"All the way off."

Omar's eyes flashed with anger, and in one swift yank, he pulled the shirt over his head. The bones on his thin shoulders protruded.

Murphy gazed at his back. "Stand up and turn around."

Chin shoved out, Omar obeyed, exposing his back to the camera. The skin was stretched tight across the shoulder blades, chocolate brown but crisscrossed with long jagged ridges. Green sucked in his breath. Scar tissue from long ago. Inflicted by whom, he wondered. By his father? Or by some sadistic thug in the refugee camp where he'd begun his life?

No wonder the man had not wanted to undress.

Sullivan nudged his elbow. "Look at his left upper arm."

Green shifted his attention and saw what had Sullivan and Levesque so excited. Three much more recent scars—purplish, weltlike and barely healed. Like the marks of fingernails dragged over flesh.

Levesque waited until Omar had his shirt back on before reentering the room. "How did you get those injuries on your arm?"

Omar shrugged. "I don't know. When I fell, I guess."

"You fell on your arm?"

"Like I said, I don't remember. I must have. Unless—" He broke off, eyes shuttered.

"Unless what?"

"Nothing."

Levesque waited a moment, but he had retreated behind his immobility. She removed the shoes from the table, and in their place she laid the evidence bin with Omar's clothes and sneakers. It seemed to Green that Omar ceased to breathe as he stared at them, like a man caught in a cobra's stare.

"Do you know what luminol is?"

The young man said nothing.

"It's a chemical that when you spray it on something and shine a UV light, any trace of blood shows up. Here's your freshly washed hoodie. Looks not bad, eh? A little stained, maybe, but who'd know?" She flipped open her laptop and slipped in Ident's CD. In no time, the luminol photo of the shirt filled the screen. She swivelled it so that he could see. "Here's what your shirt looks like under luminol."

The screen was black except for luminescent blotches of blue. In the centre, three bright patches an inch or two in diameter, and on the edges a series of paler smears. Levesque let Omar contemplate the image in silence. He ran his tongue around his lips and swallowed, seeming unable to moisten his mouth enough to talk.

"How did the blood get on your hoodie?"

"Like I said, I fell. Gave myself a nosebleed."

Levesque pressed a button, and the image changed to the sneakers. An even brighter blue lit up the screen. "These are your sneakers. See there is blood on the bottom of them. How would you get blood on the bottom from a nosebleed?"

"I don't know. Maybe I stepped in it afterwards."

"You stepped in it all right, after Dr. Rosenthal was bleeding all over the pavement."

"No! I never saw him!"

"The RCMP lab is already doing DNA tests on the blood, Omar. You know about DNA?"

He nodded, again apparently robbed of voice.

"That will tie you to Dr. Rosenthal's body." She shifted subtly, leaned forward and deepened her voice. Not threatening, more companionable. "But we know you didn't act alone. Maybe it wasn't even your idea, you just found yourself caught up in someone else's mess. It was all Nadif's idea, wasn't it?"

Omar didn't reply, merely stared at his brand-new sneakers on the table, less in reproach than in bewilderment.

"We want the real bad guy to get his proper punishment, not you. You've never even been in trouble with the law, Omar. Why ruin your life for a man who doesn't deserve it?"

"Nadif didn't have anything to do with it."

"With what?"

"With Saturday night. With...with my fall."

"He's on the video."

"He went home early."

"He had the shoes, Omar. He ratted you out. What kind of friend is that?"

"I don't know. I don't remember anything about shoes, an old man, anything!"

Green could see that the young man was backing himself up against the wall, shutting down and clinging to the story he had first offered. He looked bewildered but immovable. Green searched his face and his body language for signs of capitulation, a tacit admission of guilt or defeat. There was none. He didn't even object to giving a DNA sample when Levesque asked.

Levesque pressed on, reworking the ground, ticking off all the bits of evidence in rapid succession, hammering away at his resistance. Tears glistened in his eyes, his chin quivered, but still he stuck to his story. For the next two hours she worked away, until his lawyer, hastily called up by his father, arrived to demand an end.

As Omar was being led away, he passed by Green in the hallway. For an instant, he raised his large, limpid eyes to Green's. He looked haunted, cornered. In his gaze, however, was a question. A hint of doubt. Or guilt.

In that moment, it was Green's turn to feel confused.

Ten

Green was still puzzling over that look when he returned to the squad room, too late to catch even the tail end of his committee meeting. Waiting at his office door was the Major Crimes clerk with a business card in her hand. She handed it to him and told him the gentleman was waiting downstairs for him in the lobby.

Green glanced at the card, which was plain white but slightly grimy at the edges, as though it had been used many times. G.R. Verne LLB, barrister and solicitor, in simple black letters with an address off Montreal Road in the crime-ridden heart of Vanier. Yet Green had never heard of him. Either he was straight out of law school, or he'd never graced the criminal court.

The latter, Green decided when the clerk showed Verne into his office. The lawyer looked as if he'd been before the bar for fifty years, each one weighing more heavily than the last. His back was bowed by the weight of a hundred extra pounds, which hung on his frame in billowing folds. His frayed brown suit shone at the elbows and collar, and an odour of sweat and mothballs wafted around him. He wheezed as he wedged himself into Green's tiny guest chair, set his briefcase on the floor and propped his cane against the desk. He contemplated the room but didn't speak while he caught his breath.

"What can I do for you, Mr. Verne?"

Verne leaned over to unsnap his briefcase and extracted a sheaf of legal documents. "I expected to hear from you before this," he said, his lips forming a loose pout. "But since I didn't, I decided I'd better... I am the executor of Samuel Rosenthal's estate."

Green masked his surprise. Verne was not the lawyer named in the will they had found in the dead man's apartment, nor did he look as if he'd ever handled an estate worth millions in his life. Green wondered whether Levesque had even followed up. "I'm glad you came in, Mr. Verne. We've been having trouble locating Dr. Rosenthal's son, or any other relatives."

"There are none. Besides the son, that is. Here's his address." Verne produced another sheet of paper and handed it across the desk. An address in Palo Alto, California, different from the Baltimore address the FBI had. Another of his six houses, perhaps?

"What can you tell me about the son?" Green asked.

"A spoiled, hothouse only child who turned into an ambitious, self-centred man. Intellectually brilliant but socially bankrupt. Everyone who doesn't worship at the temple of David's self-importance is cast aside. His father, three wives, and I don't know how many employers."

Green couldn't resist a smile. "You're quite a fan."

Verne laughed, a wheezy rumble that ended in a cough. "Neither was Sam. He recognized the mistake he'd made with his son. Hence the new will." Verne tapped the papers.

Green perked up. "He didn't leave half his estate to his son?"

"Not a penny. He felt his money would be better spent on charities and on other worthy causes that really needed it. Perhaps as penance for inflicting his son on the world."

Maybe a bit of spite too, Green thought. In his experience, wealthy people who left all their money to charities had revenge as well as philanthropy on their minds. He wondered if vengeance ran in the family. "Did they ever see each other?"

"David couldn't make time in his busy schedule. No, I stand corrected. He made two days for his mother, after she died. Never mind that she took two years to die."

"Did David know his father had disinherited him? Would he be the type to hold a grudge?"

Verne's eyebrows shot up, becoming lost in the web of wrinkles on his brow. "My goodness, is that what you think?"

"Obvious question. His son was a chief beneficiary of the earlier will, but cut out of this later one."

Verne relaxed and emitted another phlegmy chuckle. "Sam wasn't even on David's radar. David has his own biomedical engineering company now. He's a millionaire many times over, even has contracts with the U.S. military."

Sometimes it's not about the money, Green thought, especially when family feuds are involved. He thought of the empty file marked "will" in Rosenthal's apartment. Had someone tried to get rid of the newer will?

"Were you close to Sam?"

Verne's levity vanished, and his baggy eyes grew sad. "Not really, but perhaps as close as anyone gets. Sam was a private man."

"Always, or since his wife died?"

"Always. I suspect Evelyn was the only person who ever got inside. Not that he was mean. He was always a gentleman, polite and friendly, but...simply self-contained. I think losing Evelyn cut him adrift."

It occurred to Green that he should contact Levesque to give her the son's address and to invite her in on the interview. But just as quickly, he squelched the idea. She's busy, he thought, polishing up the murder charge against Omar Adams. He leaned back in his chair and nodded at the document which Verne had placed on the desk. "When was this will made?"

"Just this past spring."

Green tried to remember the details of the previous will, which had been drafted just after his wife's death. "Why change his will now? His son has been out of his life for years."

Verne hesitated, his lips working. "To understand that, you have to understand Sam's change of heart. He didn't so much want to cut his son out as he wanted to compensate some people."

"Compensate who?"

"The beneficiaries named in the will."

"I thought you said he left it all to charities. Worthy causes."

"Worthy causes, yes. But some of those were people."

Green sat forward with a thud. "Who?"

Verne reached into his briefcase and withdrew a single sheet of paper. He studied it for a moment before handing it over to Green. It was a photocopy of a single page of the will, listing six names. None of them were familiar, but that was hardly surprising. Most of them would have dated from ten years ago. Three were female, three male, and the surnames ran the gamut from French Canadian to Arabic.

"Who are these people?"

"Patients of his."

Green remembered what Sharon had speculated. "Wasn't he retired?"

Verne hesitated, then raised his pudgy hand in an equivocating gesture. "He still dabbled. But most of these were former patients. From years ago."

"And what was Rosenthal compensating them for?"

"For what he had come to see as his professional mistakes."

It felt like grappling with riddles. As if something important was dancing just out of reach. "What professional mistakes?"

Verne pursed his lips. "In the interests of maintaining their privacy, I'd rather not say."

"There's no attorney-client privilege here. These people aren't your clients."

"No, but their private health information is confidential."

Green quelled his frustration. The old lawyer was far too wily to be bullied, so he tried another tack. "What's Rosenthal's estate worth?"

Verne danced around that question too. "Well, he owns several properties, and I'd have to look at his current investment portfolio..."

"Ballpark?"

"Six million and change."

"Of which these people get how much?"

"He still left half that amount to endow the cancer research chair and a few other charities, but the remainder is divided equally among these six. Which means..." Verne paused as if to calculate, although Green suspected he already knew to the penny how much each stood to inherit. "Almost $500,000."

Green leaned in, trying to hide his excitement. "Do these individuals know they're being compensated to the tune of half a million dollars each?"

"I didn't tell them, although of course I will now." He paused thoughtfully. "And I doubt Sam would have. He wanted this kept very quiet."

"To maintain their privacy?"

A rueful smile played across Verne's thick lips. "To avoid lawsuits."

Green studied the list, wondering whether Verne knew something he was unwilling to share directly. He phrased his next question carefully. "Do you know if any of these individuals had a criminal past? Or a potential for violence?"

Verne splayed his hands in a gesture of ignorance. "I have nothing more than their names and dates of birth. Not even their addresses, although I've set my secretary to work on that. But..." his lips worked as if he were mentally chewing over an idea, "That's why I brought the list to your attention. They are vulnerable people who have been wronged. And even if they weren't psychiatric patients, half a million can be a hell of a motive."

*   *   *

Levesque barely seemed to be listening as Green filled her and Sullivan in on his meeting with Verne. She was too polite and savvy to defy him openly, but when she filed the list of former patients in with her case notes and assured him she would do background checks, Green sensed no urgency in her tone. She was triumphantly putting the finishing touches on her case against Omar, and the new will had no place in it at all.

Green dismissed her irritably but beckoned Sullivan to stay. "What's Gibbs working on?" he asked. He had spotted the tech wizard bent over his computer.

Sullivan sank into the guest chair with a weary sigh. "He's working up a case for court."

"If anyone can dig up info on these people, it's him."

"You're not convinced it's the Somalis? Pretty strong case."

"I know, and maybe it *is* them. But all our high-profile

miscarriages of justice have occurred because the police jumped to conclusions too early. Dr. Rosenthal treated all these people and may in fact have been treating them at the time of his murder. It has to be investigated."

"It will be, Mike."

"But now Levesque wants to prove she's right, and it makes her blind. Don't give her enough rope to hang the wrong person, Brian."

Sullivan's face flushed red as he hauled himself to his feet. More than one person's ego is involved here, Green thought. He watched Sullivan stop by Gibbs's desk to speak to him briefly and to hand him a copy of the list. Gibbs glanced at it, set it aside, and continued with his work. When Green looked out at the end of the day, Gibbs had gone home, and the list was still sitting at the edge of his desk. Annoyed, Green snatched it up on his way to the elevator.

He spent the evening playing endless games of Snakes and Ladders with his son, who never liked to lose. It took three bedtime stories to mellow him sufficiently to coax him into bed. Hannah by some miracle was doing homework, and Sharon was not yet back from work. A perfect time to have a peek at the list.

When he and Sharon had been allotting rooms in the rambling old house they'd bought, there had been only two possible places for a home office. One, a damp, windowless room in the basement and the other a minuscule sunroom which the previous owner had tacked onto the back of the house. It barely accommodated a desk, a chair and a filing cabinet, but cheerful sun blazed in for most of the day. It had won hands down.

Insulation had not been a priority with the do-it-yourself builder, however, so at ten o'clock on a bracing September evening, Green could almost see his breath as he booted up his laptop. He plugged in the baseboard heater, zippered his fleece up to his neck and studied the names, debating where to start. He was no Bob Gibbs, the virtual world still being something of an alien landscape to him, but he finally settled on a quick search of 411 listings in the Ottawa area to see who among the six was still living there.

After fifteen minutes on the computer and the phone, he had found no trace of two. Four others had Ottawa-area addresses. Two of these were not definitive because the initials were too common, but it was a start. He launched a Google search of the first of the Ottawa residents, Caitlin O'Malley. Google identified dozens of Caitlin O'Malleys, among them a magician and a bride, but all lived in the United States, Ireland or New Zealand. The only promising hit was a Caitlin O'Malley who had co-authored a mathematics paper at the University of Ottawa. Hardly murderous stuff. In contrast, "Victor Ikes" yielded over a thousand hits, including a Wikipedia entry for an actor who'd been in a few B-grade independent films and one short-lived TV series before apparently vanishing from public view a few years ago.

Green browsed a few other fan-based entertainment sites for more information on Ikes, uncovering rumours of drug addiction, rehab, wild parties, flashes of brilliance and long black bouts of depression. There were no reports of violence, but the internet was hardly an exhaustive or even accurate source. At least this Victor Ikes had some psychiatric issues, and even more to the point, he currently lived in Ottawa.

On a hunch, Green phoned Dispatch to check the Ottawa Police internal database. If any of the six had had contact with police, even as a witness or victim, that report would be on the Records Management System. Three of the six names produced hits. A Caitlin O'Malley had been picked up once in a sweep of squeegee kids but released without charge and more recently for creating a disturbance. The responding officers had taken her to the Ottawa Hospital ER for a psychiatric assessment. Certainly a more promising possibility than the math whiz.

Victor Ikes' results were even more promising; the database yielded sixteen hits covering nine separate incidents. The dispatcher rhymed them off rapidly. Victor had been the perpetrator in eight incidents and the victim in one. Green jotted down the offences—driving while impaired, creating a disturbance, uttering threats against his neighbour, assault in a bar fight... a list of petty offences that suggested a life of drugs and instability. Charges had been laid three times, resulting in guilty pleas twice, for which he'd been handed discharges conditional on seeking treatment for his problems. Perhaps the presiding judge had been a fan of B-movies.

The one victim report was a 911 call reporting a suicide attempt. Victor Ikes had been found unresponsive in his bedroom by his mother and had been transported to the Ottawa Hospital. Green put a star beside Ikes' name. With his history of psychiatric problems and penchant for aggressive outbursts, the man certainly belonged on any credible list of suspects.

In the distance he heard the front door open and close. Modo, who'd been snoozing on top of Green's feet, struggled to attention and lumbered out of the room. The mistress was home, relegating Green instantly to second fiddle. He listened as keys clinked in the dish on the hall table, shoes thudded against the back of the closet and the fridge door opened. He made some final notes, thanked the dispatcher and hung up just as Sharon appeared behind him with an open container of peach yogurt in her hand.

She kissed the top of his head. "Everything under control here?"

"Mmm. We had a marathon of Snakes and Ladders. Our son doesn't handle losing well."

"Really. I wonder where he got that from." She peered over his shoulder at his laptop. "What are you doing?"

"Nothing, now that you're here." He closed the laptop.

She chuckled. "You back meddling in the trenches?"

"No. Well... Just trying to speed things up. Sam Rosenthal's murder has taken an unusual turn. It appears he left millions of dollars to former patients."

"That was nice of him. Why?"

"Guilt, his lawyer says. He obviously thought they deserved it more than his selfish son."

A faint frown darkened her eyes. She watched him in silence for a moment. "Don't go off on a witch hunt, Mike."

"What do you mean?"

"Don't go assuming just because they're patients that they're all crazy killers. People with mental illnesses have enough struggles without fighting that myth."

"You know me better than that," he said, but the protest sounded feeble even to his ears. That's exactly what he had assumed, as had Rabbi Tolner and even the lawyer Verne. After years in the trenches, he knew that the greatest evil lay among the greedy, the lazy and the just plain heartless.

Still, it paid to listen for zebras.

*   *   *

Canada 411 listed Victor Ikes' address as an apartment unit on Eccles Avenue, just off Preston Street. The area was still called Little Italy, even though it had been more like Little Vietnam or Little Cambodia over the last twenty years. It was a mixed neighbourhood now, with gentrified renos and patches of exquisite garden sprouting up among the converted rooming houses and rundown cottages. More importantly, it was right on Green's route from his home to the station. At eight o'clock in the morning, he might well wake the man up, but at least he was likely to catch him at home.

When he finally answered the buzzer, Victor Ikes looked as if he'd never actually gone to bed. He was dressed in torn, dirty jeans, a faded Tea Party sweatshirt and fluffy pink slippers. He looked slack-jawed and hollow-eyed, like a man who'd slept too little and lived too hard for the last twenty years. When Green identified himself, he scowled.

"You got a warrant?" The door started to shut.

Green stuck his foot in the opening. "I'm not here for that. I'd like to speak to you about Dr. Samuel Rosenthal."

Ikes staggered back and reached for the door frame. "What does he want!"

Green noted the present tense. Cunning or uninformed? "When did you last see him?"

"I stopped going to that quack years ago."

"How many years?"

"Eight? Ten? Before I moved to Toronto."

"And you're sure you haven't seen him recently."

A door opened inside, followed by a phlegmy intake of breath. Cheap floral perfume wafted through the doorway an instant before a woman appeared behind Victor, tugging a pink bathrobe across her pendulous breasts. She was built like a Sherman tank, almost six feet tall with shoulders to match. Her face looked like a botched botox job, and over-bleached hair hung in her eyes. Her feet, incongruously, were bare, perhaps to show off her bright pink, half-inch toenails. Wouldn't want to meet those at the bottom of a cold bed, Green thought.

"Vic, don't answer that," she snapped, bulldozing him aside with her elbow. "The police have no business asking about your personal medical history."

She had a faint English accent that reminded Green of *Coronation Street.* "Are you his mother?" he asked. When she didn't answer, he introduced himself and explained that he was collecting background information on Dr. Rosenthal. She had obviously read the papers, for she narrowed her eyes warily.

"We haven't seen the man in years, good riddance, so we can't help you."

"I'm interested in the types of treatments he provided, not in your son personally. May I come in?"

"Why are you interested in that?"

"Because there seem to be quite a few people dissatisfied with his services."

"And you figure one of us smashed his head in, is that it?"

Victor gasped. His hollow eyes bulged. "Dr. Sam is dead?"

Green said nothing, waiting for the mother to enlighten him. She waved a dismissive hand.

"Yeah, yeah, I caught it on the news. Didn't want to upset you, hones." She turned to Green. "I can tell you what you need, but I don't want Vic upset."

"Just a few questions," Green said, summoning his most harmless expression.

She stepped back, muttering under her breath, and headed back inside. "At least let me get my tea."

She didn't offer any to Green, nor even to her son, but Green followed her into a tiny, oppressively hot living room. Blinds were drawn tight against the morning sun. The air was stale with booze, cigarette smoke, and the stench of old clothes and dishes that seemed to clutter every surface. He pushed some magazines aside so that he could squeeze into a corner of the sofa.

Victor was pacing restlessly, staring at the floor and twirling a cigarette in his fingers. "I liked him," he said finally. "Bastard didn't know what the fuck he was doing, but at least he listened. More than I can say for the shrink I have now. Ten minutes in and out of his office, 'eating okay, sleeping okay, no voices, good, here's your new prescription.'"

"But at least you're well," his mother said, emerging from the kitchen with a cup of steaming liquid and an unlit cigarette.

"I'm not well, Mother," Victor said. "I'm keeping a lid on. That's different."

Mrs. Ikes' face hardened. She'd put on a slash of pink lipstick, most of which was now on the rim of her cup. She landed onto the sofa with a thud, nearly sending Green off the other end. "We don't pay him to be a nice guy. That quack nearly cost my son his life."

Victor's pacing increased. "Sometimes this so-called life hardly feels worth saving. Dr. Sam gave me hope, he made me feel worthwhile and energized, not like some chemical reject with parts missing in my brain."

"He should have known better. He was supposed to be a trained specialist in diseases of the mind, not a guru with some half-baked theory from Tibet. And that's the thing, Vic. You have a disease, no different than diabetes or high blood pressure, and you don't talk yourself out of those. You take medication to correct the problem." She eyed him shrewdly as he continued to pace. "Goddamn it, Vic, you went off them again, didn't you?"

He stopped pacing. Looked trapped. "Just while I do this

audition, Mum. I need that energy, that edge. The drugs kill it."

"That edge is called mania. And you know what happens next." She sighed and swivelled to face Green. "It took me years to undo the damage that quack did by telling him all this stuff was part of his 'natural state'. That maybe his black days were the price to be paid for the 'pingpong brilliance of his manic mind', Rosenthal called it. And that he could learn to manage his excesses with fish oil and mind control. Rubbish. Victor is bipolar. His good-for-nothing father, who blew his brains out at thirty-four, was bipolar. Victor was on track to do the same thing if I hadn't put my foot down."

"What happened?" Green asked.

Mrs. Ikes lit the cigarette with tremulous hands and dragged the smoke deep into her lungs. Green tried not to cough as smoke curled his way. "I knew something was wrong," she said, puffs of smoke escaping with every word. "I could see the swings—the drug binges, the wild parties for days on end, then the weeks he couldn't get out of bed. But I was only his mum. My opinion didn't count. Vic was an adult, Rosenthal said, and he could make his own decisions. Rosenthal wouldn't even talk to me, wouldn't return my phone calls. Patient confidentiality, he said."

"He knew you were part of the problem, Mum. Not letting me grow up, always expecting the worst of me, hiding all the knives and razors and pills—"

"I did that to keep you alive! In spite of yourself and that quack!"

"Fuck it. You never did get it." Victor resumed pacing.

Mrs. Ikes drew in another hit of smoke. Behind the hank of hair, her eyes were bleak. "But he managed to get pills anyway. Legal and illegal, he took the whole lot at once. Ended up in hospital, where he lay in a coma for a week, and

I had a chance to have a good long chat with the doctor in charge. That's how we got him on proper meds and back on an even keel." She glowered at her son. "Most of the time. But the brain damage was done. Vic has short-term memory problems now, and he has a tough time memorizing his lines."

"It's the drugs, Mum. I keep telling you. They deaden my mind."

"No, it's not, Vic. It's the—" She clamped her mouth shut and shook her head as if to spare her son further. "Anyway, you get the picture, Detective. That's all water under the bridge. I hated that damn Jew for years, and I'm not sorry he's dead. But neither of us took a hammer to his head."

*   *   *

Sullivan winced when Green related the story, but Green just grinned.

"I got my own back. I was going to tell them about the half million-dollar inheritance, which it looks as if they can really use, but I decided they could wait. You have to feel for the woman, though. For both of them."

"You planning to do this with all six beneficiaries on the list?"

"No, Gibbs can do that. I was just getting a sense of the nature and scope of the problem." He sobered. "It's big. For people with a serious mental illness, every day can be a struggle. They're vulnerable and desperate, and they put their trust in Rosenthal. If he betrayed them in some way... That's a powerful motive, Brian. That new will was stolen from Rosenthal's apartment, so somebody knew about those bequests. Levesque needs to take this more seriously."

Sullivan passed a weary hand over his face, as if wishing

the problem would simply go away. Then he nodded. "You're right. But I'm not sure Gibbs is the right one for the job."

He didn't elaborate, but he didn't need to. Both men had watched Gibbs wrestle with his own emotional demons over the past year and a half. His progress, though considerable, was fragile, and his own emotional grip still tenuous. Green heard the sound of the elevator door, and through his half-open door he saw the reason for that progress—Detective Sue Peters, making her slow, careful way into the squad room. He was getting used to the sight, but it still tightened his chest. Eighteen months after her near fatal beating, she was still a ghost of her former self. Her fiery red hair had been shaved for the neurosurgery and had grown back a bland brown, and her clunky, bulldozer stride had been replaced by a cautious shuffle. By sheer determination and fury, she had learned to walk without a cane, but Green could tell it was a precarious triumph.

Despite Gibbs's best culinary efforts, she was twenty pounds lighter and had had to buy a whole new wardrobe. Gone were the garish checkered suits and fuchsia jackets that had clashed so defiantly with her hair. She was wearing a blue turtleneck sweater—the better to cover her scars, Green suspected—and loose-fitting grey slacks.

She looked infinitely older.

When she saw them through the open doorway, however, she smiled the same broad, infectious grin she'd always had, now a little lopsided. "Good morning, boys!"

Same irreverent spirit too, Green thought, surprised at his own relief. Sullivan and he exchanged questioning glances, and Sullivan gestured to indicate that it was Green's call.

He strolled over. "Sue, have you got an assignment for today?"

She had reached her desk and was easing herself into the

chair. Although she was only on duty three half days a week, Green had assigned her a desk of her own. Part of her mental recovery.

"I'm entering the Rosenthal case on VICLAS."

Entering all the details of a homicide investigation onto the national RCMP violent crimes database was a tedious but necessary job. "Feel like a break?" he said. He realized belatedly that he'd left his notes and list of the beneficiaries at home, but he handed Sue a fresh copy, filling her in on what he remembered. "We're looking for background and current whereabouts," he said.

Sue grinned and booted up her computer. "Do you want me to call any of them directly?"

Green hesitated. Peters' interviewing skills used to resemble a bull in a china shop. Sullivan intervened before he could find a tactful reply. "Report to me or the Inspector before you do that. We may not want to tip them off."

Peters' disappointment was visible on her face, but unlike the old days, she turned to her computer without a word of protest.

Eleven

Sharon woke uncharacteristically early but lay in bed awhile, revelling in the silence of the house. Morning sunlight filtered through the pale bedroom blind, washing the room in muted gold. She had always loved the evening shift at the hospital, not only for its freedom from the daytime bustle, but also for these morning hours alone. Thank God for car pools. With Tony at school, she had complete solitude for the first time in years. Her thoughts drifted to the question that had been tantalizing her for months. Did she really want to change that? Did she really want to add to the crazy, crammed, conflicting press of their lives?

She ran her hand over her stomach, remembering the early feelings of pregnancy. The tiny flutter in her belly, the lush, heavy sensuality of her breasts. Morning sickness had barely been an issue with Tony. The pregnancy had been enjoyable, secret, feminine in a primal way she'd never experienced before. She had loved that growing life from her first moment of awareness. Surely she would love the next one just as much.

The question was—would Mike? He was an only child and a workaholic, already reeling from the demands of wife, daughter, son and father. Would he? He'd been avoiding the subject every time she'd drifted near. But while they vacillated, she could hear the fading tick of her biological clock. She was nearing her fifth decade. Mike was in the middle of his. They couldn't afford the luxury of time much longer.

She rolled out of bed, stumbled downstairs into the kitchen and confronted the cold, empty coffee pot. Banishing a twinge of annoyance, she brewed up a pot. While she waited for it to drip through, she hunted for the morning *Citizen,* surprised to discover it was still rolled up on the front porch. Mike must have been in quite a hurry that morning to race out before his morning fix of either coffee or the headlines. She poured a cup, carried it into the sunroom and sank into the easy chair by the sunny window. Peace. Perfection. She unfolded the paper and glanced at the headline about the interrogation of a young Somali man for the murder of Sam Rosenthal.

She read the story from top to bottom, along with the two short sidebars on the life of the young "person of interest". Omar Adams' story surprised her. Unlike most of Ottawa's Somali community, he had not come to Canada as a refugee from the terrifying brutality in his lawless homeland. His father had been a soldier in the Canadian Airborne Regiment during their ill-fated peacekeeping mission in Somalia. Stories of the Airborne's torture and murder of a Somali teenager had led to the abrupt termination of the mission and the disbanding of the regiment in disgrace.

Yet Omar's father, who was a sergeant with the mission at the time, seemed to have followed a more honourable path. His mother had been an orphaned village girl who'd been taken in to provide domestic services on the base. I can just imagine what those services entailed, Sharon thought. When she became pregnant, Omar's father enrolled in Islamic studies and took care of both her and the baby. When the regiment was recalled, he married her just before the last plane left, then battled red tape to get her and Omar to Canada, describing it as one small gesture to right the many wrongs. Omar spent his first four years in a Somali refugee camp in the desert before the final approvals came through, but at least he and his mother were able to cling to hope.

"This is a mistake," Mr. Adams was quoted as saying of his son's arrest. "Omar was in a camp, but he has always had a loving, safe family environment. There is absolutely no way he would have beaten anyone in the manner the police allege. Not in spite of what he might have witnessed as a young child, but because of it."

The official police statement was far less generous. They were continuing to gather evidence but were already confident that the evidence to date could support a charge.

Sharon put the paper down thoughtfully. Her gaze drifted to Mike's computer desk. If the police were so confident, why had he been hard at work at midnight the night before, researching the former patients of the dead man? Despite his assurances, she still had her doubts about his motives. Psychiatric patients made easy targets in the minds not only of the public but even of policy makers and police. The words "nuts", "crazy" and "psycho" were tossed around callously by people who knew nothing of the genuine struggles and silent suffering of those coping to overcome mental illness. It was disheartening to find fragments of that prejudice in someone who should know better.

The laptop was gone, but Mike's notes were still on the desk. She rose guiltily and went over to glance at his progress.

The typed list of names was scribbled over with question marks, comments and addresses in Mike's handwriting. She knew she shouldn't look and was just trying to tear herself away when a name stopped her cold. She frowned. What on earth could it mean? Could there be a connection? As she deciphered Green's pencilled notes, her confusion grew. She knew of a way to get the answers, but the question was...

Even if she did know, what could she do?

*   *   *

Green was elbow deep in neglected paperwork when the phone rang at his side. Gratefully he pounced on it. A girl's breathy, singsong voice came through.

"Hi. Um...is Inspector Green there?"

Green tried to place the voice but failed. He identified himself.

"This is Lindsay Corsin? You gave me your card? I rent an apartment above Dr. Rosenthal?"

Green readjusted his focus with surprise. "Yes, Lindsay. How can I help you?"

"I don't know if it's important? I mean, like if he's allowed? I watch *Law and Order,* and... Anyway, I thought I should call. Let you know, in case."

"Know what?"

"There's someone in Dr. Rosenthal's apartment. A man. He's got a van, and he's taking paintings and stuff out."

Possibilities raced through Green's mind. The apartment had never been a crime scene, at least as part of the murder investigation, so technically this didn't constitute tampering with a crime scene. Yet the only person with legal access to the place was dead, and it had been the scene of an earlier break and enter.

"What does he look like?"

"He's very tall, looks fit—at least for a guy his age."

"Which is?"

"Oh, I'm not so good with that. Over forty? His hair is going grey. He's got one of those old-fashioned beards that makes him look like a professor?"

"Clothes?" He was already grabbing his jacket, keys and gun, but paused to jot down her reply. "I'm sending a patrol

136

car, and I'm on my way myself. Wait for me."

"But—"

"Stay out of sight and wait."

He'd barely disconnected when he phoned dispatch and ordered a cruiser to check out an intruder at the Nelson Street address. He rattled off the description Lindsay had given. The man didn't sound like your standard B&E specialist, but Green had been surprised too many times to rush to judgment.

Sandy Hill was an exasperating maze of one-way streets and road construction that left him cursing by the time he finally rounded the corner onto Nelson Street. A cruiser was parked at the curb, and the officers were chatting with Lindsay on the front walk. A nondescript white panel van sat at the curb behind the cruiser. Lindsay looked frailer than ever, her pale skin almost translucent and her large eyes circled by blue. She hugged her frilly purple jacket around her thin frame, but it was scant protection against the bracing autumn wind that swept down the street in a swirl of dead leaves.

She looked guilty when she saw Green. "He left before they got here," she said. "I thought of stopping him, but I was too scared. He looked so angry."

He put his hand on her arm and felt her bones through the thin fabric. "You did the right thing. Which way did he go?"

She nodded up the street towards Rideau, barely a block away although a road barrier blocked the path. "That way. He was walking. That's his van there."

Green walked over to the van, noting the Ontario license plate and the discount rental sticker. He jotted down the number and handed it to one of the unformed officers. "Phone the rental company and ask who rented it. If they give you grief, tell them it's involved in a burglary."

The uniformed officer trotted up to her cruiser. Green circled the van, peering into windows. In the dark interior he could just make out some boxes stacked against one side and a collection of paintings leaning against the other. On the passenger seat was an open map, a well-worn suede jacket, and a crumpled bag from Starbucks.

The officer returned from her car. "The company rented it out yesterday to a company called Vivotech."

"Name?"

"That's all they had, sir. The man paid for a week with a wad of cash to cover the security deposit, and they didn't get a name." The uniformed officer grinned. "They're eager to cooperate, sir. The manager said he looked like a fine, upstanding citizen. How were they to know?"

Green nodded. Of course they were eager to cooperate, after violating just about every rental rule in the book. Lindsay was still standing on the walk, shivering. For the first time he noticed her frayed cuffs and the holes in her sneakers. He signalled to the uniformed officer and handed her his card.

"I want you to pull around the corner and set up surveillance on the house and the van. I have to leave for a bit, but if our man shows up, give me a call on my cell. Don't approach him unless he tries to leave again."

The officer bounded off again, her eyes shining. Probably the most excitement she's had all week, Green thought. He took Lindsay's elbow and felt the girl shrink back. Did she distrust all men, or just cops? Releasing her, he gestured to his car. "Let's wait in my car. It will be warmer."

She hesitated then picked up her bag in acquiescence. Inside, he turned the heater up, but she sat stiffly with her backpack on her lap like a shield. She had a single silver stud in her left nostril but otherwise she wore no jewellery or make-up. The backpack bulged with the weight of her books, and one of the zippers was broken.

"Do you have time for lunch?" he asked, trying to ease into the suggestion. "I haven't eaten yet."

The girl didn't answer, but her mouth worked convulsively as if already savouring the food.

"My treat," he added as he started the car.

"Why?"

He drove the circuitous route down to Rideau Street and pulled into the parking lot at Harvey's. Only then, with the smells of charbroiled hamburgers and fresh fries drifting in through the window, did he answer her. "Because I think you can help. You notice things. People. Maybe even more than you realize."

Once they were settled into a booth by the window, Green watched her devour the hamburger and wondered what else she was sacrificing to attend university. "Where are you from?"

Her head shot up, mouth full of fries. "Why?"

He shrugged easily. "Just remembering my own university years. I had my parents to live with and a full-time job as a rookie patrolman, but I still had trouble paying for it all."

She managed a thin smile. "OSAP. I'll be paying the government back until I'm ninety."

"It's not enough to live on, is it?"

She shook her head. "I had a job in an art store till they tore it down to build a condo. Dr. Rosenthal was pretty good about the rent, even when I missed a month." She hung her head and fiddled with the zipper of her bag. Took a deep, wistful breath. "I'm from Timmins. Never thought I'd miss it..."

Green waited.

"Here, you don't know anybody. You don't know who to

trust. Truth is, I wasn't exactly telling the whole truth when I said I never talked to Dr. Rosenthal. He tried to talk to me lots of times." She paused to push all the crumbs into a pile in the middle of the plate then picked them up with a wet finger. Green pushed his plate of half-finished fries towards her, but she shook her head.

"I didn't know he was a psychiatrist. I thought he was coming on to me. He asked if I was eating all right, and he told me I should never skip breakfast. He even bought me groceries once. Fruits and yogurt and oatmeal and stuff. He came into my room to put them in my cupboards, and he checked in my fridge." She squirmed. "He told me he never had a daughter. No grandchildren either, so he had nobody to worry about. I thought it was creepy. Because of..." She stopped and reached over to take the smallest fry from his plate.

"Because of?"

"Well, there were other girls, you see. At least one that I saw. And they were, you know...hookers. Sometimes he'd bring them home from his walks. Other times they'd come to visit him on their own. This one girl came every week, and she looked young enough to be his granddaughter. I even wondered how many times can an old guy get it up, you know. But she kept coming over."

Green had been listening casually as she filled in the lonely details of the victim, but now he grew alert. "When did you first see her?"

She shrugged. Picked up another fry. "I went home to Timmins for the summer, so I don't know about then, but for sure she was there last spring when I was pulling all-nighters to finish papers and exams. I could hear them talking, sometimes half the night."

"You said she was young but looked like a prostitute. Can

you remember what she looked like?"

"Tall, skinny, long messy brown hair. She seemed jumpy, like she was scared of something. Whenever she visited, she checked all around, even inside the garbage bins, before she went inside. She might have been a street person, but she had some nice things. Better than I can afford. A fur jacket, nice leather boots. I figured he was buying stuff for her. He fed her too. I could hear the kettle whistle like he was making her tea. That's why I figured he was coming on to me."

"Did you see her last Saturday night? The night he died?"

She froze, another fry halfway to her open mouth. She laid it down and thrust back from the table. "She wasn't a killer! She was a scared kid, not much older than me."

He held up a soothing hand. "I'm not saying she was. But she may be able to help us. If she was with him, she may have seen something."

She shook her head. "No. Anyway, she wasn't with him. I didn't see her. He went out for his long walk by himself."

"What time was that?"

"Late. Way after midnight. I think it was because he couldn't sleep."

Maybe, he thought. But maybe it was because he had gone looking for the mystery girl.

Twelve

Staff Sergeant Brian Sullivan was swallowing his third Rolaids when his cellphone rang. He was sitting at his desk with his feet up, reviewing Levesque's case to date against Omar Adams. She wanted to pick him up and lay formal first degree murder charges as soon as possible, so she was hounding Ident and the RCMP lab to speed up their analyses.

Even without the final forensics, the case against Omar was impressive. Sullivan could see this was not the blind miscarriage of justice that Green feared, but a carefully reasoned conclusion from the facts. All that was missing was a bloody baseball bat with Omar's prints on it. Even the Somali community was not protesting his innocence. Green suspected they were so tired of their own unruly youth tarring their reputations as new Canadians that they were reserving their outrage for members they believed to be unfairly targeted. Clearly Omar did not fit the bill.

Granted, his father was white, which made the boy an anomaly in the conservative Muslim community. But so far, his father had not screamed racial profiling but instead had quietly hired the best Jewish defence lawyer in the city, as if he knew the boy needed every advantage he could muster. The lawyer had a reputation for finding the tiniest crack in the Crown's case and driving an eighteen-wheeler through it with reasonable doubt. Sullivan wanted to make sure the case was crack-proof.

He debated letting his voicemail pick up until he saw the

name on the call display. He glanced at his watch. Two p.m. This better be quick. "Yeah, Mike. What's up?"

"I've got a witness who says Rosenthal got together with a prostitute most Saturday nights—"

Sullivan suppressed the urge to say "Good for him!" He wondered if he'd be up for that when he was seventy-five years old. Recently he'd sometimes found it a struggle at forty-six. He held his breath as he waited for the heartburn medication to do its work.

"You there?"

"Yeah," he managed. Over the phone he could hear the background sounds of people chatting and voices calling. What the hell was Green up to? "What about it? So he was out on the street hoping to score?"

"There was a sex trade worker caught on the pawn shop surveillance tape. Levesque has a picture of her. Not a very good one, but it might be enough for this witness to ID her."

Sullivan thought fast. The hooker might have seen something. This might be the extra nail Levesque needed to crack-proof her case. "I'll pass this tip on to Levesque and see if she's had any luck ID'ing the woman on the tape. If not, we'll send someone else out to ask around tonight. If she's a regular, we might even spot her."

"Screech recognized her, I'm positive, but he didn't want to rat on her. He watches out for most of the girls, especially the young ones."

"Okay, I'll send—"

"I want this nailed down ASAP, Brian. Show the photo to Screech again on your way. Use your Irish charm and try to shake a few facts loose from the old bugger. Then bring a photo line-up over to Rosenthal's place so my witness can look at it."

Sullivan shifted cautiously. The heartburn was worse, and he wasn't sure he could walk to the car, let alone interview witnesses. "Mike, I'm beat. Sean has a big hockey game tonight in Brockville, and I'm driving. I was hoping to book off early."

"You can. Right after we do the photo line-up."

"What's the rush? Your witness going somewhere?"

"No, but the prostitute might."

"It's Friday night. She'll be at her post drumming up business."

There was a beep on the line. "Hold on," Green said, and the line clicked, engulfing Sullivan in silence. He used the few seconds to lean back and savour the moment of peace. When Green came back on the line, his tone was urgent. Almost angry. "Listen, I gotta go. Talk to Screech, then meet me at the Nelson Street address."

The line clicked dead, leaving Sullivan little choice but to pop another Rolaids and haul himself to his feet.

The traffic on Rideau Street was crushing. Because it was the Friday before the most glorious weekend for fall foliage in the Gatineau Hills, the rush hour exodus across the river into Quebec had begun early. The homebound cars mingled with transport trucks amid the perennial road construction, snarling King Edward Avenue and backing up onto Rideau. Sullivan put on his emergency flashers to almost no avail and finally drove down the bus lane in the wrong direction in order to reach Screech, who was sitting cross-legged on the sidewalk in his spot of choice by the liquor store. He gave those who dropped the occasional quarter into his Tim Hortons cup no illusions about what he would spend it on.

Screech recoiled instinctively into a ball as Sullivan jumped his pick-up half up on the curb and climbed out. His fearful look gave way to a smile as he recognized the big detective.

"Hey, Sarge." He held up his cup. "Spare a loonie for a dying man?"

Sullivan laughed. It had been Screech's line since he'd hit the city ten years earlier. That and his snaggle-toothed smile netted him a fairly good take most days. Sullivan squatted and dropped a toonie in the cup.

"I may have more somewhere. First things first." Sullivan held out the photo of the prostitute. He didn't recognize her himself, but he'd been off the street too long, and faces changed rapidly in that business. "My buddy the inspector says you recognized this girl."

Screech scrunched up his old, shoe-leathery face, looking blank. "No, I didn't. I said no."

"But your eyes said yes. You gotta give him credit for some brains, that's how he made inspector."

Still Screech shook his head. Sullivan's legs felt like jelly, and the heartburn was worse. Spreading. Fuck, he was tired. What the hell bug had he picked up? He sat on the pavement and propped himself against the wall next to the vagrant. "Come on, Screech. She may be in danger if she saw something Saturday night. Or if the killer thinks she did."

Screech chewed his gums and ran his tongue around his caked lips. He cast a longing glance at the liquor store, and Sullivan twisted to pull his wallet out of his pocket. Pain knifed through his shoulder. Goddamn Green, he thought. He dangled the wallet in view but didn't open it.

"She's not a regular," Screech said. "But I seen her around."

"How long?"

He squinted. "Who counts? Springtime? She has a fur coat. Fake for sure, but nice. Mostly on Saturdays. Best crowds. I figured she had a home somewheres."

"Name?"

He shook his head. "Never got beyond Foxy, on account of the fur. Don't know what the johns called her."

Foxy was better than nothing, Sullivan thought, taking ten dollars from his wallet. If she was in the police database, that name would catch her. "Have you ever seen her with the murder victim?"

Screech plucked the bill from Sullivan's fingers and stuffed it directly into his pocket out of sight. It was still early in the day, but Sullivan saw he had nearly enough to visit the liquor store and send himself into his nightly oblivion. He was already looking vague, as if his brain had fired its quota of neurons.

"Screech?"

"Maybe," Screech replied eventually. "I seen him with some others, the young ones. Brings them a coffee, a bite to eat. Just for talk." He shrugged. "Well, he's old, eh?"

"Was she around that night, when he was killed?"

Screech's expression closed. "I didn't see nothing. I was in my sleeping bag. But I heard..." a sly look flitted across his face, "bunch of black punks shouting to her. Mighta been the ones that killed him. I seen in the papers. She was screaming help, get away from me."

Earlier in the week Levesque had released the photos of the four gang suspects to the press with the usual police nonsense about wanting to eliminate them from their inquiries. Sullivan was surprised that Screech had even glanced at the newspaper, but then street people were full of surprises.

He felt a surge of energy. This was an interesting twist. Coincidence was rare in detective work, and if this Foxy had been both a special girl to Rosenthal and the victim of unwanted overtures by the main suspects, that put a new spin on things. Had Rosenthal stopped to intervene? Or had the boys come back to exact revenge for their earlier humiliation at her hands?

Sullivan hauled himself to his feet, massaging his stiff hand and breathing lightly to avoid the pain. Wishing Screech good luck, he got into his truck and flipped the flashers on. The sooner he got this information to Green, the sooner he could go home to bed. A sliver of fear was creeping into his gut.

*   *   *

After Green had finished the call to Sullivan, he ducked back inside Harvey's to find Lindsay dumping her tray into the trash station and preparing to leave. She smiled shyly.

"Thank you for lunch. I'd better get to class now."

"Wait. I have an officer coming over to show you some photos." He led her out to his staff car. "We'll meet him back at the house, because the intruder you saw earlier in Rosenthal's apartment is back. The surveillance officer just called."

Lindsay's face grew pinched. She looked trapped, like a child in water way over her head. Green guessed the cause. "You'll wait with the patrol officer in my car. He won't even see you. Once you've had a look at the photos, the officer will drive you to school."

She had no argument left, so she hung her head meekly and buckled her seatbelt as he slammed on the accelerator. When he pulled up in front of the house, all appeared quiet. The white van was still in place, but the antique oak door to Rosenthal's house was ajar. After instructing Lindsay to stay out of sight, Green walked back and hopped into the surveillance cruiser.

"I called you as soon as he arrived," the patrol woman said. "He's been in there about ten minutes."

"Loading things into his van?"

"No, sir. He hasn't come out at all."

"What was he wearing? Carrying?"

"Jeans, a black shirt and a red fleece vest. Not carrying anything."

Green pondered his options. The man did not appear to have a weapon, although no one knew what he had already stashed inside. Green sent the patrol woman's junior partner back to sit with Lindsay and directed the patrol woman to accompany him. Together they slipped into the house and listened at the interior door. Nothing but the creak of floors and the rustling of what sounded like papers. Green banged on the door.

There was no answer. The faint sound of movement ceased. Green knocked again, his best, authoritative police knock. He heard a curse, footsteps, and the door flew open. The man looming before him was well over six feet, trim, handsome and lithe on his feet despite his grey hair. He peered down at Green irritably.

"Yes?"

Green flashed his badge and pushed past him into the room. A quick scan revealed that some of the paintings were gone and that the filing cabinet drawers were open. Stacks of papers littered the mahogany dining table.

"Who are you?" Green snapped.

"And who the hell are you?"

"You're trespassing, sir. Please answer the question."

"I'm Dr. David Rosenthal. I have every right to be here."

"Pleased to meet you, Dr. Rosenthal. I'm Inspector Green, in charge of your father's investigation. These premises are still under police authority—" A small lie, but the man got his back up. "Nothing is to be touched or removed until we release it."

"It's my property! I'm his heir."

"The disposition of his property is a matter for the courts, and his executor. Surely, Dr. Rosenthal, you're aware of proper procedure."

Rosenthal grunted and turned away. "I've already spoken to his lawyer. There's nothing valuable here. I'm taking a few personal papers and some paintings my mother bought years ago."

"Why did you not contact the police when you heard of your father's death? You must have known we wanted to speak to you."

"Oh, I'm sorry if I violated proper procedure. I was reacting to my father's death."

"Yet the first thing you do upon arriving in town is to try to spirit things out of his apartment."

"*My* things. Therefore mine to take. And I resent your insinuations. I didn't 'spirit' them. I don't have a lot of time to pick up what little I want of this." He flicked his hand to encompass the elegant but shabby old-fashioned furniture.

Green was tempted to tell him about the new will, which he either didn't know about or was pretending not to know about. But he resisted the cheap gesture of retaliation. There would come a better time for that. Instead he asked for some identification. After a pause, Rosenthal produced his passport. American. Green studied it for a few seconds longer than necessary, flipping through the pages to see the visas and customs stamps. The ex-wife was right; the man travelled all over the world.

Rosenthal said nothing, feigning disinterest. Green thought it telling that he had expressed no curiosity about his father's case, not even asking how he'd died, let alone at whose hand.

"I understand you and your father were estranged."

Rosenthal tucked his passport back into his pocket as if buying himself time. "Is that a crime up here?"

"I'm wondering why you didn't contact the police for details when you arrived."

"I got all the details I needed online." He grimaced. "Sounded like a pointless mugging by a couple of immigrant thugs. Now, if you'll excuse me—"

"Nonetheless, sir—"

"Am I under arrest here? Because otherwise I'd like you to leave. You're trespassing—"

Green's temper flashed, but he clamped it down. He wanted Rosenthal to lose his temper, not himself. "No, *you're* trespassing, Mr. Rosenthal. And refusing to answer police questions—"

"Because I know they'll be pointless!" Rosenthal shot back. "I haven't seen my father in ten years, we didn't communicate, he didn't even know he has a grandson! I have no idea what he was doing with his life or who his friends or enemies are, although I bet there are few of the former. The man had lots of time for broken souls, but plain ordinary human warmth was in short supply. I don't recall ever meeting a single genuine friend of his growing up. I have no idea who might have killed him and frankly I don't give a rat's ass—"

"Then why refuse—"

"Because I'm not an idiot. I know you'll be trying to pin this on me. The only son, a high flyer, caught in the middle of the global economic meltdown, estranged from his father but set to inherit the father's millions. I know cops. Imagination is not a big requirement of the job. I figured up here in this keystone cop backwater, I'd be your number one suspect!"

Green burst out laughing. "I'm sorry. You'd be the darling of my superiors. They don't like my imagination either."

Rosenthal darkened from red to purple. He stepped forward as if to take a swing, then checked himself. Drawing himself up, he stepped backwards with a mock bow. "There you go. I expect I've answered all your questions."

"All but one," said Green, still smiling. "Where were you on the night of September—"

A prolonged horn blared outside. Distant but approaching fast. Instantly alert to trouble, Green and the patrolwoman rushed to the bay window. Metal flashed in the sun as Brian Sullivan's brand new black Chevy pick-up slewed across the lawn on the corner and rocketed towards them at full speed, horn blasting. The patrol woman cried aloud, while Green stood frozen, unable to move as before his horrified eyes, the truck smashed headlong into Green's staff car, obliterating the back end.

The bang shattered the calm of the street. Glass and metal flew from the impact and ricocheted off other vehicles in the road. The horn stopped abruptly, replaced by an ominous hiss.

Green came alive. "Call 911!" he screamed at the shocked officer beside him. Not waiting for a response, he raced outside, vaguely aware of Rosenthal at his heels. Neighbours too ran from their houses towards the scene.

Smoke and steam were hissing from the tangled wreckage. The stink of rubber and raw gasoline filled the air. "Stay back, stay back!" Green shouted at the neighbours. "Get pillows and blankets."

At first Green could see nothing in Sullivan's truck except the ballooning air bag, but as the bag deflated, he could see Sullivan wedged in the driver's side, his head slumped forward on the dash. The truck's powerful front grill was crushed, and the hood was folded like a tent, but the cab looked intact. "Thank God, thank God", the words raced unbidden through his mind.

In the next instant, he realized the truck's cab was sitting on top of his crushed staff car. He reached the car and peered inside. The entire rear passenger compartment was folded in on itself beneath the cab, and he could just make out the bloodied head and shoulders of the junior patrolman. Of Lindsay, there was no sign. His hopes lifted faintly. Perhaps she had given up the wait.

He tried the doors. Jammed tight. He ran around the car and peered through the shattered window at a carnage of blood and glass. This time he caught a glimpse of a single, blood-soaked frilly purple cuff. Fuck!

"I need help here!" a deep voice bellowed. Green glanced back to see Rosenthal trying to haul Sullivan's inert, two hundred-and-fifty-pound body through the shattered glass window of the driver's door. "There's no pulse!" he snapped, slamming his fist into Sullivan's chest.

Green abandoned the staff car and raced to help him, snagging a hefty young onlooker to help in the rescue. Sullivan's body was eerily limp, his face ashen and his eyes slightly open. Their sightless gaze sent a shaft of horror down Green's spine.

The four men heaved and hauled to wrestle the body free, until finally it flopped like a limp sack onto the pavement. Without a second's hesitation, Rosenthal leaped astride him, performing CPR. His focus was absolute as he shouted out commands.

Green felt Sullivan's neck for a pulse, praying to a nameless god. Nothing. He heard the distant sirens. One. Two. Three. Soon the street was awash in red strobe lights and emergency workers swarmed the scene. He left Sullivan's side to speak to the one in charge. Firefighters descended on the crushed car and paramedics took over at Sullivan's side, hooking up their monitors and preparing the defibrillator. More ambulances were called in, along with the jaws of life.

Sullivan was rushed away first, surrounded by tubes, wires

and a cluster of very grave, purposeful paramedics. As they left, they gave Green a single curt headshake. As he watched the ambulance scream off with full lights and siren, he fought a lump in his throat. At least Sullivan was alive. They had established a heartbeat. Of sorts.

It took an hour to free the junior patrolman and load him into another ambulance. He was bloodied and unconscious, but at least this time the paramedics had flashed a thumbs up as they drove away.

The jaws of life took a long time to unpeel the metal, wire and blood-soaked upholstery from the broken body of Lindsay Corsin. She had been sitting on the right side of the back seat beside the patrolman, waiting for Green. As he had asked her to. The right side had taken the brunt of Sullivan's truck.

The firefighters and paramedics who had fought to free her stood in a small circle around her, reduced to silence. Green wanted to scream, weep, run for miles in howling abandon. Instead he called the coroner, Superintendent Devine, and the Chief's office. Then he began the painful job of contacting the university to track down Lindsay Corsin's next of kin.

Thirteen

Rideau Psychiatric Hospital was a sprawling collection of buildings set helter skelter amid grassy nooks and towering trees which glowed orange and red in the afternoon sun. Sharon's ward was on the sixth floor of one of the main buildings, modern and brightened by large windows that looked out over the grounds. She arrived fifteen minutes early for her evening shift, snatched up Caitlin O'Malley's chart off the cart, and sequestered herself in the back room off the nursing station. The chart was thick, testament to the number of admissions the woman had had.

Sharon wasn't sure what she was looking for. Evidence somewhere of a connection to Dr. Rosenthal, of mistreatment or misdiagnosis on his part. Something to explain why her name was on the list of Rosenthal's beneficiaries in his will.

The resident's history on her admission summary documented a sad but all too familiar struggle. Caitlin's psychiatric problems had begun eight years ago, when she had started hearing voices and come to believe she was the love child of God and Prime Minister Jean Chrétien. She had been picked up by the RCMP outside the Prime Minister's residence at 24 Sussex Drive, where she was parading with a placard that read "Dad, let me come home."

She had been twenty years old at the time and a student of mathematics at the University of Ottawa. She'd been diagnosed with paranoid schizophrenia. A six-week inpatient stint and a prescription for olanzapine had set her back on the right track, and she had completed her degree, snagging a husband in the process. Her husband was a born-again Christian and soon had her attending his church and seeking the healing hands of the visiting evangelical minister. He'd pronounced her cured, she'd thrown away her meds and six months later was outside Stornoway, the home of the Official Opposition, claiming that she'd been misled by Satan. Opposition leader Stephen Harper was her father, and her mother was a siren who had seduced him in the middle of an Alberta canola field. Only Stephen Harper could exorcise the evil in her genes.

Sharon suppressed a rueful laugh. The resident, the wide-eyed rookie Dr. Janic, had recorded all this delusional material in colourful detail, probably uncertain which nuggets of information might be important to her diagnostic profile. This time a couple of other diagnoses were tossed around, including manic episode, and a cocktail of anti-psychotic and mood-stabilizing drugs was prescribed. In the process, she divorced her husband, her father was put in charge, and a community treatment order was issued to force her to take her medications and attend support sessions. Staff shortages and lack of resources doomed that plan before the ink was even dry, and Caitlin spent a few months on the lam on the streets of Toronto before her father found her and brought her back into the family fold.

The father had obviously tried to keep her stable, because he had hooked her up with a respected private psychiatrist, and her next admission was not until two years later. This time, she had abandoned her meds and was living on the streets of Montreal with a dog and a crack addict twice her age. Renewed contact with her father's psychiatrist friend, a prescription for a more powerful drug, and Caitlin was back at home enrolled in graduate school.

The new drug had dangerous side effects and would have required much closer medical monitoring, but there were no further notations in the chart until her admission three days ago. Things had obviously deteriorated, however. She'd been picked up by the police, who originally thought she was a regular prostitute until they had her in the cellblock. She curled up in the corner by the toilet, wrapped her arms over her head, and started to rock. Silent, unresponsive, but terrified the moment anyone approached. It had taken six officers, an ambulance, and a shot of halperidol to get her to the emergency room at the Ottawa Hospital.

Sharon leafed through the file again more carefully, but there was no mention of Dr. Rosenthal. He had never been her treating psychiatrist, nor had she ever given his name to emergency room staff.

The door opened, and the head nurse stuck her head in. Show time. Sharon arranged to have Caitlin O'Malley assigned to her. The young woman was much more settled now, the day nurse was happy to report, and it appeared the powerful anti-psychotic medications were beginning to take effect. She was no longer pacing and agitated, and she was able to communicate simple needs.

After the shift handover was complete, Sharon ventured onto the ward and walked down the long hall, which was painted a cheerful apple green and tiled in a warm beige linoleum. She stopped to talk to a group of patients in the sunroom, but Caitlin was not among them. Sharon found her in the room she shared with another woman. Caitlin's bed was nearest the window, which looked out through safety bars at a glorious orange maple. Caitlin, however, was curled up against the wall in the corner of her bed, her sheet pulled up to her chin and her eyes pressed shut.

She was a tall, slender woman with a heart-shaped face and pallid skin that showed the ravages of poor diet. Her hair had been freshly washed, and it fluffed about her face in wispy strands, but it was a long time since it had seen a stylist. The Gothic black was growing out, revealing two inches of chestnut brown roots.

Sharon tapped on the open door and called her name softly. Caitlin didn't move, but her eyes pressed more tightly shut. As Sharon approached, she saw tears leaking from the corners of the lids. She sat down gently on the bed.

"Caitlin? Remember me? I'm Sharon, your nurse this evening. How are you feeling?"

Caitlin moved her head back and forth.

"Sad? Something you want to talk about?"

"I feel dead." It was a mere whisper through dry, cracked lips.

"The meds?"

This time a faint shake of the head.

Sharon reached for the plastic water glass on the night table by her bed. "Do you want a drink?"

Caitlin opened her eyes and focussed slowly on the room. She looked across at her roommate's empty bed, her gaze taking in the photos and the vase of flowers on the night table, then her own empty table, before settling on Sharon. Her eyes were bleary, the pallid grey of a cloudy day, but there was a glimmer of knowledge in them. She allowed Sharon to hold the glass to her lips, then sank down on the pillow again. Slowly fresh tears welled.

"I don't want to live like this."

It was a statement Sharon heard often, and sometimes her pat words of encouragement felt inadequate. Even flippant.

She had never walked in a schizophrenic's shoes, never felt the terror of their shifting, unreal world nor the mind-numbing half-life of the cure. Never faced the social rejection nor the uncertain future of broken hopes and lost dreams. Never lived under the spectre of an illness that lurked inside ready to spin their minds and lives out of control once again.

Caitlin was a highly intelligent woman. In her lucid times, she would know that every relapse could lead her further down the road of no return.

"Why am I here?" Caitlin asked.

Sharon hesitated. It was a question with layers of meaning, and she wasn't sure which one Caitlin intended. She chose the wisest response. "You're here to make you well again. You can be well, Caitlin."

Caitlin frowned. "No, I can't. I am who I am. Crazy."

"But you can also be well. You have been before."

"It's all pretend. Would you have made Joan of Arc well, so she wouldn't hear the messages she was put on earth to hear?"

The reasoning brain was returning, Sharon observed. Not only the ability to form coherent sentences but to apply logic. She sidestepped the challenge. "Did you see your doctor today?"

"My doctor? No, not mine, but my father's choice for me. My father, who can't see and therefore can't believe. Just as lesser minds can't see the warping of the universe or the relativity of time. My father's doctor would have shot Einstein full of chlorpromazine, and there would be no atomic bomb. Just a math retard playing with blocks on the floor."

Sharon hesitated. The woman's mental state was still very fragile, and she had no right to shove her back over the brink with the wrong question. She tried to frame it harmlessly.

"Doctors do good things too. You must have met some who helped."

Caitlin blinked rapidly, as if Sharon had shocked her. "Met? Yes, walking mercies. But they don't teach that at shrink school. Only the brain, not the mind. Not the soul."

Sharon ventured further. "It's nice to meet a doctor who treats you like a whole person."

Caitlin sat up at the far edge of her bed. "No one can know the whole. Even angels can't know, but can only walk with you on the journey."

"Have you met anyone who walked with you?"

She recoiled, her grey eyes darkening as if prelude to a storm. "Why?"

"Well..." Why indeed, Sharon thought, still feeling her way along her tightrope. "Maybe they could still help."

"Still. All still." The woman pressed her eyes shut, and a small moan escaped her lips.

Sharon began a mental retreat. "Do you want—?"

"No!" Caitlin's hand shot out and knocked the water glass out of Sharon's hand, drenching the wall and Sharon's clothes. "Don't trick me! Gone, gone, go, go, out, out, spots and all!"

One question too many, Sharon thought as she backed away to stand at the door, watching carefully to see whether her retreat would be enough or whether another shot of meds was in order.

* * *

It was three hours before Green could get to the hospital to check on Sullivan and the patrolman. He was delayed at the scene dealing with the duty inspector, the collision investigation unit, and various other members of the brass, including Barbara Devine, who demanded to be kept informed of every detail pertaining to Lindsay Corsin's death. Because the girl had been waiting in the back of Green's staff car, on his instructions, and she had been killed by another police officer, a Special Investigations team would be convened from outside the Ottawa Police Services to determine if there was any blame to be laid. Devine wanted no surprises.

Green was being peppered from all sides, including from the media, who lined the police cordon three deep in places. Zoom lenses were trained on the twisted wreckage of his car, no doubt picking up Lindsay's blood that had pooled on the sidewalk. Green forced himself to focus. There were tasks to be done, families to be notified and reports to be given. He could help no one if he dwelled on the memory of his friend's inert body as it was whisked into the ambulance, nor on the bloody body of the lonely young girl from Timmins who had perished because of him.

Throughout it all, he was aware of David Rosenthal, who like himself had been treated by the paramedics at the scene for hand lacerations from the broken truck window but who had refused their recommendation to go to the hospital. He chose instead to stay at the scene answering police questions and providing a far more lucid account of the crash than Green could muster. The paramedics credited him with the fact that Sullivan had even survived for the ambulance ride.

"I've had medical training," he told the investigators. "I just never practiced, because I prefer research. I don't know where the strength came from. I work out regularly, and I do a lot of sports, but nothing to explain hauling a two hundred-and-fifty-pound man through the window of a truck."

Adrenaline, Green thought, recognizing the signs of it in his own body. The racing heart, hyper-alertness, sense of readiness and need for action. They lasted until he was finally able to climb into a cab and go to the hospital. En route, like a wave crashing on the shore, his strength crumbled, leaving him weak-kneed and tremulous. His hands throbbed beneath the bandages. He got out of the cab at the emergency entrance to the Civic Campus and paused to lean against the rough brick wall by the door. He forced deep breaths. He couldn't let up yet. On the other side of that door, a crisis was still unfolding. Sullivan was one of the most deeply loved and respected officers on the force. Green had been fielding calls to his cellphone all afternoon from worried officers. He knew the hospital waiting room would be full.

And then there was Mary.

Mary Sullivan was Brian's high-school sweetheart, who at eighteen had followed him to the city from her farm outside Eganville, who had put up with the stress, shift work and long, gut-wrenching hours the job demanded. Who had given him support and correction in equal measure, along with three children now in their teens. She'd learned resilience on her rocky, hard-scrabble farm, and when things got tough, Mary got fighting mad.

Mary was going to be furious. Green took a final, bracing breath, pushed open the glass doors and walked into the emergency room. The waiting area was filled with people slouched in chairs, reading a book, trying to doze, or pacing nervously. The quiet was punctuated by the rattle of carts and the staccato chatter of the hospital's paging system, but otherwise the atmosphere was routine. There was not a police officer in sight.

"They transferred him over to the Heart Institute," the admissions clerk told him, then fired off directions about the maze of corridors and stairways he should follow. He got lost twice and ended up wandering the back parking lot in a daze, staring at the sprawl of aging, interconnected, red brick buildings that comprised the hospital. He spotted the entranceway to the Heart Institute by chance.

Inside the surgical waiting room, he found the bedlam he was expecting. The nurses had apparently given up efforts to cull the crowd. Dozens of officers, some in uniform, others in plain clothes or off duty, crammed into every seat and stood leaning against the walls, sipping coffee and talking about anything to stave off thought as they waited for news.

Green heard snippets of conversation. "The new goalie—", "Sens game last night?", "The guy blew point one nine!", "If Devine gets it—"

There was no sign of Mary, but Green spotted Gibbs and waded through the crowd to his side. A few hands reached out to pat his shoulder as he passed. A few faces registered surprise.

Gibbs mirrored the surprise of others. "You okay, sir?"

"Why wouldn't I be?"

"I heard it was your car he hit."

So that was one of the rumours buzzing around. Green waved an impatient hand. "But I wasn't in it." Gibbs looked pale and wan. Like himself, Gibbs fought grim memories when he was in a hospital. "What's the latest news?"

"Touch and go, sir. They rushed him into surgery. That balloon thing they do."

"Balloon?" Green tried to think through his exhaustion. "You mean angioplasty?"

"Yeah. They're throwing everything they have at him, but the nurses here aren't telling us much. All the guys think that's a bad sign."

Green dared not think too hard. In all his experiences in hospital waiting rooms, he'd found nurses only too eager to share reassuring news, but when the news was bad, they clammed up and let the doctor carry the ball.

He was still grappling to make sense of Gibbs's words. "What's wrong with his heart?"

Gibbs's Adam's apple bobbed. "He had a heart attack, that's what caused the crash. The accident itself barely hurt him at all."

Green's mind reeled. He thought back over the days, indeed the weeks, before the accident. Now with the clarity of hindsight, all the warning signs had been there screaming to be noticed. The high blood pressure, the fatigue, and constant popping of antacids. But the man was only forty-six! Who thought of heart disease in a forty-six-year-old who'd been an athlete all his life?

Other officers approached him, some with sympathies and others with questions. After the fact, everyone was an armchair physician.

"I didn't think he was looking too good."

"I noticed his weight was creeping up."

"It's the stress. My uncle was only forty-two when he dropped dead, and he didn't have an ounce of fat."

A wave of claustrophobia washed over Green. He detached himself from the crowd and walked outside, sucking in the cool autumn air gratefully. On a patch of grass nearby, a group of smokers huddled against the cold. Green shook his head at the irony.

The door opened behind him, and he turned to see the tall, cadaverous figure of Superintendent Adam Jules. Jules had been his boss for years before being replaced by Barbara Devine, and he had been both his mentor and his chief advocate in the inner chambers of the force. He had rescued Green from Patrol and brought him into Investigations, where his intelligence, obsessive drive and unorthodox viewpoint were assets. He had also paired him up with Brian Sullivan. Now he gave Green a melancholy smile. "How are you holding up, Michael?"

"Worried," Green said. He felt precarious and off-balance. "But Brian's a strong man, and this is a state-of-the-art facility. He'll pull through."

Jules dipped his lean, equine head in agreement. The grim line of his lips was the only hint of his own distress, but Green knew that the austere, solitary bachelor felt the threat to one of his own more keenly than he would ever show. He had nurtured all their careers.

"Tragic about the young woman," he said now. "No one's fault, but still..."

He didn't elaborate. Jules never said two words when one would do. Both of them knew the self-recrimination that Green and Sullivan would feel.

"Has the OPP located the family?" Green asked, anxious to fill the void where feelings massed. "The university only had an aunt's name."

Jules nodded. "The girl was an orphan. Living on her own since she was sixteen and couldn't wait to leave the place behind. Aunt's been milking the media and talking about lawsuits, but the OPP officer who delivered the news didn't see much grief."

"Poor girl's probably worth more to her dead than alive," Green said, then regretted it. A girl's life had ended, and cynicism had no place in the mourning of her. "But I'll call in the morning. We should send flowers and make a donation. And if things settle down around here, I'd like to attend her funeral. I feel..."

Jules nodded, then pursed his lips cautiously. "Anything

that's going to come back to bite you?"

Green shot him a quick glance. Had Jules been sent by the brass to get the whole story out of him, so they could ready their defences? Once again he felt shame for his uncharitable reaction. Jules was not a lackey. He had always stood up for his officers, even under pressure from the brass.

He shook his head. "She was waiting to view a photo line-up Brian was bringing over."

"Why was he in his own vehicle on police business?"

Green caught his breath. His frazzled mind raced over all the possible complications of using a personal vehicle on duty. The damage to Sullivan's beloved new truck likely wouldn't be covered by his insurance, but was there anything else? Any other liability Sullivan would face if the girl's family sued?

"I believe he was going straight home afterwards. He..." Green's throat closed unexpectedly. "He said he was tired."

The glass door slammed open with a whoosh behind them and Mary Sullivan stormed out, all fear and fury. She was immaculately dressed in the power suit and suede overcoat of a successful real estate agent, but her carrot-red hair stood straight up as if she had been pulling it, and her mascara had streaked down her cheeks. Her face grew crimson at the sight of him.

He reached out. "Mary, I—"

She slashed his arms away. "Goddamn you, Mike. Goddamn you! He was afraid to tell you. Afraid to disappoint you! And now look!"

He opened his mouth to ask her "tell me what?", but Jules' quiet voice cut him off.

"How is he?"

Caught off guard, Mary flicked a glance at Jules before slamming Green again with her rage. "He's alive. Maybe. But he's probably lost fifteen per cent of his heart function and

God knows how much of his brain. He's in a coma because this job bled the life out of him, and *you* let it happen. No, you demanded it. You know what? No more. Whatever is left of him—if he ever wakes up—he's mine!"

Fourteen

A black, moonless night had fallen by the time Green could stand the wait no longer. He'd never been good at hospitals, with their grim portent of death. Medical updates kept drifting in, but the essentials remained the same. His best friend hung between life and death, his recovery far from assured. He might never again be the man Green had known, the man who listened to his wild flights into zebra land with a bemused smile, only to gently, patiently remind him of the facts. The man who understood his passion for justice and his determination to beat the bad guys. The man who'd been content to let him lead but who had always watched his back.

The man who'd forgiven him a hundred times in their years together. This time, for his worst transgression of all, there might never be that chance.

Green walked the streets blindly, unable and unwilling to think. Memories of the crash kept sweeping through him—the raw shriek of metal, the stench of burning rubber, the taste of dread in his throat. And Mary lashing out in rage and pain. "You demanded it!"

On his belt he felt his cellphone vibrate and he snatched it up, terrified of news. Private caller, the ID said. Cautiously he answered.

"Mike? I just heard on the news! Where are you?"

Sharon's voice. Relief flooded through him. "Just outside the hospital, taking a break."

"How's Brian?

Green filled her in, clipped and professional, in his best cop's voice.

Sharon was silent a moment. "How are you holding up?"

"I'm... I'm..." His throat closed.

"I'm going to ask to sign out early. It's pretty quiet here now. I'll get someone else to do my rounds."

He didn't protest. He raised his head to look westward down the quiet residential street. She was there, less than a kilometre away. He wanted to rush to her. Never go back inside, never face the grim faces of the nurses and the reproachful faces of his colleagues. He had a reputation for driving his officers hard.

He tried to sound solicitous of her safety. "I'm on Ruskin Avenue. Walk straight along it and I'll meet you."

The traffic along the narrow residential streets was still heavy as hospital visitors came and went, and the headlights cast the landscape in harsh, constantly shifting shadows. He saw her first as a tiny figure backlit by an approaching car, and he quickened his pace. When they met, she said nothing. She merely reached up to wrap him in her arms. He pressed her to him.

"Brian's a strong man," she said eventually. "The doctors always give the worst case scenario."

He pulled away. "He was down a long time. I've been replaying the scene. I think he lost consciousness and slumped forward on the horn. That horn was sounding for at least fifteen seconds before he hit my car. Another minute or two for us to reach the truck and realize what was wrong. Two minutes to pull him out of the truck—"

"Time always slows down when you're dealing with a crisis. It probably wasn't that long."

He shook his head. "Ambulance response time from 911 call to arrival was five minutes. That much we do know. And we know his heart stopped several times en route to the hospital."

"But he was getting CPR," she said. "And he's alive. That's already a huge plus in cardiac arrest cases."

"But for what? To be an invalid? A vegetable?"

She slipped her arm through his as they walked down the street. "We don't know that. Let's hope."

"And if he wakes up, he's going to know he killed a twenty-year-old girl. He has to live with that."

"I know, and that's tragic. Poor girl. But it was an accident, hardly his fault."

Green gazed up through the tall, brooding trees into the sky. Pinpoints of starlight showered the inky expanse. So far away. Some long dead. "I think he may have known he was in trouble," he began slowly. "Mary said he was afraid to tell me. She didn't say what, but maybe he knew he wasn't well." He shook his head impatiently. "Anyway, it doesn't matter. Because of us, that girl is dead. She was an innocent kid just trying to help the investigation. I put her in harm's way, and Brian killed her. We can't either of us escape—" He broke off. Took a deep, ragged breath.

Sharon stopped him and drew him to a nearby bench on the edge of the hospital grounds. She took his hands in hers. She said nothing, but he felt his defences slowly crumble. He wanted to flee, to scream, to drive a knife into his insides to gut out the pain.

"Brian came because I insisted. He knew there was something wrong, but he pushed his limits because I insisted. He had that heart attack because I—"

"He would have had that heart attack anyway, honey.

Maybe when he was driving 100k an hour on the Queensway, taking a bunch of other innocent drivers with him."

"But this was an innocent girl who was there because I put her there. She didn't even want to stay, because she was late for class, but once again, I insisted."

She scrutinized him in the darkness for a moment, then sighed. "This was in connection to the Rosenthal case?"

He nodded. "She was going to ID a young woman who had regular visits with Rosenthal. Brian was bringing a photo line-up to show her. Because, damn it, I couldn't wait till tomorrow. Levesque is all set to railroad the Somali kid, and I was determined to find out who this mystery woman was and what she had to do with the murder."

Sharon pulled back, her gaze probing. "What did she look like?"

"I don't know. Another stupid thing. I didn't even get a decent description from Lindsay, only that she thought the woman was young and a prostitute. I've been out of the trenches for so long, I don't even follow basic procedures!"

"What makes you think the woman has anything to do with Rosenthal's death?"

"Nothing specific. It's just a coincidence that has to be clarified. The woman apparently visited Rosenthal at his apartment most Saturday nights. We don't know if it was for sex or—"

"He was pretty old."

Green shot her a glance but squelched a protest. "He'd also been known to try to help people. One of my street sources says he kept an eye on the street kids. Anyway, for whatever reason, this woman was a regular visitor, but the night he died, she didn't show. But a sex trade worker was seen on video close to the scene."

Sharon shivered and rubbed her arms. The night wind had picked up. "Do you have the photos from Brian's line-up?"

He was jolted. "Probably still in the truck. When we hauled him out of the truck, he had nothing with him." He swung on her, energized. "The truck was towed to our forensic bays, waiting for the Special Investigations team to take a look at it. We should get the photos out of it. They're crucial to the Rosenthal case."

"Are there other people who can identify this mystery woman?"

"Maybe others in the apartment building. It's worth showing the line-up to them."

To his surprise, she stood up. "How far are these forensic bays?"

"Down at headquarters."

"We'll take my car. I'll drive."

He flexed his bandaged hands. "No, I can—"

"You're in shock, Mike. I'll drive."

"But what about Tony? Hannah?"

"Hannah is more than capable." Sharon was heading down the street when she turned and slipped her arm through his to pull him along. "Come on, Mike. This is one way I can share the burden a bit with you."

He felt his steps quicken. It would fill the long, agonizing hours of waiting, and it would give him a much-needed focus. It would ensure that what Lindsay started did not die with her, and give him something to report to Sullivan when he finally woke up.

*   *   *

"Oh my God." Sharon breathed the words with awe. They

171

were standing inside the first forensic bay in front of what was left of Green's beige Impala staff car. It was still sitting on the flatbed tow truck, awaiting the first of the forensic collision specialists. Involuntarily she reached over to clutch his arm. "You could have been in there."

Amid the despair and self-recrimination of the past six hours, that thought had never occurred to him. His reaction now surprised him. If only he had been, instead of Lindsay Corsin.

"It's hard to be comforted when a young woman is dead and a rookie patrolman faces months of rehab."

"How is he?"

The ambulance had taken the young man to a different hospital, but his partner had been phoning in with regular updates. "Broken bones, ruptured spleen, concussion. Not to mention every inch of his body is in pain from the impact." He studied the jagged hunk of metal in the brilliant light of the overhead beams. The truck had hit the rear right corner, and its higher bumper had ridden right up over the trunk, crushing the rear and side windows. The vehicle parked in front of the Impala had blocked its forward momentum, causing it to crumple like an accordion.

Sitting on the right side, Lindsay hadn't stood a chance, as the relentless bumper, having demolished the trunk and the seat back, zeroed in on her skull. Sullivan must never see this, Green thought.

The duty officer was standing at their side with the sign-in log in his hand. He shook his head. "Hell of a mess. I see it all the time when these supersized pick-ups and SUVs hit passenger cars. Even worse with the tractor trailers, of course. We'd have been scraping her up off the pavement."

Green gave him a sharp look before turning to look at the

pick-up in the next bay. Sullivan's new pride and joy, intended to carry him not only out to deer hunting camp but well into his retirement years as well. It had sustained almost no damage beyond the shattered windows and the crumpled grill, but Green doubted Sullivan would ever be able to look at it again. He could still see the bloody threads of his jacket caught on the glass shards of the driver's window.

Sharon was still holding his arm and her grip tightened. "You pulled him out through there?"

It looked impossible, yet he barely remembered the strain, only the desperation. And something else. David Rosenthal hammering Sullivan's chest with a sharp blow, a risky move that can do more harm than good at the hands of a novice. Not for the first time, Green wondered what would have happened to Sullivan if Rosenthal hadn't been there.

He shivered and strode briskly up to the cab of the pick-up. He peered inside and there, strewn across the floor of the passenger side was a sheaf of papers. He was about to grasp the passenger side handle when his years of training kicked in.

"Has Ident been here to photograph all this?"

The duty officer shook his head. "Tomorrow, they said. They're still at the scene."

Green remembered the pair of them consulting with the collision investigators and fanning out over the scene. They had videoed and photographed every inch of the crash site, including the truck, from every angle, inside and out. That ought to be enough. He grappled with the handle in his bandaged hands and began to search through the papers, lifting the edges carefully so as not to disturb the array of photos.

It was a good line-up. They were all photos of young women in partial profile, most of them stock photos from police archives doctored to appear amateurish. Only one did he recognize—the grainy photo of the hooker from the pawn shop security camera. He hesitated only a fraction of a second before scooping the photos back into their folder and taking them all out of the truck. It went against all procedure, but he was the boss of this whole section; he didn't have to seek permission.

Sharon had been pressing in, peering over his shoulder. Now as he straightened up, she looked at him expectantly. "How do the photos look?"

"It might be hard to identify the woman, but it's worth a try." He signed the duty officer's log and headed out of the garage."

Sharon scrambled to follow him. "What now?"

He glanced at his watch. Nine thirty. "Now's as good a time as ever. Maybe I can catch some of the other tenants at home." He glanced at her. "If you want to go home, my own car is right over there. I should be able to drive."

She was eyeing the folder with alarm, as if she were worried about his obsessive state. But paradoxically, he felt better than he had since the accident. He had something to do. But she shook her head as she opened the driver's door. "I'm not letting you out of my sight. You're post-traumatic, and whether you know it or not, your judgement is impaired."

He snorted but didn't rise to the bait. What did she think twenty-five years on the force had taught him? Instead, he let her drive while he turned his attention to the photo. The photography tech had done a nice job of cleaning up the prostitute's image. Green could make out a fur coat falling open over her chest and long, loose hair framing a pale, delicate face. On second inspection, she didn't look as young as he'd thought. Her facial muscles carved valleys that gave her the apprehensive yet defiant expression of a woman who's spent years on guard against something ill-defined and hostile.

They were stopped at a red light, and he sensed Sharon's eyes straying to the photo curiously. He held it up for her. "With every street person there's a story to be told."

"How do you know it's a street person?"

"I don't. But she was out on Rideau Street by herself dressed like pretty much every other street prostitute, around the time of Sam Rosenthal's murder. Hardly the time for a regular stroll."

Sharon said nothing, instead dedicating herself to the challenge of navigating downtown on a Friday night. The streets were full of young people walking in clusters, some headed for the clubs, others on cellphones trying to make plans, some perhaps even going to spend much needed time at the university library. Nelson Street was still partially cordoned off as the last of the investigators measured marks on the pavement and sampled minuscule bits of debris, all to aid them in their reconstruction of the accident. The crowds of onlookers had long gone, and Number 235 had a dark, forlorn look. Two of its five occupants were dead.

Two of the other occupants were not home, but a light shone in the window of the top floor. He and Sharon climbed the stairs, and as they drew nearer, Green heard the chatter of a young child and the sound of running water. Eventually an East Indian man answered the door with a pyjama-clad toddler on his hip. He looked damp from exertion, and his expression was wary. Probably understandable, given the murder, the break-in and the accident outside the building.

When he spotted Green's badge, his wariness vanished. "I already told the police everything I know," he said in a precise Indian accent. "I wasn't here, and my wife was in the back. All she heard was a bang."

"It's not about the accident, sir. I have some questions about Dr. Rosenthal."

"I'm very sorry about him. His son was already here earlier, telling my wife he was going to sell the building." The man's eyes flashed with anger. "I have only six months left on my course work, then I return to Sri Lanka. It is very inconvenient for us."

"I wouldn't worry just yet. I would wait for the official word from the estate executor," Green remarked drily. "May I have your and your wife's names for my records?"

Dutifully the man supplied the names, spelling the impossibly long surname without being asked. "Most people call me Dharma. Please come in."

Inside, the tiny gabled apartment smelled of spices. Green recognized the furniture as second-hand IKEA, but bright colours and knickknacks were everywhere and plastic toys littered the floor. Dharma shoved these aside hastily with his toe and gestured Green and Sharon to a small sofa covered with an ornate red throw. Even before they sat down, Dharma was offering them tea. Sharon moved to decline, but Green suspected that hospitality was important to the man. Dharma shouted their order, presumably to his wife in the back.

"Thank you for taking the time," Green began. "I'm making inquiries about people who visited Dr. Rosenthal in recent weeks."

"Oh well, I'm not here very often. My wife would be the one, but she's usually very busy with the children."

"Perhaps we could ask her?"

"She doesn't speak English very well, and she's very shy."

"You could translate." Green waited until finally Dharma, looking flustered, went out to fetch his wife. A rapid-fire discussion ensued, and when Dharma reappeared, he had a pretty, dark-haired girl in tow who looked younger than Hannah. She was dressed in colourful flowing pants with a matching top, and she held a small baby in a sling around her waist. She struggled to balance the tea on a tray.

Sharon reached out. "Would you like me to hold the baby?"

The woman looked alarmed when her husband translated, but dutifully allowed Sharon to lift the baby from the sling. Sharon tickled the baby's cheek and cooed. "What's your name?"

Green's felt a twinge of uneasiness as he watched her cradle the baby, but the husband was beaming. "Her name is Jewel," he said. The wife bent to serve the tea. It was a sweet, milky brew that set Green's teeth on edge, but Sharon seemed in heaven. Only once everyone had been served did Green come back to the question at hand.

"Did you ever see Dr. Rosenthal have any visitors in the last three months or so?"

After an exchange with his wife, Dharma replied, "Sometimes two or three men. He was a very quiet man."

"What about young women?"

Even before the translation, Dharma's wife stiffened. She started to shake her head. "Please," Green said. "No one is in trouble. But if you saw any young women..."

Dharma and his wife had another lively exchange before Dharma turned to them apologetically. "My wife is embarrassed. Dr. Rosenthal was a kind man, and my wife does not want to bring shame."

"He helped people, especially young people. It's important that we find them."

"I am very busy with the children," his wife managed. Green took the photos out of his folder and laid them out one at a time on the coffee table.

"Tell me if any of these women visited him."

They both leaned forward. Green watched the wife's expression closely as he revealed each photo. She paused to dwell a little longer on the photo from the video, but ultimately she passed on.

"They are not very good quality," Dharma offered dubiously.

"I know," Green said. "And we won't be going to court on your identification. But we do need to know who the woman is. She may have witnessed something."

"She could be in danger?" Dharma asked.

Green gave a non-committal shrug, which seemed to be enough for Dharma, who embarked on another long discussion. Finally his wife learned forward to tap the photo of the mystery prostitute.

"My wife isn't sure, you understand, but she thinks she has seen this woman. Many times, coming and going from Dr. Rosenthal's apartment." He paused. "Often late at night, when she is feeding the baby."

"Did she see Dr. Rosenthal at these times?"

"Yes. He comes out to put the woman in the cab."

Green perked up. "What cab company?"

Another exchange. "She doesn't remember."

"One last question. Did you see her last Saturday night? The night he died?"

No, she had not, but she had gone to bed early and the baby had not wakened.

As they said their goodbyes and picked their way down the steep, dark staircase, Green's thoughts were already racing ahead, planning the next line of inquiry.

Outside, the cold night air hit them after the stifling heat of the apartment. Sharon had been quiet, but now she broke in on his thoughts. "What's your next move?"

"Find her, obviously. She's a crucial piece of the puzzle."

She unlocked the car and climbed in. "How will you find her?"

"Usual ways. Ask around the street, contact the cab companies and our informants." He glanced at his watch, which read ten thirty. "Drop me at the station, and I'll get myself home. If I move fast enough, I can get this photo out into the patrol cars and onto the streets while the night time regulars are still out and about. Someone may know her."

"And if not?"

"Well, if worst comes to worst, there's always the media."

She frowned, drew a breath as if to speak, then shook her head. She remained silent as she navigated the stop-and-go Friday night traffic through the Elgin Street club district. He sensed she had more to say, but he had his own worries. Not the least of which was the riskiness of releasing the photo to the media.

Until he knew what role she played, he might be putting another young woman at risk.

Fifteen

Green lay awake half the night, staring at the ceiling. He replayed the accident, the frantic aftermath, and every word of his last conversation with Sullivan. The shy, wistful face of Lindsay Corsin rose unbidden in his thoughts, along with the young patrol officer who might never return to full duty again. At three thirty in the morning, he slipped out of bed, tiptoed downstairs and poured himself a hefty shot of scotch. Half an hour later, he fell into a fitful sleep on the living room sofa.

He awoke with a start at seven a.m. to the sound of his cellphone ringing. Sullivan! After a mad scramble, he located it under the jumble of his jacket and snatched it up. Not the hospital but Sergeant Levesque. In her outrage, her accent was more marked.

"Detective Gibbs just call me this morning. He want to clarify the orders you left last night. I would appreciate this too. What orders? Sir."

"It was important to act quickly. I left you a voicemail message. I suggest you check it."

"Sir, with respect, I can't run the case like this."

Oh, get off your high horse, Green wanted to snap, but instead he sidestepped. "What's the news on Brian Sullivan?"

"I don't know yet. I just got Gibbs's call—"

"Meet me at the station in an hour," he said. "By then we may have some responses to the bulletin, and I'll fill you in."

"But this is my day off."

Green didn't trust himself to respond civilly, so he said nothing. After a moment, she seemed to realize her mistake. "Very well, sir."

Green was showered, shaved, dressed and out the door in fifteen minutes, juggling a fresh travel mug of coffee. Ten minutes later, he was illegally parked in the loading zone and was dashing through the front door of the Heart Institute.

Even at seven thirty on a Saturday morning, the cardiac care unit bustled with activity. Every moment held a potential life and death drama, so doctors swept through the cubicles on rounds with a full complement of students in tow. Nurses scurried on rubber-soled shoes, equipment trolleys rattled and everywhere was the incessant beep and hiss of machines. The waiting room, however, was almost empty; the police officers had obviously ceased their vigil, and even Mary Sullivan was nowhere in sight.

"She spent the night by his side," explained the nurse who came to speak to him. "We finally persuaded her to go home to get some rest and pick up some things for him."

"How is he?"

The nurse hesitated. "Are you family?"

Green considered the question. Sullivan was his family. "Closer than most. I'm his boss and his oldest friend."

She brightened. "Oh, are you Inspector Green?"

When he nodded, she put her hand on his arm. "He was asking about you."

Green's joy set him floating. "He's conscious?"

"Just woke up. He said only five people were allowed to visit him—his wife, three kids, and you. Normally, we would only allow immediate family, but... I'm married to a fire fighter myself, and I know."

Green couldn't trust his voice, so he bobbed his head

several times. She smiled. "Do you want to see him? Only for five minutes, and don't let him get agitated."

Sullivan was in a private cubicle barely large enough for his hospital bed, a guest chair and all the monitors and paraphernalia that sustained him. Green hated hospitals. Even after twenty years, the sounds and smells, the wan figures languishing in beds, all brought back memories of his mother's long, futile fight with cancer, and of his own vigils at her bedside. He'd been helpless to ease her pain or to halt her inexorable drift towards death. Back then, as now, the streets teeming with life and danger had been his refuge.

Sullivan lay slightly propped by pillows to ease the pressure on his heart. His eyes were closed, but he looked relaxed and pink with health. Green felt a rush of relief at the sight. The small bandage on Sullivan's forehead and the slight redness on his nose and cheeks from the airbag were the only visible reminders of yesterday's ordeal. Beside him, his heart monitor tracked a steady beat.

The nurse checked the dials on his monitor and the drip of his IV before nodding to Green and heading out the door. Sullivan opened his eyes and stared at Green a long moment without a hint of recognition.

Green felt a niggle of fear. He smiled nervously. "Hey. You gave us a scare."

Sullivan didn't return the smile. "What did I do, Mike?"

"What do you mean?"

"I mean I don't remember, and no one will tell me."

Green sat in the guest chair, mindful of the nurse's warning. "What did they tell you?"

"Don't play mind games with me, Mike. I remember talking to Screech, I remember pain..." He reached up to touch the bandage on his forehead. Green saw that he had bandages on his forearms as well. He tried to slip his own hands out of view. "Did I crash my truck?"

"Look, they're only giving me five minutes. I want to know how you are. What do the doctors say?"

Sullivan's eyes remained locked on his. Understanding dawned in them. "Fuck. Did I hurt anyone?"

The heart monitor picked up its pace. Green cast about nervously for a change of topic. "I got the photo line-up with the hooker from your truck, and we're working on an ID." He watched in alarm as the jagged line leaped up. He leaned forward, trying to sound soothing. "I just want you to concentrate on getting better. Everything is under control on the job. I'm going to supervise the case personally until you're better."

Sullivan sank back amid his pillows. Slowly he shook his head back and forth. "I'm a washout, Mike."

"Nonsense. Lots of guys come back better than new after angioplasty."

"I can't concentrate, I can't breathe without pain—" He broke off, his chin quivering. "I've got three kids I won't see walk down the aisle—"

"You've just had a heart attack! Give yourself some time, man."

"I'm forty-six years old, and I'm an old man."

"My father is an old man. And he's lived with heart disease for years." Green leaned forward and dodged the IV tube to squeeze Sullivan's forearm. For the first time, Sullivan's gaze caught the bandage on Green's hand. His heart monitor spiked, and he pressed his eyes closed. "I did crash my truck, didn't I? And since everyone is pussyfooting around and won't tell me the goddamn truth, I have to assume it's bad. So unless you're prepared to be straight with me, you can just take your false cheer and get the hell out."

"Brian, I can't—"

"Won't."

Green took a deep breath. "I will tell you, once I get the details—"

The nurse popped back into the room. "Time's up, gentlemen. Mr. Sullivan needs his rest."

"I don't!" Sullivan began, but his protest sounded feeble.

The nurse reached for his pulse. "The doctor's orders are very specific, and he's the boss." She turned to Green, keeping the bright smile on her face, but he could see the warning in her eyes. He stood up and gave Sullivan a final thumbs up.

"I'll be back," he said as he fled. Feeling a traitor and a fraud.

Outside, he found Mary Sullivan leaning against his Subaru with her arms folded. She looked haggard and drawn, dressed, not in her usual Real Estate Agent power suit, but in black sweats emblazoned with the logo of her son's hockey team.

"I hope to hell you didn't tell him, Mike."

Green was surprised, for Mary didn't allow a single profanity in her home full of teenagers. "He already suspects something."

"So you told him."

"No, I didn't. But I don't see how we can keep it from him. It's all over the news."

"Then we have to keep him away from the news. His heart can't take it."

"But he asks."

"Then lie to him," she snapped, pushing herself away from his car.

"I can't lie to him," Green retorted. "Our friendship deserves better than that."

"And you think our marriage doesn't? If you can't do that much for him, then stay away. He needs forty-eight hours to stabilize."

He headed around the car to the driver's side, too angry to trust himself further. Mary didn't need an argument with him on top of all she was handling.

But she wasn't done. "Damn it, Mike, he idolizes you! He puts himself at risk for you. If you weren't his boss, he'd have moved to a less demanding section the minute his blood pressure started to climb."

He took a deep breath. "I won't lie, and I won't stay away. But I will try to stall when he asks. But for God's sake, between you and his doctors, figure out a way to tell him."

*   *   *

Green was still upset when he reached the police station, where he found an impatient Sergeant Levesque parked outside his door. She wore blue jeans and a battered leather jacket, but with her blond hair pulled back in a simple ponytail, she still managed to look like a model. She glanced pointedly at her watch.

"I've sent out a fresh bulletin to the patrols in the market, and I've assigned a team to check with cab companies. Uniform has been showing those video stills around the Byward Market all week without success, but they'll try again." She paused just long enough for her skepticism to show through. "Is there anything else you want me to do, sir?"

Green unlocked his office and ushered her in. "Look, Marie Claire, I'm not a hard-ass. This case is proving to be much more complicated than our original theory. Staff Sergeant Sullivan has a lot of respect for you. The best way we can help him recover is to work together and solve this case as fast as we can. Bring him some good news."

"We have a suspect, sir. He's at home, just waiting for

formal charges to be laid. The Crown has so much confidence in our evidence that she's ready to go for arraignment first thing Monday. The defence will walk all over her if they learn we're still looking for suspects."

Green held onto his fraying temper with an effort. "We have a son who has been disinherited and a mystery woman who was known to the victim and who was present on Rideau Street shortly before he died. We need to eliminate them both as suspects, or the defence will walk all over us at trial."

That seemed to reach her, for she frowned down at her hands clasped in her lap. Before she could speak further, his phone buzzed. The duty officer on the front desk was an old warrior drifting towards retirement. After years on patrol, very little phased him, but he sounded rattled. Perhaps Sullivan's brush with death has unnerved us all, Green thought.

"I knew you were in, Inspector, so I thought I'd run this by you. There's a Mr. Frank Adams here, claims to be Omar's father, and he's demanding to speak to the Chief of Detectives."

"That would be Superintendent Devine."

"Well, I know that, and I tried to tell him it was Saturday, but he's not taking no for an answer. He's pacing back and forth across the lobby, clicking his heels and threatening to go to the media. Ex-military. I can spot them a mile off."

Green glanced at Levesque. This might be interesting. He told the duty officer that he and Sergeant Levesque would be down shortly.

"The father will lie through his teeth to protect his son," Levesque protested once Green had filled her in. "He's already given a false alibi."

Green didn't bother with a reply as he led the way down the back stairs to the lobby. His first glimpse of Omar's father was a surprise. Omar was so black that Green had forgotten the father was white, his skin so pale it was almost translucent. His shaved head glistened like a skull, and a network of fine blue veins ran beneath the skin of his forehead and neck. His blue eyes were like the sky on a misty morning, so light they were haunting. Soulless.

Green felt the man appraising him coolly as he introduced Levesque and himself. The handshake too was devoid of warmth. Green ushered them all into a small, featureless room off the lobby.

"I asked to speak to the Chief of Detectives."

"I'm the senior supervising officer," Green replied.

"A middleman," said Adams with contempt. "I know how it works. Just enough power to carry out orders and take the blame. Not enough to call the shots."

Green felt his temper flare. I've taken enough crap for a Saturday morning, he thought. "I call the shots in Major Crimes, Mr. Adams. What is it you want?"

Adams fixed him with his empty eyes for five seconds before he blinked and shifted in his chair. "I want the police department to stop railroading my son. He gets caught in a couple of minor lies, in the wrong place and at the wrong time, and because he's black, he's guilty. If you're going to play the race card with my son's life, I'll have the black community so up in arms that the whole justice system will come to a halt. You think the O.J. Simpson trial was a circus?"

"There's a solid circumstantial case against your son, but the courts will—"

"Bullshit. If he wasn't black, there's no way it would have gone this far."

Levesque leaned forward and placed her elbows on the table. Sensing she was about to erupt, Green changed direction. "We're still investigating, Mr. Adams. Believe me, I want to make sure we have the right person too." He paused, trying to soften his tone. "Do you have information that you think would help your son's case?"

"Why should I tell you a damn thing?"

"Because I'm the one in a position to help. I've spent twenty-five years tracking down murderers, and it's important to me that the guilty ones pay."

Adams' eyes flickered. He glanced at Levesque but said nothing.

"There is something, isn't there? If it helps your son..."

Adams flexed his right fist, forming ropes of muscle along his forearm. His jaw tightened, and a vein pulsed at his temple. "I don't have much faith in middlemen—the military drummed that out of me—but I'll tell you this because you said you want to get at the truth. My son is not a killer. He's a physical coward, he could no more cave a man's head in than he could pull the wings off a fly. We live in a tough neighbourhood where it's pretty damn hard for a kid to avoid violence. Either you're beating others up or you're getting beaten. You either join the tough guys or they eat you for a snack. This starts about senior kindergarten on the playground."

Adams raised his head to stare at the wall opposite. His eyes were bleak now. "I chose to live where we do so my kids would know the real world, so I'm not making excuses. I tried to toughen the boy up, but it was no use. Omar used to get beaten up all the time, until he figured out how to hang out with the tough guys. He's smarter than he looks, my boy. He's not in a gang, he doesn't do bad things, but he gets some protection by hanging around with a few who live on our street. I've tried to stop it, because I know someday they're going to make him pay his dues, but you can't ride a twenty-year-old two-four-seven."

Green sensed Levesque beginning to fidget at his side. He

wanted to kick her under the table. The man was telling a story, and he had to tell it his way.

"Friday night, he sneaked out. I knew he was gone, and I was listening for him to come home. I always do. Kids get knifed on buses, they stumble drunk into the paths of trucks." He paused as though circling the core of his story. "Omar came home at five to three in the morning. I heard someone a block away, running, and I looked out the living room window and saw him run smack into a hydro pole. Knocked him over, and he went sprawling into the street. When he came in the house, he was bleeding like a pig. I thought his nose was broken. He was drunker than I'd ever seen him. Stumble down, passing out drunk."

Adams switched his gaze to Green. "Even if Omar was the type to beat up old men, there was no way, that night, he could have landed an effective blow."

"Was he alone when you saw him in the street?"

"Yeah. He was out with his friends, but they'd split up."

"Did you speak to him when he came in?"

"Tried to, but he was beyond hearing. I figured he'd better just sleep it off."

"Did you do anything else?"

Adams frowned. "What do you mean?"

Green shrugged. "Did you touch him, help him upstairs?"

"I don't see why that's important."

Green let the silence lengthen, suspecting there was more to the story. He'd seen the scars on Omar's back, no doubt part of Adams's "toughening up" techniques.

"Well, I did grab him."

"Grabbed him how?"

"By the arms. He was so piss drunk, I was trying to get his attention."

Green stood up and faced him. "Show me."

Adams recoiled in surprise. He stood up warily, taller and heavier than Green. Omar was also at least four inches taller than Green, but he hoped the comparison would suffice. Adams reached across and grasped Green lightly by the upper arms.

"That's it? Just gently like that?"

Adams dropped his hands. "Well, no, I was mad. It was three a.m. I grabbed him hard."

"Shook him?"

"Maybe a little, to get his attention. But he was beyond that. He just pulled away."

"And?"

"And went upstairs."

"What did you do?"

"Just let him go. No point in anything else."

Green returned to his seat and turned to face Adams gravely. "Mr. Adams, your son's back is crisscrossed with scars. Like he's been beaten. For years, I'd say."

Deep red spread slowly up Adams's neck and face. He flexed his fist again, and for an instant Green thought he was going to punch him. "Like I said, he used to get beaten up in school as a kid."

"These looked like lashes from a belt."

"What's the relevance? Trying to pin the 'abused kid turns abuser' label on him?"

"No, just trying to explain the marks on his body."

Adams jutted out his chin. "You think you know. Hard-ass military father from the Airborne, and we all know what those cowboys were like. Probably figured a little harsh discipline never hurts, builds character. That's what you think."

Green said nothing. He knew Adams would set him straight without prompting.

"I never laid a hand on that boy. At least not a serious hand. Beyond that, you can think what you like."

Green pondered his choice of words, his refusal to name the culprit or even to admit there was one. As if he were protecting someone. Green took a shot in the dark. "I've seen mothers do some pretty violent things to their children in a fit of rage."

Adams said nothing, but the fist flexed.

"Somalia was a terrifyingly brutal place—"

"Still is."

"Some women suffered unspeakable violence. Sometimes the only way they can lash out is at others who are even more vulnerable than themselves."

Adams snorted. "Pop psychology. Same crap all the white, middle-class social workers dish out. Gemalla has panic attacks, she has flashbacks and hallucinations, but she beat Omar so he wouldn't turn out like his father—" He snapped his jaw shut.

Green masked his surprise. "You?"

"Not me." He shot Green a sharp look. "Omar doesn't know. How can you tell a boy he's the product of some rebel thug who raped your mother when she was thirteen years old. After he'd beheaded her father before her eyes. When Omar was little, she swore she could see that thug mocking her through Omar's eyes." He smiled, a tight, twisted smile. "I don't know why she thinks that. Omar is all her—timid and gentle. Not a single drop of that sadistic bastard's blood runs through his veins."

Maybe not, Green thought, but that timid, gentle mother had, in repeated fits of rage, laid open the flesh on the back of her child.

Sixteen

Levesque was surprisingly quiet as she and Green headed back upstairs to the squad room. At the top of the stairs, she shot him an oblique glance. "He could have seen the marks on Omar's arms and made up the story about grabbing him to cover it."

Green nodded. It was possible, even probable given the man's protective instincts. But nevertheless it was one more piece of evidence weighing down the scale of reasonable doubt. However, he was even more intrigued by the father's other revelation. Between his mother's abusive rage and his father's efforts to toughen him up, the young man might well be a powder keg. Alcohol, peer pressure and the taunts of a defiant victim—had all that been the match?

"Maybe," he replied, "but in the meantime keep on top of the news coming in about our mystery hooker. She could be an important player. And if you're hoping to beef up the case against your suspect, I suggest you rattle the cage of his buddy Nadif. He's already shown a healthy appetite for self-preservation."

Levesque frowned as she tried to recast his words in her own language. Her English was normally so good that he forgot it wasn't her mother tongue. "Any suggestions, sir?"

Her request was unexpected, but he could detect no hidden mockery. "You might want to check his phone wiretaps."

"Those have been useless. He uses a cellphone for his private calls. He must know he's being tapped, because there's nothing but his mother talking to friends and his father discussing Somali association business. Everything is very controlled."

"But they can't control incoming calls. I suggest you keep on top of it. You never know."

"Sir..." She stared back at the elevator door longingly. "This is Saturday. There's no crisis that the guys on duty can't address. I want to visit Staff Sergeant Sullivan. Also I have a daughter. She's starting figure skating lessons next week, and last year's skates are too small."

Green was about to tell her that the updates she needed would take less than half an hour, but he stopped himself. He thought of Brian Sullivan fitting one last thing into his already long day, of Mary saying he could never say no to Green.

Inside his office, he could hear his own phone ringing. What the hell is this? It was his Saturday too, not Grand Central Station. All he wanted was to hug his own children and go for a long walk with them in the leaves. He debated not answering, but anxiety won out. It could be about Sullivan.

"No problem," he said to Levesque as he opened his door. "You can get the duty detectives to contact you if anything important turns up."

It was not about Sullivan. It took Green a few seconds to place the wheezy, age-frayed voice at the other end of the line.

"I'm glad I caught you in. I wasn't sure who else I should ask."

"What can I do for you, Mr. Verne?"

"Sorry. Yes, it's George Verne. I've just had a very unsettling visitor. It didn't seem worth a 911 call, but I did want to get a police opinion."

Green sat down and snatched a piece of paper from the pile on his desk. A memo from Devine. He flipped it over to its blank side, pen poised. "What visitor?"

"David Rosenthal, Sam's son. Very irate, very threatening."

"Threatening what? Physical violence?"

"Well, no. Lawsuits. But have you seen the man? He's built like a lumberjack. He's got at least an eight-inch advantage on me."

"Where is he now?"

"Gone. Stormed out. Broke the window on my office door when he slammed it."

"Did he say he'd be back?"

"Oh, yes. In an hour, once I'd had time to consider his proposal and to locate the information he wanted about the will."

Green glanced at his watch. Eleven o'clock. In the chaos of yesterday evening, he'd lost track of David Rosenthal. The man had stayed around to give his report to the police and had even shown up at the Heart Institute to find out how Sullivan was doing, revealing a more empathetic side than Green had suspected. However, at some point in the long evening vigil, he had slipped away before Green had even thought to ask where he was staying.

Green clawed back in his memory to his meeting with the man just before the accident. There were still questions he wanted to ask, not the least of which were when had he arrived in town and what had he been doing last Saturday night between midnight and four a.m.

"I'm going to send a cruiser over immediately, Mr. Verne—"

"Then you consider him dangerous as well?"

"Just a precaution. I don't know him. But I'm also on my way over there myself. You can fill me in on the whole story once I get there."

Green took his own Subaru, planning to go home afterwards, and drove quickly east along the Queensway to Vanier. Like most police officers, he knew every shabby corner of the old neighbourhood, where legitimate businesses and the working poor struggled for dominance amid the drug dens and flophouses. As he turned onto the side street listed on Verne's business card, he spotted a cruiser parked conspicuously outside a three-storey house. The red brick was blackened with age, but the green paint on the double entrance doors was fresh. A row of rusty brass buzzers lined the wall beside the door. He stopped by the cruiser, leaned in the window and introduced himself. The patrols snapped alert.

"Pull around the corner a little more out of sight. I don't want to spook this individual."

Once the officers had complied, Green squeezed around the overgrown cedars blocking half the walkway and rang the bell beside Verne's name. The names on the other buzzers gave little hint as to their business. AMX Ltée., B.P. Père et Fils... As he waited, Green scanned the building, which was more invincible than it first appeared. It was guarded by a well-known alarm company and appeared to have sensors on the windows and doors. The door had a peephole and deadbolt.

Eventually he heard the sound of a cane thumping along the floor inside, followed by prolonged wheezing on the other side of the door, presumably while Verne sized him up through the peephole. Finally, the deadbolt clicked and the door swung open. Verne peered out, alarm racing across his face.

"Where is the cruiser? It was here a moment ago."

"Around the corner. You're safe."

Verne turned and began the slow process of returning to his office without another word. The outer reception area was little more than a walk-in closet with a desk, a computer, a full wall of filing cabinets, and two small chairs which evidently served as a waiting room. The furniture, Green noticed, was mostly grey metal government surplus.

They passed through the broken office door into a slightly larger room beyond. Glass crunched underfoot, and Verne scowled. "He's going to pay for that. For the clean-up as well. Obviously I can't do it."

Verne's office was a curious mixture of old elegance and new functionality. A carved oak desk and leather swivel chair sat in front of the window, and a wall of built-in bookcases contained a lifetime of leather-bound law books. A network of stainless steel railings ran from the door to his desk and along the length of the bookcases. Green understood their purpose when Verne hooked his cane on the coat rack behind the door and held the rail to traverse the room to his desk.

He smiled thinly as he eased into his chair. "It works."

Green chose one of the two client chairs opposite him. "Now maybe you should start at the beginning, Mr. Verne. From your first moment of contact with David Rosenthal."

"I had some warning. I was at my desk catching up on paperwork. I live just upstairs, although few know it." He twisted and pointed to the wall of books. "Behind there is an elevator that leads up to my flat on the second floor. It's not much, but over the years I have remodelled it to suit my needs. I own this whole building, you see, although few people know that either."

Green thought of the minutes ticking away before Rosenthal's return. "So you were in the office here, catching up on paperwork."

"And I got a phone call from Elliot Solquist, a colleague who'd drawn up Sam's earlier will. He was the original executor of the estate, so he'd initiated a will search as the first step in that process. That turned up my later will, of course. Therefore, when David Rosenthal arrived at his office this morning, he had to tell him there was a new will." Verne paused to catch his breath, wheezing into the silence.

Green tried not to drum his fingers. "How did he take it?"

"Extremely poorly. He demanded to know who I was, what kind of practice I had, what mental state his father had been in. To which Elliot replied that he hadn't laid eyes on Sam Rosenthal since he'd handled some property transactions for him nine years ago, at which time he'd seemed of perfectly sound mind. David didn't let him off easily. He implied that Elliot knew the contents of the new will and had deliberately kept them from him. When that didn't fly, he implied that Elliot must have been incompetent, since Sam hadn't asked him to handle the new will."

"Why didn't Sam use him for the new will?"

Verne raised his palms to gesture eloquently around the room. "Do I look like part of the establishment or the circles Sam Rosenthal would have moved in? Elliot and he had been long-time friends and colleagues. In the old days Sam often testified for clients of Solquist's firm. I, on the other hand, have a reputation for my *pro bono* work on behalf of the disabled. In fact, I first met Sam when he brought a young patient in to see me who wanted to contest a declaration of mental incapacity. It didn't proceed, but I think Sam was impressed by my counsel. He wanted anonymity to make these bequests without questions being asked or objections raised. He did tell me that many of his colleagues hadn't approved of his new approach to treatment. I assumed Elliot fell into that category."

Green nodded. He knew Elliot Solquist by reputation as a senior partner in one of the most influential, politically connected firms in the city. Not exactly the underdog's lawyer. "Did Mr. Solquist feel threatened at any point in this morning's meeting with David?"

Verne chuckled. "Elliot doesn't feel threatened. He possesses a state-of-the-art security system and a direct line to the police chief himself. But he is aware of my more pedestrian circumstances, and David was pretty heated after fifteen minutes of Elliot's legendary stonewalling. Hence he phoned to warn me. When David arrived, I had the general gist of the will ready for him."

Verne's levity faded, and he had to stop again to catch his breath. "To say he was angry is to understate the case. He was incandescent. This was a man clearly used to getting his own way and quite prepared to terrorize those who stand in his way. A bully of the first order. He didn't even try to use charm or diplomacy. He walked in here, took one look around, and asked how the hell his father had even found me. That did not dispose me kindly towards him. I told him that my health required me to operate on a modest, part-time basis, but it by no means affected my faculties nor my acumen as an attorney. On the contrary, I told him, his father was obviously aware of my advocacy work for the disabled and had chosen me to help him implement his wishes."

"And he threatened you with lawsuits? Claiming what—undue influence?"

"Not then. Not yet. He wanted to know the contents of the will, when it was made and what his father's state of mind had been at the time. From his questions, I suspected he hadn't had contact with his father in years but was wondering whether his father was depressed or senile. Whether, living alone and missing his wife, he'd become needy, so that his judgment was impaired and easily manipulated by clever con men."

"Meaning you?"

Verne chuckled again, causing a coughing fit. Spittle formed at the corner of his mouth, which he wiped away with a stained handkerchief. When he had spent himself, he draped over his desk and dragged air into his lungs. "He said he certainly intended to look into the charitable causes that I represent, to see whether any of them benefited from the new will. All to be part of his lawsuit, I imagine. But first he'll contest the will."

"Using Elliot Solquist?"

"Elliot turned him down. Conflict of interest, the sly old bugger. But David wasn't content just to go after me. Until this point he'd primarily acted like an abrasive bully. Now he wanted the names and addresses of the new beneficiaries."

"The six patients?"

Verne nodded. "He intends to prove they unduly influenced his father and took advantage of his vulnerability. A psychopathic individual, for example, who was faking mental illness for his own purposes."

"Some would argue that the psychopath is mentally ill."

"But not someone who is treatable by conventional methods. Not someone that Sam Rosenthal would have undertaken to help. But David was convinced that his father had been conned by a psychopath into giving half a million dollars to himself and to other needy sufferers."

Green leaned forward and looked at him keenly. "You discussed this will with Sam. You helped him draft it, perhaps even chose the amounts and the beneficiaries."

Verne looked affronted. "Not those. We decided on six, and Sam came up with the names."

"Did you ever sense he was being influenced by someone? That maybe he was depressed and wasn't thinking straight?"

Verne whipped his head back and forth, his jowls jiggling. "Sam was adamant that he owed it to these people because his poor treatment advice had cost them in health, happiness and life success. I wanted him to choose more than six. I've seen what a sudden, huge financial windfall like a legal settlement or a lottery win can do to a person used to barely scraping by. But Sam wanted the half million each. That's ten years of an ordinary man's annual salary, he said. Ten years that he'd deprived them of. He was very rational, Inspector Green."

"And you told this to David Rosenthal?"

"I did. He still wanted names and addresses. I told him—and I was cognizant of the fact that he was much larger than me and incensed, but I knew Sam would not want them bullied—that since he was not the beneficiary of the will, he had no automatic right to the knowledge of its contents."

"And he's given you one hour to reconsider and provide him with the names."

"That's right." Verne glanced up at the antique Roman numeral clock that hung over the door. "A time limit that expired five minutes ago, I note."

"Perhaps he's consulting other counsel."

The phone on Verne's desk rang, a shrill old-fashioned ring that made Green jump in his seat. Verne lifted the receiver, spoke, listened, and shot Green a knowing look. "My decision remains the same, Mr. Rosenthal. My advice is to retain counsel in order to examine your options." With that, the old lawyer hung up and gave Green a satisfied smile. "The crisis has been averted. He spotted your police cruiser around the corner and decided not to come up."

"Did he sound calmer?"

"I suspect David Rosenthal doesn't calm easily. He'll be on the lookout for another way to get hold of those names. My worry is that there could be a copy of Sam's will in his apartment somewhere."

*   *   *

Green hurried down into the street and around the corner to the cruiser. "Did you see anyone approach the premises a few minutes ago? A tall man, maybe?"

The constable in the driver's seat looked up from his coffee thermos and glanced at his partner questioningly. They shook their heads in unison. "No one's come near since you went in, sir."

"Did anyone drive by?"

"A few vehicles. Cars, couple of vans, a pick-up."

"And a delivery truck," his partner added.

"A plain white van?"

"Don't think so." The driver frowned. "Come to think of it, one guy did slow. I thought he was looking for an address. Then he took off in a hurry."

"What make of vehicle?"

"Green Camry."

Possibly a red herring, Green thought, but worth following up. "Did you get a look at the driver?"

"Just a brief one. White, beard, grey hair..."

Bingo, Green thought. David Rosenthal had a new car. "Which direction did he go?"

The driver pointed towards Montreal Road, a main thoroughfare where David would be swallowed up in traffic instantly. Green returned to his own car and pulled his cellphone from his pocket. If Sam Rosenthal's new will was in his apartment, David had not found it during his visit the day before. He might go back for a second look.

Green sat in his car, toying with his cellphone. If David found the will and its list of new beneficiaries, what would he do? Was he angry enough, and foolhardy enough, to go after them? Green knew that so far he didn't have enough concrete evidence to justify picking David up, even as a stall tactic. There were vague threats and ultimatums, but neither Verne nor Solquist had laid any complaints or expressed fears strong enough to justify any sort of charge.

There was one course of action open to him, however, but George Verne would have to take it. As executor of Sam Rosenthal's estate, he had the power to order the locks changed on the dead man's apartment to prevent removal of assets. It was probably closing the barn door after the horses were long gone, but it was a start, he thought as he dialled the old lawyer's number.

Afterwards he was just steering the Subaru back towards home, hoping to catch a couple of hours with Tony and Sharon before her evening shift, when his phone rang again. Once more, he thought as he answered, and I'm going to turn the thing off.

It was Levesque, sounding excited.

Seventeen

I was thinking you want to hear this, sir," Levesque said when she greeted him at the basement entrance to the police station fifteen minutes later. There was a bounce in her stride as she led the way to the large room where the electronic surveillance teams were housed. Banks of computers and monitors lined the aisles like the workings of a giant high tech firm. Their footsteps were muffled by carpeting as they headed to a small cubicle in the audio surveillance corner, passing technicians with headsets who fiddled with dials and recorders. Levesque stopped in front of an automatic wiretap recorder. The technician waiting for them handed Green a headset.

"This came in about an hour ago from the Hassan wiretap. It sounded hot, so I let Marie Claire know." The technician flashed her a warm smile, which she ignored. Better stick with your own age bracket, Green thought. At close to fifty with a paunch, a wife and four kids in college, the guy hadn't a hope. Green slipped on the headphones, and the technician ran the tape.

The sound of ringing, followed by a male voice saying hello. Young, Green thought.

"Nadif?"

"Who is this?" Slow. Wary.

"It's Omar's father, you piece of shit."

"Mr. Adams!" Alarm now. "Don't—"

"I'll do the talking."

"Sure, but why don't I come over."

"This won't take long. I just want you to know—"

"Wait!"

Green chuckled. Nadif knew his phone was being tapped, and he was trying to stem the tide.

"You made a big mistake when you tried to drop Omar in it—"

"Omar's my friend!"

"Yeah, some friend. It should be you going to jail, you little rat."

"No one's going to jail, Mr. Adams. It's all a mistake."

"Sure. Just so you know, you'll get yours back. Omar's remembering things. The hooker? The knife? Soon it's going to be you—"

The line clicked abruptly. Nadif had finally had the sense to slam the phone down. Too late.

Levesque was smiling in triumph as Green peeled the headphones off. "I knew those punks were involved," she said.

Green looked at the technician. "Anything after this?"

The man shook his head. "That tap's been stone cold. Nada." He looked apologetically at Levesque. If he'd found a single incriminating word, Green realized, he would have reported it to her, just for the pleasure of having her near.

Levesque was fairly dancing, her blue eyes bright above pink cheeks. Green remembered that feeling, that moment when the case begins to break open. He felt his own pulse quicken, but he held up a cautioning hand.

"What this proves is not that the two were involved, but that Omar has been holding out on us. Or he's remembering more details about that night."

"Absolutely. Either way, I'm going to have him picked up

for further questioning."

Green glanced at his watch. "When?"

"As soon as I get upstairs."

Green hesitated. She was so caught up in the case that she'd forgotten it was Saturday. Her time with her daughter. Yet this time, the haste was premature. "The other thing the tape proves is that the prostitute is important. We need to find her and get her statement before you have another run at Omar. Any word yet on who and where she is?"

Levesque scowled, her eyes clouding. "Not yet."

"Let's just check the latest." Green turned to head back to the exit, remembering at the last minute to thank the technician. It was something Sullivan would have done, always mindful to show respect and appreciation for those under him. In his headlong rush to solve the case, Green often forgot that others existed.

Up in the squad room, Green made some phone calls to the hospital and to Sharon while Levesque busied herself gathering updates. Sharon was surprisingly gentle and understanding when he apologized for being delayed by the demands of the case.

"How's Brian?" she asked immediately.

He was taken aback. How well she knows me, he thought. Work has always been my escape route. He filled her in on his disastrous morning encounters with Brian and with Mary.

"The only thing you can do for him, honey, is to be there when he does learn the truth."

He grimaced. "Being there" had never been his forte. "The best thing I can do for him right now is solve this case," he countered, "and it looks as if it's cracking open a bit."

There was a silence, then, "Have you identified that photo Brian had?"

"Not yet. We're working on it, especially now—" He broke off as a dreadful thought struck him. He glanced through his open office door to see Levesque striding towards him. "Look, I have to go now. I'll fill you in when I get home."

Levesque came in shaking her head. Before he could voice his fear, she said, "As I thought, some progress but nothing exceptional. A bus driver on the number two route recognized her, says he often picks her up in the Beacon Hill area and drops her off on Rideau Street."

Green considered this information. Beacon Hill was a mixed but largely middle-class residential area in the east end of the city, featuring older homes with established families and stable, modest incomes. There were some lower income and subsidized rental properties, but it was hardly the area one would expect a young street prostitute to live in.

"Anything else?"

"Our guys spoke to one Blueline cabbie who remembers picking her up several times at the Nelson Street address—"

"Ahah!"

She shook her head. "Most times he just delivered her to Rideau Street. Dr. Rosenthal would hand him the money and give him an address—the cabbie didn't remember it, but it was somewhere in the east end."

"Well, it would be in their log."

"No, because as soon as they drove off, the woman would tell him to drop her on Rideau Street, and she'd ask him for the extra money."

Green processed the implications. "So the good doctor was trying to help her, but she was playing him."

She shrugged. "Probably she had a habit to feed. A lot of basically decent girls can find themselves in a bad corner."

The glimpse of compassion surprised him. "Anyone on

the streets give any more leads?"

She nodded. "She's a familiar face. She's been around for a few months, off and on, but she's not homeless. That's to say, the outreach people don't know her, and she never uses the shelters or kitchens."

"No. My guess is she goes back to a regular home in Beacon Hill."

"Maybe tonight... It's Saturday night, she might put in an appearance. I can tell the patrols to keep an eye out. She'll surface eventually."

"We can't wait for eventually. I want you to release that photo to the news media. We can get it on the local news websites and maybe on TV bulletins right away."

"But sir, that may drive her underground. By tonight we should—"

"We can't afford to wait." Levesque was frowning at him, puzzled. "Think about it, Marie Claire. Omar's father has just tipped off Nadif that Omar remembers a hooker. We don't know how she fits into the murder scenario, but we can bet one thing. If she was there, if the boys think she saw anything, then Nadif will be looking for her. He'll want to find her as badly as we do, and he's not as nice as we are. So we'd better find her first."

*　　*　　*

Green rounded the corner into the hospital waiting room and stopped in surprise. The small TV in the corner was on mute, but the crime scene on Rideau Street filled the screen. A moment later, the grainy photo from the pawn shop video flashed up. That was fast, Green thought.

The waiting room was nearly empty. Only a couple of

seats were filled by visitors likely waiting for medical updates. He located the remote control on the table nearby and hunted among the various buttons for one that would turn on the sound.

"The woman is not a suspect," the TV suddenly blasted. "But police are interested in questioning her about the events of last Saturday night, when the seventy-five-year-old retired psychiatrist was assaulted on Rideau Street."

The visitors glared, and Green hammered the volume button. "As of today, the police have few leads. Anyone with any information concerning the identity or whereabouts of the woman in this photo is asked to phone Ottawa Police at 613-555-2333." The camera then panned out over footage of yesterday's crash, focussing on the crushed remains of the Impala beneath the pick-up truck. "The investigation took an even more tragic turn yesterday when a motor vehicle crash killed one of the police witnesses, a young University of Ottawa woman from Timmins who lived in Dr. Rosenthal's building. Two Ottawa Police officers were also injured in the crash, which occurred when—"

A groan sounded behind him and Green whirled around to see Sullivan standing at the entrance to the room with his IV pole. Sullivan sagged against the wall, his face grey with horror.

Green leaped to his side. "Jeez, Brian! What are you doing out of bed?"

Sullivan was shaking his head back and forth. "I knew it. I knew it. I fucking knew it."

Green dragged him to a chair and thrust him into it. Sullivan bent forward, trembling. His breath came in deep, shuddering gasps. Green looked frantically around for a staff person, but the halls were empty. He clutched Sullivan's arm.

"You feeling all right? Dizzy? Any pain?"

"They're supposed to walk," came a voice from the corner, where an elderly woman sat reading a book.

"Feeling all right?" Sullivan said. "I just killed a woman, Mike."

"That was an accident."

"That was me! Losing control, passing out! That was this fucking useless body! Killing some poor kid who should have had sixty good years of life left in her."

Green groped for Sullivan's pulse. Not that he would know what he was feeling, but at least he could tell how fast it was going. Where the hell were all the doctors! And why were they letting him wander around unattended?

Sullivan shook off his hand. "Do you think I give a fuck about me right now? Did you see it? Tell me what the hell happened!"

Green thought fast. He wanted to shout for help, he wanted above all to be anywhere but here, forced to tell his friend the worst news of his life. He took a deep breath to slow his own racing heart and tried to project a soothing command. "Okay. I will tell you. But first I need you to sit back, breathe deeply, and calm down. Let me go get a nurse—"

"No! They'll try to stop you from telling me, like they have all day. Don't you think I already suspected the worst? That I'd killed people? Maybe mowed down a mother and her half dozen little kids? Why do you think I came out here? So I could see what they were hiding!" Sullivan sat back, his blue eyes blazing and his face now bright red. "I'm calm enough. You fucking tell me."

"You did not kill half a dozen little kids." Green searched for a way to ease into the revelation. "You were bringing me a photo line-up to show my witness, a young woman who rented from Rosenthal. You remember that?"

Sullivan nodded. "I remember preparing the line-up, stopping to talk to Screech—"

"Do you remember what he said?"

Sullivan nodded. "I asked him about the mystery woman. He..." Sullivan frowned as if searching through the cobwebs of his memory. "He called her Foxy, because she wore a fur coat in the cold weather."

Green's thoughts raced. A fur coat wasn't conclusive, but it fit the comfortably middle-class neighbourhood of Beacon Hill. Sullivan's colour was marginally better—pink now instead of fuchsia—as he set his mind to work.

"He thinks our suspects hit on her, and she told them to bugger off. That's all I remember." He flinched as if in pain and the grey horror returned to his face. Green felt his own pulse spike. "What did I do, Mike?"

"You lost control—probably passed out as you said—and hit the police car I'd parked in front of Rosenthal's place. That's all you hit. Unfortunately—" Here Green paused, fighting a sudden tightness in his chest. "I had left my witness in the back seat to wait for me while I spoke..." He stopped. No point in complicating things. Sullivan needed to rest, not become more embroiled in the case. "She was in the car."

"And I killed her."

"Your truck killed her."

A strangled grunt escaped Sullivan's lips. "Fuck you, Mike. You can't make this go away. I knew I was in trouble. I'd been in pain all morning. My gut was churning, and I'd been ignoring it for weeks. Got an appointment with my GP for some time in the next decade. I was actually going home early yesterday—"

"But I made you do one last stop."

Sullivan shook his head. "No, that's Mary's take. I chose this.

210

I chose to ignore the pain, climb behind the wheel of the truck, and set that five thousand-pound death machine in motion."

"You couldn't have known what would happen."

"Of course I could have known! How many times have we seen that scenario? Guy thinks it could never happen to him, just heartburn, and boom! I should have pulled over when I felt the light-headedness, and my muscles not obeying me any more..." He stopped. Frowned. "As things closed in, I do remember thinking 'there's a parked car. If I can just hit that.'"

Green felt sick. Tears were brimming in Sullivan's eyes, and Green felt his own throat constrict. He babbled to stave off thought. "You were doing the best you could. And if that girl hadn't been there, if I hadn't put her there—"

"No! You can't take this off me, Mike!"

"She didn't want to wait. I insisted."

Sullivan was staring at the floor, his hands hanging limply between his knees and a single tear running down to the tip of his nose. "The difference is, you couldn't have known. I should have. That's why you'll be able to sleep again. Maybe not tonight, but eventually. I won't."

Eighteen

Green started his car, leaned his forehead on the steering wheel and breathed deeply to wrestle his emotions under control. This was no one's fault, he told himself over and over, but he knew it would take more than words to shake the profound guilt they both felt. Sullivan's doctor had ordered him back to bed and prescribed a mild sedative. He was fast asleep before Green was even out the door.

Green had no such oblivion. He wanted nothing more than a few hours with his family, playing with Tony in the park and sharing his distress with Sharon. But she was headed for work soon. At most, he'd be able to steal an hour with her, but not unless he hurried. Finally he fished his cellphone out of his pocket and dialled Levesque's cell. She picked up after the second ring.

"Where are you?" he asked.

"Still at the station."

"Good. According to Screech, the homeless man on that street corner, our four punks tried to pick up the hooker that Saturday night. Probably shortly after that video was taken. So when you do bring Omar in for further questioning—"

"He's on his way."

"What!"

"A cruiser has just picked him up. I'm setting the video up now."

Green bit back his outrage. What had happened to his

request that she hold off until they had the hooker's story? The woman was insubordinate as well as stubborn. A strangely familiar combination, he conceded with a ghost of a smile, glancing at his watch. It was at most a fifteen-minute drive from Omar Adams' house to the police headquarters. Even allowing for paperwork formalities, Omar would get to the interview room before he did.

"Sir? Do you want to observe?"

Green was surprised that she was asking. They were making progress. He thought of his family waiting for him at home and of Sharon's comforting arms and unflappable common sense. By the time he finished at the police station, she would be long gone to work.

"I do. Hold off until I get there."

Twenty minutes later he found Levesque in the video control room, watching Omar on camera as she prepared her questions. The young man had adopted his trademark pose, sitting very still with his eyes closed and his arms folded as if in meditation. His expression betrayed no emotion, but he looked gaunt and strained, as if sleep had eluded him recently.

He didn't move a muscle all the time that Green and Levesque looked over her questions, but Green sensed he was attuned to every sound. His eyes flew open the instant Levesque and Charbonneau entered the room. His nostrils flared as he wrestled to bring his fear under control. Green watched while Levesque led him through some preliminary instructions about the process and repeated the caution before asking if he wished to add anything to his previous statement. Omar shook his head.

"My Dad's hotshot lawyer charges a thousand bucks to walk in the door. I don't need him here. I've got nothing to say to you."

Levesque hid her smile and made a show of consulting her notes. "We have some new evidence. I want to give you a chance to respond. We have a witness who says you have remembered more things about that night."

"I remember nothing! I had some beer, some bad weed, and I went home. I fell on my way home."

"The witness says you ran into a hydro pole."

Omar frowned. He sat very still a few seconds, then shrugged. "Maybe."

"The witness also says you were running at the time."

"I don't remember."

"Running like you were scared. Like you were running from something."

"Well, that's news to me."

"You don't remember running down Nelson and along Clarence Street, running smack into a hydro pole and landing in the street?"

Omar was shaking his head, but a shard of memory seemed to have broken loose. He looked off-balance. Uncertain. "Maybe."

Levesque jotted some notes and studied her file. In the corner, Charbonneau stood by the door, taking notes. They both continued to scribble as the silence lengthened.

"We have another witness who saw you that night, Omar. Saw you approach a prostitute on the corner near where Dr. Rosenthal was killed."

"I don't remember."

"Yes, you do. Maybe not all the details, but you remember the hooker." Levesque laid the picture of the mystery woman on the table. "Does she ring any bells?"

Omar stared at the picture and swallowed, his Adam's apple travelling up and down his lean, curved neck. "She looks familiar. We might have talked to her."

"About what?"

"About... You know. We were wasted."

"Looking for action?"

He inclined his head. "I don't remember much. It was mostly Nadif's idea."

"What was she like? Nice? Friendly?"

He shrugged. "I remember weird. She was yelling. Nadif said..." He rubbed his face. Blinked his eyes. "I remember he said he'd work a deal."

"And then what happened? Did you all have sex with her?"

"I don't remember. I don't think..." Omar stopped. His eyes widened, and he seemed to press back against the wall.

"What are you remembering?"

"I was wasted! Dizzy. Sick! I just wanted to get away."

"From what?"

"I didn't want it. I'm not like that."

Levesque laughed. "Omar, it was Saturday night. You were wasted, on the make. You expect me to believe you turned down a perfectly good chance to get laid because 'you're not like that'? She's a hooker! She invited you!"

Omar thrust his lower lip out. "I don't remember. I don't remember what happened with her."

"Your first time?"

He flinched. "No."

"Sad not to remember your first time."

He scowled. Glanced at Charbonneau as if for rescue, but finding nothing but a stone wall, he sat back in his chair and folded his arms. "Maybe I did her, maybe I didn't. But whatever I did, it's not a crime."

"Does your father beat you, Omar?"

He stiffened. "What? No!"

"Never hurt you or tried to toughen you up?"

"He's tough, but he doesn't hit or anything. There's lots of ways to be tough."

"What other ways?"

Omar scowled. "What the fuck does it matter?"

"He calls you a coward. He said you never had the nerve to fight, never even to defend yourself."

"He's full of shit."

"Have you ever been in a fight? Ever used your fists?"

"I'm not an idiot. You think you'll get me bragging, maybe even admitting I beat up helpless old men."

Point to Omar, Green thought. He's smarter than he seems. This time it was Levesque's turn to shrug. She looked supremely uninterested. "Even the most cowardly, crapped-upon worm turns eventually. Lashes back. I just asked if you ever did."

"I never had to," Omar snapped back. "I learned to outsmart the old man and outlast him. Only an idiot lashes out, and that only gets him in trouble."

"So you get other people in trouble instead, is that it? People who aren't as smart as you, like Nadif and Yusuf."

"No!" Omar leaned forward, his dark eyes sparking. "There's enough moronic violence in this world. Enough people living in fear, enough people lashing out and taking revenge. I can't stop it, but I don't have to add to it. Not because I'm a coward, but because it has to stop somewhere."

Green was fascinated by this new glimpse of Omar. An intelligent, impassioned Omar. He leaned into the microphone. "Now's the time to ask about his mother."

Levesque didn't miss a beat. "Are you talking about your mother, Omar?"

The young man jerked back. "What?"

"Enough people lashing out, taking revenge? You mean her?"

216

"My mother's seen the worst of it."

"And given the worst of it."

Omar was silent. However, he didn't look puzzled, Green noted.

"Did she give the worst of it?"

"My mother has nightmares, yes. She hides all the knives in the house and sees enemies everywhere on the street."

"What about even inside the house?"

"My father protects her."

"She gave you those beatings on your back, didn't she."

"I got beaten in Somalia."

"Those are more recent than that."

Green leaned into the microphone again. "Show more sympathy."

In response, Levesque frowned faintly. "Your mother couldn't help herself, could she?"

Omar's breathing grew ragged, and his large eyes shuttered. "Ask your fucking questions, but leave my mother out of this."

"It must have made you angry. Even if you understood what she was going through, you were only a child. She was supposed to love you."

Omar's hand slammed on the table, making both Levesque and Charbonneau jump. "How many families have perfect mothers and fathers? I have a mother. She loves me. The violence isn't her fault, that's why it has to stop."

It was not the answer any of them expected. Levesque consulted her notes, looking for ammunition to push him further. Green watched Omar, trying to sort out the implications of what he'd said. Omar had let a rare glimpse of himself show through. Intelligence, passion, principle. Not a dumb gangsta wannabe, but a young man in search of a cause.

Green headed down the hall and opened the interrogation room door, startling all three of them in the room. Without introducing himself, he leaned on the table. "What violence must stop, Omar?"

Levesque looked outraged, Omar merely bewildered. "Violence everywhere."

"Everywhere? Here in Canada? Africa? The Middle East?"

"Everywhere."

"But some places are worse than others, right? Some countries are worse than others. They hold all the cards—money, power, the biggest armies, the most modern weapons. Right?"

"I don't know what you're talking about."

"How does one simple person like yourself fight all the violence and injustice in the world? You take a stand. You do something, however small, to attack the people who are destroying the world." Green took the only other chair in the room, beside Levesque and opposite Omar. "I understand how it happens. How you feel. You love your mother, and you know she's lived through unspeakable pain. Pain that she took out on you when you were too young and innocent to understand. You saw how your father tried to shield her. But it wasn't enough, was it? The world is full of people doing cruel and violent things to innocent people. Believe me, I understand how that makes a son feel."

Omar was watching him warily. "If you're trying to make me say some people deserve to be punished, sometimes I feel like that, but I resist it. That's how the violence keeps going around. And it still doesn't make me lash out at helpless old men."

"Not helpless. Sam Rosenthal was a fighter. He fought you back."

"He was still an old man."

"He was also a Jew." Green dropped the word like a feather into the silence.

Omar blinked. "A Jew?"

"You knew that. You ripped the religious chain from his neck."

"You think I'd attack him because he was a Jew?"

"A lot of people think the Jews have done some pretty awful things to innocent people."

Beside him, Levesque sucked in her breath. Green forced himself not to look at her. Not to break the spell.

Omar wet his lips. "The Jews have suffered a lot themselves. They're the perfect example of what violence does to people."

"Like your mother."

"Yes, like my mother. I'd never beat up a Jew just because of what they've done."

"How do you know?" Green countered, leaning in. "If you don't remember, how do you know you didn't? Just like your mother, maybe you lost control. You were drunk, wasted, and finally all that anger burst out."

*   *   *

Minutes later Levesque stormed into Green's office, leaving Omar Adams in the interrogation room. Green was on the phone trying to reach Deepak, the head of the Hate Crimes Unit. It was Saturday, but one could always hope. He watched as she wrestled her outrage under control. Caution, and concern for her future, finally won.

"I thought you believed he was innocent, sir. Now you think he's perpetrated a hate crime?"

Deepak's voice mail kicked in. Green hung up and

weighed his thoughts before answering. In fact, he hadn't a clue what the truth was. He had a mystery prostitute with a personal connection to the victim, he had the victim's son on the loose with a secret agenda of his own, he had a known gang member with a history of assault, and now he had a physically and emotionally brutalized young man looking for a scapegoat for his troubles. Green had been prepared to dismiss Omar Adams as a suspect, but now he was not so sure.

In the old days, he would have rehashed the case in detail with Brian Sullivan over a couple of beers and a smoked meat. Thinking of that, his chest tightened. Those days might be gone forever. For now, he was on his own.

Finally, he chose to equivocate. "I'm exploring possibilities, Marie Claire, that's all. These are leads to follow up. Until we know exactly what happened that night and how all the players fit into the picture, we need to keep pursuing all the leads."

"Fine, but I want to detain Mr. Adams in the meantime."

"That's premature."

"With all due respect—"

"First, you need to find David Rosenthal and the mystery prostitute. Now that her photo has been released, we should be hearing from the public any minute. And you need to talk to Deepak of Hate Crimes about Omar."

She glanced at her watch pointedly. The two pink spots of fury on her cheeks were fading, but her tone was icy. "How much more do you want me to do on Saturday afternoon?"

He sighed. Another lost era. Sullivan and he would have stayed on the case until they had personally tracked down the loose ends. They would have hounded colleagues and witnesses and suspects, in their own homes if necessary. But with an effort, he stifled his frustration. That attitude had cost Sullivan dearly. Now even he, Green, had to go home, because Sharon had already left for work and Hannah, the fall-back babysitter, would be drumming her fingers with impatience. Her Saturday social life awaited. And Tony was waiting for his dad to play.

"You can assign those tasks to the weekend staff however you want, just get Hate Crimes started on Omar's background." He stopped abruptly. "When you searched the Adams's house, did you find a computer?"

She shook her head. "They had one, but it was broken."

"All the same, have it brought in and ask the tech guys to search it. Chances are Omar still has an email account and uses the internet at the library or school. He may even have a Facebook or MySpace page. Get the tech guys on that too."

She'd been jotting reluctant notes, but now she frowned. "Why?"

"Because if this guy harbours extremist views, or any views at all regarding politics in the Middle East, they're going to show up somewhere. On chatrooms, listserves, in posts to various websites. A lot of people feel anonymous on the web and feel safe to vent the worst kind of hatred, especially when they're with like-minded individuals. Get Deepak and Criminal Intelligence's help to tell you where to look. They'll know all the Jihadist and Islamist websites. There are thousands."

Her eyebrows shot up. "Now you think he's a terrorist?"

"No, I don't. But he may be a confused, angry young man looking for a place to vent."

She looked doubtful as she wrote in her notebook. "This could take weeks and be a total waste of time."

He merely looked at her, and in the end she slipped her notebook in her purse without further protest. A quick study, he noted with satisfaction, who was learning that in murder, he left no stone unturned.

Nineteen

Sharon stood in the nursing station and studied the inpatient charts with dismay. She had arrived ten minutes early, full of apprehension and resolve. All day she'd been rehearsing how she would handle Caitlin O'Malley. The woman had still been very fragile the night before, but she had been responding to her meds amazingly fast. Perhaps by this afternoon, her thinking would be coherent enough and her paranoia blunted enough that Sharon could ask her straight out about her relationship with Dr. Rosenthal.

She couldn't ask about her presence on Rideau Street or her possible witnessing of his murder, or even about her prostitution activities, because she, Sharon, wasn't supposed to know about any of that. But she could at least ask about Rosenthal himself, whether he'd ever treated her and whether she'd continued to see him. If Caitlin's paranoia didn't kick in, she might even venture further. Her hope was to encourage the woman to go to the police voluntarily and tell them what she knew about that night. If necessary, Sharon would facilitate the contact with Mike. That was far preferable to violating her ethical and legal obligations by informing Mike herself.

When she'd arrived on shift, she'd immediately gone to check Caitlin's chart to see what kind of day the woman had had, only to discover the chart was nowhere to be found.

"Oh, she was discharged today," said the day nurse, who

was just changing into her street shoes to go off duty. "Dr. Janic has the chart."

"Discharged! Already?" Sharon was flabbergasted. The woman had been frankly psychotic only a few days earlier.

The head nurse overheard the comment and drew her aside. "None of us were too happy about it, but the seventy-two-hour assessment period was over. The father called her private psychiatrist, and he told Dr. Janic to sign the discharge papers."

Sharon winced. Dr. Janic was the psychiatric resident on duty over the weekend, a fresh-faced first year ninny with all the experience and common sense of a door knob. The private psychiatrist had seen her only once over the past few days, choosing instead to dictate his orders over the phone. He would have had to take the resident's word for her miraculous recovery.

"Voluntary? Not even a community treatment order?"

The older woman shrugged at the folly of her superiors.

"When did this happen?"

"Just happened. I'm surprised you didn't run into them in the parking lot."

"But why? I mean, why risk her recovery? She's proved she's not too compliant with her meds when she's out."

"Well, that's the thing. The father came in here this afternoon claiming that there had been a mistake, that she had been taking her meds and had missed at most a couple of days—"

"That's not enough to become that ill."

"I know that, and so should he. He's been dealing with her illness for eight years. But whatever his motives, he said she was much better now, but she was upset about being back in hospital. He was sure she would complete her recovery much faster in her own home under their care."

Sharon thought of Caitlin working Rideau Street at two in the morning. "Do they plan to supervise her twenty-four hours a day?"

"He said they would, at least for the next two months to make sure she's okay." The head nurse lowered her voice still further. "Listen, Mr. O'Malley is a lawyer, and he can be very intimidating. Makes you feel like you're on the witness stand being cross-examined. Poor Dr. Janic just rolled over for him. Accepted his assurances and his voiced concern for his daughter."

Something in the nurse's tone caught Sharon's ear. "You don't think it's genuine?"

The head nurse frowned. "Sharon, I never said this, because I can't substantiate a single word. I think something's up. Earlier in the week, when we first called her parents and he came in to see her, he was so grateful she was here and we were taking care of her. You remember how she was raving on. She didn't want to be here, because we were all robots controlled by Lucifer. Her father was very firm. 'You stay, you take the pills they give you, and you tell the doctor everything that's going on.'"

Sharon nodded. She had met the father the day after Caitlin's admission, and he'd been both angry at his daughter and concerned for her recovery. In the past year, she'd been doing so well, he'd said. She wanted some freedom. How could they keep a twenty-eight year old captive in her own home? She was entitled to some life, and her parents wanted her to have some friends, some independence and some goals of her own. They had thought she'd do her part. She'd promised to take her meds and see the doctor regularly.

"I remember the father didn't like being duped," Sharon said. "He'd tried to trust her, and she'd lied."

The head nurse rolled her eyes. "But honestly, what did he expect? She's a paranoid schizophrenic. She's going to lie if she has to in order to keep her secrets. That father still doesn't really understand that his little girl—the intelligent, rational girl whom he still remembers—is no longer there. That the disease and the woman can no longer be separated."

The head nurse's lips were pursed, and behind her wire frame glasses, her eyes were hard. Sharon debated what to say. The woman had seen too many patients come back through the revolving door when fragile psyches were sent out into a world too complex and lonely for them to master. She'd become an exceptional organizer and manager, but she had never been a mother. She'd never had to deal with the emotional yearnings and heartbreak that went along with parenting those fragile souls.

Sharon tried to make her voice soft. "That's because when she's well, that intelligent, rational woman comes back to him, at least in glimpses. And he always hopes she'll stay."

The nurse clucked her tongue. "Wishful thinking, or to be more precise, classic denial. That's what he had in spades today. He came in here on a mission from the moment he got off the elevator. I'm betting Caitlin phoned him and laid on a story about feeling much better—" The nurse paused, her skepticism clearing. "And she *was* better. We were all remarking how well she'd done in such a short time. She was responding appropriately, with no evidence of hallucinations or thought disorder. If she still thought we were robots, she was keeping her opinion to herself. But she was far from out of the woods. That's what paranoids do. The minute they're recompensated enough to pull it together, they hide their craziness. That's where we were with Caitlin today, I'm convinced of it. She still thinks we're robots out to get her, but she's just well enough to be able to fake it. And Daddy, in full denial, bought it hook, line and sinker."

"Well," Sharon said, "as long as she's been discharged with some proper meds and outpatient follow-up—"

"No groups, no outreach, just Daddy's psychiatrist friend."

The nurse's tone said it all. Recovery meant so much more than monitoring of medication. It meant support, encouragement, coaching and even the friendship and understanding of peers. The loving intentions of family were crucial but not enough. Caitlin's history had already proved that.

What now? Sharon thought. She still couldn't tell Mike of the woman's identity without seriously violating patient confidentiality, and with a father like Patrick O'Malley, she wasn't eager to step into that quagmire.

But unless Caitlin was identified soon, Sharon would be faced with an even bigger dilemma. Because now, not only did she know who the mystery hooker in the photo was, but the woman was on the loose again, believing some crazy delusion about an invasion of satanic robots.

*　　*　　*

As Green waited for the elevator, his thoughts already yearned for home. He knew it would be some time yet. He had to visit the injured patrol officer in hospital first, to express his regret and to see how the young man was coping. He had been at Lindsay's side when the poor girl had died, and Green knew the terror of that moment would haunt him long after his broken bones had healed.

After that, there was the Heart Institute before he could even contemplate the comforts of home. How he wished Sharon was there. He wanted to discuss Omar with her in order to get her opinion on his abuse and his repressed rage. Would such a person, passionately committed to the principles of non-violence but faced with impossibly conflicting feelings for the woman who had borne him, who both loved him and hated him, who soothed him and beat him... Would such a man be capable of explosive rage committed in a kind of automaton state? Afterwards, would he block out all memory of the attack, so that he truly believed himself innocent?

Green knew what Sharon would say—an unequivocal yes. He'd watched enough expert psychiatrists on the stand and studied enough abnormal psychology in his graduate criminology courses to know all about the phenomenon of displacement. The technical term for scapegoating, in which a person who can't tolerate their anger at one person, displaces it onto someone else instead. Tyrants the world over used it to keep their restive subjects in line. Hitler had been proof of how well it could work.

Green also knew the mind was capable of amazing distortions. It would block out intolerable memories, and in extreme cases it could literally split itself in parts. Dissociation this severe usually happened only after prolonged, horrific abuse with no means of escape except through detaching oneself mentally from the experience. He wasn't sure he understood it all, but Sharon had described several such patients over the years. Sometimes the abused patients had created alternative personalities, and in less extreme cases they had simply wiped the hours or days of abuse from their memories. Could Omar have done that?

If Omar was charged, the Crown or the Defence might seek formal psychiatric assessment, either as a means of challenging his competence and criminal intent, or as a means of explaining the viciousness of the attack by a heretofore peaceful young man. But meanwhile, in a pinch, Sharon might be able to shed considerable light on the case. He resigned himself to being patient and waiting for her to return home from work.

The elevator door slid open, and Levesque stepped out with a cherubic young man in tow. He was clean-shaven and spit-polished, sporting a navy blue suit and matching powder blue tie, and on his face was a beatific grin that looked pasted on and wobbly at the corners. Levesque herself wore a grin, but hers was real. Triumphant.

Green stood his ground, one hand on the elevator door. "Hello, Sergeant Levesque."

She nodded and tried to sidle past. Green blocked the man and extended his hand. "I'm Inspector Green. And you are...?"

"Adrian Crugar." The man pumped Green's hand, making his teeth rattle.

A scowl replaced Levesque's triumphant grin. "Mr. Crugar thinks he may know the identity of our mystery woman," she muttered.

"Oh?" Green arched an eyebrow. A John perhaps, despite the born-again smile?

"Well, I'm not a hundred per cent sure," Adrian interjected. "It's not a very clear photo, and I haven't seen her in a few years. If it isn't her, I don't want to get her in trouble. She's had more than her share."

Green turned and gestured down the hall toward one of the interview rooms. The squad room was almost empty in the late Saturday afternoon, but there was a lone detective pecking at his computer in the middle. Hoping to pry much more out of him than an identification, Green wanted Adrian Crugar to relax without distractions. As if determined not to let Green take over, Levesque led the way.

Once they were settled in the interview room, Levesque laid the photo on the table. The Ident photographer had done her best to clean up the image, but it was still shadowy. With the woman's face partially obscured by her hair, Green thought a definitive identification might take a miracle.

Adrian was frowning unhappily. "See, she didn't have long hair when I knew her, and she wasn't that thin. It's the way she is holding herself, that tilt of her chin, that makes me think... You don't have any other photos of her I could look at?"

Levesque was shaking her head when Green interrupted. "Maybe you can play him that section of the video tape. Sometimes movement helps."

Adrian's eyes lit up. "Yeah."

Levesque half-rose, looking from Green to Crugar warily. She seemed to find no way to refuse, for she headed out the door. Green reached for her file. A brief glance showed that she'd recorded no details about the young man beyond his name. He clicked open her pen. "Just some information for our records, sir?"

The man supplied his full name, date of birth, an address in the far-flung eastern suburb of Orleans, and employment as an assistant loans officer at Scotiabank in Orleans. The man lives and works in Orleans, Green thought, a long way from the inner city throb of the Byward Market, but only a short hop across the open pastures of the Greenbelt from Beacon Hill. He was about to ask if he ever went to Beacon Hill when the door opened and Levesque reappeared, carrying her laptop and a CD. She shot Green a suspicious look but said nothing.

Together they hunched over the laptop and watched the grainy images move across the screen. As the prostitute appeared, first her stiletto boots, white jeans, stylish shoulder bag and finally her fur jacket and swoop of hair, Green heard Adrian suck in his breath. He sat awhile in silence once the scrap of tape was done.

"Oh, my goodness." Adrian's chin wobbled, and tears brimmed. "What has happened to her?"

"Do you recognize her?" Levesque asked.

He nodded, sucking breath into his lungs. "I think it's Caitlin. I—I gave her that handbag."

"Caitlin who?"

"Well, probably O'Malley now."

"Spell it." Levesque took down every letter. "Do you know her address?"

He shook his head. "I only know her parents' place. They live in Rothwell Heights. Patrick O'Malley is a big name attorney."

Rothwell Heights was an exclusive enclave of wealthy homes on huge natural lots near the Ottawa River. Certainly a neighbourhood befitting a "big name" attorney. More importantly, it was adjacent to Beacon Hill and quite possibly on the same bus route. Patrick O'Malley's name rang a loud bell in Green's memory. A specialist in personal injury litigation, Patrick O'Malley sued people for a living, which would go far towards financing a home in Rothwell Heights. There was another distant bell ringing in Green's memory as well, but he couldn't place it. Annoyed, he rifled through his thoughts.

"How do you know Caitlin O'Malley?" Levesque was asking.

"I used to be married to her. The smartest, most exciting girl I've ever known. We were both too young, and her father never approved. Caitlin had...a gift, but she couldn't always harness it. It scared her sometimes, overwhelmed her and threw her off course." He paused, his eyes narrowing at the pain of the memory. "She developed a few problems, and her father had a different idea of how to help her. I thought a loving husband, a supportive community and a trust in God's greater plan would get her through it, but her father wanted her stuffed full of drugs."

Green started as the memory clicked into place. Caitlin O'Malley! One of the six beneficiaries of Rosenthal's will! His thoughts raced afield.

Levesque did not appear to have made the connection as she plowed ahead. "Do you know anything about her recent activities? Her current whereabouts?"

Adrian shook his head. "I haven't seen her in four years. She had a breakdown, and her father took me to court. He had himself declared responsible for her health care and got a court order barring me from seeing her. I was a danger to her health and safety." A flash of anger tightened Adrian's jaw, but he quickly quelled it. "That made the breakdown so much worse. I loved her. I never made her feel like a failure the way her father did. Who was to say she was crazy? All through history, God has spoken to a select few. We used to call them saints, not lunatics."

Levesque pursed her lips. "Yes, but science—"

Green nudged her foot imperceptibly, but Adrian was not distracted. "Definitions only. Evil is in all of us. Caitlin felt so alone trying to fight it until she met me. When she lost me..." He took a deep, steadying breath to fight back fresh tears. "I'm sorry, this is something that has haunted me for years. I should have fought harder for her, but I was just out of school, and I had no money and no friends in the courts like he had. But I think when she lost me—when I gave up the fight—she lost her only friend. Her only hope." He gestured weakly to the laptop screen. "And now look at her."

Green tried to recall what else he knew about Patrick

O'Malley. The man was a local success story and philanthropist who'd been consolidating his network of friends in high places since his early years at St. Patrick's, once Ottawa's most prestigious Catholic college. Adrian Crugar wouldn't have stood a chance.

Masking his excitement, he stepped into the silence. "What was her diagnosis, do you know?"

Adrian dragged himself back from the past to focus on Green's words. "Lots of them. Schizophrenic, bipolar, borderline—whatever that is. How she hated the labels and all the different meds the doctors tried. They made her fat, they gave her the shakes, they made her feel weird inside. She was afraid they were killing her brain cells."

"Does the name Dr. Samuel Rosenthal mean anything to you?"

"The man who was murdered?" When Green nodded, he shook his head.

"He was never one of her treating psychiatrists?"

"Not that I know of. But once her father cut me off, I never knew what was going on. Friends would pass stuff on, rumours they'd heard. She's back in school, she's earned her PhD, she's on the streets. It seemed like a real roller coaster. She probably had lots of psychiatrists, because I'm sure Mr. O'Malley fired them every time she had trouble. Dr. Rosenthal could have been one of them."

Green studied the man closely. He looked genuinely distressed, and he had one of those open, honest faces that made lying impossible. Yet there was something... something he was holding back. "What else do you want to tell us?" he asked gently.

Adrian dropped his gaze. Flushed. "She phoned me six months ago, the first time in four years. I didn't speak to her.

I was out, and she left a message on my machine. She sounded good, she said she wanted me to know she was doing well and finally taking charge of her life. She'd found her own lawyer and was going to stand up to her father. That was all."

"Did you call her back?"

He flushed even more deeply. "I was just starting a new relationship, and I thought... God help me, Caitlin can be so draining. But the new relationship didn't work out, and when I went to return her call, the number was out of service."

Twenty

Levesque navigated the unmarked Impala with one hand. A misty drizzle coated the landscape in a drab grey sheen, and Green peered through the rain-spattered windshield, trying to read the house numbers.

It had been Levesque's idea to pay a cold call to Caitlin O'Malley's father, even though evening was almost upon them, her daughter's skates were a distant memory, and she claimed to have a dinner engagement. Green had been champing at the bit to follow up on Adrian Crugar's lead, but once they'd escorted the young man out, he had deliberately refrained from suggesting it. Mary Sullivan's indictment still rang in his ears. "You demanded it!" His obsession had already cost his friend dearly. Nothing on the job was worth that price.

Whether Levesque had sensed his underlying impatience to follow up or whether she herself had caught the bug, this time it was she who was not content to delegate the job, she who insisted on doing it herself.

Police work did not often bring Green into the cluster of winding, hilly streets known as Rothwell Heights, where sprawling mansions were tucked artfully into the hillsides, camouflaged by huge trees and sweeping gardens. Green thought of the decayed, litter-strewn corner where Screech and the mystery hooker spent their nights. If Caitlin O'Malley was that woman, her life had gone into free fall.

Mental illness could do that, of course.

"Here it is," Levesque said as she drew to a stop at the curb. Green looked at the house, a rambling, west-coast style bungalow set well back from the road. Behind it, thick woods dropped away into a ravine of reds and golds muted under the grey sky. A silver BMW sports car sat in the driveway in front of the three-car garage. Green scanned the windows but saw no movement behind the sheer curtains as he and Levesque strode up to the door.

"Your call," he said quietly as they rang the bell, sending a melodic church bell peeling through the house. A small dog set up a frenzied barking, obscuring all other sound. No one answered the door, however. Green stepped back to peer in the front bay window while Levesque leaned once more on the bell. The dog reached a frantic pitch just inside, partially masking the sound of the automatic garage door. The roar of a car startled them, and they swung around to see a late model Lexus SUV shoot backwards down the drive and swerve into the street, narrowly missing their Impala. Green caught a brief glimpse of a thin, long-haired woman behind the wheel.

"*Sacrifice!*" Levesque shouted, sprinting back down to the Impala. She had started the engine and was gunning away from the curb before Green could even yank his door shut. He clung to the shoulder handle while she slewed through the twists of the winding road. The tires slithered as they struggled for purchase on the pavement slick with rain and sodden leaves.

Thankfully, because of the rain, there were no pets or small children to contend with, but Levesque had to dodge the occasional bike, each time with a muttered "*calice*" or "*tabernac*". Green refrained from advice. She was a good driver; she kept the Lexus in view but made no attempt to catch it.

There were few access roads out of this maze of streets, and no matter where the woman fled, she would likely end up at the same intersection. Green dialled the com centre and requested back-up to intercept the Lexus once it reached the major arterial of Blair Road. Levesque relaxed marginally but still drove hunched forward, gripping the wheel with both hands. She risked a glance at Green.

"You think it was Caitlin?"

"I couldn't tell," he said, "but it's a strong possibility. People don't usually take off on the police unless they have something to hide."

She was silent while she negotiated a four-way stop sign. The Lexus had blown right through it, but cross traffic stopped Levesque from taking the same risk. The Lexus disappeared from view up ahead.

"I wonder how she knew we were police," she mused as she gunned forward again.

Green didn't bother to answer. Plain clothes and an unmarked car did not disguise the aura of authority that street people and criminals instinctively seemed to recognize on sight. Perhaps as an attractive young woman, Levesque had encountered that less often, but Sullivan could not step into a room without everyone falling silent.

On the straight stretch of road up ahead, the Lexus was visible again, along with the stop sign marking Blair Road. Green frowned. There was still no sign of police cruisers. The Lexus approached the stop sign, where two cars waited ahead of her. Cross traffic streamed by, sparse but steady. Green sucked in his breath as the Lexus brake lights came on and it slewed sideways. He could imagine the panicked driver fighting with the wheel. As it hurtled towards the cars at the stop sign, the Lexus jumped the curb, ran through a hedge and a signpost, and flew off the curb again. It landed with a thump on Blair Road, inches in front of a delivery truck. Horns blared and tires screamed. The Lexus roared ahead.

Levesque raced towards the stop sign, where the two cars still sat as if stunned. She glanced across at Green, seeking permission. Still no cruiser in sight, which was hardly a surprise. In this remote corner of the city, hemmed in by the sprawling National Research Complex, the Ottawa River and the Greenbelt, a routine patrol car was likely to pass by less than once a week.

He shrugged. "Go for it. She's already paved the way."

Levesque flicked on her emergency lights and deftly steered towards the demolished hedge. Broken branches tore at the undercarriage, but she managed to avoid the signpost, which was bent in two. She swerved back onto the road in front of the startled driver of a Hyundai.

Green was already studying the map, tracing their route north towards the Ottawa River. "She's not going far. Blair Road dead-ends just before the parkway. Unless she wants to get trapped in another maze of residential crescents, she'll end up—" He broke off as they crested the hill just in time to see her brake lights disappearing down a small road on the left.

Levesque cursed. "Where does that go?"

He squinted at the map. "Under the parkway to a parking lot by the river. There's nothing there but a boat ramp and bike trail through the bush."

"Not much of an escape plan." Levesque muttered as she swerved onto the side road.

They found her in the parking lot, standing on the boat ramp in the rain, peering out into the roiling chop of the river. She turned at the sound of gravel crunching under their wheels and watched without moving as they climbed out of the car.

The woman was tall and slender, dressed in an elegant, red leather coat and hastily wound white silk scarf that did nothing to offset her pale, pinched face. At first glance, the resemblance to the photo was so strong that Green thought it was Caitlin, but as he drew closer, he could make out crow's feet around her eyes and deeply etched furrows in her brow.

"Mrs. O'Malley?" he guessed, extending his hand. Beside him, Levesque had her badge ready.

The woman glanced at the badge and Green's hand but said nothing. Her nostrils flared with fear, but her scowl was defiant. A strong odour of Scotch wafted around her.

"I'm Inspector Green, and this is my colleague Sergeant Levesque." He made a show of glancing up at the damp sky. "Let's speak inside my vehicle."

"Why were you chasing me?" she demanded.

"Why were you running?" Levesque countered. Not the approach Green would have used, but he resisted the urge to glare at her.

"Because you were chasing me."

"You didn't answer the door," Levesque said. "You sneaked out and took off—"

"I didn't know you were the police!" the woman snapped. "Not until I saw your red flashing lights."

"Who did you think we were?"

Mrs. O'Malley clamped her jaw shut. She was trembling in her thin leather coat. Green stepped in front of Levesque and took the frightened woman's elbow. "Come, let's talk in the car."

This time the woman responded and allowed him to guide her into the rear of the Impala. He slipped in beside her, leaving Levesque no choice but the front seat. She twisted around and draped her arm over the seat back, scowling.

In the small confines of the car, the smell of booze was

almost dizzying. Black mascara was smudged beneath her eyes, but otherwise she wore no make-up. Her brown hair, long and uncombed, showed half an inch of grey roots. Green could see the telltale web of broken capillaries in her eyes and across her cheeks. Drink had been this woman's companion for a long time. He tried for a gentle smile. "Why don't you start at the beginning? Why were you afraid of someone coming to the door?"

"What is this—good cop, bad cop?"

"You're not in trouble, Mrs. O'Malley. We were simply coming to your house to ask about your daughter Caitlin."

The woman heaved a deep, defeated groan. "So you've identified her."

He nodded. "We want to talk to her about an incident she may have witnessed—"

"Dr. Rosenthal's murder."

"Did you know him?"

She shook her head. "We saw the news clip."

"He wasn't one of the psychiatrists who treated your daughter over the years?"

"You make that sound like she's a revolving door," she snapped, then dropped her gaze to wipe a rain drop off her jacket. "Which she was. A revolving door with more advice and prescriptions than we knew what to do with."

"Did he treat her?"

Vague apprehension flitted across her face, as if some ill-defined fear were niggling. "Not unless she saw him during one of her more outlandish stints when she wouldn't talk to us for months on end."

"Do you know what she was doing on Rideau Street on the night he was killed?"

She swallowed and ran her tongue around her chapped lips,

as if yearning for a drink. "My daughter is a very ill woman. She has battled schizophrenia for eight years, and sometimes it makes her turn on those who care about her the most. My husband used to comb the streets for her, staying out all night. He visited the shelters and volunteered at the Shepherds of Good Hope, thinking maybe someday he'd look up from his soup pot, and there she'd be. Every time we heard of a car accident or rape or unidentified overdose, we'd be terrified."

Green waited while the woman brushed every rain drop from her coat and scrubbed at an invisible stain. "I suppose she was...soliciting again. It paid the bills. We stopped giving her money, because she'd give it all away to every bum and addict she came across. Or she'd buy something ridiculous like a mink coat that would be stolen the next day. One of her psychiatrists explained that soliciting gives Caitlin some independence. Some power, for God's sake. We tried everything to stop it. Community treatment orders that she ignored, fancy private hospitals in the U.S. We even had her committed to an institution for awhile, so at least she'd be cared for, but in the final analysis, we decided we had only two options. Bar her from the house and live in constant fear of a phone call from you folks or the morgue, or let her come and go on her own terms."

"So does she live at home?"

"We still keep her room ready, but she's more an occasional visitor. My husband still tries. He still tries to reason with her. I..." The woman pressed her eyes shut and waved a dismissive hand. "Some days I'm beyond caring any more. But it's hard for a father to accept his little princess selling her body on the street."

Green felt a wave of sorrow for them both. He remembered his own desperation when Hannah had been out of control, staying out all night, sleeping with God knows what pimply-faced punk, and swallowing dangerous drugs by the handful. Through perseverance, patience, and a hope he often doubted, she'd come around. However, she did not have a mind-altering illness.

"Was she at home when we called at the house just now?" Levesque asked, and Green saw the implication he'd overlooked, that perhaps the mother had fled to draw the police away from her daughter. But Mrs. O'Malley shook her head. Offered no alternative.

"Do you know where she is?"

"No."

"She's not in trouble," Green said. "If fact, if she saw something, she may be in danger."

The woman stiffened. "Why?"

Green didn't answer but instead took a guess. "She has been in touch, hasn't she? Is she scared?"

He could see the woman teetering on the brink. She looked exhausted from years of battling the complexities of her daughter's psyche.

"We only want to help her," Levesque interjected, just as the woman began moving her lips. Mrs. O'Malley shot her a disbelieving look and pressed her lips closed. Inwardly, Green cursed.

"I don't know where she is," Mrs. O'Malley said. "But she would be scared. She would have seen her picture splashed all over the news, and she'd know that every police officer on every corner would be looking for her." A ghost of a smile twitched her lips. "A paranoid's nightmare."

"Where would she go if she was on the run?" Green asked.

"I don't know that she's on the run. I just know how her mind works. She'll think nowhere is safe. She has a thing about satellite surveillance, Google Earth, wireless signals. She thinks they're all part of the Devil's network, and we're fools not to be suspicious. Sometimes she even convinces me. Besides..." She paused, doubt flickering in her bloodshot blue eyes.

"Besides what?"

"Did you guys phone this morning, looking for her?"

Green's senses grew alert. "It wasn't us. Who phoned?"

"I don't know. Some man with a big, booming voice who said he was an old friend of Caitlin's." She grunted. "That put me on guard immediately. Caitlin doesn't have any old friends whom she hasn't driven away with her craziness."

"Was there a caller ID?"

"It said 'private caller'. Normally I don't answer, but Patrick wanted to keep the line open in case—" She broke off, but Green understood. Against all rationality, you hope they'll call.

"What time was this?"

"Eleven thirty. Just before I usually walk the dog."

Green and Levesque exchanged glances. Eleven thirty was after the internal police bulletin had been issued but before the photo had been circulated to the media. Someone had known her name and address even before seeing the photo. Green asked Mrs. O'Malley to repeat the conversation as precisely as she could.

"Not much of a conversation. He asked if she still lived there, and when I asked who he was, he said he was an old friend who really wanted to get in touch with her, and did I know where he could reach her. I said she hadn't been in touch for some time, but he didn't sound as if he believed me. He said that doesn't sound like Caitlin, which is when I knew he was lying, because it's exactly like Caitlin. He had a loud voice and a laugh that sounded forced. I admit I was unnerved. I waited quite awhile before I took the dog out. When I came back, as I was walking up the street, I saw a car parked in front of the house. Was that one of yours?"

"What kind of car?" Green asked, his mind exploring possibilities.

"A regular car. Dark green. I'm not good with makes, but I don't think it was out of the ordinary."

"Did you see anyone in it?"

She nodded. "I gather that wasn't you people? I could make out someone in the driver's seat, but from where I was, that was all. The windows were tinted."

"What happened next?"

"I stayed where I was. Pretended Zoë was doing her business. He stayed a couple of minutes and then he drove off really fast."

"He?"

"It certainly looked like a man. I had a quick glimpse of him climbing into the car when I first rounded the corner. I think he may have rung the doorbell. But it was alarming how he sat there afterwards, as if he were spying." She pressed a shaky hand to her lips. "I've always feared that some day one of the unsavoury characters my daughter consorts with..."

Green felt a flood of understanding. No wonder the woman had fled when he and Levesque came calling. "Did you report this to the police?"

"No, Patrick didn't think it was worthwhile. Anyway, right after that we saw Caitlin's photo on TV, and we figured that perhaps it was the police. But if it wasn't..."

"Your husband was home at the time of this visit?"

"Yes, but he was in the backyard planting tulip bulbs, and he didn't hear the bell."

Green thought of the silver sports car in the drive. "Is he

home now? Perhaps he saw something useful."

She shook her head. "He went out right after we saw the story on TV. Probably out looking for her." She paused, vague apprehension crossing her face again. "I think the strange visit worried him."

Him and me both, Green thought. "Can you tell us anything at all about the man? Such as his clothes or his voice? Did he sound old or young on the phone? Did he use sophisticated language or..."

"He sounded plain. Rather like a used car salesman. Although..." She cocked her head. "It's nothing I can put my finger on, but he seemed to have a very slight accent. I couldn't tell you what kind."

Twenty-One

The setting sun was peeking out from under the cloud cover by the time Levesque and Green had finished with Mrs. O'Malley and headed back downtown to the station. The whole sky was an eerie pink. Green spent the drive on his cellphone, trying to track down the dark green car. Neither the families of Omar Adams or Nadif Hassan owned such a car, but David Rosenthal was still a mystery. He and his white van were registered at the hotel he had given to the crash investigators, but neither had been seen all day.

Green had a bad feeling about the stranger who had come looking for Caitlin. Had the police's own efforts to identify her on the street tipped off the killer that she might be a threat? Had the police inadvertently placed her in harm's way? Once they arrived back at the station, he sent Levesque home to her dinner engagement while he headed straight down to speak to the duty sergeant for the Central District.

"We need to step up our efforts to find this young woman. We now have a name—Caitlin O'Malley—and a possible street name, Foxy." He handed his colleague a new photo that Mrs. O'Malley had given him of Caitlin smiling in her graduation photo. Although not classically pretty, the young woman looked proud and full of hope. The sergeant studied the photo, his expression softening. Within minutes, he had it scanned and sent out to the in-car computers.

"You figure she's downtown somewhere?" he asked.

"She's probably on the run, but her mother swears they haven't seen her or given her money, so I figure she'll be trying to make some. The fastest means she knows is soliciting, so that's where we should concentrate our efforts. The Byward, Vanier, maybe even as far west as Gladstone and Hintonburg." Green stopped to consider other avenues open to them. "We should assume she knows we're looking for her, but she doesn't know that someone else is looking for her too. I don't know if she's streetwise enough to figure that out. I also don't know how rational she is. She may be right out of her tree."

"Dangerous?"

"Well, she is a paranoid schizophrenic, so depending on how she's interpreting things... The mother says she's never been violent, but maybe she's never been this frightened before. It appears that she and Dr. Rosenthal were close. If she did witness something last Saturday night, she may have become completely unhinged."

"Gotcha." The sergeant reached for his computer again. "I'm going to send out special instructions to the guys to make sure they get back-up before approaching her. And to take her to Emerg if she loses it, instead of bringing her here."

Green turned to leave. He felt bone-tired. "I want to be informed the minute you have any word."

"What about her home? You want some surveillance on that in case she goes there?"

Green weighed the pros and cons. A car, even an unmarked one, would be so conspicuous on that quiet street that it would likely scare Caitlin off entirely. At the end of the afternoon discussion, the mother had seemed convinced of the possible danger to her daughter and of the police's desire to help. She had his cellphone number and had promised to contact him if she had any news.

On the other hand, parents often had their own solutions. "Do regular drive-bys, and if Patrol spots any signs of unusual activity, phone me."

Finally, gratefully, Green headed out into the night. He stopped first at the General Hospital to visit the young patrol officer and was relieved to find him in fairly good spirits, surrounded by flowers and cards. The mood was less upbeat at the Heart Institute. Sullivan was dozing and not to be disturbed. He'd been agitated and medically unstable much of the day, prompting the doctor to order more sedation and slap a ban on visitors outside the immediate family.

"His wife's on guard in the lounge," said the nurse with a knowing tilt of her head towards the waiting room. "No one's getting past her, least of all you."

"But his health—is it improving?"

"He's stable now. That's good news. Beyond that, you'll have to speak to his wife."

Green steeled himself. He was frayed and exhausted, the adrenaline of the hunt still pumping uselessly through his veins. He doubted he had the strength for Mary's rage, yet he owed her that. He owed Sullivan that.

She was curled in a soft-backed vinyl chair by the wall, her head propped on a pillow and a hospital blanket draped over her. She'd made no effort with her make-up or hair, leaving her vulnerability on show. She looked asleep, oblivious to the couple who chatted quietly in the opposite corner, but when Green entered the room, her eyes flew open. She stared at him, her expression cold.

"How are you holding up, Mary?"

"He's had a bad day, thanks to you."

"I know." He sat down opposite her. "He would have heard it on TV anyway. I'm glad I was there, to give some perspective."

"We wanted forty-eight hours, Mike. So his heart wouldn't go haywire."

"Did it?"

Her lips drew tight. "No. We were lucky, if you can call it that."

"He's a strong man, Mary. He's survived this, he came out of the coma without any obvious damage, his heart is hanging in—"

"But he'll never be the same." She threw off her blanket and leaned forward. "Whatever you do, let him make the decisions he has to about his future. This is not about you this time, Mike. So you just step out of the way. Be a friend. If you know how."

He told himself it was Mary's fear talking. She had nearly lost her husband, and now she was fighting tooth and nail to keep him safe. But her words were still smarting when he arrived home to be greeted by an exuberant four-year-old, a large dog wagging her tail shyly, and a teenage daughter all dressed up and ready to go out the door.

Hannah stiffened when he wrapped her in his arms, but she was too startled to protest. He kissed her head as he pressed her close. She had cost him many sleepless nights, but slowly an intelligent, self-sufficient young woman was emerging. Considering the parent-child minefield of broken lives and hopes, he was incredibly lucky to have her.

"It's been a really rough couple of days," he said when he could trust himself. "Thank you for helping out. And for being you."

She twisted away to peer at him dubiously. The black eyeliner was back tonight, but not the death's door make-up. "It's okay, Mike. Do you need me tonight?"

It was on the tip of his tongue to say, "I could use the company," but instead he shook his head. Ruffled his son's dark hair. "No, we'll manage. Go have a good time."

She paused on the threshold, and he wondered if there was a hint of reluctance in her parting. Had he made a mistake in sending her away?

More likely wishful thinking, he decided as he fetched Modo's leash and Tony's jacket, and the three of them set off for a walk. The rain had blown over, leaving another starlit night with a threat of frost. Tony held his hand and skipped along the sidewalk, chattering about the Nintendo Wii his friend had just received for his birthday and reminding Green that his own birthday was less than two months away. Four years old, and already the gaming culture had its hold.

Avoiding Snakes and Ladders this time, father and son spent the evening building an elaborate space station from the hundreds of lego pieces that littered the living room floor. Throughout it all and the bedtime stories that followed, Green kept half an ear tuned for his cellphone, hoping for news that Caitlin O'Malley had been found. By midnight, he figured the prostitution street scene should be at its height, and he struggled to stay awake. Modo was snoozing at his feet, and *The Daily Show* was blaring from the TV when Sharon arrived home. She kicked off her shoes and peered into the living room, smiling in surprise.

"You're still awake!"

"I'm waiting for some news from Patrol." He muted the television. Stifling a yawn, he ambled stiffly over to kiss her.

She seemed distracted. "Why?"

He returned to sink back on the sofa with a sigh. "We've identified that woman in the photo you saw last night, but we haven't found her. I have Uniforms out scouring known prostitution areas."

"So she is a prostitute."

He shook his head. "She's actually a math PhD, but she's

mentally ill. She turns to prostitution sometimes when she's on the street."

Sharon slowly uncoiled her scarf from her neck. "Did you check her home?"

"Her parents haven't seen her. That's not unusual, according to the mother."

She hung up her scarf and jacket. "Is it so urgent? I mean that you have an APB out on her?"

"Someone else is apparently looking for her too. It may be the killer looking to eliminate a witness. We need to find her first."

Sharon said nothing as she disappeared into the kitchen. He checked his phone yet again to make sure the battery was still charged. She reappeared with a dish of ice cream and a glass of red wine. "Want some?"

He shook his head. "My mind is fried as it is."

She sat down beside him and ate a spoonful of ice cream. She looked worried, and he brushed a lock of hair from her eyes. "Hard shift?"

"I've been wondering whether to tell you this. It's kind of unethical—well, no, it *is* unethical. That woman's name, is it Caitlin O'Malley?"

He swung on her, eyes wide. "You know her?"

"She was admitted to Six North this week. She's the one I mentioned to you, who came in through emergency, off her meds and extremely agitated."

He sat up excitedly and reached for his phone. "I should call the hospital to put some protection on her."

She laid a hand on his arm. "No, Mike. Wait."

"I won't say you told me, honey. In fact I'll get Levesque to make the call. But bottom line, I don't want anyone getting to her."

Sharon had been shaking her head impatiently. "She's

gone. She was discharged this afternoon."

He was flabbergasted. "After less than a week?"

"The nurses were equally appalled, believe me, but her father assured us he could take care of her."

"Her father!"

She nodded. "He came and signed her out this afternoon."

"What time?"

"Just before my shift. About two thirty."

Green's mind raced over the time line. That was before his encounter with Caitlin O'Malley's mother. Either the woman didn't know what her husband had done and they hadn't arrived home yet, or she'd been lying through her teeth.

Whichever the case, the parents had some explaining to do. More than six hours had elapsed since his conversation with Mrs. O'Malley. Six hours for Patrick to arrive home with Caitlin, six hours for them to settle her in and take stock. Mrs. O'Malley had Green's phone number and knew damn well that he was waiting for news on Caitlin's whereabouts.

He reached for his phone again and this time dialled the official surveillance unit. These guys knew how to be inconspicuous. No suits, no late-model, spit-polished Impalas. They would pick a vehicle to blend in.

The sergeant on duty sounded harried. Saturday night was a busy one in surveillance.

"Have you got bodies you can spare?"

"Life or death?" the sergeant grumbled.

Green chuckled. "Maybe. I want unmarked surveillance on Patrick O'Malley's house on Rothwell Drive, and I want a notation of every single movement inside the house, upstairs and down."

Twenty-Two

For the second day in a row, Green was up at seven a.m., this time dragging himself downstairs and fumbling around the kitchen to brew sufficient caffeine to sustain him. His dreams had once again been tortured by visions of the crash, of Lindsay's crushed body and Sullivan's grey face. He forced them aside with an effort and slumped at the table with a huge mug of French roast in his hand, trying to sort out the priorities of the morning. Despite his worries about Sullivan and the young patrolman, and his concern for Lindsay Corsin's family, he realized, once enough caffeine had penetrated his neurons, that safety of the public came first. He phoned downtown to get an update on the surveillance of Caitlin O'Malley's house.

There was not much news. The surveillance team reported that the lights were out when they arrived, and although they had come on briefly in a downstairs room at 2:36, 3:20 and 4:57 a.m., no one had entered or left the premises all night.

Someone had a restless night, Green thought, which was hardly surprising under the circumstances. Through the sheer curtains, the surveillance team had been able to establish the movement of at least two people inside, but not three. The team also reported one vehicle visible in the driveway—a BMW sports car registered to Patrick O'Malley. The garage doors were closed, however, and Green knew the Lexus was probably inside. The Motor Vehicle Licensing

Bureau listed a third vehicle in the family, this one a Lincoln Town car registered to the law firm of O'Malley, Hendrickson and Potts. Without a search warrant or a clandestine peek, however, there was no way to determine whether it was also in the garage.

Green sipped his coffee, considering the facts. The vehicles were in exactly the same configuration as yesterday. The surveillance team had seen no usual activity at the house, other than evidence that someone had been awake a few times. Furthermore, they had seen only two people, not three. Was Caitlin even there?

Abruptly, another sinister possibility jumped into his mind. What if Caitlin had not left the hospital with her father after all? Someone else had been looking for her yesterday, someone who was tall and drove a dark green sedan.

On impulse, he looked up the O'Malley phone number and dialled. The phone rang four times before switching to voicemail. Green listened to a man's clipped, authoritative voice and left a message asking them to call him immediately. Afterwards he hung up, feeling queasy. He needed to know if Caitlin was safe. If the O'Malleys refused to cooperate, another search warrant would be needed to confirm that Caitlin was being sequestered there. No judge—no matter how police-friendly—would take on O'Malley, Hendrickson and Potts without considerably more ammunition.

Sharon came into the kitchen, poured herself some coffee and tossed the morning *Citizen* on the table. "Caitlin's front page news."

Green snatched up the paper. There, above the fold on the first page, was the fuzzy video photo along with the caption "Police seek woman as possible witness to slaying". The article itself, short on facts but long on speculation, included the hint that the woman was a known prostitute hiding from gang members implicated in the murder. "Caitlin O'Malley, only child of prominent Rothwell Heights attorney Patrick O'Malley, is a troubled woman grappling with health issues," the article said.

"Who gave them this shit!" Green exclaimed, thrusting the paper aside in alarm. It was an empty question. Like cops, reporters had their own network of informants on the street. Now, because of their hunger for headlines, not only did the actual killer know there was a potential eyewitness to the killing, but he had her name and picture, along with a fairly good lead on her location.

"The man who picked up Caitlin yesterday—are the nurses sure it was her father?"

Sharon frowned at him, puzzled. "Well, I wasn't there but—"

"What did he look like?"

"I don't know, Mike, but surely..." Sharon's eyes widened. "You think someone else took her? But—but Caitlin's father is well known. He visited every day, and he's a prominent lawyer in town. Who would be brazen enough to pull that off?"

"I don't know if anyone did. I just can't confirm she's at home right now."

"But why would she go off with a man pretending to be her father? She's paranoid—she'd never go along with it."

Green snatched up the phone again and dialled the Major Crimes Unit. He was lucky enough to snag Gibbs just coming in.

"Pull a photo of Patrick O'Malley off the internet and show it to the nurses who were on day shift at the Rideau Psychiatric Hospital yesterday. We need him confirmed as the man who signed Caitlin O'Malley out."

After he'd signed off, he felt Sharon's incredulous gaze

upon him. "This is crazy. Who else could it be? It would have to be someone white and middle-aged. Your main suspects are young and black."

"The most obvious person is David Rosenthal, the dead man's son. He's a completely unknown entity in this whole situation. We do know he was estranged from his father and anxious to get his hands on his money. He did not appear to know his father had changed his will, and he became outraged when he learned he was getting nothing. I think he was at the O'Malley house yesterday, looking for Caitlin." He considered what little he knew about David Rosenthal. "He's a man of tremendous physical strength, quite capable of beating someone to death. He's also a man of action, used to going after what he wants. But..." Green shook his head slowly. "I didn't get any sense of guilt or regret from him. If he'd killed his father, I'd expect some distress."

"Unless he's a psychopath."

Green pondered the idea. Despite all David's arrogance and contempt for lesser beings, Green had a secret liking for the man. Perhaps liking was too strong a word. Esteem. David had been the first on the spot to save Sullivan's life and had stayed around to see how all the victims were faring before he dropped out of sight again. Surely those were signs of a man who cared.

Yet psychopaths made excellent heroes, because they were without fear and acted without the complex self-doubts that hampered more sensitive people. Furthermore, a display of caring would be well within the acting range of an intelligent psychopath. Perhaps Green was blinded by the man's heroic gesture that had saved his friend's life.

Green contacted Gibbs again, relieved to catch the young detective before he headed out to Rideau Psychiatric. "Who else is there in the squad room?"

"Just Sergeant Collins."

Green hesitated. It would take too long to brief Collins on the background of the case and would tread too hard on Levesque's toes. Levesque was probably still in bed sleeping off the effects of her hot date. The woman was entitled to some time free of the job.

"When you're finished at the hospital, I want you to do some background inquiries on David Rosenthal. First I want to know exactly when he crossed the border and secondly if he has any history of violent or criminal activity in the U.S." True psychopaths had trouble keeping their nature completely under wraps and often had a chequered history of driving violations, neighbourhood conflicts and minor disputes. The United States' patchwork of law enforcement jurisdictions would make it a nightmare to track them down, but if anyone could, it was Gibbs.

"On Sunday, sir?"

Green knew the dismay had nothing to do with laziness. Official agencies would be on skeleton staff. "Do what you can. Oh! And check with the Rent-Me car agency to see if he exchanged a white van for a dark green sedan yesterday."

A brief silence. "W-would it be all right, sir, if Detective Peters came in to help me? She likes t-to be busy."

Another reason for Gibbs' reluctance, Green realized, reminding himself that all his detectives had lives. Including himself, he thought when he hung up to find Sharon eyeing him dubiously.

"A dark green sedan? Sounds like a Le Carré novel."

"A man driving a dark green sedan paid a visit to the O'Malley house yesterday. Spooked the mother out completely."

Sharon sipped her coffee. "But that could be anyone. A door-to-door salesman or canvasser for charity."

"It could be, but Mrs. O'Malley didn't seem to think so."

Sharon looked skeptical, a sentiment he was beginning to share. This was turning into a bad spy novel with a young woman in peril and mysterious figures slipping in and out of the shadows. Had Caitlin left the hospital with her father, or had she been abducted by another white, middle-aged man? Was that the same man who had called at her home earlier in a dark green sedan, or were there two different men both out to get her? What for? To find out what she knew? To protect her, or to silence her?

Equally important, how did this mystery man know who and where she was, even before her photo had been released to the media?

"Did Caitlin have any visitors other than her parents during her stay at Rideau Psychiatric?" he asked.

"What, like a young black male wearing a hoodie and giant shoes?"

He laughed. "Anyone."

"Not that I know of. Just her father, who came every night."

"Could someone have called to ask how she was?"

"Yes, but they would get no information, not even confirmation that she was there."

He turned the problem over and over in his mind. It was probably a wild goose chase, but he had to explore it. "Let's assume the killer realized that a prostitute working that street corner had witnessed the murder. He'd be trying to find her. He'd ask around on the street and probably come back to see if he could find her another night. But how would he know she was at Rideau Psychiatric?"

Sharon's face registered a belated memory. "Well, Mike, you guys arrested her. Picked her up in the market a couple of days later. Lots of bystanders probably witnessed that."

He stared at her. "What? The Ottawa Police?"

"Yes. She was agitated and ranting, scaring passersby with stories of blood and Satan. Eventually you guys shipped her to Emerg."

Green slammed his hand on the table. "Why the fuck did no one tell me! What kind of morons do we have on Patrol that they didn't think there was a connection? We're turning over rocks looking for a hooker in the market, and meanwhile they've just picked up one who's ranting about blood?" He was about to grab the phone again, this time to ream out the duty sergeant of Central Division, but he stopped himself and forced a couple of deep breaths. He began to cobble together the chain of events.

"There were probably lots of witnesses to this arrest, maybe even the killer himself. That may in fact be how he knew Caitlin was a threat to him. It would be reasonable for him to assume the patrol officers took her to Emerg, also reasonable to assume she'd be transferred to a psychiatric facility."

"Rideau Psychiatric is the biggest facility," Sharon added.

He nodded. "But how would he know where to find her, without her name?"

"Maybe by checking out each ward," she said. "He could pretend to be visiting someone else. It might take him a few days, but once he saw her, he'd have his answer."

"And her name?"

Sharon shrugged. "It depends how resourceful he is, and how trustworthy he looks."

Green pictured David Rosenthal, white, middle-aged, and well-educated, striding confidently onto a ward with a clipboard in hand and a doctor title to back him up. "I bet he could just ask," he said.

Screech snarled and yanked his new sleeping bag more tightly over his head. Green squatted at his side, balancing a fresh cup of Tim Hortons coffee in one hand as he shook the man's shoulder with the other.

"Screech, wake up."

"Fuck off!"

Green pulled the sleeping bag back to uncover the old vagrant, who pressed his eyes shut against the invading sunlight. Dried spittle flecked his beard, and yellow mucous oozed from his eyes. Green held the coffee under his nose.

"Foxy needs your help. She may be in danger. I need your eyes on the street, so sit up and take this. Please."

It took some coaxing, but finally the old man was propped against the brick wall, clutching the coffee with both tremulous hands.

"This better be good," he muttered. "Disturbing a man in the middle of his sleep."

"You remember the night Foxy got arrested? Did you see that?"

"Foxy?" Screech's eyes clouded over.

Green prodded him. "Yeah, your Foxy—the working girl with the fur coat. A patrol car picked her up last Tuesday night. Ten o'clock in the evening, in that parking lot right over there." Green gestured across the parking lot to a building painted sky blue and surrounded by crumbling pavement intended for client parking but more frequently used for drug deals and fast sex. A cluster of garbage bins, recycling bins and dumpsters lined the back of the building, which housed a discount hair salon in its death throes. The building itself looked on the verge of being condemned.

Screech swivelled his head to follow Green's finger. The caffeine began to penetrate, and slowly a frown creased his leathery brow. "Yeah, I seen it. More like heard it. It were enough to wake the dead. Started off just telling people they were all going to die, then they were all dead." Screech shook his head. "Poor Foxy, always did have a bad view of things. That night all the folks was evil, out to trick her. She was up and down the sidewalk jabbering and scaring off my business. Anyway, they came and got her. Fought them like a wildcat. I never seen her that bad." He swivelled back to Green. "You got a loonie for a dying man?"

His eyes were runny and criss-crossed with spidery red, but Green could see the telltale yellow tinge of liver disease. He felt a fatalistic sorrow. He took out a five-dollar bill.

"This is very important. Was there anyone else hanging around watching her, who might have witnessed her arrest? A John maybe, or just a curious guy?"

Screech blinked. "What arrest?"

"Foxy's. Did anyone see Foxy get picked up?"

Screech shrugged. "Lots of guys. Peak cruising hour."

"Anybody try to intervene?"

The vagrant scrunched up his nose in bafflement. "Mix in," Green amended.

Screech locked his gaze on the five-dollar bill. "Sure. Maybe."

The hand holding the coffee cup began to droop, spilling some of the hot liquid on Screech's leg. He didn't flinch. Gently Green eased the cup back up towards his lips. Wondering whether he was wasting his time, he pulled a sheaf of photos out of an envelope. He'd downloaded some of them from the internet, but they made a passable lineup. David Rosenthal from his company website, Patrick O'Malley from a recent fundraising gala, and three recent victims of fatal crashes. He held the photos up one by one.

"Did you see any of these guys on the night she was arrested?"

Screech studied them all, blinking slowly and flicking his gaze at the money frequently, as if afraid it would vanish. "I was pretty busy, like," he began. He looked unhappy at the prospect of losing his payment. Then his face brightened. "That one. I seen that one. Not that night."

Green glanced at the photo of Patrick O'Malley. "When?"

Screech wagged his head in bafflement. "Coupla nights later? He was around awhile. Parked his car at the beer store. Asked me the same thing as you."

"What exactly did he ask?"

"If I seen the girl get arrested. If anyone else did."

What's this all about? Green wondered. "What did you tell him?"

"That I was busy. He asked if she left anything, then or another night." He slurped his coffee. "Didn't like the look of him, didn't want Foxy in trouble, so I said no. He went looking anyway."

Green almost dropped the photo. "Looking for what?"

"Beats me. He was looking through all them garbage cans, dirty job for a fancy man like that, got a silver sports car and all."

"What did he find?"

Screech fixed his gaze on Green's face. "You gonna give me that five or not? Mr. Fancy pants gave me a twenty."

Green put the five away and took out a twenty. "For this, I expect a straight answer. What did he find in the garbage?"

"Nothing."

"Nothing?"

Screech scowled. "Didn't I say that? He looked in corners, he opened up bags. Nothing."

Green grasped his arm and began to haul him to his feet. "Show me where he was looking."

Grumbling, Screech stumbled upright and turned to the wall. "Need a piss."

The man stank of urine and sweat. "Later. Show me."

Green cajoled him across the street into the vacant parking lot still cluttered with the detritus of last night. Screech shuffled over the cracked asphalt, oblivious to the condoms, needles, and crumpled bits of foil. At a row of dumpsters by the back of the building, he stopped.

"I ain't getting up in them dumpsters."

Green dragged a chunk of broken cinderblock over and peered inside the first dumpster. It was almost empty, containing a rancid collection of plastic bags, take-out boxes and loose garbage. He did the same with all the dumpsters, to no effect. He made a mental note to check the pick-up schedule.

"You're telling me he went through all these?"

"Yep. And further down the street too. He was some determined." Screech's eyes strayed to Green's pocket. "Gave me another twenty before he took off."

Green laughed as he tucked two twenties into Screech's shirt. "You watch you don't spend that all in one place, eh?"

Even before he'd returned to his car, Green was on the phone calling Gibbs. Surely the young man had managed to finish his interviews at Rideau Psychiatric. It was time to talk to Patrick O'Malley.

Twenty-Three

Bob Gibbs had needed less than ten minutes to locate a good photo of Patrick O'Malley on the web. A simple Google search of Ottawa and his name generated hundreds of images, many of him handing over cheques at fundraising galas, giving keynote addresses at corporate gatherings, and commanding the centre of boardroom portraits. Patrick O'Malley was a busy man. Besides being a prominent civil litigation lawyer, he was also on numerous charitable and social service boards such as The Children's Aid Society and The Children's Wish Foundation. He must have a soft spot for children, Gibbs reflected.

From his thinning grey hair and deeply etched face, Gibbs guessed that he was close to sixty, although in his tailored suits, he was still a handsome figure. But the camera captured something in his eyes that unnerved Gibbs. A challenge, an icy control. Gibbs hoped he never had to meet him on the witness stand.

He printed off a couple of friendlier photos and tucked them into a file, glancing at his watch as he prepared to leave the station. It was still too early to phone Sue Peters, who fatigued easily and needed at least ten hours' rest at night. He would make the quick trip out to the hospital and perhaps drop by her place with coffee and muffins on his way back. If she was up to it, they could both spend some time at the station researching David Rosenthal. The overtime would come in useful for the big plans he had.

Gibbs had only visited an inpatient ward at Rideau Psychiatric Hospital a handful of times in his career, and he was always taken aback by how different it was from a regular ward. Gone were the white coats and officious trappings of authority that separated patients from staff, gone were the ubiquitous IV poles, wheelchairs, and monitors crammed into the rooms and the carts and guerneys that cluttered the tile halls.

Gone, most strikingly, was the smell of disinfectant, fear and disease. In its place was the friendly cheer of nurses, the chatter of TVs and the sense of shelter and calm. Gibbs knew that every one of the patients sitting in the lounge or walking the halls was desperately ill, but there was not a bandage or a walker to be seen.

Sunday morning was a quiet time on the ward. Many patients were still in bed, and when Gibbs got off the elevator, two staff members were sitting in the nursing station working on charts. They seemed happy for the diversion and for the chance to shed some light on the mystery.

Gibbs did not consider himself old—in fact, he battled the image of a baby-faced choirboy in the unit—but he felt old beside the pair who greeted him now. One sported a wedding ring but otherwise had the pink cheeks and ponytail of a high school cheerleader. The other one, with a name tag Zoë Wark, still had a mouthful of braces.

"The nurse in charge is down the hall dealing with a patient," said the cheerleader, whose name tag said Jessica Derkson. "She may be awhile."

"All I require is a simple ID," Gibbs said, privately thinking that he might get more out of them without the senior nurse.

"So it *is* Caitlin!" Zoe exclaimed. "I was so shocked when I saw the photo on the news last night. Makes you wonder if all her talk about blood and stuff was real!"

Gibbs pounced on the opening. Green would have been

proud. "What did she say? Anything that could help in the investigation?"

"Oh, it was mostly word salad," Jessica interjected. "Gibberish. Blood, Lucifer, radio waves orbiting the earth."

"She seemed really upset," Zoe said. "And no wonder, if the poor thing witnessed that murder. She kept hugging herself and shaking her head. Almost like she was trying to wipe out the memory."

Jessica frowned. "I don't think we should read anything into all that. She was extremely delusional. I was amazed when they let her go yesterday."

"She wasn't ready?" Gibbs asked.

"Absolutely not. She was just beginning to respond to her meds. She needed a stable, stress-free environment for quite some time yet."

"But we're just nurses," Zoe piped in, flashing Gibbs a smile full of wires.

"She was signed out into the care of her father, right?" Gibbs asked. "She wasn't just let free."

"Technically yes," Zoe said. "But nothing stops her from walking out on her father the minute she gets home. She's done it before."

"I don't think he'll let her," Jessica said. "He seemed pretty determined yesterday."

Gibbs thought of the steely-eyed stare in Patrick O'Malley's photos. He doubted anyone crossed the man without a serious fight. "Just for the record, can you describe the man who signed her out?"

Jessica rattled off a clear, concise description that fit O'Malley perfectly, right down to the pale grey eyes. Gibbs showed them the photo, and both confirmed his identity without a second's doubt.

"Those eyes unnerved me," Zoe said.

"But you could tell he cared about her," Jessica countered. "He visited her every day, met with staff, brought her some nice comfy clothes from home. She'd arrived with nothing but—" Jessica broke off.

"Skank clothes," Zoe supplied. Jessica frowned. "Well, what else would you call six-inch heels and jeans so tight they—"

"We shouldn't be talking about this," Jessica said. "She's a patient."

Zoe flushed and looked about to crawl into a hole. Gibbs hunted about for a way to keep them talking. At least he hadn't taken a note. Hadn't even taken out his notebook, another technique Inspector Green had taught him. "So you feel confident that her father will take good care of her in her own home?"

"Oh, yes, he assured the doctor of that," Jessica said. "I overheard his conversation with her treating psychiatrist. Old friends, it sounded like. He told the father to pick up the phone and call him directly if he needed to."

"We never met the mother, though," Zoe added. "She never once came to visit, so I don't know how supportive—"

Jessica cut her off. "I'm sure everything will be fine. But if you want to talk to Caitlin..." she drew herself up and seemed to recover the full force of her professionalism, "would you wait a few days? She's very fragile. Even in the most loving, supportive home environment, she may find the trauma of that evening too stressful to relive."

Gibbs was feeling very pleased with himself as he thanked the nurses and ducked back into the elevator without so much as a glimpse of the nurse in charge. He knew he had pried more personal information out of them than they ever should have revealed. He went back to his car. Time to report his news to Inspector Green, and then... On to Sue Peters.

His phone rang before he could dial out. To his dismay, it was Sergeant Levesque, sounding fuzzy, as if she'd just woken up. "Anything important on the search for Caitlin O'Malley so far, Bob?"

Gibbs hesitated. He hated squad room politics, because somehow they always managed to bite him in the ass. While he searched for a safe answer, she added, "I see that Inspector Green ordered surveillance on her father's house last night."

"Yes, ma'am, and he asked me to follow up with—"

"I know, the nurses at the hospital. What did you find?"

Gibbs relaxed fractionally. At least Inspector Green had kept her informed, rather than doing his usual end run. He summarized his interview with the nurses.

"So our witness is probably safe and sound at her parents' home." She paused. "Did Inspector Green ask you to do anything else this morning?"

"Background on David Rosenthal. I was going to ask Detective Peters to help. Is that all right with you, ma'am?"

"That's fine. Go ahead with that, and leave this hospital information with me. I'll pass it on to Inspector Green when I speak with him."

Her voice cut like a whip now, like she'd woken up in a hurry. Gibbs was more than happy to step out of the line of fire between her and Green. After a totally unnecessary apology, for which he privately cursed himself, he hung up and set off for Sue Peters' apartment. Breakfast with Sue followed by a leisurely drive back to the station and a morning spent in companionable silence tracking David Rosenthal through cyberspace. That was the police work he loved.

He and Sue had just arrived in the squad room an hour later, however, when his phone buzzed. It was Collins, the detective sergeant on duty. "Got a man. Down in the lobby. To see you." He spoke like a train jolting along a rusty track. "Cabbie, called in earlier about your mystery ID. Sounded important. Told him to come on in."

"Did you notify Sergeant Levesque?"

"No. Knew you were on."

More squad room politics. Gibbs glanced at Sue and hauled himself tall. Before getting all worked up about who should know what, maybe he should hear what the cabbie's important news was.

Hamid Farahani's dark eyes danced with curiosity as Gibbs ushered him into the squad room. He reminded Gibbs of a spider monkey he'd seen once on the Nature Channel, all scrawny limbs and tufts of black hair. He talked so fast that Gibbs struggled to understand his guttural Middle Eastern accent. Slowly he learned that Farahani drove a taxi for Blueline, but only at night, to supplement his income while he tried to expand his small shwarma take-out shop into a viable restaurant. In this economy, probably not the best idea, but... Farahani raised his spider arms expressively.

Gibbs finally saw an opening. "You phoned the police because you recognized the woman in the photo?"

Farahani's head bobbed. "I want to do my civic duty." A pause. "But I'm wondering, is there some money for this?"

"If your story checks out, I'll have to ask—"

The man held up his hand. "I do my duty anyway. I only ask because, well, I am trying to start my business, and on *CSI*...."

"I understand, sir. Why don't you start by telling me how you recognize this woman." He laid the photo line-up Sullivan had prepared on his desk. Because the pawn shop photo had been splashed all over the news, he had removed it and substituted Caitlin's graduation photo. "Just to confirm, point out the woman you picked up."

Farahani looked at all the photos, a deep furrow working its way into his brow. "She is not here. That photo is not here."

"But do you recognize the woman in any of these photos?"

The long spidery fingers hovered over the photos, pausing a long time over the graduation photo before picking it up. "This one, possibly. She looked very different that night in my cab."

Gibbs made some notes and packed away the photos. "When did you see her, and where?"

"Last Saturday night, the night that man was killed. I'm sorry, I didn't see a connection before, because I picked her up in Vanier, more than a kilometre away. I thought she was a working girl. She dressed like a hooker, so I thought she was working Montreal Road. The girls along that strip, they are everywhere. Used to be even worse. All the side streets, all the alleys. You can't believe what I was seeing. Friday and Saturday nights, men call me all the way from Kanata and Nepean. Where are they going to find girls on the streets out there? It's all behind fancy glass doors, booked by cellphone. But down here in the city, if you don't want a trail..."

Farahani looked pleased with himself, like he was acting as guide to a dangerous but titillating world. Gibbs could sense Sue Peters grinning. Time to bring the man back to earth. "Did this woman phone for a cab?"

"No, no, I see her. She is walking along Montreal Road, holding herself like this." He jumped up and gripped his stomach as he hobbled across the room. "Like she was hurt. It is dangerous that time in the night."

"What time was this?"

"3:20 a.m., sir. I check my log today."

"And what direction was she walking?"

"East, to St. Laurent Boulevard."

And ultimately towards Rothwell Heights, Gibbs thought, although it would be a really long walk. "What did you do?"

"I stop. First I slow down. I was worried. A young woman alone on the street at that hour and dressed in nothing, only a black bra and jeans. I asked her where is she going, and she said she is walking home. I offered her a lift." Farahani paused. He looked nervous. "I have two daughters, younger, but I hope if ever they are in trouble..."

"And she accepted the lift?"

"When she got in the back, I see she is very upset, making no sense, and her jeans are..." He makes a gesture towards his crotch. "I see some blood there. I asked what happened, but she only shakes her head. I want to take her to hospital, but she says no, just take me home."

"What address did she give you?"

Farahani looked at his notes. "1714 Montreal Road. Near Blair Road in Beacon Hill. Much too far walking." He waved his hands to signal distance. "She has no money, but I say it doesn't matter. I get her home safe."

Gibbs recorded the address then carefully closed his notebook. All the time he was thanking the man and escorting him back downstairs, he was thinking ahead. Caitlin had been captured on video on Rideau Street an hour earlier, at 2:10 a.m. What had happened during that hour, and why had the woman walked over a kilometre from the site of the murder? Had she been sexually assaulted, and even if she had, what did it have to do with the murder of Sam Rosenthal?

The minute he was back in the squad room, he picked up the telephone. Inspector Green needed to know this.

*   *   *

Green propped his notebook against his steering wheel and jotted notes as Gibbs reported his interview with the cabbie. He frowned as he wrote down the address. "That's not Patrick O'Malley's address."

"No, sir. It's a townhouse unit in a large, low-rent complex. Sue Peters is looking it up now to see who owns it. But I think it's a red herring, sir."

"How so?"

"It's just across the street from the back of the neighbourhood where her father lives. I think she didn't want the cabbie to know where she lived, so she had him drop her on a main street nearby. Maybe she didn't want to draw attention to herself by pulling up outside her father's place in a cab at three thirty in the morning either."

Green pictured the quiet street, at that hour almost certainly asleep. Nonetheless, there might be some nosy insomniac peeking out the curtains to see what shenanigans the O'Malley family was up to at that hour. Given Caitlin's erratic history and her mother's drinking, he imagined the gossip had been fairly fierce over the years.

"What about the nurses, Bob? Did you get the father's photo over to the hospital?"

There was a pause. "Oh, yes, sir. I'm sorry, sir. I—I reported in to Sergeant Levesque. She s-said she would tell you."

Green squinted through the windshield as he wrestled his temper under control. This was not Gibbs' battle.

"I'm sure she'll call," Gibbs rushed on to fill the silence. "She was at home, sounded like she just woke up. Or something."

Despite his annoyance, Green had to smile. He could almost hear the young detective's embarrassment through the phone line. From the sound of it, Levesque had managed a successful dinner date after all.

His annoyance dissipated entirely as Gibbs' described his visit to the hospital. With his gentle manner, the kid was developing quite a talent for drawing people out. But in the midst of all the concern about Caitlin's fragile mental health, no one had asked the very crucial question—why now? Why had Patrick O'Malley suddenly shown up at the hospital that afternoon and insisted on taking his daughter home? Insisted to the point of interrupting her psychiatrist in the middle of his weekend off. What had sent him into a panic? The photo of his daughter released to the media that afternoon?

"The nurses were pretty surprised she'd been discharged," Gibbs was saying. "She's still very ill, they said, and they asked if we could hold off interviewing her for awhile."

Green peered at his watch. It was edging towards midday. Sharon was going to sue for divorce, if she didn't murder him outright. He'd promised to take Tony and his new kindergarten buddy bicycling on their brand new two-wheelers today. And to tackle the yard. There were two massive maples and an oak in the backyard, and if he ignored nature much longer, the house might totally disappear under their leaves.

"Not possible. But it's Patrick O'Malley I really want to talk to right now. As soon as Sergeant Levesque shows up at the station, have her give me a call."

Twenty-Four

Green leaned on his rake and stared at the back yard with dismay. After an hour, six bags brimming with leaves were already lined up at the curb, but the yard looked untouched. The task was not helped, of course, by the enthusiastic contribution of Tony, his friend, and Modo, who were making a game of jumping in the leaf pile. It was amazing what havoc two little boys and one huge dog could create.

From inside the house, he heard the distant ringing of the phone. A moment later, Sharon emerged, pouting darkly. She surveyed the leaf-strewn chaos wordlessly before she handed him the phone. About time, he thought, tossing the rake aside. No one should get to spend the whole day in bed.

To his surprise, the dessicated voice of Lyle Cunningham came through the phone. "Gibbs said I should call you. He thought you'd want to know right away that we've got two interesting results back about Rosenthal's cane. First, the tissue and blood on the tip of it. Levesque wanted me to expedite that analysis, so I rode the RCMP lab hard. They can't give me DNA yet—that'll be another few weeks—but they did do some tissue typing for starters, so we could focus our inquiries. The good news—the blood is Type B negative."

Green's excitement jumped. Type B negative was rare and could go a long way to eliminating suspects quickly.

"The bad news," Cunningham continued before Green could muster a comment, "is that none of your four suspects, including Omar Adams and Nadif Hassan, are Type B. However, your victim is."

"So he was hit with his own cane?" Green pictured the blows to the head, which according to MacPhail were caused by a long cylindrical instrument. "Could it have been the murder weapon?"

"I highly doubt it. You could hit someone hard enough to stun them or knock them down, especially a frail old man, but I can't see the cane having the strength to break the skull without snapping in two itself."

Green agreed. "But let's run it by Dr. MacPhail for confirmation."

"I will tomorrow. Especially in light of my other finding." Even the normally deadpan Cunningham sounded excited. "When I realized someone else had wielded the cane to strike Dr. Rosenthal, I took another very careful look at the handle and the shaft. I had checked it for prints before, but I should have been more thorough. My mistake."

Green struggled to hear over Modo's barking and Tony's shrieks of glee. He edged into the house, bringing a cascade of leaves with him. "What? You found a print?"

"The cane is covered in latents, mostly unusable. But I did find a partial on the shaft under the handle. Right index finger. If you're gripping the cane in your right hand in order to swing it, your right index finger would press pretty hard on the wood in exactly that spot."

Green's disappointment vanished. "A partial? Enough for a match?"

"Yes, indeed." Cunningham chuckled. "A gift-wrapped present for the lovely Sergeant Levesque. Omar Adams."

*　　*　　*

Omar Adams was sitting on the floor of the bathroom, propped against the bathtub. The morning's *Ottawa Citizen* was spread out on the tiles in front of him. Since the police had searched the house and pulled him in for interrogation, his father had been buying every newspaper in the city, including the French *Le Droit* and tuning into the radio news every hour. Omar found the reporting terrifying. The newspapers invented what they didn't know and created ridiculous stories out of the tiniest coincidences. He tried not to read them.

This morning's paper, however, caught his attention from the first page. "Police seek woman as possible witness to slaying". The name Caitlin O'Malley meant nothing to him, but the photo jolted him. He snatched the paper from the kitchen table where his father had left it and raced upstairs with it. He chose the bathroom as the only place where he could lock the door and read in peace without the eagle eye of the old man and the peppering questions of his brothers.

He read the article for the third time. The woman was supposed to be in hiding from known gang members. Did Nadif know anything about her? What the hell could she possibly have seen? He stared a long time at the fuzzy photo.

He knew this woman.

Slowly a memory drifted into focus of the woman leaning against a brick wall in the shadows off the main street. She was tall, her head bent forward talking to someone, her hair tumbling down. She wore white jeans and a fur jacket that hung open at the front. Underneath, nothing but a black lace bra.

His heart pounded with fear. He shut his eyes, half trying to remember, half to forget. Nadif had spotted her from down the block. He'd boasted to them, his tongue flicking. As they got closer, Omar remembered shouting. Swearing. High-pitched and frightened. Nadif shouting too.

There was someone else too. The old drunk? Someone yelling at him to stop and grabbing his arm. Stinging pain on his arms and back. Pain like he hadn't felt in years. He remembered grabbing something smooth and round, swinging it. Flailing, tearing at flesh. Then steel flashing in the shadows. A knife?

That's when he'd turned around to run.

In the bathroom, he scrambled up and flung himself over the toilet bowl just in time. Heaved until his gut ached and tears ran down his cheeks. Fuck! Had they done it? Had he been part of that? He remembered the feel of the slippery round shaft in his hand, the swoosh of it rushing through the air. He clutched his head and started to cry. Was he going to rot in jail for the rest of his life? Was he going to be raped and beaten and used like a woman in the jungle of the prison yard? He'd done nothing but defend himself. But Nadif, that murderous bastard, must have had his fucking knife.

He stumbled to his feet, doused his face with cold water and dried his tears. Stared at himself in the mirror. I ran away, he told himself. I ran away because I'm a chicken shit coward that freaks at the sight of blood. I didn't beat the old man's head to a pulp.

He opened the bathroom door and peered out. The hall was quiet. No one had heard a thing. His brothers were excitedly playing their video game and from downstairs came the drone of his parents talking. Omar slipped down the stairs and stopped in the front hall, hardly daring to breathe. His parents were in the kitchen arguing in Somali about money. He knew it was because of him. Because of the high-priced Jew lawyer his father had hired. He'd been against it, but his father said it was the smartest move. Besides them being the sharpest lawyers, it was like hiring a woman to defend you on a rape.

He pulled on his sneakers, snatched his jacket and slipped out the front door, trying to shut it as silently as he could. He was still grounded, and his father would kill him if he caught him. Dead eyes for a week.

It was bright and cold out. He squinted up and down the street, adjusting to the sunlight. Now that he was out here, he needed to figure out his next move. Should he ask Nadif? He shivered at the thought. Nadif scared him. Even when they hung out, Nadif scared him. He'd knifed that kid in the Rideau Centre on a dare, for no other reason than the guy made a crack about Nadif's girlfriend. "Hey, ho, you ever get tired of Nadif, I'll show you what a good time really is."

Yusuf. That was the guy to ask. Yusuf had a scary side too, but it was mostly show. Imitating music videos and tramping around in gangsta clothes. All fucking hot air. Yusuf wanted to be Nadif, but he'd never stabbed anybody. Maybe this had freaked him out too.

Omar started down the street towards Yusuf's house. It was a long walk across Rideau Street and way down through Sandy Hill almost to the Queensway, but this was one time a cellphone wasn't enough. He had to see Yusuf's face.

When he'd gone a little more than two blocks, he heard footsteps behind him. Laughter. He turned to look. Nadif was walking up the street about a block behind, cool as could be, with four of his gangster friends. Today they were all wearing the black bandannas of the Lowertown Crips.

"Hey, Omar! Where you going?" Nadif shouted. The others flashed big grins. They walked five abreast like commandoes sweeping the streets.

"Buy something for my mom." He turned to continue his walk.

"Aw." More laughter. The five picked up their pace. "Wait up, we'll help you."

Omar smelled danger. A couple of the others had their hands in their pockets. They were slouching along like they didn't have a care in the world, but Omar knew some of them packed handguns. Nadif was a pussycat compared to them. He had called in the big muscle.

"I'm late. Thanks, anyway!" He began to walk as fast as he could. Behind him he heard running. He risked a glance and saw they were closing the gap. Giving up the "everything's cool" act, he began to sprint. The traffic light at Rideau Street was visible up ahead, but so far away. Could he make it? He was skinny, and he was fast, much better at running than at fighting. For once, tough guy muscle didn't matter. He raced full tilt up the block, dodging cars, strollers and old ladies with shopping carts, expecting a bullet to zing past his head at any second.

Behind him, footsteps thundered. Curses flew. If he could just reach Rideau Street, he could get lost in the crowds and maybe duck into a shop...

But the sidewalks along Rideau Street were deserted. What the fuck, he thought as he hurtled down the street. Where was everybody in this useless town? At church? He thought of flagging down a car—any car—but a small voice of caution said no. If these guys were going to open fire, they wouldn't care if there was a dozen innocent people in their way.

He dashed across four lanes of traffic and flung himself through the doors of a delicatessen he knew was open. A Jewish delicatessen. Of all the fucking luck, he thought. Inside, he ran down the narrow aisle past the counters of deli food, ignoring the shouts of the guy behind the cash, and ducked through the doorway into the restaurant part, which was full of people and clattering with noise. He made a direct line for the bathroom. Without a second's hesitation, he burst into the Ladies' Room, muttered a quick sorry to the woman at the mirror and slammed himself into a bathroom stall. He pressed the bolt shut, stood up on the toilet, and listened. Prayed he wouldn't hear footsteps, or worse, gunshots. Prayed the woman at the mirror wouldn't rush out into the restaurant screaming "There's a man in the bathroom!"

Astonishingly, there was silence. He heard the soft creak of the door as the woman slipped out of the room, the murmur of voices beyond as people began to react. He strained to hear over his ragged breath, but could only make out frightened fragments. Cops, 911, gun... After an eternity, his breathing quieted and his heart slowed to a heavy thump. He groped in his pocket, dragged out his cellphone, and punched in a single digit on his speed dial.

"Dad?" His voice quavered. Shattered. "Can you come get me?"

*   *   *

As soon as Cunningham signed off, Green phoned Levesque. Enough lying around in bed, no matter how nice the company. He updated her on the Ident officer's news and set up a meeting with her at the station to plan their next move. He gave her an hour to say goodbye to what's-his-name and get dressed, which also gave him time to jump into the shower to wash the dirt and sweat off. Sharon was sitting on the bed waiting for him when he emerged from the shower. He dropped a quick kiss on her head as he walked by.

"Sorry, honey, I don't know how long I'll be. At least I got some leaves off the ground."

"So Omar Adams is the guilty party after all?"

He stopped, a pair of T-shirts in hand. He'd barely had time to process the idea. "That's where the evidence points."

She shook her head in disgust. "A stupid mugging by a bunch of hyped-up punks. What a waste of a life. Are you going to arrest him?"

"Probably. I want to get him off the streets ASAP, in case he goes after Caitlin." He picked the cleanest shirt and pulled it on. "The kid's an enigma. On the surface he plays a 'peace and non-violence' guy, but he was raised by a no-nonsense military father and an unstable, abusive mother. He doesn't appear to be part of the local street gang, although the others are to various degrees. He can turtle in on himself and block out the outside world, and in interrogation, he claimed he didn't remember a thing about that night. He's either very good at hiding who he is, or he's a seriously screwed-up kid who snapped." He began rooting through the closet for his belt. "I'm leaning towards the latter. I've also got CrimIntel looking into possible jihadist connections. So far he hasn't shown up on their radar. This kid is adrift, on the fringes of groups without belonging anywhere." He paused, switching to his search in earnest.

Sharon reached under a pile of clothes and pulled out his belt. "Gangs are more likely. With parents like that, he probably feels powerless, put down and victimized for things that weren't his fault. Gangs would give him friendship, protection, excitement, a chance for payback, and most importantly, a place to belong. He's probably struggling in the mainstream white world of school, jobs, women..."

Green was familiar with all the social theories about the appeal of gang membership, and he knew Omar fit many of the criteria, yet his gut reaction was negative. "But the kid seems frightened of violence. He hasn't developed a tough, 'don't feel anything' attitude yet. Gangs may offer a haven, but they are still violent and predatory. They have initiation rites—"

"Could this have been an initiation rite?"

"Maybe. An initiation rite gone wrong." He turned the idea over in his mind as he did up his belt. "But usually the rites are within their own criminal world—like against a rival gang—or a property crime. Omar is more the type of kid you see addicted to violent online gaming, where he can be brutal and cut people down, but it's victimless. Virtual."

"That satisfies up to a point, Mike, but when it's all imaginary, the person is still left feeling powerless and aggrieved in the real world."

He turned to her, excited. "That's why the internet jihadi stuff. It's the best of both worlds. You plot, you share fantasies of murder and revenge, you may even meet to pick targets and start preparations. But until you actually blow something up, it's all imaginary, and the victims you fantasize about are far removed. Jihadism also gives your violence a noble cover."

"Is he religious?"

Green shook his head. "CrimIntel's looking into that too. So far we have no evidence of that. He dresses like your average gangster punk straight out of a Geto Boys hiphop album. But jihadists typically don't come from religious backgrounds and in fact are so poorly informed about Islam that they are easy prey for manipulative radical imams." He glanced at his watch. "Luckily all we have to do today is charge him. We'll have lots of time to pull together the background before his day in court. And who knows, maybe with this new evidence linking him directly to the assault, he'll crack and tell us what really happened. If he's faking amnesia, this might scare him into flipping on his friends. And if he really is blocking it all out, the sight of the cane may open the flood gates."

From the downstairs hall, he heard the dim ringing of his cellphone. He contemplated not answering, but after four rings, Tony came bouncing up the stairs, shouting and brandishing the phone. "It's for you, Daddy! She says it's very, very important!"

Green glanced at the ID. Levesque. "Change of plans," she said. "Meet me outside Nate's Deli."

Twenty-Five

By the time Green arrived at Nate's Deli, Rideau Street was a parking lot, and the entire block had been cordoned off by police cruisers and yellow tape. A group of civilians stood off to one side outside the cordon, being interviewed by uniformed officers. Restaurant patrons, Green surmised. Black-clad officers from the Tactical Unit blocked the entrance to the deli, and a quick scan revealed more of them positioned on the roofs and corners of surrounding buildings. A tall, ramrod straight man was arguing with the officers at the door, gesturing wildly and demanding entry. Green recognized Frank Adams.

"He's not dangerous!" Adams yelled. "I'm telling you, he's scared. He called me to come get him."

"We're just following procedure, sir," the tactical commander replied in a patient monotone. "No one's going to get hurt. First we need to ensure that everyone is evacuated from the premises, then we'll check on your son. We have a negotiator on his way."

"He doesn't need a negotiator, you id—" Adams stopped himself just short of the insult. "He's hiding. He says five guys from the Lowertown Crips are after him. Have you bothered looking for them?"

"There was no one fitting that description in the street when the police arrived, sir. And as you can see—" he gestured towards the motley collection of mostly pot-bellied, middle-aged patrons, "no one among the restaurant customers either."

"Then let me in to talk to him. I promise I'll bring him out."

"I can't let you do that, sir, but once the negotiator arrives—"

"Oh, for fuck's sake!" Adams roared. He's going to accomplish nothing with this by-the-book crew except maybe get himself arrested, thought Green, and he pushed forward through the throng. Tactical officers moved to stop him, bristling with rifles and armour, but Green flicked open his badge. Adams saw him about twenty feet away.

"Will you tell these cowboys that Omar is no threat!"

Green approached calmly. "Your son is scared and cornered, Mr. Adams. That makes him unpredictable. Does he have a firearm?"

"Fuck you guys! He's harmless."

"Possibly, but this is no time for guesses. You have four firearms registered to you. Does he have access to any of them?"

Adams looked startled. "You checked up on me?"

Green didn't answer, and after a moment's thought, Adams deflated. "I keep them out at the Rifle Club. They have no place in a family home."

"What about knives?"

"He doesn't own a knife. I keep telling you, he hates violence."

Green held up a soothing hand. "Look, Mr. Adams, you may be right. But I also have to tell you that parents are often the last to know what their young people are up to. Does he spend time on the internet?"

"Our computer is broken. You know that. You've been through my entire fucking house."

"At the library then, or at an internet café."

Adams shrugged. "Maybe to check his email and his Facebook page. He's not an internet nut, doesn't even play PlayStation much any more."

"How does he spend his time?"

"We shouldn't be wasting time on this now. We should be getting him out!"

"The more time he has to calm down, the better. And the more we know about him, the better we can defuse this. His time?"

Adams folded his arms sullenly. "He has a part-time job at the Loblaws in Vanier—the usual grunt work stocking shelves and pushing carts. He's studying at Adult High School. I keep him busy. Less time for trouble that way."

"Does he attend church? Mosque?"

Suspicion flickered across Adams's face. Beside him, the tactical commander leaned in intently at the mention of the word "mosque".

"Mosque? What's that got to do with anything?" Adams's scowl blackened to outrage. "My boy's not in there because he's a Muslim terrorist! He's got Nadif Hassan and his thugs after him, trying to kill him because he can rat them out on that murder!"

Green hid his excitement. "He told you that?"

"No, but I'm guessing. He was reading the paper this morning about that hooker who's a witness? I bet Nadif is running damage control."

"How did Omar call you? On his cellphone?" When Adams nodded, Green raised his hands in disbelief. "Why don't you just call him back?"

"We did," the tactical commander said. "The suspect is not answering his phone. Word is he may be barricaded in the Ladies' room."

The Tactical Unit was simply following procedure. They had secured the perimeter, evacuated the area and were waiting to initiate communication. Green cupped his hands to the front window and peered into the now deserted restaurant. He could see no movement through the glass, but somewhere inside, a scared young man was hiding, while outside, a dozen commandos trained their rifles on the door.

Green drew the Tac commander out of the father's earshot. "I don't believe this requires a negotiator. Let me go inside. I know the layout of this place, and the ladies' bathroom is on the far side. I'll talk to him as soon as I'm close enough for him to hear. He knows me."

"Sir, I can't let you do that."

"There are several walls and two doors that will serve as cover."

"Too risky. We can't confirm his location, his state of mind, or whether he's armed."

Green looked up at the grim, expressionless face of the commander. Going strictly by procedure, the man was absolutely correct. Omar was, at this point in the murder investigation, their most credible suspect, a young man who had snapped and flown into a rage so violent that he didn't even remember it. He was now at the end of the road, trapped between the threat of jail and the street justice of his gang friends. There was no way to know whether he was cowering in the corner of the restaurant or lying in wait with a gun.

Yet Green could not shake the image of the bewildered and immovable young man in the interview room. A young man who not only claimed to hate violence, but, according to his father, feared it. In all the enigma this young man presented, Green felt sure of only one thing; the boy needed a lifeline. If they followed procedure instead, he would panic. Cornered by an army of black-clad officers armed to the teeth and all intent on railroading him into a murder charge, there was no telling what he might do.

"You come with me," Green said. "Just you, and try not to

point that thing at my back. The rest of your team can follow and be ready to move up at a second's notice, but I don't think it will be necessary."

"I'm not authorizing—"

Green pushed the rifle aside, eased open the door and slipped into the restaurant. Swing music from the forties played softly in the background, muffling their movements, and the familiar smell of smoked meat and garlic dills filled his nostrils.

Emptiness yawned before him. Green stood inside the door, straining to hear any furtive sounds. Despite his display of confidence, his heart hammered against his ribs, and his mouth was so dry he could barely speak. He prayed he was right about this enigmatic contradiction of a boy.

He heard nothing but muted trumpet crooning a seductive tune. Louis Armstrong, Green thought. Keeping his Glock hidden at his side, he crouched low. No point making himself a huge target.

"Omar?" he called, his voice ricocheting around the empty room. "It's Inspector Green. Can you hear me?"

There was no answer. Satchmo played on.

"I'm coming in to get you out of here. You're safe, Nadif is gone. There's no one outside but the police and your father."

Still no answer. Green crept down the aisle past the deli counter with its briskets of smoked meat and piles of *latkes* and white fish. He peeked around the door frame into the restaurant and peered up and down, trying to see under tables and behind booths. Nothing. He took a deep breath. Across the room on his left, in a recessed area behind an outer door, was the entrance to the Men's and Ladies' washrooms. If Omar was hiding inside the recess, he would be impossible to see until they opened the door.

Behind him, the tactical officer was almost treading on his heels. Green could feel his hot breath on his neck. So far, however, the commander had not interfered. Green signalled his intention to cross the room to the far wall, which would bring him close to the recess. The commander nodded and waited, rifle trained ahead as Green hurried across the room. He pressed himself against the far wall.

"Omar? I'm outside the bathroom. I know you're scared, but you're safe. Nadif can't get to you. I promise we'll protect you. There are lots of police out looking for Nadif, and we'll catch him. So talk to me, Omar. I'm right here to help you."

Still silence. Green felt a tremor of fear in his gut. The longer Omar went without answering, the less hopeful the outcome. The boy was resisting help. What was he planning, holed up in the bathroom?

"Once you're out, once you're safe, we can talk about all the rest. I want to hear the whole story, Omar. Your side. I know you're not like Nadif. We can work this out."

Louis Armstrong played obliviously on through the silent room. His trumpet quavered, high and melancholy. Green pressed gently on the door, which swung open an inch without a noise. The commander rushed to Green's side and tapped his shoulder. He slipped a small camera through the gap.

Nothing. Inside, both men's and women's washroom doors were closed. Green glanced at the man. Readied his own gun questioningly. The commander signalled to the Ladies' room, and both men flung open the door at once. They dropped down and froze just inside.

The room was empty. Four stalls, three gaping open. The commander searched each rapidly, poking his gun inside. Empty. They both looked at the door to the fourth stall. Pressed against it. Locked.

"Omar? You in there?"

Silence. Not even the stifled intake of breath. Green got on his hands and knees to slip the camera under the door, praying he wouldn't get a bullet in the face. The stall was empty.

The tactical commander radioed his team, and they conducted a thorough search of the whole place, including the kitchen and the supply cellar. Omar was nowhere to be found, but off the kitchen, a service door was propped open by a pail to encourage a breeze. The service door opened onto the back parking lot, but right beside the door was a fire escape leading up to a series of rambling rooftops.

"He didn't trust you guys!" Frank Adams raged when he learned the news. "In the end, he didn't trust you could ever keep him safe!"

*   *   *

The tactical commander lambasted his team for failing to block the fire escape when they secured the perimeter, but Green suspected Omar had fled long before the team even set up. He strode through the back parking lots, trying to trace the escape route the young man had probably taken. There were drain pipes, cables, ledges and low hanging roofs, all of which would be easy routes for a young, agile fugitive who was desperate enough. Omar Adams was long gone, and it was impossible to know where.

Levesque joined him as he stood in the back alley. "No question about his guilt now, is there, sir?"

"Scared people run too, Marie Claire."

She thrust out her lower lip in a disapproving pout. "Where do you think he went?"

"Friends? Friends of friends? Obviously he can't rely on Nadif and his buddies to protect him." Green mulled over the events of the day. "If he isn't guilty, he may be trying to clear himself. Trying to find Caitlin O'Malley to find out what she saw."

"Or if he is guilty, to kill her," she replied.

He acknowledged the harsh fact reluctantly. "Good thing we have that surveillance on her father's house."

Levesque said nothing, but her sudden quiet unnerved him. "What?" he asked.

"I took the surveillance off that house this morning."

Green whirled on her. "What the fuck for?"

She shrugged, her pout deepening. "When we learned it was her father who picked her up, and we got the forensics on Omar Adams—"

"You figured it didn't matter? That her life no longer mattered?"

"No, sir. I didn't consider her in danger."

He spun on his heel, not trusting himself to reply. Regardless of whether Omar was after her, Nadif certainly would be after this morning's news article. Nadif was desperately running around the city covering his tracks, with the help of his gangster friends. Levesque was a dangerous fool to have put a power struggle ahead of civilian safety.

He rounded the front of the restaurant and caught sight of the duty inspector on his radio, no doubt in complex negotiations with the Com Centre as they coordinated the city-wide search not only for Omar Adams but also for his pursuers. Green rapped on the duty inspector's window to get the man's attention. Inspector Doyle raised his finger irritably, signalling for him to wait. Green rapped again, then opened the door without waiting.

"Get a unit over to 180 Rothwell Drive ASAP. We have a witness needing protection, and Omar and Nadif may be on their way there."

He waited to make sure the call went out then phoned the O'Malley residence. After four rings, the machine kicked in. Green called again, but still no one picked up. Not in, or screening calls from the Ottawa Police? He left a message urging caution and suggesting they vacate the premises for a few hours.

Afterwards he grabbed Levesque's elbow. "We're not done with this," he snapped. "But for now, let's get out to the O'Malley house. I've got some questions for Mr. O'Malley anyway."

Rothwell Drive was still deserted when they rounded the curve into view of the house. So much for the ASAP part of my order, Green thought. Fortunately there was no sign of Nadif or his threatening pals either. Five black males with bandannas would face a tough challenge trying to sneak up on the house in any case. Diversity was hardly one of the neighbourhood's strong points.

Like its neighbours, the O'Malley house looked sleek and serene, the curtains drawn, the garage door closed, and the silver sports car sitting alone in the drive. Either the SUV and the Lincoln Town Car were in the garage, or the family was away. This time he directed Levesque to park diagonally behind the sports car to block an unexpected exit. Then he told her to go around to cover the back door.

She didn't budge. "Aren't we going to wait for the uniforms?"

"I'm not expecting the family to come out shooting," he retorted, his temper still raw. Did the damn woman have to question every simple order?

She shrugged and started down the flagstone path to the back. Inside he heard a heavy thump and the muffled, furious yapping of a dog. At least someone was home. He pressed the bell and listened as the dog yapping crescendoed and footsteps thudded down the upstairs. Came close to the front door then receded. It sounded like a lot of footsteps for just one person. Green felt a prickle of alarm.

From the back, he heard a crash, shouts and a scream. He tore around the side of the house, wrestling his gun from its holster. Levesque was sprawled on her stomach beside the French doors which gaped ajar onto the patio, their glass shattered. Blood stained her blond hair and oozed onto the flagstones.

At the rear of the yard, disappearing over the ornamental black fence, was a young man in baggy pants and massive shoes which snagged on the fence post, sending him plunging head first on the other side. Green raced to the fence, but by the time he reached it, the man had disappeared. Behind the O'Malley house was nothing but a thickly wooded ravine, tipped orange and yellow in the autumn sun.

Green whipped out his cellphone as he flung himself down at Levesque's side. Not again, not again, this can't be happening! All because of my goddamn temper!

The young woman was stirring. She moaned as she reached up to touch her head. "Don't move," he whispered and snapped out information to the 911 operator. "Officer down, send ambulance and police back-up. At least one suspect fleeing northeast on foot. Set up roadblocks in and out of the neighbourhood and send search teams including K-9 to the wooded ravine backing on Rothwell Drive."

"What's the status of the downed officer?" the dispatcher demanded.

Levesque was struggling to sit up, staring in disbelief at the blood on her hands. Conscious, all extremities moving, he reported with relief. He stripped off his jacket and tried to wrap it around her, but she shoved it off.

"I'm sorry, Marie Claire. You were right, we should have

waited. Can you give us a description?"

"Tall, black, late teens or early twenties." Her teeth chattered. "Wearing the Lowertown Crips colours."

"Omar or Nadif?"

She gestured to her face. "He had a bandanna over his face. He rushed the door. There was maybe more than one of them, I don't remember. *Ah maudit, ça fait mal!*"

"The ambulance and patrols are on their way, Inspector," the dispatcher said. "What are the officer's injuries?"

"She's bleeding from the head, but responsive and coherent."

"I'm fine!" Levesque snapped. "A little hit on the head, that's all."

"Green!" bellowed the deep, throaty voice of the duty inspector over the phone. "What the fuck's going on!"

"We arrived at the home of that potential witness and surprised an intruder. Perhaps more than one..." Green's voice trailed off as he stared through the open door into the quiet house. Even the dog had fallen silent. His heart rose in his throat. What had happened to the O'Malleys?

"Armed?" Doyle snapped.

Green wrenched his gaze from the interior and repeated the question to Levesque. She nodded. "He hit me with a pistol butt."

Green felt a wave of nausea. How close he had come to losing an officer yet again, all because of his impatience! Doyle was talking again, peppering him with questions about the neighbourhood and the suspects. In the distance, sirens began to wail. Still no sound emerged from the house.

"Listen, Doyle," he said. "Dispatch another ambulance to the house. I don't know what's happened yet, but I'm getting a bad feeling."

He heard a siren shriek down the street and come to a

stop. Squeezing Levesque's hand, he rushed around to intercept the responders, two young constables in a cruiser. Leading them to the back of the house, he found Levesque struggling to her feet, propping herself unsteadily against the wall. He ordered her to sit down again and motioned to one of the constables to stay with her.

Gesturing to the other to follow him, he withdrew his Glock again and pointed through the French doors into the house. Levesque's eyes widened. "Sir!" she whispered hoarsely. "It's too dangerous. Someone may still be hiding inside."

"Possibly. But there may be injured parties in there as well. As soon as back-up comes, send them in. But we can't wait."

With a bravado he didn't feel, he stepped inside. The room was designed for comfort, with thick broadloom and huge, overstuffed recliners grouped around a sleek black fireplace. A high definition TV covered almost half the opposite wall, and bookshelves lined the other three walls. The room was empty. He and the constable hurried across, their footsteps muffled by the deep pile. On one side of the entertainment room was a study lined with leatherbound legal volumes, and on the other a granite and stainless steel kitchen. The kitchen was cluttered with pots on the stove and plates of salad on the counter, as if the family had been surprised in the middle of lunch.

Green felt goosebumps down his arms. He stood in the hallway trying to listen. The dog had resumed its frantic barking from somewhere upstairs. The intruders must have locked it up, Green realized, which showed a modicum of restraint. Some gangsters would simply have shot it dead.

Through the kitchen window, he saw the paramedics arrive, and soon two more constables joined the search of the house. Green directed the newcomers into the basement while he and the first constable continued on the main floor.

Living room, dining room, both glossy hardwood and sleek leather. Both empty. There were cushions on the floor, and newspapers scattered casually on the tables, but no signs of struggle. Oil paintings hung undisturbed on the walls and the fine china and silverware in the glass cabinets had not been touched. The hall closets bulged with fur and leather coats.

Whatever the intruders were after, they had paid no attention to the commercial riches at their fingertips.

On the carpet at the base of the spiral staircase, Green detected the first real sign of trouble—a small, reddish brown smear clinging to the rich cream fibres. Green sucked in his breath. He pulled some neoprene gloves from his pocket and gestured to the constable to follow suit as they crept up the stairs. More stains at the top and a long smear along the wall, barely visible against the antique plum paint.

On the landing at the top of the stairs, they confronted the entrances to four bedrooms and a closed door, behind which the dog was scratching and whining. Green left the dog where it was as they rapidly checked each room. The first was a neat bedroom all sunny yellow, the second an all-purpose room in complete disarray. A sewing table, an artist's easel, open jars of paint and scraps of fabric all over the floor.

The third bedroom was also in chaos. Painted soft pink, it was almost entirely papered in photos from magazines, many curled and yellowed with age. Not the posters of rock stars and punk heroes that decorated Hannah's room, but photos of planets, moon phases and stellar constellations. The bed was unmade and strewn with papers. Clothes, shoes and books littered the hardwood floor. The closet door gaped open, revealing more boxes of files half emptied on the floor. Was the occupant simply messy, or had someone been searching for something?

The final bedroom was set apart at the end of the hall. A

crystal chandelier hung from the ceiling over the double entry doors which were ajar, revealing a Persian carpet also strewn with clothes. In the gloom of the shuttered windows, only the foot of the massive, frilly bed was visible. At the last second, he hesitated before pushing open the door. This is how cops got shot, by blundering into an unknown situation unprepared. All his instincts screamed danger, yet could they afford to wait? He signalled to the constable, and placed his hand on the door. Inched it open. From within, nothing but silence. Stillness. A familiar smell wafted through the gap. His gut tightened as he steeled himself for the sight.

The woman was lying on the floor by the bed, half underneath as if she'd been trying to get away. Her head was thrown back in a paroxysm of horror, her lips curled back over her teeth and her eyes, already clouding over, bulged. Her chest was a mass of blood that had pooled beneath her and spread red through the brilliant jewel tones of the Persian carpet.

Green raced over to check the woman and sagged against the bed in shock. Not what he was expecting, but no less a tragedy. In their brutal quest to silence Caitlin O'Malley, the Lowertown Crips had murdered her mother. A woman with long brown hair and a delicate, heart-shaped face, who looked young enough in a poor light, or a fuzzy photo, to pass for her daughter.

Twenty-Six

Within an hour, every available police officer had been recalled to duty. The com centre crackled with activity as search teams were dispatched to comb every inch of terrain between Lowertown and Rothwell Heights. Omar, Nadif and all the members of the Lowertown Crips were in their sights. Informants were squeezed, gang associates questioned and all affiliated gang hideouts were raided. In Rothwell Heights, officers canvassed every neighbour within blocks. The media dogged their every move in what had become an international crime drama.

Throughout it all, Green worried most about what had become of Patrick and Caitlin O'Malley. Had they witnessed the mother's murder and somehow escaped with their lives? Surely if Patrick O'Malley were alive, he would contact the police. The longer the silence, the greater Green's sense of foreboding. Nonetheless he tried to maintain his optimism as he raced to keep up with the reports flying in from all quarters. Lou Paquette and his Ident team had sealed off the entire O'Malley house, and Green had set up a temporary command post in the neighbour's house while he waited for the official white truck. Levesque had been treated at the scene but had refused the paramedics' recommendation of a check-up at the hospital. Instead she sat in the neighbour's kitchen with a huge white bandage around her head.

The break came at 4:17 p.m. in the form of a triumphant call from a patrol officer in Vanier that five young black males had been spotted washing themselves in the Rideau River. At the cruiser's approach, the group had scattered along the bike path, but after radioing for back-up the officer had kept one of them in her sights with the help of local dog walkers.

Nadif was finally cornered by three uniformed teams converging on the park from opposite directions. He had contemplated his only means of escape, the shallow, fast-moving river, and had surrendered without a fight. Two of his accomplices were apprehended a few minutes later running through a back street of Vanier. Green ordered them all stripped and every scrap of clothing handed over to Ident, then had them all placed in different interview rooms to wait for him. Under other circumstances, he would have preferred to let them stew in the cell block for awhile, perhaps even overnight, to give Ident time to provide some ammunition for the interrogation. But today there was not that luxury. Not with Patrick O'Malley and his daughter missing and Omar still on the loose.

On the way back to the station, Green drove while Levesque furtively massaged her temples. "I want you checked out at the hospital," Green said.

She closed her eyes. "I'm fine! Do you think I would miss this moment, when we finally crack this case wide open, just because of a little headache?"

"All the same, Marie Claire," he said gently, "you're in no shape to conduct an interrogation."

"I just want to be there, okay? You can do the questioning, but I want to sit in. It's my first case, sir! And if I hadn't removed the surveillance—" She broke off.

He glanced across at her. Her eyes were glassy and her cheeks flushed, whether from pain, shock or self-recrimination, he didn't know. But he understood what this apprehension meant to her.

"Afterwards," he said, "I'm driving you to emerg personally."

"Afterwards you can buy me a stiff drink."

He laughed, the first moment of levity since the horrific discovery of Annabeth O'Malley's body. Marie Claire wasn't the only one wrestling with regrets. Green's gut was tight with a dread he barely dared to acknowledge. A dread that had been lurking since his first glimpse of the blood on the stairs. What if Levesque was right? What if Omar was the killer, and he had released a killer back onto the streets? Had Green misread the man so badly that it had cost at least one woman, perhaps more, her life?

At the station he shoved the doubts from his mind and assigned teams to interview the two accomplices while he prepared to face down Nadif himself. As he gathered his props for the interview, he gave Levesque time to change her blood-stained jacket and wash up. The second floor was abuzz with officers and civilian employees hunched over phones and computers, tracking the investigation.

Even dressed in cellblock-issue white scrubs with paper slippers on his feet, Nadif still presented a handsome figure. His eyes were dark with apprehension, but he kept his flawless features expressionless as he watched Green and Levesque sit down. Green dictated the preliminaries for the tape and embarked on the requisite caution. Before he was even halfway through it, Nadif interrupted.

"I want to talk to my lawyer."

Without a word, Green handed him the phone. Not surprisingly, the young man dialled the number from memory, then rolled his eyes while it rang. Green heard the voicemail kick in and Nadif cursed. He left a terse message asking the man to come to the station, then hung up.

Green smiled at him sympathetically. "Sunday afternoon. Bad time for lawyers. You could be waiting a long time."

Nadif shrugged. "I got time."

"True. Or..." Green laid his file folder on the table. "We could clear up a few things while we're waiting. You see, two of your buddies are down the hall talking to my colleagues. You might want to get your story in before they pin it all on you. Things won't look so rosy when you're staring down twenty-five years to life."

"No crime in playing in the river."

"Mrs. O'Malley's murder was a messy one. You know what that means? Lots of interesting bits of evidence for our Ident team to discover. And believe me, they will. They'll be there for days going over every carpet fibre and speck of blood. And what do you think they'll find on your clothes? On the soles of your shoes? I heard you running through their house. One fibre from their carpet in the treads of your sneakers, and you're toast, Nadif."

"I don't even know who this Mrs. O'Malley is. I was in the park with my friends."

"The mother of the prostitute you guys assaulted last weekend. You killed the wrong person, buddy."

A spasm of surprise crossed Nadif's face, but he said nothing.

"You're piling them up, Nadif." Green took out a sheaf of photos and laid the one of Caitlin on the table. "Sexual assault of Caitlin O'Malley..." He laid three photos of Sam Rosenthal's bloodied body alongside it, including a close-up of his battered head. "Murder of the old man who came to her aid. Murder committed in the course of a criminal act is an automatic first degree. Assaulting a police officer, breaking and entering..." He laid down two photos of Annabeth O'Malley's body. "Another first degree murder charge."

"You got nothing on me, or you'd be charging me."

"Patience, Nadif. Forensics takes time. Let's start with the original murder. We just got the results back today on the old man's cane. We have blood on the tip and fingerprints on the shaft." He added Ident's enlarged photos of the cane to the line-up. "But we know you didn't act alone. We know your friends Yusuf and Omar were involved. With your previous record and your age, you're facing the most serious prison time, but if you cooperate—"

"I'm not ratting!"

"If you cooperate first, that's going to show the judge you're remorseful. I know this didn't start off as a murder, Nadif. I know you just wanted to get laid, but she turned you down. Who knows why, that's what she was there for, right? Maybe it was because she didn't want a foursome, or because you were black. Whatever, she told you to get lost, and things got ugly. When the old man Rosenthal showed up, they got out of control. He was fighting you, you grabbed his cane to stop him, you hit him back..."

Surprise and fear flitted across Nadif's face as the scenario unfolded. Finally he burst in to stop the barrage. "Like I said, it wasn't me. You got me mixed up with some other black dude."

Green shrugged. "And like I said, I'm just giving you the first chance to cooperate, because you're in the deepest. Do you think your buddies down the hall will keep you out of it? Or Yusuf? How about Omar Adams? Omar's scared to death, you know he's never been in trouble before. How long before he cracks and tells us the whole story? Only he's going to paint himself in the best light. He's going to say it was your idea to proposition the hooker, you who got mad and grabbed her—"

"We didn't proposition no hooker! We didn't lay a finger on her!"

"But you saw her. You talked to her."

Nadif whipped his head back and forth.

"We have a witness who heard her telling you to leave her alone."

The young man was staring at the bloody photo of Rosenthal as if mesmerized. "This is fucked."

"What's fucked?"

"It didn't go down like that."

"Then how did it go down?"

Resolutely, Nadif said nothing.

Green shuffled the photos. "This is your chance, Nadif. Because the others are going to say it was you who grabbed the old man's cane, you who smashed him over the head—"

"That wasn't me, that was fucking Omar!"

The words reverberated around the room. Nadif froze. Green leaned and tapped the close-up of Rosenthal's head. "Omar did this?"

A convulsive swallow. "He went berserk! He smashed the guy till he went down."

"And what did the rest of you do?"

"Nothing."

"The man's head was a pulp, Nadif. A cane can't do that."

"We didn't do nothing! Maybe Yusuf landed a couple of kicks, I don't remember. But we didn't kill him. He didn't—" Nadif stabbed at the close-up, his lips trembling, "he didn't look like that."

"So when did you steal his stuff? Before or after you kicked his head in?"

Nadif said nothing. His eyes were wide as he stared at the close-up.

"Come on, you took his shoes."

"Omar took his watch!"

"We found no watch in our search of his house."

"Then he got rid of it. But he yanked it off his wrist. The

dude was batshit crazy, I tell you!"

"But after Rosenthal was down on the ground, you took off his shoes and his rings. Stole the sleeping bag off a homeless man—"

Nadif jerked back as if slapped. "What?"

"He was wrapped in a sleeping bag."

"We didn't do that!" The young man whipped his head back and forth. "Something's fucked here. That picture ain't right. He must have crawled over there, because we didn't leave him there."

"But you did beat him up, steal his shoes, watch, rings, and the chain around his neck."

"Omar ripped that off. Called the guy a fucking Jew." Nadif held up his hand. "I got nothing against Jews, but like I said, Omar was apeshit. Started whacking away at the guy. Freaked himself right out and took off like a cannonball after that." Too late, Nadif froze.

The words hung in the air. Green leaned in. "Let me get this straight. Omar took off before the rest of you did?"

Nadif shrugged, as if it were a minor detail.

"What was the woman doing all this time?"

"Nothing. I think she took off. She got us into this fucking mess, and then she takes off."

"But you knew she was a witness. You knew she could finger you. That's why you went to her house."

"Like I said, I think she ran off when the trouble started."

"But you had to be sure, so you went looking for her."

"I had nothing to do with that."

"Come on, Nadif, things are closing in on you. The hooker has been identified, and you knew it was a matter of time before Omar cracked. That's why you went looking for him this morning."

"He's my friend!"

"And when he ran away, you chased him."

"He's my friend," Nadif repeated. "I just wanted to talk to him."

"Uh-huh. To make sure he kept his mouth shut about the hooker."

Nadif shrugged. He was sitting with his arms crossed, half turned from the table as if avoiding the sight of the photos laid out on it.

"And when you couldn't get to him, you went after her." He laid out some preliminary photos that Ident had taken of fibres, fingerprints and blood stains in the O'Malley house, including one on the frame of the French patio door. "Forensics is going to place you at the scene, Nadif. The poor woman was killed in her own bedroom."

"I didn't do that. Maybe we did beat the old guy up a bit, defending ourselves, but—" He pointed to the old man's battered body. "I didn't do that either." He sat back, his eyes shut and his arms falling limp at his sides. Green recognized defeat. He leaned in.

"If you didn't, then save yourself. Tell me what did happen with the old man."

Nadif sighed. He wagged his head slowly. When he finally spoke, his voice was a monotone. "He had it coming. He was the one hassling that bitch. We just went in to help, and he turned on us. When he went down, we stole a couple of things off him, and we took off. He was alive. Moaning, even. But who was going to believe us, eh? Four black homeys up against some fancy old Jewish doctor with a cane? Who's going to believe he'd go after a whore? I knew we didn't kill him, but you guys were busy stacking the deck, so I figured we had to find her. See if she knew what happened. That's why we were at her house. We went in the back way, because who's gonna let four black dudes in if we ring the bell all polite like. We thought there was nobody home, but the dog was going ballistic, and we were afraid it might bite us. Lucky it was stuck in the bathroom. We were checking out the place—"

"Lots of nice stuff to steal?"

He flicked his gaze at Green but didn't deny it. Instead he gripped the table as if to steady himself. "We were just looking around, to make sure she wasn't asleep, like, and we opened the door and went in the bedroom. She was already there, on the floor." He stabbed his finger on the photograph. "Just like that."

"Already dead?"

He shook his head sharply. "Don't know. Just then the doorbell rang, and one of the guys said 'Cops', and we knew we had to get out of there. I mean..." He opened his large, dark eyes wide and stared at Green. "Were you going to believe us? That we walked in and the lady's already dead, and some other killer is walking around out there holding all the cards?"

Green held his gaze for a good ten seconds. Was this a premiere performance, or the truth?

"Who, Nadif?"

Nadif shrugged. "If I knew, I'd be giving him to you, wrapped up in a bow."

"The night you beat up Rosenthal, did you see anyone else around?"

"Just an old drunk down the street, but he was passed out cold."

"What about today, when you arrived at the O'Malley house? Did you see anyone around?"

"We came in the back, over the fence. The place was dead." Nadif's jaw twitched in a grimace. "Quiet."

"Any vehicles?"

"Nothing. I don't know, man! Maybe Omar came back to finish him off. Like I said, I saw a whole new side of him last Saturday night. Who knows what he'd do?"

*   *   *

Levesque had lost much of her colour by the time they had wrapped up Nadif's interview and returned him to the cellblock. While Green remained at the interview table, sorting through impressions, she leaned her head back against the wall and closed her eyes.

"Do you believe him, sir?"

Green turned the question over in his mind. Nadif was a self-serving liar, manipulator and thug. There was no reason to believe him other than a niggle of doubt in Green's gut. If Nadif had really wanted to put police off his scent and lend substance to his lie, he would have invented a mystery third suspect—someone hanging around in the shadows while Rosenthal was being attacked, or some indefinable vehicle cruising slowly past the scene.

But if not Nadif, then who? Green's thoughts roamed afield to other plausible suspects. Omar, who had Nadif's vote, was certainly high on the list, but even Nadif had let slip that he fled before the rest of them. According to Omar's father, he was still running when he reached home that night. Furthermore, he was so impaired that he was barely upright.

Green returned to the few inconsistencies that had surfaced in Nadif's testimony. If he was to be believed, after the initial assault, someone else had taken the time to beat Rosenthal as he lay moaning and drag him into the lee of a building to conceal him from the street. That person also had the presence of mind to steal Screech's sleeping bag and wrap the body to further delay its discovery.

Hardly the actions of a drunk, freaked out youth.

Yet if there was a third suspect, what would have been the motive for such a crime? Not self-defence or robbery or flash rage. This was a calculated assault on a helpless man. Someone had wanted him dead.

Green shook his head impatiently. What were the chances of the real killer stumbling upon the mugging and seizing the opportunity to finish the job? That required a ludicrous stroke of luck. How would the killer have known that Rosenthal would be on Rideau Street at that unlikely hour? How would he have known that Rosenthal would get into a dispute with a bunch of punks out for sport?

Green pressed his fingers to his temple, trying to force his thoughts into focus. He needed a coffee. He needed Sullivan, who would have listened to his wild speculations and patiently brought the facts into line. Levesque, exhausted and physically brutalized, was no substitute.

In his scramble to keep up with the unfolding case, Green could think of only two ways that his unlikely "third suspect" scenario could work. Either the real killer had been lying in wait on Rideau Street waiting to ambush him, or he had followed Rosenthal from his house, looking for the chance to strike unseen and disappear without a trace. Either scenario relied heavily on pure serendipity. In the first, how would the killer even know Rosenthal would show up on Rideau Street at that time and place? The second was more plausible, although the killer could not have known that the four punks would make his task so much easier.

The obvious suspect was David Rosenthal. His whereabouts at the time of the murder were still unknown. Furthermore, his behaviour had been very odd. He had tried to remove papers from his father's house even before touching base with the police about his father's death, he had become incensed when he'd learned he wasn't inheriting a penny, and most ominously he'd tried to contact Caitlin O'Malley, the one witness who might be able to identify him.

Abruptly Green shoved his chair back and stood up. "We need to check what Sue Peters and Bob have managed to dig up on David Rosenthal."

Levesque didn't move, beyond opening one eye. Green softened. "You're going to hospital. I'll get one of the guys to take you."

She shook her head gingerly, wincing at the pain. "Everyone's busy. I just need a little sleep. I'll join you in fifteen minutes."

He eyed her uneasily. Concussion was a tricky injury, invisible and often undetectable. Sleep was unwise. But before he could overrule her, she said, "I'm not going to sit in the ER for ten hours waiting to see some med student and catching every bug going around. Not when I can spend that time on the case."

He didn't argue further but left her with the silent vow to check on her in ten minutes. Any sign of wooziness or slurring, and she would be off by ambulance. Back in the squad room he found Peters and Gibbs bent over their computers.

"Any news on the searches?"

Both heads shook in unison. Omar, Caitlin and Patrick had all dropped out of sight. Patrick's known friends and associates had all been contacted, to no avail.

"What have you learned about David Rosenthal?"

Gibbs' eyes lit. He spun away from his computer and groped through the stack of print-outs and post-its on his desk. "Lots! Customs has him entering Canada on Sept. 23

through Pearson International..."

Green did a quick calculation and his hopes fell. "That's three days after his father's murder. Shortly after we contacted the FBI."

"Yes, sir. But he could have entered the country earlier at one of the smaller road crossings, and it didn't get in the system."

Green looked dubious. "And what? He went back out again to make an official entry?"

"Yessir." Gibbs pawed through paper and flourished the one he wanted. "Because it looks like he's broke. He lost millions in the global collapse last year when companies cancelled contracts. He makes cutting-edge prosthetics for injured soldiers, and he had invested up the yingyang to develop them. He's been selling off personal assets to keep the core of his company alive. Three houses so far."

So Dr. David Rosenthal certainly had motive, Green thought, even though his opportunity was questionable. "Have we found him yet?"

"No. We do know he's been to the morgue and arranged for his father's funeral. It's tomorrow, out at the Jewish cemetery. But he hasn't been at his hotel whenever we checked."

Green thought of the dozens of officers already deployed in the searches. One more demand, and the duty inspector would have a heart attack. "Put surveillance on the hotel," he said. "We need to contain this guy. As long as there may still be a killer on the loose, Caitlin and even Omar are in danger. No leads at all on their whereabouts? Friends? Obscure hotels?"

At a nearby work station, Sue Peters waved her hand excitedly. She was on the phone, jotting notes and nodding. As Green and Gibbs hurried over, she slammed the phone down and swivelled her chair triumphantly. "I think I found them! You remember that address where the cabbie dropped Caitlin off?"

"Montreal Road?" Green asked. "Near her home?"

"1714 Montreal Road. It's a low-cost rental unit. I checked all the tenants, there and nearby. Nada. Students, new immigrants, single moms. The usual."

Green's eyes narrowed. "Who owns it?"

Peters grinned. "I thought of that, but no cigar. It's a property development firm. But! On a Google Earth search, I saw there's another house right beside it. 1710 Montreal Road. It's a little post-war bungalow slated for demolition and in the middle of a zoning dispute. It's listed as empty and water and hydro are disconnected. But guess who owns it?"

"Patrick O'Malley?"

"Bingo. And what's more, I was just talking to one of the tenants at 1714 who remembers the last occupants. Newlyweds named Caitlin and Adrian."

Green sucked in his breath. "Take me home," Caitlin had told the cabbie that night, and this must have been what she meant. Not her father's place but the home she'd shared, however briefly, with the man she'd loved. If Patrick had brought her there after her discharge from hospital, that would explain why the mother knew nothing about it.

Rapidly he considered his courses of action. Annabeth O'Malley's name had not been released to the media, but film and camera crews were crawling over the neighbourhood, and the conclusion would be obvious; something catastrophic had happened at the O'Malley home.

If Caitlin and her father were without power, it was possible they hadn't seen the news, but more likely Patrick O'Malley had a wireless laptop or Blackberry which would keep him plugged into the outside world. He and Caitlin had to be informed of the mother's murder as soon as possible.

On the other hand, a cruiser at full lights and siren would be a traumatic way to learn the awful news. No matter how difficult, they deserved to hear it from the investigating officers themselves. The hideaway was so obscure that it was unlikely either Omar or David Rosenthal would be able to find them.

In the end he decided on a compromise. He asked Dispatch to send a cruiser to watch the little house quietly until he arrived. When he went to rouse Levesque, she was sleeping slumped over the table, but to his relief she became instantly alert and coherent.

"Of course I'm coming," she said, already on her feet before he'd finished briefing her. She swayed but caught herself quickly, shaking off his helping hand with a scowl. Back in the squad room, he signalled to Gibbs. "Round up an available detective and follow us. And I want EMT back-up in case we need assistance. Caitlin is pretty unstable mentally."

Sue Peters pushed herself to her feet, trying to hide her stiffness from sitting so long. "How about me?"

Green felt a pang of regret. She wasn't cleared for field duty and would be of little help if physical restraint was required. He saw her excitement fade to defeat as he hesitated.

"Someday, Sue," he said. "Meanwhile you hold down the fort for us here. Omar and David Rosenthal are still out there, and we need to keep on top of their searches."

As the two staff cars headed eastward in convoy onto the Queensway, Green turned the case over in his mind with dissatisfaction. They were missing some part of the puzzle, and other pieces didn't fit. Maybe those pieces were irrelevant and weren't meant to fit, but he wasn't comfortable being unable to form the whole picture. What about the break-in at

Rosenthal's apartment the week before his death? What about the theft of his laptop and personal papers? Why had Patrick O'Malley visited the scene of the murder several days later, asking about witnesses and going through garbage? Why had he suddenly whisked Caitlin from the hospital before she was well, and why had he told his wife nothing about it?

No matter how the pieces were sorted, Patrick O'Malley seemed to loom larger in the picture than Green had envisaged.

They were fast approaching the Blair Road exit ramp when his cellphone rang. Expecting an update, he pressed the "hands-free" button and was surprised when the wheezy, measured voice of George Verne filled the car. "Sorry to disturb your day off, Inspector, but I find myself in possession of another piece of information that may be relevant to your investigation. Or not. But here I'm on dubious ethical ground. *Entre nous?*"

Green glanced at Levesque and laid a finger to his lips. "What is it, Mr. Verne?"

"I purchased an *Ottawa Citizen* to read with my afternoon coffee at the office, and lo and behold, I see a familiar face on the cover."

"You know Caitlin O'Malley?"

"I do. She was never actually a client of mine in the sense of officially retaining my services, but she did consult me."

"When was this?"

"In March of this year. The case I mentioned to you, when I first met Sam Rosenthal. He brought her to see me. He was encouraging her to explore her legal recourses against her father, who'd managed to have himself appointed her guardian. Effectively, he controlled her finances, her holdings, and her medical treatment. She was under a mandatory community treatment order to follow a medication regime, and the last time she'd defied it, her father had sent the police after her."

Green nearly missed the Blair Road exit. He gripped the steering wheel, fighting both the car and his excitement. "So Rosenthal was treating her?"

"I don't know about that, but he was prepared to testify on her behalf. A Consent and Capacity Review Board had turned down her appeal, and she wanted to pursue the matter in the courts."

"To do what?"

"To have her father's guardianship and power of attorney revoked. She was quite adamant. A very bright woman who wanted out from under her father's thumb."

"But you didn't take the case?"

"In the end it didn't proceed. Sam Rosenthal merely said later, when he came to make the new will, that it had been ill-advised. I had cautioned them that although I would be delighted to take the case, she should be prepared for an ugly, upsetting battle. Patrick O'Malley doesn't take prisoners, and her psychiatric history was not a thing of beauty."

Green thanked him for the information and disconnected to see Levesque already processing the implications. "So there was no love lost between Sam Rosenthal and Patrick O'Malley," she said.

Green was already on the same track. Was it possible? Could Patrick have resorted to murder to keep Rosenthal from his daughter? It explained why Patrick had returned to the murder scene several days later, to find out if anyone had seen her and to look for telltale evidence. It explained his whisking Caitlin away from the hospital once her photo had been released. Anything to prevent the police from finding her and questioning her about Rosenthal's murder, for given her unstable mental state and her antipathy towards him, she couldn't be relied on to protect him. It even explained her panicked flight from the murder scene and her choice of 1714 Montreal Road instead of her father's address. Sam Rosenthal had been her ally, and she'd been running from her father. In her confused and terrified state, she'd chosen the one place she'd ever felt safe from him.

A new and sinister fear swept over Green. If Patrick O'Malley had killed Sam Rosenthal, he was a desperate man running scared as the truth closed in. Once a successful, respected lawyer, he was now threatened with losing it all. How far would he go? He had already lied to his wife and kept Caitlin's hospitalization a secret from her. Had he also killed her once she guessed the truth? And what would he do to his only child who, although beloved, could bring his whole world down?

"We need to get there ASAP," he said, flipping on the emergency lights and stomping on the gas. "He may not be hiding her at all. He may have taken her there to kill her."

Levesque didn't argue, didn't even ask for an explanation. He felt a swell of satisfaction when instead she reached for his cellphone and ordered immediate back-up.

The little bungalow was tucked between a low-rise strip mall and the cluster of townhouses that included 1714 Montreal Road. Once it had probably been one of several low-cost, post-war country homes scattered along the road out of town, but the burgeoning city had expanded around it, surrounding it with disparate, ill-matched neighbours. An oak that looked at least fifty years old dominated the front yard, and overgrown cedars obscured the porch. A huge "No Trespassing" sign hung in the front window. Because traffic was light, Green killed the red flashing lights and coasted by, his gaze scouring the property. There was no sign of life and no vehicle in the drive, but a narrow, rutted lane led around the back to a ramshackle shed barely visible from the street. If Patrick was smart enough—and Green suspected he was—he would store his Town Car in the shed and hide all traces of his presence, even from satellite and aerial surveillance.

Green pulled into the adjacent townhouse parking lot and tucked the Impala out of sight behind the complex. Gibbs drew up behind, and the four detectives climbed out of the car.

"Are we waiting for the back-up, sir?" Levesque asked. The late afternoon sun was slanting in over the townhouse rooftops, washing her in a rich gold glow, but it could not hide the lines of fatigue and fear on her face. She was in no shape to be charging into the house on full alert, not knowing what danger Patrick might present.

He nodded. "Get them to meet us here on the east side of the townhouse complex."

"What about the Tactical Unit?"

Green had been vacillating on that score. Patrick was supposed to be an intelligent, rational man, who would surely know when he'd reached the end of his options. Yet what kind of intelligent, rational man would stab his own wife, not in a rage born of jealousy and despair as most wife-killers did, but in a cold-blooded move to silence her?

He nodded. "Let's call them in too. You wait here to coordinate it, and you—" he pointed to the detective accompanying Gibbs, "watch the front door of the bungalow. Gibbs and I will take a preliminary look around the back to see if Patrick's car is there."

Levesque blanched. "But sir!"

"We'll stay out of sight, don't worry. And my cellphone will be on vibrate. Back in ten."

He didn't give her more time to object but headed around

the back of the complex. A couple of dogs started barking as they passed behind small, fenced patios mostly abandoned to old bicycles, barbeques and broken furniture. Behind one, however, they found a young woman and her toddler picking cherry tomatoes from a sprawling tomato plant just outside her allotted space. She dropped her bowl in fear at their approach, spilling bright red tomatoes all over the grass. Her son squealed with delight and she recoiled, pulling him to her. Green placed his finger to his lips, showed her his badge and drew her inside the shelter of her fence. A pretty oasis of flowers, garden art and a child's wading pool full of floating plastic toys greeted them.

She propped her child on her hip, only marginally less suspicious. He gestured to the bungalow, whose roof was barely visible above the lilac bushes and thistle that had taken over the lot. "Have you seen any signs of activity in or around that house?"

She hesitated. "That's been abandoned as long as I've lived here."

"Yes, I know, but has anyone been staying there in the past few days?"

The son squirmed, but she pressed him even closer. "What's this about? Is something wrong?"

"No. We're looking for a young woman who may be in danger, and our information is that she may be staying there."

"Danger? What kind of danger?"

Green cursed himself for letting too much slip. "We'd like to talk to her, that's all. She may have some information. Have you seen her?"

"She says she owns the place, and one day she's going to build her dream house there."

Green hid his excitement. "You've talked to her? When?"

Finally trusting enough, the woman set her squirming son down, and he toddled off towards the tomatoes with a shriek.

"Last month? She's been there on and off for a few months. Looked like she'd seen better days, so I figured what's the harm?"

A few months was a long time to be without water or electricity, Green thought. The young mother was frowning as if debating whether to add something.

Green encouraged her gently. "Concerns?"

"It's just... She *has* been acting weird lately. Like she's scared of someone. At first she seemed pretty nice, not exactly friendly like, but she'd borrow water from me sometimes or play with my little boy. But recently when she goes there, she sneaks in the back way around behind the strip mall like she doesn't want to be seen. And she hardly ever comes out of the house, just sneaks out at night, and she keeps the windows covered up so you can't see in. She won't answer when I say hello, just looks the other way like she doesn't want to be seen."

"Did you ever see anyone else visit? A man, for example?"

"She's not there all the time. I think her father tried to visit, but they don't get on. A few months ago when we used to talk, she told me he's a lawyer and he's trying to tear her house down."

"Is someone there now? Did you see a white Town Car, for example?"

She bit her lip, looking distressed. "I was out so I didn't see anyone arrive, but I think I heard some sound—maybe voices? A couple of hours ago."

"Male or female?"

"I couldn't tell. Just a low murmur. But it surprised me, because she's usually alone."

Green's scalp prickled with dread. "You've been extremely helpful. For now, would you please take your child in your house, lock the doors, and stay inside until we give you the all-clear."

Her eyes widened. "There *is* danger!" she gasped, snatching up her child again.

"Just as a precaution."

"Fuck," she breathed. "You read about these things, but you never think it will ever happen!"

Green watched to ensure she and her son were safely inside before returning to Gibbs. His eyes scoured the windows of the abandoned bungalow for signs of movement within, but they were all opaque, merely reflecting the late afternoon sun and the pale blue sky. He signalled Gibbs to follow as he continued around to the back.

The yard was enclosed by a dilapidated wooden fence with numerous broken slats. He slipped between them and fought his way through the tangle of overgrown lilac on the other side. The centre of the yard was surprisingly orderly. The thistle and goldenrod had been cut back, and a propane barbeque sat on a small patch of gravel. Laid out in patterns on the grass around it were odd stone circles, and an elaborate geometric system of steel pipes wove between them like a post-modern sculpture.

Green dashed across the yard to the shed, crouching low to obtain partial cover from the brush that surrounded the clearing. Thorns clawed at him. Ignoring the scratches, he pressed himself against the rear of the shed and waited for Gibbs. Together they breathed deeply to slow their hearts and to listen through the silence. Nothing but the screeching of a flock of birds in the oak tree. Closer by, a squirrel watched them balefully from a fencepost.

Gibbs nodded towards the steel pipes. "What do you suppose that is, sir? A water system?"

Green shook his head. "It's not connected anywhere. Looks almost like an old-fashioned TV antenna, but who knows?" He turned to examine the shed. Its roof was bowed, threatening imminent collapse, and paint flaked off its weathered wood siding. A small window at the back was crisscrossed with cobwebs but by cupping his hand Green was able to distinguish a glint of glass and chrome inside. As his eyes adjusted, the full shape of the Lincoln Town Car emerged.

Fuck.

Green pressed himself against the back wall of the shed, out of sight, and dialled Levesque to tell her that Patrick O'Malley was indeed inside.

"The Tactical Unit has arrived," she said. "They're setting up a perimeter and planning their approach. Any sign of the subjects?"

Green peered around the corner of the shed and scanned the house. The windows were all covered on the inside by what looked like plywood sheets, but the patio door was uncovered and provided a glimpse into the room beyond.

"Let me get a little closer, and I'll see if I can identify where they are."

"Sir, that's a job for the Tac—"

"I'll get back to you ASAP." He hung up on her protests, then squeezed through the shrubs to the far side of the shed, using it as cover while he approached the back of the house. When he reached the front of the shed, he sprinted the short distance to the back corner of the house and flattened himself against the rough brick wall, straining to hear over the hammering of his heart. Nothing. No voices, no footsteps.

Too silent.

He signalled for Gibbs to follow, and together they crept along the back wall until they reached the edge of the patio door, then dropped to a crouch to make a less visible target. Pressed against the cold stone of the patio slabs, Green inched forward and peeked through the dust-streaked glass. The room was packed with junk. Not the usual couch and chairs but a broken baby stroller, several upside down lampshades arranged in a circle, a shopping cart plastered with "no trespassing" signs, and an old dog bed buried in broken Barbie dolls in the corner. And around every doorway and window, more steel piping. Green knew enough about the quirks of the schizophrenic mind not to even try for a logical explanation.

Still no sound.

He reached up to test the door and felt it slide beneath his cautious push. The door was not locked. He hesitated, trying to muffle his ragged breath. The Tac commander was waiting for a report. Green needed to let the unit do its job, yet listening through the slit in the door, he could sense no threat. Fear crawled through him, not of what might happen but of what had already happened.

He took out his Glock and stared at it, cold and heavy in his hand. He hated it but knew he needed at least this precaution. Behind him, he heard Gibbs suck in his breath. Before he could protest, Green pressed his finger to his lips. Eyes huge with apprehension, Gibbs took out his own Glock.

Green slid the door back and slipped inside, assailed instantly by the stench of unwashed clothes, urine and rotten food. Now, within the confines of the tiny house, he heard a sound like the rustling of papers. With Gibbs' tense breath in his ear, he crept towards the sound, past a gutted shell that had once been a kitchen and towards a doorway at the front. The door was torn off its hinges and propped against the wall. The sound was clearer now, not the rustling of paper but the soft, sibilant sound of breath. A person weeping.

Green readied his Glock and stepped through the archway. He took a few seconds to make out the shapes in the darkened room. The only furniture was a single cast-iron bed in the corner, made up with a frilly pink duvet and matching pillow. A woman lay on the bed, her hands at her sides and her eyes closed. Her long brown hair fanned out on the pillow as if spread by a tender hand.

She was still. Too still. Green's heart leaped in his throat, and he stepped forward in horror.

Patrick O'Malley sat on the floor by the head of the bed, stroking her hand with his thumb. At the sound of Green's entry, he raised his ravaged face. Didn't attack, didn't even cry out in surprise.

"Please," he said, "let her be."

Twenty-Seven

Violet darkness had descended. The back-up and emergency response teams had been released, and Levesque had finally been despatched to hospital. While MacPhail and the Ident team did their job inside the house, Patrick paced the little clearing in the backyard. The Tac Unit had set up floodlights, and Green had scrounged three battered lawn chairs from the shed to form a make-shift interview room, but Patrick seemed unable to sit still. He ran his fine, manicured fingers through his greying hair as he circled the yard. His shadow raced in spooky shapes across the dark brush beyond.

"Caitlin has been very ill for a long time," he said, "but I never, never imagined that she was capable of murder. All I've ever tried to do was protect her."

Green eyed him skeptically. He felt profoundly weary and sick at heart. A young woman lay dead inside the house because he had failed to put the pieces together in time. No matter the cause or the reason, that was a tragedy.

Dr. MacPhail's preliminary examination had revealed ligature marks on Caitlin's wrists and bruising on her arms, but no signs of injury that would explain her death. Two prescription bottles sat empty on the floor by the bed, their labels revealing that they were sleeping pills prescribed for Annabeth O'Malley. Also on the floor was a glass with traces of a clear liquid, probably the water used to wash down the pills. Lyle Cunningham had already told Green that a clear set of useable latents could be lifted from the glass and one from the bottle. Green suspected they would be Caitlin's. Even if he were guilty, Patrick was too clever for such an obvious oversight. He would have set every detail of the stage.

If this was a performance, however, it was Oscar-worthy. Patrick looked like an old man, his face carved in haggard lines by the harsh lights. He was shrivelled and grey with grief, yet driven by a desperate urge to talk. To be understood.

"So you're saying that your daughter killed Samuel Rosenthal?"

Patrick stopped. Bowed his head in faint assent. "And my wife. God help me, I didn't see that coming." Tears sprang to his eyes. "You always hope...she'll get better, you know?"

"But what reason would she have? Dr. Rosenthal was helping her."

He drew himself up, shook his head angrily as if to banish his weakness and strode over to open the door to the shed.

"Hold it!" Green snapped. Three detectives stepped forward to block his path.

Patrick sighed. "I want to show you something."

Inside, sitting in the trunk of his Lincoln Town Car, was a box of files and a laptop in a black case. Green glimpsed the name "Caitlin O'Malley" on the tab of one file.

"These belong to Dr. Rosenthal. I found them inside Caitlin's bedroom yesterday, hidden in the back of her closet. I was going to turn it all over to you later, that's why it's in the trunk of my car. I wasn't concealing evidence, merely...giving her time." He raised his hand, ran it through his hair distractedly. "I couldn't break the password on the computer, but the file told me all I needed to know. Rosenthal had been keeping progress notes on her for a year, ever since he encountered her one night in the Market. At first I think he was documenting her progress without the anti-psychotics so that they would have evidence in her suit against me." He plucked Caitlin's file from the box and thrust it at Green before turning away to resume his pacing, a little off-kilter like a drunk. Green placed the file unopened in his lap, too weary to read it. His stomach churned, and the floodlights were giving him a headache. Instead, he waited for the story to resume.

"Samuel Rosenthal was the agent of his own death." For the first time Patrick's voice shook with outrage. "Such extraordinary hubris, to believe he understood her, that he understood schizophrenia and the dark, toxic brew that washed her mind. The man was supposed to be an experienced doctor! If he hadn't believed that the brilliant reaches of her mind were more important than sober, stifled sanity—'unfettered insight', he called it—she would still have been on her clozapine, and she would not have become delusional again."

He flicked a restless hand at the file in Green's lap. "Last spring it seems he realized his mistake. He began trying to persuade her to go back on the anti-psychotic. But a paranoid, by their very nature, sees conspiracies instead of truth. She resisted. She thought he was being influenced by Lucifer, who was trying to destroy her gift. So he started meeting her every week so that he could persuade her to take at least a little bit of medication. Enough to keep away the worst of the scary voices, he told her, but not enough to interfere with her divine gift or her so-called destiny."

He stumbled a little on the stony ground and cast a sharp look at Green as if expecting disbelief.

"Divine gift?" was all Green said.

Patrick steadied himself. "Caitlin thought her intelligence was being channelled from God through outer space. That's what these are for." He waved at the network of steel pipes. "She had all the answers, you know. If millions of people pray to God and think God speaks to them, why not her? Why does her belief make her crazy? In fact, it was her lunatic evangelical husband and his preacher friend who put the idea of Lucifer in her head. Listen to God, they said, destroy Satan. Who was I, the voice of reason, the heretic, in all this? Caitlin has always fought me, even before she got sick. I was already the bad guy. Dr. Rosenthal took a different approach. He didn't argue with her, he went along with it. He seemed to be trying to keep track of how ill she was while still keeping her trust." He tilted his head to gaze at the darkening sky and drew a deep breath. "Foolish, foolish man, trying to outwit a brilliant paranoid."

A random piece of Green's puzzle clicked into place. "She got suspicious and broke into his apartment to steal his files. Somehow he gave himself away."

Patrick nodded. "Apparently, two weeks ago Dr. Rosenthal phoned me. I knew nothing of his meetings with Caitlin, and as you'd imagine, I wasn't kindly disposed towards the man who'd planned to take me to court. Worse, he was encouraging my child to explore her sick, delusional world. I was out, but Annabeth must have taken the message. Annabeth is... To be blunt, she's an alcoholic, has been for years, and both her memory and her judgement are impaired. She never gave me the message, but I'm guessing Caitlin found it or saw his number on Call Display. That would be enough to fuel her paranoia."

"How did you find out he called?"

He gestured to the file again. "The call is documented in there. Rosenthal had come full circle. He wanted to discuss enlisting my support to have her hospitalized. Committed, if need be. In Caitlin's eyes, that would be the ultimate betrayal. Rosenthal had joined me on the dark side."

Patrick's words hung in the silence. Night had settled in, sprinkling the sky with pale stars. Green's numb exhaustion robbed his brain of thought. Patrick told a convincing story, but he was a skilled storyteller, well practiced in the art of persuading judges and juries to believe his version of a case.

"She's not a very powerful woman," he said quietly. "How did she kill him?"

Patrick's face twisted. "You know how strong a person is when they're fighting for their life? Caitlin thought she was. She carries a length of this steel piping in her handbag wherever she goes, to help her hear God. She came home last Saturday night in a state, bloody and half-naked. No coat, no handbag, no steel pipe. When I read in the paper that Rosenthal had been beaten with a heavy bat, I began to fear... I searched all over for her things—the whole house, this place, even the murder scene, but I couldn't find them. She must have thrown them away. In the river, maybe?"

Green tried to recall the bits of information they had learned about the moments surrounding Rosenthal's death. Caitlin waiting in the alleyway, talking to someone. The four Somalis coming down the street, hopped up on drink and drugs. Caitlin screaming "help, get away from me." The fight, the robbery, and an hour later, Caitlin walking down Montreal Road towards home, with no fur coat or handbag. Just her bra and jeans, stained with blood.

There were still many questions, many pieces to fill in, but at this point Green needed to read Rosenthal's file and review the forensics being collected at the scenes. But before he could terminate the interview, there was one further question he needed to ask.

"What happened to your wife, Mr. O'Malley?"

Despite being a seasoned cross-examiner, Patrick was clearly not expecting the switch in direction. He stopped pacing and sank into a chair, his head in his hands. "Do we have to do this now? I'm so physically and emotionally drained that I can barely put my thoughts in order. Of course, that's what you want, I expect."

"I just want the truth."

Patrick stared into the blackness beyond the floodlights. Whereas before he'd seemed desperate to talk, now he had to dig deep to muster the last of his strength. "Annabeth, as I said, was not a strong person. She had given up on our daughter. Given up fighting for her health, I should say. To spare her, I hadn't told her about Caitlin's latest hospitalization nor about the files I found in her room. But she knew something was wrong when Caitlin's picture appeared on the news, and you showed up looking for her. By the time I brought Caitlin back home from the hospital yesterday, she was already well into the sauce. She didn't want to hide Caitlin from the police. Caitlin must have heard us arguing about it this morning, because while I was downstairs making them some brunch, she went into our bedroom. Annabeth was still in bed..." He paused, his throat working. "I don't know exactly what happened. All I heard was screaming and doors slamming, which I'd heard many times before. But when I went back upstairs to see why the dog was barking, there she was dead on the floor. And my girl was back in her room, washing her hands."

"Why didn't you call 911?"

Patrick shook his head helplessly. "That was my first instinct. But in that split second when I saw Caitlin frantically scrubbing her hands, I couldn't. I knew Annabeth was dead. There was no changing that. But my daughter still needed me." He looked across at Green bleakly. His eyes were dry, beyond the relief of tears. "She didn't resist, you know. She knew she'd gone beyond. That small part of her mind that Caitlin still controlled—my Caitlin—knew this was irrevocable. I bound her hands, because I couldn't be sure, but she came with me... here... almost eagerly. I unbound her. We sat. We talked. About what she'd done and what lay in store for her. Trial, stigma, locked wards, and the unbearable choice between staying crazy or living with the horror of what she'd done."

He looked across at the bungalow, where the murmuring of the forensic investigators could still be heard. "She chose this way. And after all the destruction she'd caused, I couldn't stand in her way."

*　　*　　*

"I think you made a mistake not to charge him, at least as an accessory," Levesque said unexpectedly. She was propped up in a bed in the Civic ER, her head wrapped in fresh white gauze. She looked pink with outrage. "He protected his daughter when he knew what she'd done. Because of him, his wife is dead. And Lindsay Corsin! We should throw the book at him."

Green's thoughts were still reliving a father's bleak despair, and he took a moment to shift his focus. Not only Lindsay Corsin, but Constable Rikert and Brian Sullivan. Patrick O'Malley's decision had cost a lot of people.

He nodded. "I know. And maybe we will, but we've done enough for today. He's in the cellblock, so he's not going anywhere. Believe me, he knows what a horrible mistake he made. Under the circumstances I'm more worried about suicide."

"Horrible mistake? You're assuming that story he told you is true? Maybe he killed his wife *and* his kid, got rid of both his big problems, and now he's one step away from walking free."

Green felt a flash of anger. "I'm not assuming. Never assume. Wait for the forensics and autopsy evidence. But so far we do have one piece of evidence from the Rothwell house—that phone message the mother supposedly took. Lou Paquette's partner found it crumpled up in the waste basket in Caitlin's room."

"But Patrick could have planted it!"

"That's why I asked Lou to put a rush on the prints they lifted off it—they belong to the mother, and Caitlin."

Levesque frowned. "So she crumpled the note. That's one little thing."

"But it does support Patrick's story. I had a quick look at Dr. Rosenthal's notes, and so far what I read also supports Patrick's story. Rosenthal was obviously worried about Caitlin. Even a full week earlier, he feared she might be headed for a full psychotic break. She was very paranoid about people around her, including him and her father. She was beginning to believe they were black knights of Lucifer, but she was still rational enough to carry out a sophisticated plan of retaliation. He was concerned, in fact, that his minimal doses of medication might be making her more dangerous by keeping her sane enough to carry out her delusions more effectively."

"That still doesn't eliminate her father as a suspect. He already read the notes himself, so of course he'll make his story consistent. But what about the sexual assault? What about the cabbie picking her up crying and bleeding?"

"The cabbie said she was half naked, bloody and upset. He assumed the sexual assault, she never said it. The blood on her could have been Rosenthal's."

Levesque grunted in disbelief. "Convenient that the steel pipe and the handbag are both missing. We only have Patrick O'Malley's word they ever existed."

He studied her ruefully. Her head rested against the pillow, her jaw was slack, but unlike him, her thoughts were still clear, and her eyes burned with excitement. Her take on Patrick O'Malley was far less forgiving than his, perhaps because she'd never been a parent struggling to manage a child whose life was careening out of control. Reluctantly he inclined his head to acknowledge her point. "Tomorrow we'll get another chance at him, Marie Claire. By that time forensics may have more answers, and we'll have had time to study the files. But for now, your brain needs a rest."

* * *

To his surprise, Sullivan greeted the theory with equal skepticism. He was sitting up in his guest chair after refusing to lie in bed any longer. Green was hoping the resolution of the case, albeit tragic, would take his mind off himself.

"So that skin and bones woman managed to beat Rosenthal to death?" Sullivan said.

"Looks that way."

"But using what? Where's the weapon?"

Green hesitated. He'd left Levesque grumbling in her ER cubicle, surrounded by snuffles and bandaged limbs, while he'd dropped in for a quick visit to Sullivan. It was nearly midnight, and he'd promised the nurses on his eternal soul not to discuss the case. They hadn't reckoned with Sullivan, however, who was thirsty for the diversion. Green decided a few more details couldn't hurt, so he told him about the steel pipe.

"Tomorrow I'll order a search of the route she took," he

added, "including the Rideau River below the Montreal Road Bridge. We might get lucky."

Sullivan chuckled. "Right. And how many officers do we have to spare for this?" His laughter faded, and he grew thoughtful. "Steel pipe from the house? That sounds almost premeditated."

"Apparently she always carried it with her, to help her hear God," he said, "but I have been playing with the possibility that the murder *was* planned, at least partly. Let's assume father's scenario for the moment. Caitlin discovered that Rosenthal had contacted her father and she became suspicious, so she broke into his house to steal his files. There she found Rosenthal's notes on how he and her father were planning to have her committed. God knows what her paranoid mind made of that. She would certainly have seen him as a threat in the days before his death. And look at the circumstances of his death. She always went to see him on Friday nights, but that night she didn't show up. I think she knew he would go out to look for her, and so she was ready with the steel pipe." Literally God fending off Lucifer, he thought, but kept the more demented elements of the story to himself.

"But what about Nadif Hassan and company? They're the ones who started it all."

"I'm out on a limb here, but I'm thinking we may have that backwards. I've been putting together the bits we know from Screech and Nadif. Screech says he heard her say 'help, get away from me'. But he didn't see who she was talking to, because he was hiding. We assumed it was Nadif, but what if it was Rosenthal himself? Nadif also heard her shout for help. He's fuzzy on the details, because he's pretty much wasted on some bad street drug, but he says Rosenthal was hassling her, and he and his friends only went in to help."

"But Mike, come on! Nadif's credibility is—"

"I know, but let's see where this goes. Let's say she was hiding in the alleyway waiting for Rosenthal. When he showed up, he tried to persuade her to come home with him, and they argue. Then she spotted the Somalis coming along the street, noisy and drunk, and she sees her chance to get them involved. So she calls help, screams like she's being attacked, and in they charge."

"So you're saying she set them up?"

Green hesitated. He was way beyond the known facts, way beyond his expertise, but it seemed too devious for a devout young woman who believed in the voice of God. "We may never know if it was a deliberate set-up, or if she just wanted their help to fight Lucifer."

Sullivan looked dubious, searching for holes in Green's tattered theory. It almost felt like old times again. "Either way, it sounds mighty clever and well-organized for someone on the brink of psychosis."

"I know. I admit there are still a lot of holes to plug. As to her being organized enough to carry out the murder, I'll leave that to the shrinks to explain. She was psychotic, but she was also very smart. Rosenthal himself said in his notes that his minimal meds might be keeping her just sane enough to be dangerous."

"But Mike, that's a lot of luck, those punks coming along at exactly the right moment."

"If they hadn't, she would have done the job by herself. That was probably her original plan; they just made it easier."

"Assuming she's the killer at all."

Green hesitated. "Well...yeah. Bottom line, she was a confused, desperate young woman who thought she was fighting for her life."

Sullivan sagged back in his chair with a sigh, and Green

felt a stab of concern. He had stayed too long and dragged Sullivan far too deeply into the case. He stood up.

"Anyway, I should go before the nurses have my head. I told Marie Claire I'd drive her home when they discharge her."

Interest flared again in Sullivan's weary eyes. "How's she working out?"

"She's a pain in the ass. Contrary, controlling, know-it-all..."

"Uh-huh."

Green laughed. "Touché. But she's not you—"

"Don't even go there, Mike. I'm done. The Big Guy sent me that message loud and clear."

Green didn't argue. Midnight, barely two days after a life-threatening ordeal, was not the time to persuade him. Green could afford to wait. If three days of enforced bed rest had Sullivan craving details on the case like an addict his next fix, Green suspected he would persuade himself.

Twenty-Eight

The day of Sam Rosenthal's funeral dawned gloriously sunny and warm. No wind disturbed the gilded, leafy canopy of maples and oaks that stood sentinel over the small community of gravestones in the rural cemetery. Grey squirrels scampered about, snatching acorns and racing up into the trees. Green arrived unexpectedly early, having made good time on the back country roads, and he found the small chapel barely half full. The mostly elderly mourners gathered in clusters and traded hushed gossip about Sam's life and lurid death.

David Rosenthal stood near the front, looking stiff and ill-at-ease as his father's acquaintances filed past offering condolences. He wore the traditional mourner's black tie, cut to symbolize the tearing of garments, and it contrasted oddly with his brown cords, suede jacket and steel-toed boots. Standing at least a head taller than the crowd, he spotted Green easily and detached himself to join him. He grabbed Green's elbow and steered him outside to a private corner of the garden.

"I was going to call you today. I've been a fucking moron the past few days, and I apologize."

Green masked his surprise. "I didn't take it personally, Dr. Rosenthal. Losing a loved one to murder is an awful shock."

"Yeah, well, I've never been good at tact. Been told that often enough, starting with my father." David extricated a thin sheaf of folded papers from his inner jacket pocket. "I found these in my father's desk. I think they're as close to a death-bed accusation as you'll ever get."

Green glanced at the dense, handwritten pages. One was an annotated list of people and the other some notes about Caitlin O'Malley, including one dated the night of his death. The handwriting was spidery and difficult to read. "Is this why you went looking for her on Saturday?"

David's gaze flickered with surprise. He seemed about to protest, then thought better. "I should have gone to you instead, but I didn't recognize their significance. I figured that was the list of my father's beneficiaries, and I wanted to see her for myself, to see if she was conning him." He shrugged. "That's my style, Inspector. I see something needs doing, I do it."

"Thanks to that style, my best friend is still alive." Tempted as he was to try to decipher the notes, Green slipped them into his pocket of his leather jacket for later study. He took out a plastic evidence bag. "I have something for you too. It's broken, but I know a good jeweller."

David's tangled brows shot up. "My mother's Star of David."

Green nodded. "The inscription says *To life and hope, my darling.* It seems fitting."

David took it from the bag and held it up by its chain. It spun lazily. A peculiar mix of resentment and regret flitted across his face. "She didn't choose life, you know. She hated the chemo. It might have bought her a couple of years, but it made her so sick that she decided what was it worth, this life she had left? So she took up some macrobiotic diet and meditation to fight the cancer with her mind. It didn't work, but my father told me it gave her the best few months she could have asked for. At the time I was so furious at him, I didn't even hang around for *shiva.* But now..."

Footsteps crunched on the gravel path, and both men turned to see Rabbi Tolner approaching. He looked spry and tanned, wearing a rumpled suit that was now too big for him and a black *yarmulke* perched on the top of his shiny pate.

"It's time, David."

Back inside, the funeral was quick. Tolner whipped through the formalities, leading the mourners through some traditional prayers and speaking briefly about his own admiration for the deceased before inviting David Rosenthal up to give the eulogy. David strode to the lectern and pulled out a crumpled sheet of paper from his back pocket. Even from a distance, Green could see it was heavily scribbled over in red. The speech had not come easily to him. He smoothed it out, surveyed the crowd of expectant faces and took a deep breath.

"Most of you are luckier than me. You knew my father. Growing up with Samuel Rosenthal, learned student of the mind, was a challenging task for a little boy who was blessed with his father's brains and stubbornness but not his wisdom. Like any child, I was self-absorbed and defiant but also hurt by what I felt was the crushing burden of his expectations. My father's compassion for his patients, his devotion to their care and well-being, his forgiveness of their sins—none of that was accorded to me. I say this not to criticize him but to show how poorly I understood him. Neither my father nor I were very good at explaining ourselves, least of all to each other."

Grey heads bent in the congregation, whispers were exchanged and frowns suppressed. The unrest seemed to galvanize David.

"In the past seventy-two hours, I've been reading his private papers and now have an idea where he was coming from. It made me feel better, I'm only sorry it took till now, when he's gone.

"I chose a career in biomedical engineering for the simple reason that, although the challenges are huge, the wiring extraordinarily small and the connections infinitely complex, at least they are physical. I can see, touch and manipulate them. The human brain is not only a thousand times more complex, with millions of synapses, receptors, and neuro-transmitters interwoven in intricate, precise patterns, but it is overlaid with human consciousness, with interpretation, understanding, and an overarching search for meaning that governs every choice we make." He glanced up and cleared his throat nervously before returning to his notes. Green had to smile in admiration. The speech was far more polished than the man, proof of what he could do when he brought the full force of his intellect to a task. He pictured David labouring over every word.

"This is hardly a new idea," David said. "Religious scholars, existential philosophers and Eastern mystics have been trumpeting the notion for centuries. But in his later years my father tried to cultivate it in that most sterile of soils, modern psychiatry. While most of his colleagues preferred to tinker with receptors and neuro-transmitters through the use of drugs, my father understood that to become truly well, his patients had to stay in charge of that search for meaning. How they understood their world, how they defined their illness and how they chose to manage it was more crucial to their recovery than the right dose of the latest wonder drug.

"I don't think he was foolish enough to believe that mental illness was merely a state of mind or that medication had no role to play, but he came to abhor our pill-popping shortcuts and our tendency to define every deviation from the mean as a disorder to be corrected. Once in my childhood, some doctor diagnosed me as ADHD. This was undoubtedly true, for it caused me a lot of grief—disciplinary trouble in school, conflicts with my parents and friends, for example. It still costs me, in relationships and in financial and career stability. But it is also a gift that allows me greater vision to imagine what's possible, greater courage to take the needed risks, and greater energy to carry them through. I was perhaps my father's first guinea pig, to see whether I could understand and channel the challenges of my brain and to incorporate them into who I was and where I was going, rather than simply drugging them away."

David's voice had picked up confidence. The audience unrest was gone now, each listener barely moving as he turned over the page.

"Paradoxically, a person defined only by their synapses and neuro-transmitters is diminished when an expert deems these physical functions to be defective. That's why the halls and outpatient waiting rooms of psychiatric hospitals are filled with people who feel like failures. There's a huge sense of inadequacy that needs to be overcome. My father's goal was to try to connect with the person inside the illness, to listen to them and to draw out their hopes and fears and challenges. His hope was to be a partner with them to fight for those things they felt were not only healthy and fulfilling but also provided mastery and meaning to their life.

"Finding that balance was often a case of trial and error, and towards the end, my father recognized he had sometimes tipped the balance too far. Ultimately, such an error cost him his life, and even more tragically, the lives of others. But despite this, I hope we can all applaud the inspiration he provides all of us to look ahead with hope. In his own words, he believed that even inside the darkest, sickest brain, that messy little enigma—the thinking mind—was the ultimate agent of recovery."

*　*　*

A message not just for mental illness but for all of us, Green thought as he made his way back to the station after the service. A hokey idea, this need for meaning. For Sullivan, it would determine the ultimate path of his recovery. For Sharon, it rose from deep inside her biological core—a clarion call that scared the hell out of him. He'd been ambivalent about another child since Sharon's first subtle hints, but Sullivan's brush with death had added another layer of doubt which he knew he had to face. Someday.

For Levesque, however, just beginning her career in major crimes, meaning was all about catching bad guys and making them pay for their assault on social order. She would be waiting at the station to begin the next round of interviews with Patrick O'Malley. He wondered what forensics had uncovered since yesterday, and whether they would ever know what had really happened. Whether there was a bad guy to catch at the end of this chase, or just a series of tragic tales.

Omar Adams had crept back home late the night before, once the news linking Caitlin to Rosenthal's death had finally reached him, and his father had brought him into the station himself that morning. Green found them waiting when he arrived back from the funeral. The young man looked gaunt and subdued but no longer so afraid. His father sat at his side, grim and ramrod straight, but with a hint of something new in his eyes. Light.

"He wants to cooperate," Frank Adams said. "We had a long talk, and he knows it's the right thing to do. He still doesn't remember much, but now at least he knows he didn't kill that man."

"Whatever else I did..." Omar muttered, then shrugged in

acceptance as the duty sergeant led him away.

Charges would have to be laid against him, Nadif and the others. They might not have killed Rosenthal, but they had certainly beaten and robbed him. Without their help, Caitlin might not even have succeeded in her goal. Ultimately the young men needed to be held accountable for their part in the tragedy that had followed. Green doubted it would do much to deter Nadif from his path of crime, but Omar might still be turned around. As with Dr. Rosenthal's patients, the proper remedy needed to be chosen with care.

In the squad room, the sense of urgency no longer hung in the air. They were no longer hot on the trail of a villain; Nadif, Omar and Patrick were all in custody, awaiting the interview and forensic results that would construct the case for court. Levesque was busy at her desk, the white bandage already replaced by a much more fashionable flesh-coloured bandaid. She sported two black eyes that made her look wan and frail, but she counteracted the effect by wearing a tailored navy suit and for the first time ever, a subtle pink lip gloss. She'd come prepared for battle against the high-powered, charismatic lawyer.

She glanced up belatedly as Green reached his office door, then gathered up some print-outs and came to join him. "I booked the video interrogation room for Mr. O'Malley at one o'clock, sir. His lawyer, Elliot Solquist, will be joining us. I thought you'd like to know the latest forensics before that."

He sat behind his desk and scowled at the blinking voicemail light on his phone. No doubt there was a similar pile-up of messages in his email inbox as well. He gestured Levesque to a chair. "The executive summary, Marie Claire."

She smiled. "At the Rothwell Drive scene, they found the weapon used to kill the mother. An eight-inch pair of fabric shears. It was placed in the cosmetics drawer in the daughter's en suite bathroom, still covered in blood and smeared with fingerprints. Lou Paquette identified a useable one as Caitlin's."

"None from Patrick?"

She shook her head, pouting slightly as if disappointed.

"What about other prints? There were bloody handprints and footprints all over that scene."

"Still being processed. Lou says he'll be busy all month. They did find some traces of blood washed down the sink in Caitlin's bathroom."

Green thought back. "That also supports the father's version of events."

"But—!" Quickly she flipped to another report. "At the Montreal Road bungalow, Lyle Cunningham found some interesting prints on the prescription bottle and the water glass. The ones on the bottle were overlapping and partial, so he could only get enough points for a conclusive match on one. Caitlin's. But he said some of the partials might have been Patrick's."

Green waved his hand in dismissal. "Patrick might have handled his wife's sleeping pills any time. It means nothing that his prints are on it. What about the glass?"

"A couple of partial prints match Caitlin's, but—" she smiled, the pout vanishing in her triumph, "the clearest, most complete print belongs to Patrick. His right thumb."

It wasn't much to go on, Green reflected once Levesque left the office. The crumpled phone message, the fingerprints on the fabric shears, the blood in Caitlin's sink...everything was consistent with Patrick's story. Most of the puzzle pieces fit. Even Patrick's prints on the glass could be explained away.

Yet Green was left with a restless sense of unease.

He pulled out the sheaf of notes that David Rosenthal had

found in his father's apartment and smoothed them out on the desk. He bent close and slowly picked apart the doctor's scratchy handwriting, still elegant but spidery with age The first page was a list of nine names and accompanying notations. Six of the names Green recognized as beneficiaries of his will, including Caitlin's. Two other names were crossed out with the words "doing well" beside them. The final name was "David", followed by three question marks and the word "maybe". Caitlin's name also had a question mark beside it and the word 'father?'

There was no date or useful explanation on the page. If this list represented Sam Rosenthal's original deliberations about his new will, he'd later made up his mind to exclude his son and to award Caitlin the money.

The second page contained two very brief progress notes, under the heading "C. O."

Sept. 13. Patient arrived 10 p.m. Appeared anxious and fearful, denied concerns but not very talkative about herself. She asked about the High Holy Days, and what Jews did to celebrate the new year. I explained it was not a celebration but a time of reflection and atonement. For evil, she said, then talked on about bad state of world, some talk of Lucifer but denies hearing any commands from God to destroy him. Refused increase olazapine. Major concern, I tried to put some in tea but she didn't drink it. I sense increasing suspicion. I hope the mother didn't tell her about my call to her father.

Sept. 20, 1:30 a.m. Patient failed to appear for her session this evening. Even allowing for her rather loose appreciation of time, this is abnormally late, and she knows I will worry. My optimism that she would respond to my treatment approach appears to be misplaced, and her erratic and

ACKNOWLEDGEM[ENTS]

I am grateful to the numero[us]
offered their time and ex[]
story. As always, a big [thanks]
of great friends an[d]
Cameron, Ma[]
Wiken, wh[]
prose. To m[]
Thompson, a[]
their continued s[]
thanks to Mark [O.]
Service, who has provi[ded]
throughout Inspector Gr[een]
humour and insight have hel[ped]
is. Any errors in police procedu[re,]
or deliberate, are mine entirely.

Above all, I am grateful to my ch[ildren and]
family, for all that they mean to me.

This is a work of fiction and any resem[blance to]
actual people and events is unintentional. Alth[ough]
most of the Ottawa locales are real, some have be[en]
invented or altered in the interests of the story.

---

deteriorating behaviour has left me cornered fo[r]
and her future. With each relapse, the hopes for
diminish.

Her father has not yet returned my phone call. I know
cares about her in his heavy-handed, take-charge fashion. For a
parent, that moment when hope is relinquished, is the most
devastating loss of all. I will make one last effort to find her
tonight and if that fails, I will call him again tomorrow.

Green reread the last note several times. *"That moment
when hope is relinquished is the most devastating loss of all".*
His thoughts returned to Patrick's version of the events that
had unfolded that tragic Sunday afternoon. Patrick had
argued his daughter's side against his wife, who wanted to
turn her in to the police, then he'd gone down to make lunch.
He'd heard an argument from upstairs, but that was
commonplace so he thought nothing of it. He returned back
upstairs to find his wife murdered in her bedroom, and
Caitlin in her bathroom washing her hands after presumably
stashing the murder weapon in her bathroom drawer. Patrick
had chosen not to call 911, but instead to bind his daughter's
hands and bring her to the Montreal Road house. To he[r]
refuge, her one true home.

They had talked about her past and her future, her li[fe at]
a crossroads. She had reached a decision. Perhaps he ha[d]
poured the water, held the glass, emptied the pills...

The vague sense of unease clicked into foc[us.]
Caitlin's hands bound, only one person could ha[ve taken]
the bottle of sleeping pills from her mother's b[]
one person could have brought the supply of w[ater to]
wash them down.

photo by Laura Thompson, 2009

Barbara Fradkin was born in Montreal and obtained her PhD in psychology. Her work as a child psychologist has provided ample inspiration and insight for plotting murders.

Her novels featuring Ottawa Police Inspector Michael Green are *Do or Die* (2000), *Once Upon a Time* (2002), *Mist Walker* (2003), *Fifth Son* (2004), *Honour Among Men* (2006), *Dream Chasers* (2007) and now *This Thing of Darkness*. *Fifth Son* won Best Novel at the 2005 Arthur Ellis Awards, and *Honour Among Men* repeated the honour in 2007.

Fradkin lives in Ottawa, Ontario. More information on her work is online at www.barbarafradkin.com

The Inspector Green Series: